USA TODAY bestselling author **Barb Han** lives in north Texas with her very own hero-worthy husband, three beautiful children, a spunky golden retriever/standard poodle mix and too many books in her to-read pile. In her downtime, she plays video games and spends much of her time on or around a basketball court. She loves interacting with readers and is grateful for their support. You can reach her at barbhan.com

Carol Ericson is a bestselling, award-winning author of more than forty books. She has an eerie fascination for true crime stories, a love of film noir and a weakness for reality TV, all of which fuel her imagination to create her own tales of murder, mayhem and mystery. To find out more about Carol and her current projects, please visit her website at carolericson.com, 'where romance flirts with danger.'

Also by Barb Han

Also by Carol Ericson

Discover more at millsandboon.co.uk

MISSION HONEYMOON

BARB HAN

LAKESIDE MYSTERY

CAROL ERICSON

MILLS & BOON

First Published in Great Britain 2022
by Mills & Boon, an imprint of HarperCollins*Publishers* Ltd
1 London Bridge Street, London, SE1 9GF

www.harpercollins.co.uk

HarperCollins*Publishers*
1st Floor, Watermarque Building,
Ringsend Road, Dublin 4, Ireland

Mission Honeymoon © 2022 Barb Han
Lakeside Mystery © 2022 Carol Ericson

ISBN: 978-0-263-30350-6

0722

MIX
Paper from
responsible sources
FSC C007454

This book is produced from independently certified FSC™ paper to ensure responsible forest management.

For more information visit: www.harpercollins.co.uk/green

Printed and Bound in Spain using 100% Renewable electricity at CPI Black Print, Barcelona

MISSION
HONEYMOON

BARB HAN

All my love to Brandon, Jacob and Tori,
the three great loves of my life.

To Babe, my hero, for being my best friend,
greatest love and my place to call home.

I love you all with everything that I am.

Chapter One

Just breathe.

All ATF Agent Ree Sheppard felt on either side of her was a wooden box. Trapped, she wiggled her foot and felt the bottom. If she stretched out her body, the crown of her head reached the top. Her shoulders were in a permanent shrug, and she could scarcely move her arms in any direction. The space was fitted-glove tight.

The sun was high in the sky on a hot mid-September afternoon. A sliver of daylight came in through a crack where the wood didn't perfectly match up. Ree lifted her head toward it, trying to grab fresh air. Panic set in as reality gripped her. She'd been hit in the back of the head after breathing in a chemical that rendered her unconscious. Or maybe it was the other way around. She couldn't be certain. She did, however, have a monster of a headache. Based on the angle of the sun, she hadn't been out for long.

And then it dawned on her what she was inside. This was a coffin. Her lungs clawed for air as her claustrophobia took the wheel. Her chest squeezed, and she had to remind herself to slow down and breathe again. This was her worst nightmare realized.

"Sit tight, sweetheart. We'll be back for you if you make it through the day and your man cooperates," the unfamiliar male voice stated with a haughty laugh. Ree had been abducted in Dallas, where she'd returned to the apartment she was sharing with her undercover partner during their last case.

"You didn't say anything about putting her in a coffin, Lindy," a female voice stated. This one was familiar. Giselle Langley was the mistress of someone mid-level in the crime organization Ree and her partner were investigating. Giselle had helped Ree and Quint climb another rung higher toward the leader before betraying Ree earlier today by luring her outside her apartment. Unbeknownst to Giselle, her imprisoned boyfriend had arranged for her to be offered Witness Protection once this case was over. Ree and Quint were on a mission to take down one of the largest and most profitable Romanian weapon trafficking rings in Texas. Giselle's link to Vadik Gajov was meant to get them one step closer to their ultimate target, Dumitru, the man in charge and responsible for the death of an agent. Tessa Kind had not only been Quint's best friend, but she'd been pregnant. The fact that she'd been able to convince Quint not to tell their boss haunted him. Locking Dumitru behind bars for the rest of his life had become Quint's sole mission. Ree's partner and, most recently, fiancé couldn't let it go. Even though Quint didn't yet have a ring, he'd asked Ree to marry him at the conclusion of their last case and she'd said yes. Still, with Dumitru walking around free, they couldn't begin their future. Not until justice was served.

"She'll be fine until we come back for her," the male voice said.

"No," Giselle argued, and there was something in her voice that sent an icy shiver racing down Ree's spine. "Don't do it, Lindy. She won't be able to breathe."

Rolph Lindberg, a.k.a. Lindy, was on the same level as Vadik according to their desk agent, Agent James Grappell.

Vadik and Lindy both were advisors to Dumitru. Vadik was presently in jail due to a recent bust that Quint had orchestrated while Ree had been forced to play the part of party girl at Vadik's penthouse.

At the conclusion of their last case, Lindy had posed as Dumitru via a text message calling for Vadik's murder. Part of their cover story was that Quint had been released from prison recently and, therefore, would have connections inside. From what Ree gathered so far, she'd been abducted to force Quint into arranging for Vadik to be killed while locked up.

Lindy wasn't exactly known for mercy. Ree squirmed, testing the strength of the homemade coffin. She strained to check out what was happening aboveground in time for the first clump of dirt to hit the wood. She blinked as crumbs hit her in the eye.

"Stop." Giselle's voice was more agitated now. Nervous?

"Or what?" Lindy said. Another clump splattered on the outside of the encasing like a pumpkin that had been thrown off a bridge.

"I'll tell Axel," she threatened. There was far less confidence in her tone now. It had raised an octave too, which wasn't exactly encouraging from where Ree stood. "They're his friends, and he wouldn't want them treated this way."

Lindy stopped. Was he considering the plea?

"I can't leave this in the open," he finally stated. "If someone finds her, it could be worse all the way around, including for her."

"Good point," she said, then hesitated.

How about someone pull me out of this grave and open the box? How about that? Ree wanted to shout.

"She's been missing for hours already," Giselle continued after a few beats. "He'll come looking for her. What if he finds her like this?"

"Are you kidding around or just stupid?" Lindy asked.

"What are you doing with your phone?" Giselle didn't come off as offended despite the dig.

"What do you think? Taking a picture," he stated like she should have read his mind. Or was it that obvious to someone in their line of work?

"Here's the deal," Giselle started. "I'm the one who asked to meet up with her for lunch. My name is on this, and on Axel's by extension. If anything happens to her, who do you think her man will come after?" She paused as though for dramatic affect. "That's right. *Me.* And when Quint puts me in a box over this, I won't ever be coming out again. And then you'll have Axel Ivan to deal with. Is that what you want?" Giselle seemed to gain more confidence the longer she spoke. "I'm not taking a hit for this one, Lindy. Now, let her out. She'll wake up any minute now. You can leave her out here in the boondocks. Who knows how long it'll take her to walk back to Dallas? By then, he will have already done what you want."

"If I open this box and she doesn't wake up right away, she might be dealing with something worse than me," Lindy said. "There's all kinds of wildlife out here. Is that what you want? You want to come back here and find her blood and guts everywhere?"

"Well, no. Not when you put it like that." She cowered.

Ree wanted to shout. She wanted to tell Giselle to go to hell for baiting her into a meetup that ended with Ree in a coffin. Instinct told her to be quiet and be still no matter how much her lungs clawed for air and she wanted to scream.

There were a couple of important points Ree picked up on in their conversation. For one, they planned on coming back, at least. Could she spend an entire day and night out here in the middle of nowhere? She listened for sounds of vehicles or a roadway and heard nothing. Another note was that even if she was able to free herself from this box, what would she do next? They'd said they were about to leave her in an area where wildlife roamed freely. A dark thought struck her. Texas was known for snakes, spiders and all manner of insects. If they left her inside this thing, who knew what could join her?

Ree shivered at the thought. She hated snakes. Spiders weren't much better in her book. But the stabbing pain in her chest would do her in before either of those had a chance at her. After growing up with four rowdy brothers on a small ranch, Ree didn't fear a whole lot of people. Being buried alive ranked right up there beside heights and small spaces, though.

More of those calming breaths, she reminded herself as she waited to hear her fate.

"See. I'm doing her a favor by covering the box," he continued.

"How will she breathe?" Giselle asked, her voice more of a whine than anything else now.

Another splat sounded. Dirt seeped through the crevice. Ree literally thought she might hyperventilate.

"Let's get out of here," Giselle said, sounding a little panicked.

Seriously? She was the one who was freaking out? Ree had a few choice words for her so-called friend when she got out of this predicament. This seemed like a good time to remind herself she was one hundred percent successful at getting herself out of difficult situations. Granted, this was the first time she'd been *buried alive*. Those last two words caused a tremor to rock her body. Biting her tongue was near impossible.

The sound of footsteps walking away from the area sent a cold chill racing up her spine. An engine came to life. It didn't sound like a truck. Could be a sedan or SUV. Did Giselle think she was going to get away with this? Did Lindy?

Clearly, they planned to leave her there—wherever *there* was—alone. A sharp pain in the back of her head reminded her of the blow she'd taken as she was being herded into a minivan. A cloth had been placed over her mouth before the rank smell filled her senses and total darkness came. The memory caused white-hot anger to roil in her veins.

Ree silently counted to sixty, marking each passing second by straightening a finger from her fists.

It was hot. There was no air movement. The box was stifling.

Beads of sweat rolled down Ree's forehead and dampened the back of her neck. There were no sounds of life. Not yet anyway. Ree needed to get out of this box and now.

Could she shimmy down a little more and kick out the bottom? There was very little wiggle room. Maybe she could blow out her breath and bring her shoulders in. She inched down. Would it be possible to take in a deep breath and cause her shoulders to swell enough to break out? The move would be faster. She tried. Failed. More of the panic tried to take hold.

She couldn't allow her nerves to take over. An anxiety attack would only make the situation worse. Logically, she knew it. Emotions were a whole different ball game.

Another attempt at trying to get her feet to the bottom made a little more progress. She grazed the wood with the ball of her foot. More wiggling and she got her heel there too. Problem. There was no room to lift her leg high enough to get off a good stomp. At this rate, she would never get out of this awful thing. Ree expanded her lungs, pushing her shoulders hard against the crate. Shock of all shocks, there was enough give to rain dirt down on her through the crevices. She turned her head and spit out the mud crumbs.

Ree turned a little on her side and threw her right elbow up. The lid loosened. A few more elbows and she was covered in soil. She sat bolt upright and brushed it off before pushing to standing. She immediately checked her pockets for her cell. Nothing.

There wasn't much in this area except for trees to one side and a lake to the other. No road. She would have to follow the tire tracks where they'd flattened the weeds. Wasting no time, she climbed out of the shallow grave and headed toward freedom, praying she would find someone willing to help her.

QUINT STABBED HIS fingers through his thick hair as exasperation settled in. Ree had been gone for hours with no word. Her cell phone tracked to the trash can on the street outside the downtown Dallas apartment they shared for the undercover assignment that he'd insisted they take so he could get vengeance for his former partner. As their last undercover case was wrapping up, a message had come from Dumitru asking Quint to kill the person who'd been arrested during the bust. The head of the crime ring believed Quint was in jail alongside Vadik, a man Dumitru couldn't afford to have strike a plea bargain in exchange for giving up information. As it turned out, the text hadn't come from Dumitru. It had come from his secondhand man by the name of Lindy.

Putting Ree in danger due to Quint's personal need for revenge sat like a hot poker in his gut. She'd hinted she might be ready to retire her undercover career. The only reason she'd taken the last two assignments was to be the one to watch his back. She hadn't said it outright, but he knew it to be true.

James Grappell, the desk agent assigned to them, had been able to pinpoint the exact location of her phone. There was no good reason for Ree to drop her cell in the garbage. Quint had retrieved it and cleaned it off, and now it was sitting on the counter half-wrapped in a paper towel.

Ree was out there without a communication device. This was in connection to the case. No doubt in his mind. He had been asked to arrange for Vadik to die in jail. Since Quint's most recent cover story was that he'd been incarcerated and recently released, his connections on the inside should be strong and—at least to Lindy's thinking— difficult to tie back to Dumitru or any of his colleagues.

Quint had been beaten almost to a pulp a few weeks ago as part of a twisted initiation into Dumitru's crime ring.

His cell phone buzzed, still in his hand. The screen revealed an unknown caller. Since Quint could count on one hand the number of folks who had this number, he answered.

The familiar voice of his partner and fiancée came through the line. "Quint, it's me. Ree." Wind roared in the background, making it difficult to hear a word being said.

"Where are you?" he asked loudly in an attempt to speak over the noise as his pulse skyrocketed.

"On the highway, heading back to Dallas. I hitched a ride and borrowed a cell phone," she said, raising her voice. Being on the highway explained the wind tunnel sound.

"What happened and are you okay?" A half-dozen questions bottlenecked in his brain, each fighting to be the next one spoken out loud. A potent mix of anger and relief assaulted him. All he could allow himself to focus on was the fact she was alive.

"I'm good. I'll explain everything when I get there. Lock the doors, and don't respond to any messages from anyone until I'm back," she shouted. Her voice kept cutting out, but he picked up the gist of what she was saying. "Oh, and, Quint. Don't trust Giselle."

The line went dead.

Quint immediately opened his department-issued laptop as he made the call to Agent Grappell.

"She's safe," he said the second Grappell answered.

A sigh of relief came through the line.

"That's good news," Grappell said.

"All I know is she's on her way back to the apartment and told me to lock the door in the meantime," he relayed. "Get this. She told me not to trust Giselle."

"I was about to call you when my phone rang," Grappell stated. "Ree received a text at eleven forty-five this morning from the informant requesting a lunch meeting around the corner."

"Ree must not have been worried about it since she didn't text me to let me know before she left the apartment," Quint said. "I was in PT, trying to work my arm back into condition."

"She might have been in a hurry. Giselle made it seem urgent to get together but didn't give a reason as to why," Grappell informed him.

"Interesting," Quint said. "I guess I'll know the details as soon as she arrives."

"I'm not sure why she tossed her phone," Grappell said, sounding disturbed by the point.

"You and me both," Quint stated. "All I can think is that she didn't have a choice."

"As in someone did it for her?" Grappell asked.

"It's the only reason that comes to mind. She trusted

Giselle as much as an informant can be relied on," Quint stated.

"There are tracking devices on cell phones if they're lost. When she didn't turn up, someone might have figured you would trace her whereabouts," Grappell reasoned.

"Makes sense to me," Quint said. Made him mad beyond belief that someone would kidnap her right outside their apartment building.

Quint's cell buzzed, indicating a text.

"Hold on a second," he said to Grappell before checking the screen. The message was from Lindy.

Get rid of the bastard and *she* comes home *alive*.

Quint knew exactly who was in league with Giselle now. Lindy. He returned to the call with Grappell.

"Lindy wants Vadik dead, and he knows I have contacts on the inside from my recent incarceration." Of course, Lindy didn't know the entire story had been fabricated as part of Quint and Ree's cover.

"Vadik is refusing to cooperate," Grappell told Quint. "He says we can lock him in solitary confinement for the rest of his life. Dish out any punishment we want. He said he intends to beat the rap and stay aboveground."

"Then I'll just have to pay him a visit and convince him otherwise," Quint responded. He had no idea how he was going to convince Vadik to turn state's witness and allow them to fake his death, but he would figure it out if it meant bringing justice for Tessa.

First things first. He needed to see that Ree was okay. She was the only person he cared about right now.

Chapter Two

Ree had no idea if the building was being watched, so she slipped in the back and made her way up to the apartment via the service elevator. The only thing she hated worse than tight spaces was heights. The apartment on the twenty-seventh floor of a thirty-story building was a nightmare.

As the elevator dinged, she realized she didn't have her key with her. Giselle must have taken Ree's purse along with her cell phone. Ree also recalled sounding the alarm to Quint, putting him on high alert, and telling him to lock the door.

It had been one helluva day so far. She was still picking dirt out of her hair.

Quint must have heard the elevator and then checked the peephole, because she'd barely taken two steps into the hallway when he flung their door open and made a straight line to her. She crashed into him at the halfway mark, then buried her face in his chest as he walked them into the apartment before closing and locking the door.

His hands cupped her face. She blinked up at him.

"They buried me," she said, fighting the emotion trying to take over at the thought of never seeing him again.

Anger flashed in his blue eyes, and his jaw muscles clenched. "They better never touch you again. We can make an excuse to get you out of here. Say one of your family members is sick and you had to go."

"They'll see it as weakness," she reminded him. "It'll hurt the case."

He thumbed a loose tendril of hair off her face.

"I don't care, Ree," he said with an overwhelming intensity that became its own physical presence. "I can't lose you."

Those words hit her with the force of a tsunami. Neither of them could predict what would happen next. Neither could guarantee this case wouldn't go south. Neither could guarantee they would both walk away in one piece.

"Let's take ourselves off the case together," she said, knowing full well he wouldn't take her up on the offer but suggesting it anyway.

Quint didn't respond. When she pulled back and looked into his eyes, she understood why. A storm brewed behind those sapphire-blues, crystalizing them, sending fiery streaks to contrast against the whites. Those babies were the equivalent of a raging wildfire that would be impossible to put out or contain. People said eyes were the window to the soul. In Quint's case, they seemed the window to his heart.

He pressed his forehead against hers and took in an audible breath. When he exhaled, it was like he was releasing all his pent-up frustration and fear. In that moment, she understood the gravity of what he'd been going through while she'd been gone. Kidnapped. For all he knew, left for dead.

So she didn't speak either. Instead, she leaned into their connection, a connection that tethered them as an electrical current ran through her to him and back. For a split second, it was impossible to determine where he ended and she began.

Ree had no idea how long they stood there in the entryway of the apartment as though frozen in time. She didn't care. She was safe. She was home. And in that moment, she realized home was anywhere Quint was. No, she wouldn't walk away from the case, and neither would he.

Quint finally spoke first. "You must be starving and I'd like to know exactly what happened."

"I got a text from Giselle asking if I could meet her for lunch. I stepped onto the sidewalk, and a guy came out of nowhere. I was struck and the next thing I knew a rag came over my mouth. There was some kind of chemical smell that knocked me right out," she said as he walked her over to the nearest stool where she perched. "I woke up in the middle of nowhere inside a coffin to the sound of Giselle telling Lindy not to bury me alive."

Quint muttered a string of curses low and under his breath but loud enough for her to hear. "That sonofabitch."

"I'm here now," she reassured. "I'm alive and doing fine. Tired and dirty, but I'll live."

Tension radiated off Quint in waves.

"It should have been me," he ground out.

"It's over now," she said.

"I thought I lost you," he said as a mix of anger and intense sadness passed behind his eyes.

All Ree could do in that moment was lean into him as he embraced her again.

"What sounds good to you right now?" he asked after a few moments of silence.

Exhaustion set in. The only word she could say was, "Shower."

He gave a slight nod and then walked beside her to the bathroom.

"I'll have food and coffee ready when you get out." He feathered a kiss on her lips, her chin, and the base of her neck, where her pulse thumped.

Ree gave his hand a squeeze of acknowledgment before heading into the bathroom, needing to wash the dirt off her. An involuntary shiver rocked her body, thinking about being locked inside the coffin. Her hands fisted at her sides at the thought of seeing Giselle again. Ree didn't want to be in the same room with the woman. It wouldn't turn out well for Axel's girlfriend.

A shower went a long way toward making Ree feel human again. She spent another ten minutes picking splinters out of her skin where it had been exposed to the wood. The smell of fresh-brewed coffee caused her to speed up. By the time she threw on a bathrobe and sat at the bar counter, Quint was setting a plate in front of her. An omelet with the works: spinach, cheese and chives. There was toast with a smattering of jelly along with a side of fresh greens and a slice of tomato. The meal tasted as good as it smelled, and she wolfed it down in a matter of minutes.

"More?" Quint asked as he plated his own food.

"I couldn't eat another bite. Believe me, I was full halfway through." She smiled and meant it. At least she would be fine after a cup of coffee and a minute to shake off the horror of what had just happened. Quint would be recovering from his injuries for weeks if not months after what Vadik's men had done to him in the back alley of the building where Vadik lived.

"He won't cooperate," Quint informed him. "We can't make a move without his help. It's the reason you were kidnapped. They were trying to force my hand, and I can't fake his murder without his consent."

"I should have known better than to trust Giselle," Ree stated, furious with herself for the slip that could have cost her her life.

"Every agent makes mistakes, Ree," he said in a soothing tone. "Including the best like you. The trick is to not make one that leads to something permanent." He didn't say the word *death*, but it was implied. The storm brewed again. This time, he was thinking about Tessa and her unborn child.

"Did he say why?" she asked, redirecting the subject, not yet ready to let herself off the hook. No one was perfect. She was very aware of the fact. She was also reaching a point in life where she wanted to sit out on her back porch, drink coffee and watch the sunrise. Maybe while looking after a kiddo or two.

If someone had told Ree six months ago that she'd be pining for a family, she would have laughed in their face. What was so different in her life now? *Quint*, a little voice in the back of her mind stated.

Ree shoved the thought aside and watched the man she was crazy about finish chewing the bite of food in his mouth.

"Wants to stay aboveground when he beats the rap," he informed her.

She must have made quite the face, because Quint cracked a smile.

"I know. He won't. Funny how he doesn't seem to realize it," he said.

"To each his own, I guess," she said with a shrug. "We'll have to find another way to convince him."

"I told Grappell we'd like to pay Vadik a visit," Quint said.

"That's risky," she immediately pointed out. "We're still undercover. He could blow everything for us."

"It might be a chance we have to take," Quint reasoned. "Hear me out before you tell me that I've lost it."

She nodded before picking up her coffee mug and taking a sip. Instead of setting it down on the table, she rolled the warm mug around in her hands. There wasn't much that could convince her to walk into Vadik's cell and announce herself as Ree Sheppard.

"EXPOSING OUR IDENTITIES to Vadik might validate that we know how to pull off an undercover operation. Gaining his trust is more than half the battle. When he realizes we pulled the wool over his eyes and everyone around him, he might agree," Quint stated before putting a hand up, palm out, in the surrender position. Being left wondering about Ree, the sickness in the pit of his stomach that something might have happened to her, had his wheels turning. "I do realize what that means, and if I had to pull us off the case, I would."

He was considering making the request anyway. This investigation had bad mojo wrapped around it from the start. For months, he'd been stewing and plotting his revenge. It was so close now he could almost taste it. But putting Ree's life on the line to follow through with his plans held little appeal if it meant hurting or—heaven forbid—losing her.

Reality said she could walk across the street and be hit by a car tomorrow. No one knew how long they had with someone. The thought might be sobering, but it was also true. Sickness could strike at any moment. A freak accident could take her away.

He could live with those things happening. There would be no choice. He would be gutted, and he highly doubted he would ever get over the loss, but he would know in the bottom of his heart that he'd done nothing to cause it.

Keeping her on the case was another story altogether.

"Here's what I'm thinking," he said. "We walk away now, and it'll be hell for anyone else to step in. All the work we've done up to this point is a wash. Sure, a couple more bastards are behind bars. That's a good thing. Tessa and her baby are still dead, and the reason is still walk-ing around out there, getting away with it, thinking he's slick as they come."

Ree nodded before taking another sip of coffee. She chewed on the inside of her cheek, which told him she was not only listening but agreeing with his analysis.

"Without Vadik's cooperation, we lose our in and our window of opportunity," he continued.

She did the cheek thing again as she studied the rim of her mug.

"So, what if we go in and tell him exactly who we are and what we've been able to accomplish so far?" he asked.

"It could backfire," she said after a thoughtful pause.

"Or possibly work," he pointed out.

"And what if he doesn't decide to cooperate?" she asked. "As much as I want to throat-punch Giselle the next time I see her—and believe me when I say I haven't made up my mind just yet that I won't—she'll be dead for certain. It would be signing her death warrant along with Axel's and his family's should his family ever surface again."

"You're right," he admitted. "There is a whole lot that can go wrong with this plan. But we're short on options."

"This is a dangerous Hail Mary," she reasoned. "There's a whole lot on the line if the meeting doesn't go well."

"Very true," he agreed. "Axel's family is in WITSEC. It's not a guarantee no one will ever find them, but the US Marshals office has a long and successful track record of keeping their witnesses safe. Axel refuses to go in until Giselle and his son are safe."

"I agree. I have a whole lot of respect for the agency," she concurred.

"Giselle is a wild card," he admitted.

"Truer words have never been spoken," Ree said. "I thought she was pining for Axel and wishing he would get out of prison so her son would know his father. When we first met, she seemed like she wished the three of them could be a family. After spending time with her, I realize she has a very loose definition of what a family looks like."

Quint nodded. He also realized there was more to the story there, but he didn't want to derail the conversation by asking questions.

"Plus, I think she's so used to the penthouse life and being taken care of by the others that it doesn't even seem to bother her much that her son lives with her sister," Ree continued. "I bought the sad act at first. But seeing her in action at the penthouse, I'm not sure she wants the role of full-time mother."

"There are plenty of strong single women out there kicking butt and taking names," he stated. He should know. His own mother had been one of them. She'd worked two jobs to keep food on the table. They'd lived in a trailer park on the outskirts of Houston, and she'd been gone most of the time, working. Quint had been young and stupid. He got bored. Lonely. So he ended up getting into trouble when he should have been studying his backside off and picking up the slack at home. One of the times Quint got into trouble, the liaison officer at his school stepped in, realizing Quint needed a male role model in his life. Officer Jazz had been a lifesaver. He took it upon himself to speak to the school. Quint's teachers apparently came forward saying he used to be a good student and they weren't sure what happened. Jazzy, as he used to call him, didn't leave it there. He kept digging and then eventually asked if he could sit with Quint at lunch one day. Said he would like to be Quint's sponsor in a mentoring program. Quint had balked at first, but then he got into a real fix. He distinctly remembered the day he'd sat across the dining room table from his mom and saw the exhaustion and hurt in her eyes. She could barely stay awake because she'd worked all night at the hospital, changing bedpans. In that moment, it had clicked. Quint realized his mother deserved so much better from him.

The word *saint* didn't begin to cover it when it came to his mother. She sure didn't deserve to get sick and die before he could repay her for all the amazing things she'd given him and done for him growing up. Anger welled inside him as he thought about how his father had walked away from the mother of his child, not to mention the child itself. Taking in a slow breath, he flexed and released his fingers a couple of times to work out some of the tension that came with the memories.

Ree had been the first person he'd opened up to about his mother. He'd never even spoken about her to Tessa, and the two of them had been best friends. Sharing a part of his life with Ree no one else knew about and wanting to show her the small things made him realize she was different, special.

"I don't get the impression Giselle could ever be confused with being a strong woman," Ree stated with a little ire in her tone. She had every right to be angry.

"Nope," he agreed.

A visible tremor rocked Ree.

"What is it?" he asked. "Tell me what happened to you and exactly how Giselle was involved."

Chapter Three

Ree recounted the story of getting a last-minute text, practically sprinting out the door and then being kidnapped literally the minute she walked onto the street. It was broad daylight. Giselle was making a beeline toward Ree, waving. Two guys flanked her. It had all happened so fast, in spite of the fact Ree was trained to check her surroundings for clues.

The whole incident sounded like something out of a spy movie, even to her.

"These situations are rehearsed. They're good at what they do," she stated, even more frustrated someone had gotten the drop on her. She was skilled at her job too. There was no reason she should have been caught unawares. Of course, she'd learned to go with the flow a long time ago in her law enforcement career. Being undercover for the past two years had honed the lesson. As awful as these incidents could be, they often led to a break in a case. *Or a body bag one day*, she thought.

"There's a reason this ring is one of, if not *the* best weapons trafficking ring in North America," Quint said. The comment was most likely meant to ease her embarrassment at allowing herself to fall into their trap, even though the statement was true. "And letting them kidnap you was your best chance at staying alive."

Quint seemed just as upset about what she'd been through as she was. If the shoe was on the other foot, she would be frantic too.

"After they buried me in the coffin-like crate, they shoveled dirt on top," she said, pausing as the memory caused her chest to tighten. She released the breath she'd been holding. "Giselle came to my rescue. She begged Lindy to stop what he was doing and at least give me a chance to breathe."

"That was good of her, considering she was the one who betrayed you in the first place." His tone held the same rage she was experiencing.

"My thoughts exactly," she quipped. "But I have to give her props for going to bat for me. He would have buried me all the way if she hadn't stepped in, and her intervention is probably the reason I was able to push through and open the top. Otherwise, the weight might have been too heavy, and there might not have been any give."

Her body shuddered involuntarily at the thought.

"I'll kill that bastard," Quint managed to grind out. Except they both knew he wouldn't. Not if he wanted to keep his job, his pension and his self-respect.

"At least he stopped, or I might still be buried," she said with another shiver. "He said something about coming back for me if I stayed alive. I'm guessing he reached out to you shortly after to force your hand into ensuring Vadik is dead."

"Lindy planned to leave you there overnight?" Quint said. Again the jaw muscle pulsed.

"Seems so," she admitted, not real thrilled with the idea either. "At least he planned to come back. Plus, we have his timeline. For all he knows, I'm still out there buried alive."

"He was the one who reached out to say I needed to get rid of Vadik in the text message," he reminded.

"We could get him on solicitation of murder," she explained. "He would go away for a very long time on a charge like that one."

Quint nodded even though he knew as well as she did there was no way they would go through with it. Not when they could get Dumitru instead.

"That about sums up my side," she said.

"Have you made up your mind about whether or not you think we should pay Vadik a visit?" he asked.

"Are you asking my permission?" She didn't bother to hide the shock in her voice. She wasn't trying to be a jerk. He actually caught her off guard.

"No," he said, hesitating for a few seconds. Then came, "We both know this investigation wouldn't be where it is without you. We make a great undercover team." He paused for a few beats. "But I think our relationship outside of work is the most important one. At least, it is to me."

"You won't get any argument from me there," she agreed, and meant it with all her heart.

He reached over and covered her hand with his. The connection calmed her nerves a notch below panic as she relived the horrible day and the decision they needed to make about Vadik.

"If he doesn't agree, we walk away, and he gets locked up in solitary confinement," Quint continued.

"What about the case, Quint?" she asked. "Will you be able to leave it behind? You have a whole lot of history behind this one and a personal connection binding you to the outcome. Knowing you as well as I do, I find it difficult to believe you'll be able to move on without getting the closure you deserve."

Quint sat there for a long moment without saying a word. With his free hand, he took a few sips of coffee before setting the mug down near hers.

"I can't make any promises, because I don't know how I'll feel if the lead dries up," he started. "There are a whole lot of things I want to say, and believe. But you're right. I would be naive to think losing out on Dumitru after being this close wouldn't eat me alive from the inside out."

She nodded. They weren't the words she wanted to hear, but they were brutally honest.

"Then there's you to consider." He brought her hand up to his lips and placed a tender kiss on the inside of her wrist. "I've never had anyone in my life before who makes me want to come home every night. There hasn't been anyone I couldn't walk away from and get over like that." He snapped his fingers. "Until you."

"How does that change the investigation?" she asked, her body literally warming. This close, she could breathe in his spicy male scent. She'd memorized it...*him*.

"I still want to lock Dumitru behind bars and throw away the key," he admitted, the fire back and dancing in his eyes. "Make no mistake about it."

Quint took in a breath, and then slowly released it.

"But I plan to come home to you every day for the rest of our lives," he said. "And this case won't...*can't*...be the reason I don't get to."

"I want out, Quint," she stated, unsure of how he was going to react to what she had to say next. "This job. This life." She brought her eyes up to meet his. "It isn't a life, but it does overtake one."

"If you're happy, that's all I need to hear," he said. "I love you, Ree. I want to spend the rest of our lives together. I don't care what you do for a living. What we have between us is the only priority for me."

Ree took in another deep breath. Why was it so difficult for her to admit what she needed to tell him? She'd said yes when he'd asked her to marry him. He was her best friend and her everything. Shouldn't telling him be easy?

"What is it, Ree?" A look of concern darkened those stormy blue eyes.

"There's something I need to tell you," she said.

"Okay," he responded, squaring his shoulders like he was preparing to take a punch.

"I'm not sure if what I have to say will change how you feel about me in any way," she continued, searching for the right words, the right moment to speak what had been on her mind.

"You can tell me anything," he said, his brow furrowing.

Since there was no easy way to say it, she decided to go for it.

"I want kids."

Quint's jaw dropped, and she panicked.

"It doesn't have to be right away." Ree qualified her statement—a statement that had thrown Quint for a loop.

"Okay," he said, trying to process the fact they'd shifted gears into unknown territory.

"Okay?" she asked.

Quint wasn't sure how he felt about the idea. To be honest, he'd never given kids serious consideration. His life had felt lacking in a strange way recently. He'd tried to chalk it up to losing Tessa, but the feeling had been there for much longer than the past eight or nine months. He'd been restless before his partner had died and long before Ree came along. He was still trying to sort out what it all meant.

"We've been tied up with the case, so I've been focused on that recently," he said by way of explanation. The tiny muscles in her face tensed as he spoke, and he realized he was disappointing her with his response. An apology seemed in order. Except that he really didn't know where he stood on kids. Quint was certain where he *used* to stand on the subject. But a lot had changed since meeting Ree. He'd never thought he'd be eager to spend the rest of his life with someone until her.

"Forget I said anything," she quickly backpedaled. "It's too soon anyway."

It wasn't, though. He was in his forties. She was four years shy of her fortieth birthday. If they wanted kids, they probably should be thinking about them, making plans. Under normal circumstances, the idea would have made Quint's brain explode. Surprisingly enough, it didn't.

"I'd like to put the subject on hold for now," he said, and noticed the tension lines forming on her face. "Just until we figure out if we're off this case or moving full steam ahead. Okay?"

"Makes sense. We should visit Vadik," she said, but the enthusiasm was gone from her eyes. "We have plenty of time to talk about our future."

"I'll hold off responding to Lindy until we talk to Vadik," he said, figuring he needed to fire off a text to Grappell to set everything up.

"We need to find Vadik's Achilles' heel," Ree said as Quint sent off the message to their desk agent.

"He doesn't have children or a wife. At least, not obviously. They must be tucked away somewhere if they exist," Quint said.

"I didn't see any pictures or indications there were children at the penthouse. Did you?" she asked.

"No," he responded. She'd spent more time there than him, so she would have been the one to notice.

"Vadik doesn't act married either. Although we both

know the definition of marriage and relationships in their
world doesn't exactly match with ours," she continued.

Quint agreed.

"I wonder if there is anyone special in his life," she said.

"It sure would make our lives a whole lot easier if we
found someone to use as leverage," Quint agreed.

Ree sucked in a breath.

"What about a sibling?" she asked.

"I'll see what else Grappell found out about Vadik,"
Quint said. "Everything has been happening so fast, details are slipping. I should already know this."

"We're here now and we'll figure it out. I'd start with
asking about bank records," she said. "See if he sends
money to anyone on a regular basis who isn't connected
to the crime ring."

"A money exchange like that would most likely happen under the table, or he would find a way to launder
it," he said.

"True." She chewed on the inside of her cheek again.
"What do we know about the guy other than the fact that
he's high-ranking within Dumitru's organization?"

"That's all I have so far." Quint sent off another request
for personal information about Vadik. "He seems to keep
his personal life separate from his professional one."

"I don't think he lives at the penthouse full-time," she
said.

"Why is that?" he asked.

"It's a party spot, and when I went seeking out a bathroom once, I ended up in the master bedroom. It was a
basic room. There wasn't anything personal in there. I
ducked inside and checked the drawers and closet. Same
thing. There was very little in the way of clothing, and I almost tripped over a weekender bag sitting next to the door."

"Interesting," Quint stated, hoping this meant Grappell

would be able to dig up usable information on the man. Right now, all they had to use as incentive was negotiating for a lighter sentence. With a hotshot lawyer, the case against Vadik could get kicked out of court. The thought sent fire racing through Quint.

Criminals shouldn't get to roam the streets or do whatever they wanted because they had enough money to pay for the best lawyers. Don't even get him started on the ones who were part of human trafficking organizations. Vadik needed to rot in jail for his part. Quint might have jeopardized their last case by calling the bust early, but it had been worth it.

"Speaking of Vadik," Ree started. "Did Grappell update the file about the kids?"

"Yes," he said. He'd been forced to end the last case earlier than he would have liked when half a dozen kids were brought to Vadik's jewelry store along with trunks full of weapons. There'd been no way Quint could walk away from the scene and allow those children to be sold. Period.

The move had cost him valuable time that he needed to build a strong case against Vadik while working his way to Dumitru. Seeing the look in those kids' eyes had caused him to snap. All he'd been able to think about was Tessa's unborn baby and what she would have thought of him if he'd allowed children to be sold. Children he had the power to help.

So he'd done what he had to and called for the raid. He'd made a point of slipping out, getting away, and outrunning the cops who'd shown up to make the arrests. One of Vadik's colleagues had set the building on fire, destroying valuable evidence.

The case against Vadik wasn't strong, and he seemed to realize it. Gaining his cooperation without the right leverage was going to be an uphill battle. But all the cards had been played, and this was the only hope.

"She would be proud of you. You know that, right?" Ree said, breaking into his reverie.

"How do you know I was thinking about Tessa?" he asked.

"You get a look on your face," she said with a shrug. "I noticed."

"I hope she would be proud," was all he said.

"We've gone in with nothing before and come out with what we needed," Ree continued. "We make a good team."

"No arguments there," Quint agreed. So much so, he could barely imagine doing this job without her as his partner. His cell buzzed, so he checked the screen. The message was from Grappell.

"What is it?" Ree asked.

"I think we just got our leverage," Quint said, placing a call to their desk agent.

Chapter Four

"Vadik has a mother."

"I'm guessing there's more to this announcement," Ree said, considering everyone had a mom. "Even creeps like him had to come from somewhere."

"True enough. He keeps her tucked away, though," Agent Grappell continued.

"With the circles he runs in, I don't blame him for keeping his mother far away from his day-to-day life," Quint stated.

"Why not keep her at his place, though?" Ree asked, figuring the man had enough money to put security around his mother twenty-four-seven. His penthouse had more guns than a shooting range on half-price day.

"She needs full-time care," Grappell explained. "Her memory is failing, and she has health issues. He keeps her in a pricey place overlooking Lake Travis in hill country. Believe me when I say that I had to dig deep to get this information."

Ree involuntarily shivered at a couple of those words: *dig deep*. The image of the box she'd been buried in came to mind. Try as she might, shaking off the feeling that her chest was caving in was hard. She reminded herself where she was, in the apartment, safe with Quint.

Why did they have to bury her? The *one* thing she

would have the most difficult time recovering from was her claustrophobia.

Glancing down in her lap, she realized she'd subconsciously twisted her fingers together. Flexing and releasing her fingers a few times served to work off some of the tension. A couple of deep breaths later and she felt half-human again. Confronting Giselle was something Ree looked forward to. *If* she got to the woman first. Quint seemed ready to pounce the minute they laid eyes on her. A little voice in the back of Ree's mind picked that moment to remind her she wouldn't be sitting here right now if not for Giselle's intervention. The thought helped dial down the heat boiling in Ree's veins.

Grappell rattled off the address of the group home where Vadik's mother lived as Ree clued back into the conversation.

"There are only four residents in the McMansion on the hillside," Grappell continued. "There's twice as many staff as residents. There's a cook dedicated to fixing nutritious meals."

"I imagine security will be tight," Quint stated with a glance toward Ree. He sat close to her, like he didn't want her farther away than arm's reach. There was something about his physical presence that reassured her too. Like somehow life would always work out if the two of them were connected, together.

"True," Ree agreed.

"I'll see what I can do about getting the layout of the residence and the property," Grappell stated. "I'm guessing you'll want to act as soon as possible on the mother."

"If we have her, we have leverage," Quint said. "Without her, we don't have a leg to stand on."

"Vadik doesn't seem like he'll cooperate otherwise," Grappell agreed. "What are we talking about here? Removing his mother from her environment could backfire considering she needs medical care."

"Maybe we don't have to take her anywhere," Ree piped up. "Can we send in a drone and get some pictures of her on the lawn? Maybe snap a few of her in her room from the window? All we need is to see from the outside looking in and we'll have something to show Vadik. A threat to his mother would work."

"I could fake documents saying we're going to deport her," Grappell said.

"That should shake him up quite a bit," she agreed. "He must want her close to him rather than halfway around the world."

Quint was nodding, and she could practically see the wheels turning.

"How long before you can get those printouts to us?" he asked.

"A couple of hours for the digital files," Grappell stated. "A couple more for the prints."

"We can go in with pictures on our cell phones," Ree said. "All we're trying to do is shake the man up."

"Darn," Quint protested. "I like the idea of slamming a file folder down on the table with photos in it."

Ree smiled for the second time that day. Only Quint could bring out her lighter side after the day she'd had.

"Why don't you guys hunker down for the rest of tonight and let me work on this?" Grappell asked.

"I don't know," Ree started. "A middle-of-the-night visit, being yanked out of the comfort of his bed, might be just what he needs to wake up and realize we're offering him his only choice out of the mess he's made of his life."

"If his mother's health is on the line, he might not care about anything else," Quint pointed out.

"That's why we have to convince him to help us," Ree

continued. "Without us, his mother gets deported, and there's no one there to take care of her. She gets sicker. Maybe even dies while he rots in a cell." Ree snapped her fingers. "If he cooperates, we don't touch her. It's that simple."

Quint was nodding in agreement.

"It's our best bet," Grappell stated. "I'll send the drone and see if we can capture any shots of dear old mom."

"Thank you," Ree said, figuring Grappell didn't get near enough credit for everything he did for investigations like this one. He'd been their assigned agent on four cases now, all of which were leading up to Dumitru's eventual capture. At least, Ree hoped they would be able to incarcerate the man responsible for Tessa's death. Otherwise, Ree's fiancé might live in a mental prison of his own making for the rest of his life.

THEY HAD A solid lead. Quint should be happy. And yet what had happened to Ree still had him shaken up to the point he wasn't sure it was worth going on with the investigation. But stopping now wasn't an option either. Ree wouldn't want him to walk away at this point over her. She was fully capable of doing her job, and she had been doing just that this afternoon at lunchtime when she'd been abducted off the street in front of their apartment building.

Lindy was flexing, showing he could do whatever he wanted, whenever he wanted, and no one—not even Quint—would be able to stop the man. Lindy was essentially telling Quint that he could take his girlfriend in broad daylight and there wasn't squat Quint could do about it. His hand involuntarily fisted as they ended the call with Grappell. The desk agent had promised to let them know the minute he had any pictures to work with. Those pictures were going to sway Vadik into agreeing to cooperate. *They had to.*

"Hey, are you doing all right?" Ree's voice traveled over to him. He looked up at her and realized she'd been studying him. He shouldn't be surprised at this point. She seemed to be able to read his moods.

"I can't help but think I let you down today," he admitted.

"You didn't," she argued.

"If I'd been downstairs with you then—"

Ree put a hand up to stop him.

"Quint, you would step in front of a bullet for me. Don't be so hard on yourself considering you can't physically be around every second. Plus, I'm a qualified agent," she pointed out.

"You're right up there with the best I've ever worked with or come across professionally. And that's saying a whole lot," he agreed. Still, risking her life felt like the most selfish thing he would ever do. Tessa would kick his behind if she was alive. Somewhere deep down, he realized she wouldn't want him going after the guy connected to the case. So why couldn't he let it go?

The thought of walking away from this case and from his job had never appealed. He hadn't given a whole lot of thought to what he would do when he was finished putting his life on the line. Had he ever seriously considered retiring? A voice tucked in the back of his minds pointed out the fact that he never really expected to live long enough to retire.

Until Ree, he didn't have much to live for. The realization struck like stray lightning on a sunny day. Now he had someone to build a future with who felt the same. He was still figuring out kids. He'd never given them much consideration at all until Tessa had turned up pregnant, and then he'd been focused on being the stand-in dad her kiddo would need. Not once did he truly consider becoming a biological father. Ree's comment had thrown him off guard before, and he was still regaining his balance. Did he want kids?

The question had to be shelved for now. This wasn't the right time or place. Besides, all he could think about was putting Dumitru behind bars and this case in the rearview once and for all. Tessa would want him to move on. This was the only way he could sleep at night.

"Quint?" Ree's voice broke in.

"Yes," he responded.

"Where did you go just now?" she asked, still studying him.

He hoped she wasn't worried about what she'd gotten herself into by saying yes when he'd proposed.

"I'm all over the place," he admitted. "Mainly, I'm determined to wrap this case up as quickly as possible so we can move forward with life."

"I'd drink to that," she said with a warm smile. "Since you're already bouncing topics, where do you want to live after the wedding?"

"I guess I hadn't thought too much about it," he admitted. Honestly, he hadn't gotten much further than ending the case. "Where would you like to live?"

"I'd been assuming that we would live at my place, but that's not exactly fair to you," she said.

He reached over and took her hand in his. Physical contact with Ree had a way of calming the always raging storm inside him.

"I want to live wherever you are. My place isn't big enough for the two of us. I love your grounds. Moving into your home, making it ours, sounds right to me," he said.

"Are you serious?" she asked. "Because I would love that too."

"Then it's decided," he stated. "Besides, I want you to be closer to your family."

"That means a lot to me, Quint," she said. Then came a cheeky smile. "But you may live to regret it. You've met them. My mom isn't going to welcome you with open arms."

"She will if we tell her that I'm the reason you're planning on leaving undercover work," he teased.

Ree laughed, and she had a musical quality to her voice.

"You'll get even more brownie points if you tell her you put your foot down," she said with an eye roll.

He shook his head.

"I can't imagine a reason in the world your mother wouldn't be bursting with pride every time she thought about you," he said in all seriousness. "Not only are you one of the best undercover agents I've had the pleasure of working with, but you're a good person to boot. You're intelligent, quick-witted, and can hold your own. I have yet to see you back down from anyone or anything."

"That's the problem right there," she said. "My mother wanted a girlie-girl, and that has never been me."

"She is missing out on an incredible daughter," he stated. "If we ever have a girl, I hope she is just like you."

Ree shot him a look as he heard the words coming out of his own mouth. Shock didn't begin to describe his reaction to what he'd just said. She seemed to catch on to the fact he'd just spoken without thinking and clamped her mouth shut.

A text came through, breaking into the moment. Quint checked the screen. "Grappell doesn't quite have the photos of Vadik's mother yet, but he says we might not need them. As soon as Vadik's mother was mentioned, he back-pedaled and said he might be ready to talk."

"That's good." She pushed to standing. "We should go strike while the iron is hot."

Quint suppressed the urge to ask her to stay in the apartment, reminding himself she was a more than capable undercover agent. Being in love with her was like having his heart walking around outside of his chest. If he loved and wanted to protect her this way, he couldn't imagine how much more that would extend to their children.

Was he seriously considering a family?

Ree deserved to have everything she wanted, and that seemed to include little rug rats running around. Could he give that to her? Did he really have a choice? He would do anything to make her happy. Now he needed to figure out how to be just as enthusiastic at the thought as she seemed to be.

Quint grabbed the keys from the counter and then tucked his cell phone inside his back pocket.

"Give me one second to get dressed," she said before grabbing clothes and then disappearing into the bathroom. She emerged a couple of minutes later.

He walked Ree out of the apartment, to the elevator and then to the waiting SUV with his hand on the small of her back.

After surveying the parking lot, she climbed inside the vehicle. The way her jaw was set and her gaze narrowed told him she was still reeling from being kidnapped this morning. The same had happened to him, except the part about being stuffed inside a makeshift coffin. Every undercover agent who'd been on the job longer than a few years had, at one time, been abducted or lured to a questionable place in the name of a case. Quint was going to have to figure out a way to get past the fact it had happened to Ree despite how much his protective instincts flared. Besides, their future family didn't work without her.

Chapter Five

The ride to the Dallas County Corrections Department was quiet. Between the coffin and talking to Quint about possibly having babies in the future, a lot of ground had been covered. Becoming an undercover agent two years ago was the pinnacle of a hard-fought career, but the job had become her life. Preston, her ex-boyfriend who also happened to be her older brother's best friend, and her family had been right all along. The only thing she'd cared about up to this point was work. What they were missing was the fact she'd never met anyone before who made her want to consider another path.

Quint Casey was the difference. But now she needed to refocus on what they were going to say to Vadik and how the next steps of their plan might fall into place. *The sooner the better* came to mind when she thought about wrapping this one up. It was also the first time in her career that she'd followed a target over four undercover operations. The longer the two of them stayed with this, the more dangerous it became. The risk of their identity being uncovered grew with each passing day.

Quint parked the Chevy Blazer in the lot but didn't immediately exit the vehicle. He sat there, staring out the windshield, looking like he had something to say. His lips formed a grim line.

After releasing a sharp sigh, he asked, "Ready?"

This was it, she realized. After securing Vadik's help, they would enter the final steps of what had been a very long journey so far. And if they couldn't get Vadik's agreement, if this was some sort of trick to get them down here so he could spit in their faces, Quint and Ree would have to step out of the case and back into their lives. They had a wedding to look forward to and a real future. She worried it wouldn't be enough if her fiancé didn't get closure. They'd come this far. Failure wouldn't be an option to Quint no matter how often he'd said he could walk away. There'd been no conviction in his words, and she couldn't allow him to compromise or he could end up bitter. There was no way she could live with herself if she was the reason he stopped working on Tessa's case.

The desk sergeant escorted the two of them to a small room with a table and three chairs. He locked the door behind them and then disappeared. Quint tapped his finger on the tabletop as they waited. After what seemed like forever but was more like fifteen minutes, an officer brought Vadik into the room through a door on the opposite side of the room, deposited him and then indicated he would be waiting on the other side of the door.

Vadik Gajov was five-feet-nine to five-feet-ten, if Ree had to guess. He would be considered average height by European standards. Here in Dallas, he stuck out as being short.

"Have a seat, Vadik," Quint said. His gaze narrowed, and his tone left no room for doubt that he wasn't there to play.

"I like to stand." Vadik had a thick eastern European accent. His intense gray eyes settled on Ree.

Instinctively, Quint stood up, drawing attention back to himself. "Then we'll both stand."

This was a contest to see who could claim to be in control of this conversation. Vadik had already lost. She could tell from his slight pout that he was unaccustomed to be on the losing side of any matchup. Too bad. He was already behind the eight ball, and the reality he had a mother to protect put him securely at their mercy.

"Do what you want," Vadik said, crossing his arms. "Now that I know you're both cops, what do you really want?" A look of disdain radiated from dark eyes. His gaze lingered on Ree for a few seconds and his top lip curled in what looked like a growl. "You?"

"That's right. And I'm an agent not a cop. You'll get a lot further with us if you cooperate," she stated, unfazed by his reaction.

He sat there for a long moment, staring her down.

"You already know what we want. Your cooperation." Quint shifted the focus to him.

"In return for what?" Vadik asked. "What will you do for me?"

"Allow your mother to stay in the country, for one," Quint said calmly, like he was reading the Sunday paper in his house slippers with a cup of coffee nearby.

"Fine," Vadik said, brushing nonexistent lint off the sleeve of his orange jumpsuit like he had all day. "What else?"

"That's the only thing I can promise," Quint stated. "And that's pushing it."

"What if I don't agree to your terms?" Vadik asked.

"Then dear old mom gets deported and is never allowed back in the US," Quint said. "I bet you have some relatives back home who would be willing to take her in and care for her. Right, Vadik?"

He bristled and recovered almost as quickly. As much as he was trying to play his cards close to the vest, he had no power here. Still, his pride seemed like it would hold him back as much as possible.

"I'll be honest with you. Keeping my mother in this country is my greatest wish," Vadik said. "However, never being able to see her again is a knife to the chest."

Ree observed the tension lines in Vadik's forehead. She saw the deep grooves around his mouth that hadn't been there before.

"I understand," Quint said, not offering to go to bat for Vadik.

"They will kill me," Vadik said. Ree glanced at his hands and realized he'd been chewing his fingernails to the quick. The cool, penthouse-living, suit-wearing image was a far cry from the man standing in front of her now.

"They are already trying," Quint stated. "They sent me to get it done because they have no idea about my true identity. Otherwise, you'd already be dead instead of sitting in this room talking to us."

Vadik audibly gasped. "It makes no sense why they would come after me this way."

His shoulders deflated despite his chin shooting up.

"You're too close to Dumitru," Quint pointed out. "He doesn't want to risk you talking to save your own hide."

"He should know that I would never do that." Vadik's grip on his arms caused his knuckles to turn white.

"Law enforcement is circling, Vadik. He has to know some of his men, especially the ones closest to him, might turn," Quint pointed out.

Ree stayed quiet up to this point. Mainly because Vadik might love his mother, but he didn't respect women. She'd seen the way he treated them at the penthouse, not allowing them to stand at the bar because it cheapened them in his eyes. The women there were nothing more than party girls to be disposed of when they were deemed too old or no longer useful. It made Ree sick to her stomach thinking about the manner in which Vadik treated people. Looking at him now as he faced the music from a lifetime of crime, it was impossible to drum up sympathy for the man for the fact he might not see his mother again.

She did, however, feel a twinge of sadness for the elderly woman who was completely dependent on Vadik for her quality of care. Ree highly doubted any of Vadik's relatives in Romania would take her care this seriously.

There were always so many casualties in the criminal world. Ree had also seen families who knew exactly what was happening and protected their own. She assumed they were protecting their free ride since many of them lived in nice houses with no real incomes on record. Crime families had a strange dynamic, Ree thought. Her own family seemed normal by comparison, and on many levels, it was. Her mother didn't agree with Ree's career choice. Had Ree worked harder to climb the ladder out of spite? She wasn't a vengeful person, but she did push her mother's buttons at times. Now that Ree was thinking of having a family of her own, she was softening toward her mother, beginning to see a little bit of the woman's point of view.

Her mother's concern did come from a place of love and care. Ree's shoulders deflated. Had she been part of the reason for the rift? Was her brother Shane right about Ree needling her mother at the point of her insecurity?

Thinking of having a family was resetting Ree's priorities already. She could scarcely imagine what it was going to be like when she actually had kids. Maybe it was time to give her mother a break? After all, no parent was perfect, and Ree was beginning to see how difficult the job of bringing up kids was going to be. She was already second-guessing herself in the parenting department.

And then what happened if the kid turned out to be like

the thugs she put behind bars? What if she had a child just like Vadik?

Quint said he would be open to having kids. Did he realize what he might be getting into?

"IF I AGREE to these terms, will I ever see my mother again?" Vadik's question was valid. It wasn't the one he needed to be asking.

"You're dead to her either way," Quint stated. All he had to do was think about the half-dozen children Vadik had been so ready to sell to the highest bidder to be able to distance any sympathy Quint might have had. He called up the dirty and scared faces of each one because he'd burned the details into his memory. "I'm offering a way your mother can stay safe and well cared for."

"Not without money," Vadik said. "The government has already seized all my assets by now. My bank accounts are most likely frozen. How will my mother be cared for if there is no money to pay the bills?"

"How far up is she paid?" Quint could have Grappell look into the details, but he wanted to see how honest Vadik would be.

"Five years," he supplied. "Give or take."

"A lot can happen in five years," Quint pointed out. He wasn't making any promises and wouldn't. The man needed to pay for his crimes. Being kind to his aging mother didn't erase his willingness to sell innocent children who'd been stripped from their families. So, no, he didn't have a whole lot of sympathy for Vadik. Don't even get Quint started on how the man treated women in general. Being kind to his own mother did nothing to purge the rest of his sins.

Vadik paced back and forth along the back wall. All pretense he was sitting in the driver's seat of the conversation was gone now. The man was in self-preservation mode. All he seemed to care about was his mother and his own fate.

"I'll beat these charges," Vadik stated. "I have access to the best lawyers through my connections."

"You could roll the dice, but the evidence against you is strong. I've seen guys like you locked away for the rest of their lives with half this much proof. Not to mention the fact I've never lost a case when I'm the star witness," Quint said. It was true. He was an excellent witness.

Vadik frowned.

"You've never gone against my lawyers," he said. "And when I get out of this hole, I intend to stay aboveground."

"You seem to be forgetting one very important point," Quint continued. "They sent *me* to kill you already. Even if you have the best lawyers in the world, you'll never make it to trial. If I don't get the job done, they'll just send someone else."

Vadik's eyebrows drew together like he was trying to figure out how to split an atom.

"Then there's the obvious fact the government seized all your assets, and all your accounts are frozen, which is a long-winded way of pointing out that you're broke," Quint continued. "Your former employer seems ready to cut bait."

A long, drawn-out silence sat heavy in the room.

"How would it go down?" he asked, stopping in front of the same door he'd walked through minutes ago.

"It would have to be visible," Quint figured. "Probably a fake attack in the yard or in your cell. We'll plant someone to carry it out. They'll most likely use blood-like pouches the size of washing detergent pods."

When Vadik gave Quint a sideways glance, he held out his hand palm up.

"They would fit here basically," Quint explained, motioning toward his palm and drawing the shape of an egg there. It dawned on him that a man like Vadik wouldn't know how to use a washer or dryer. The guy probably hadn't lifted a finger since rising in the ranks of A-12, the organization headed by Dumitru.

"And what would that do?" Vadik's eyebrows drew together, and his lips thinned. He didn't like what he was hearing, but he was listening intently. Quint could work with that.

"Cause a burst of what looks like blood. The attacker can fit it in the palm of his hand, so when he shows a knife or sharp object, everyone will assume the blood is from you," Quint said. "It'll splatter all over you and the person attacking you, which makes it all the more believable to bystanders."

"What about others? Some might join in," Vadik said. "Try to get in a punch or a stab."

"This has to look natural but will be tightly controlled to ensure that doesn't happen." Quint noticed how careful Vadik was being while placing himself in harm's way. His thoughts snapped back to the kids at Vadik's store. Quint reminded himself to exhale. The notion of bringing kids into a world with people like Vadik running around didn't sit well. Of course, he did realize many of the kids who were kidnapped came from vulnerable situations at home. Alcoholic or neglectful parents, or both, who weren't paying attention put their kids most at risk. Then there were the older kids who ran away thinking they could get a better deal on the streets than in their own homes. Ree and Quint's children would have two parents who stuck around, provided for them and loved them.

His mind snapped to Ree's father. He'd been killed on the job while working law enforcement. Quint had toyed around with the idea of walking away from the job recently. Could he?

The last thing he wanted was to be the kind of father who disappeared for weeks on end, leaving his wife and children to worry about whether or not he was coming home. Since Tessa and her baby's death, being an undercover agent had been losing its shine anyway. What would Quint do if he left the only career he'd ever known?

"And all this is for show?" Vadik asked, interrupting Quint's thoughts. Did the man seriously believe a federal agent would set up a fake death and then actually kill him? Vadik seemed to be getting the idea of the scrutiny agents were under to do their jobs. He had to account for every bullet fired, and not just for inventory purposes. The bullet had to be traced and explained once it struck.

"It is," Quint confirmed, figuring this wasn't the time to educate Vadik on policy. "You might be struck, possibly bruised, so a lawyer will come in the room after we're finished here to explain your legal rights."

"And there's no plea bargain on the table for me?" Vadik had the boldness to ask.

All Quint had to do in order to answer that question was think about having kids of his own, or any of the many other children already born who Vadik would sell if he had a chance when he walked free again.

"No. Absolutely not. There's no way my boss would approve a deal for you," he said, knowing full well he would never even consider asking for one.

"Then there's no way I'll help you," Vadik concluded. "I'm sorry to have wasted your time."

Ree flinched ever so slightly.

Quint pushed up to standing.

"Very well then. You'll be locked in solitary confinement until our case concludes so you can't speak to anyone," Quint said, as serious as the day was long.

Quint glanced at Ree, who immediately stood. She'd

been quiet so far, and he realized why. Vadik would listen to Quint more than he would a woman. It was one of Vadik's many disgusting qualities.

Ree turned to the door and took the couple of steps. Quint reached for the handle as she spun around and then folded her arms.

"Before we go," she started, and then seemed to lock onto Vadik. "What message would you like us to give your mother?"

Chapter Six

Vadik blinked a couple of times at Ree before answering. For a long moment, it seemed like he was dumbfounded by her comment.

She provoked him. "Come on, Vad. You had to know we would leave here and go straight to her. She'll be in a holding cell at immigration before you brush your teeth for bed."

He stood a little straighter but held his tongue.

"I just hope she doesn't end up with lice like the last batch we sent over there," she continued, figuring painting a vivid picture would work better than any words ever could.

"Right," Quint piped in when Vadik kept his mouth clamped. "And then some of the elderly scratched so hard they drew blood."

"It was a mess," she said with a shrug toward Vadik. "But, hey, that's no longer our problem once we get her in the system."

Ree turned toward the exit.

"Wait," Vadik finally acquiesced. His tone gave away his intentions long before his actual words. "I'm not finished talking."

"Yes, you are," Ree said, acting unfazed. The jerk needed

to sweat it a little after being stubborn from the moment they'd walked through the door.

"Hold on," Vadik said, his tone more pleading this time. Now they were getting somewhere. He sized Ree up. "I knew you were different from the others." He let his gaze wander over her. "Too bad. We could have had a good time together."

She didn't take it personally. It probably galled him to no end that he had to cower to a woman he viewed as beneath him.

"Personally, you don't do anything for me," she quipped. "But then, you never did. So if you're ready to talk about how this will play out, we'll consider sitting down again. But you'll say, 'Yes, ma'am,' when you speak to me from now on or we walk out the door."

"You would risk your precious case?" Vadik said with disdain.

"In my world, there's more than one way to skin a cat," she countered. "You are one option." She didn't bring up the fact he was the best and quickest. Information with Vadik was on a need-to-know basis.

"You will protect my mother?" Vadik asked.

"We'll ensure her safety," Ree stated.

He issued a sharp sigh.

"Then what choice do I have?" he asked with a shrug.

"Good," she said. "We have an agreement. The lawyer will be in shortly."

Quint nodded to the guard who'd been standing at the window with his arms crossed. He unfolded his arms and retrieved Vadik. It had been a long but productive day. Everything was sore and Ree was exhausted. Time to head back to the apartment.

As soon as they stepped into the hallway and the door was closed, Quint brought Ree into an embrace.

"We need to get you home and to bed," he said, then caught the implication. "Not for that. Although I'm ready and willing the second you feel up to it."

He winked and it made her smile. His smile brought to life places that needed rest.

She pushed up to her tiptoes and pressed a kiss to his lips. She'd been wanting to do that all day.

"You'll be the first to know when I'm able," she said, then wiggled her eyebrows. "Are you ready to get out of here?"

"There's no place like home," he quipped, linking their fingers as they headed out toward the same way they had come. The desk sergeant came and unlocked the door for them before thanking them for coming by.

The ride home was short. Ree ate a ham sandwich before rinsing off in another shower. It would take a month of showers to wash off the creepy feeling of being buried alive. She threw on pajamas and hit the bed.

"I'll join you after a shower," Quint said, kissing her good-night.

She could get used to this. In fact, she *would* get used to it once this case was over and they planned their wedding. As it was now, Quint was trying to infiltrate a higher level in A-12 and get close enough to Dumitru to pin him for the crimes he committed. Was *still* committing. The arrest she prayed was coming would have to stick, so they needed to be very careful with how they went about collecting evidence. One slip could be used against them in court, allowing Dumitru to walk. Was the system flawed? Yes, she could honestly say it was.

Was it necessary to dot every *i* and cross every *t*? Absolutely yes. Did it mean some folks walked? The fact burned her up inside.

But Ree didn't want to churn over a system that needed

tweaks. All she wanted to do was think about the progress they'd made and the fact that, at some point tomorrow, Vadik would be "dead."

Kicking the case into high gear meant closing it that much faster. It was an idea Ree could get behind. In her mind, she'd already started writing her letter of resignation for her boss, Lynn Bjorn.

QUINT WOKE BEFORE REE, slipped out from underneath the covers and logged on to the system to check the status of the case. Securing Vadik's help would move the case along. He hoped. Quint needed to provide a status update to Lindy since the man was still under the impression Quint was a bad guy. Surely he would know by now that Ree was no longer in the box. Should Quint let the man sweat it? Wonder where she could be?

While the system was booting up, he circled around the counter into the kitchen and made coffee. His mind was still foggy, and he realized he hadn't checked his cell phone. He'd left it on the nightstand. Coffee came first.

The machine beeped less than three minutes after he loaded it with water and grounds. The smell alone started the wheels turning in his brain. He needed to come up with a plan on how to handle Lindy today. Giselle was a whole other story. Quint had to work hard to control his anger. Of course, any normal person in a relationship would be raging mad at this point, and rightfully so. This was an opportunity to show loyalty to Lindy. As much as it galled Quint, he would do it.

Conjuring up the image of Tessa lying in the hospital bed was normally enough to bring insta-rage boiling in his veins. Either Ree was softening him, or maybe it was the idea of picking up his life and starting a family, but he wanted peace. Peace for Tessa. Peace for her child. And peace for him.

None of what he was currently doing would bring her or the baby back. In fact, she'd most likely chew him out for sticking with a case this long. He knew the risks. He wanted justice for his former best friend and what would have been his godchild. But he was beginning to want to build his own life even more.

If any of his actions could change the past, he had no problem continuing on this course. He'd seen it this far. Leaving now would cast suspicion. It would be impossible to insert another pair of agents into the case at this point. All momentum would be lost, and it could take another two or three years to get this close to Dumitru. The situation was too hot to introduce new players if Quint and Ree walked out. Like it or not, he was stuck with this one. And, like it or not, he needed to see it through to the end.

Would Tessa kick his ever-loving backside over going in this deep and half the stuff he'd pulled to get this far? Quint smirked. He knew the answer was a resounding *hell yeah.* It was getting easier to set some of his anger at the situation aside and see reason. Was Ree the difference in this new ability?

Again, the answer was yes. Being with her made him want to strive to become a better person. He wanted to deal with the emotional baggage he'd convinced a counselor he didn't have. There was something about Ree that made her see right through him to his core. She saw the real him, flaws and all, and seemed to love him anyway.

So, yeah, he wanted to give her everything she deserved in return. Did that mean dealing with his demons so he could move away from a haunted past and have children? Yes. Did that mean reconciling the past with Tessa? Yes.

If only Ree could have met his mother, and his best

friend. Life could strip away loved ones at any moment, he realized. All he truly had was the here and now. He'd been reminded yesterday morning just how quickly someone could be stripped from his life forever.

The way folks drove in downtown Dallas, the possibility of being struck and killed by a vehicle wasn't all that far-fetched. Life was at best unpredictable and at worse cruel. And then someone like Ree had walked into his world, making him rethink everything he thought he knew about goodness and love. She was everything that was right in the world.

Movement in the adjacent bedroom meant she was waking up. He poured a second cup of coffee and brought in to her. Silky red hair splayed across the cream-colored pillowcase. She yawned and stretched her arms out before rolling over to where he sat.

"Well, hello there," she said, her sleepy voice tugging at his heartstrings. He was still trying to figure out how she'd ended up falling for a guy like him. He'd been rough around the edges when they'd met on the first case, but she'd seen something in him. The times they'd kissed had made him realize a spark had been missing from every one of the kisses he'd shared in the past.

Ree Sheppard had turned his world upside down. And he was all the better for it. She was like an angel descended from the heavens, made just for him, perfect in every way imaginable.

"Is that coffee?" she asked as he sat there, dumbstruck.

"For you." He handed over a cup as she sat up. The covers slid down to her waist, revealing the white cotton T-shirt that clung to her curves and revealed firm, full breasts pressed against the thin material.

Ree might be beautiful and have a body made for sinning, but it was her intelligence and sharp wit that had attracted him in the first place. She was the real deal of brains and beauty. Her sense of humor was right up there with his own on the rare occasion he saw it. And there had always been something about Ree that defined her, made her stand out from every other woman Quint had dated. The connection they shared was deeper and more electric than anything he'd ever known. Quint was still trying to figure out what he'd done to deserve her.

"Why so serious?" Ree asked. "Did something happen in the case?"

"No," he quickly said, not wanting her to worry before she had her first cup of coffee. "Nothing like that."

"Then what?" she asked.

He leaned forward and pressed a kiss to her full pink lips.

"I'm a lucky bastard," he said. "That's all."

Her smile could melt ice in a freezer with the door closed.

"I consider myself pretty lucky to have found you, Mr. Casey," Ree said, then took a sip of her coffee. Her tongue slicked across her lips, leaving a silky trail. It was a trail he was having a difficult time taking his eyes off of.

"How are you really feeling this morning?" he asked, needing to redirect his thoughts, because all he wanted to do was make love to his fiancée.

"Well enough to work," she said. "But not before brushing my teeth."

Quint set his cup of coffee on the nightstand as Ree disappeared into the bathroom. She returned a few moments later after the whir of her electric toothbrush did its job. She immediately took a sip of coffee before straddling him on the bed. He splayed his hand on the small of her back, holding her in place so she didn't have to balance her weight. He brought his other hand up to her face, cupping her cheek and bringing her mouth down on his.

And then he made love to the woman he could hardly wait to start his life with. Because everything up to now seemed like a warm-up to the real deal.

"Now that's the proper way to start a day," Ree teased as she gasped for air. Having had one of the best orgasms of her life, she figured this was just the beginning. They'd made love a few times on the assignment but not nearly enough, considering her fiancé had the hottest bod on the planet. She wanted to memorize every inch of him, every scar, every imperfection. Although there were very few of those on a man like Quint Casey and he was one of the rare few who made battered and bruised still look sexy.

"Agreed," he said in between deep breaths. "We need a vacation."

"I'd like a permanent one," she said with another smile. Work waited, and they couldn't stay in this position for long. For the moment, there was no other place she'd rather be than here with her head resting on his arm as it wrapped around her.

Quint's cell buzzed. He reached over to the nightstand and picked it up before checking the screen. "It looks like it's all been arranged and will go down at their breakfast this morning."

"Do we know what time breakfast is at the prison?" Ree asked, figuring their brief oasis of sanity was over.

"In about half an hour," Quint supplied.

"I guess we wait around until we get word it happened," she said. There was no way either of them could relax until it was done, so she threw off the sheets and got ready for the day.

After freshening up in the bathroom, she moved to the

kitchen and refilled their coffee mugs. She checked the fridge to see what she could throw together to eat as Quint studied the laptop screen, no doubt reading up on all the case notes and updating the file. A lot had happened in the past twenty-four hours.

Ree pulled out a carton of eggs, a quart of milk and some leftover spinach from salads they'd had. She could throw together some decent scrambled eggs with the shredded cheese she found. No one would accuse her of being a good cook, but she knew enough to feed herself on the most basic level. There was a loaf of bread, so she could make toast. No jelly, but she could always make do with a dab of butter.

A knock at the door startled them both. Her gaze flew to Quint, who immediately jumped into action. A few seconds later, he was at the door with his weapon at the ready. He peeped through the hole in the door.

"Open up, Quint," a familiar female voice pleaded. What did Giselle think she was doing here?

Chapter Seven

Anger raged inside Ree. So much so, she didn't trust herself not to jump Giselle the second Quint opened the door.

"Why should I after what you pulled?" Quint asked as Ree scurried around, securing the laptop and cell phone after taking his weapon. She pointed toward the wall of closets in the bedroom.

"Is she here?" Giselle asked.

"I think we both know you don't care what happens to my partner," he said, disdain dripping from his tone. Ree figured he didn't have to do a whole lot of acting to pull it off. She felt her own anger in a place deep in her bones. Betrayal could do that to a person.

With all the accessories in hand, she climbed into the closet in the adjacent bedroom and shut the door. Giselle needed to wonder a little while longer what happened to Ree. Her hands pressed against the wood as she crouched inside the small dark space. Memories of being surrounded by nothing but wood flooded her, and she had to remind herself to breathe as her chest squeezed. This wasn't yesterday morning. Ree could open the door at any time and be free. She repeated those thoughts until she started to believe them, and her pulse slowed down a few notches below panic.

"I'll open the door, but if there is someone waiting out

of view, Giselle, I promise you that I will hunt you down," Quint threatened.

"There isn't, and I'm taking a huge risk coming here. Open the door and hear me out," Giselle begged. "At the very least, get me out of this hallway."

Thankfully, their undercover apartment was small and open enough for Ree to be able to hear everything that was going on in the next room from the closet. She took note since she didn't exactly want her neighbors to know every time she and Quint were intimate. Then again, she hadn't heard noise from other apartments since they'd started living there. It was highly possible the walls in between places were thicker. The door would leak noise since it wasn't exactly made of hardwood. This place had a high-end look, but the contractors had cheated in spots with the materials, making it easy to hear everything inside the open-concept space.

It dawned on Ree what her next career move might be. She shelved the thought for now, but she'd always noticed the small details in a house or apartment or how she might do things differently.

"You have a helluva lot of explaining to do." Quint's voice practically boomed as she heard the door open and then close. Then came the snick of the lock.

"Is she here?" Giselle repeated, her voice sounded near frantic at this point. Still, it was impossible to forgive the woman.

"Does it look like it? Look around." Quint's voice sounded wild with worry and steeped in anger. Was this how he'd felt yesterday afternoon, realizing she was gone? Ree's heart pounded against her rib cage as she thought about what might have gone wrong and how terrible it must have been for Quint to sit on the sidelines, not knowing where she was or what she was doing. Or what might have happened to her. His mind had to have flashed back to Tessa. Did that explain his sudden change of heart on the possibility of children?

"You need to start talking and tell me where she is," he demanded.

"I—I—I don't even know where to start." From the way Giselle's voice came in and out of clarity, Ree guessed the woman was pacing. She should be very nervous being around Quint after the stunt she'd pulled. Not to mention the fact Ree and Quint had access to Axel, her boyfriend and her baby's father, who was currently in prison. He'd been the one who struck a deal for his family's safety in exchange for Giselle getting Ree and Quint in with Vadik. Once this case was resolved, Giselle and her young son would be offered Witness Protection, unbeknownst to her. Axel had arranged everything. He'd said she would agree to WITSEC after he spoke to her, which couldn't happen until Dumitru was behind bars.

"Then why are you here?" Quint's voice was the equivalent of thunder booming. It practically shook the walls when he spoke.

"Because I need you both to know I had nothing to do with what happened," Giselle said. "It wasn't my idea, and I fought hard against Lindy. With Vadik in jail right now, Lindy is having a field day."

"I know you were involved. I just don't know what you did," he said. "But she would have let her guard down because she trusted you."

The disdain in his voice permeated the space.

"I didn't have a choice. Lindy said I had to lure her out of the apartment, or he'd take little Axel away, and I'd never see my boy again. What would Axel think of me if I lost our child?" she said, her voice a mix of scared and whiny. Ree liked neither. She could, however, sympathize with a mother who was doing what she could to protect her son.

The truth was that Giselle seemed to like hanging out at Vadik's penthouse more than being home or a mother to her son—a son, she had to remind herself, who currently lived with Giselle's sister. What kind of a mother shoved her kid off to the side and then partied all the time? Not a good one. It also had Ree thinking she needed to cut her own mother a little more slack. Not that she was ready to forgive and move on, but at the very least, Ree's mother cared about her daughter's safety. The fact her mother was too judgmental about Ree's personal choices didn't diminish the fact Ree had always known she was loved. Her older brother Shane would be the first one to point it out. He was their mother's favorite, so he would know.

Ree also noted Lindy liked to hit people directly in their hearts by threatening their families or those they loved. He'd kidnapped Ree to force Quint's hand into arranging a prison murder.

"Did you ever think of what might happen to Ree?" Quint pressed.

"Of course I did. I begged Lindy not...not to..." She seemed too choked up to go on.

"Not to what?" Quint insisted.

"Put her in that coffin, bury her and leave here there to force your hand," Giselle said, pleading her own case. She was all about self-survival, and yet those statements were actually true. She had gone to bat for Ree and sounded remorseful about the situation.

Ree was going to have to find a way to let it go and move on. They'd made a deal with Axel to protect Giselle and then offer WITSEC for her and their son. Ree would have to honor that commitment no matter how much she wanted to throttle the woman.

"My girlfriend might be out there lying in a ditch some-where," he fired back. "You're taking me to the spot where you left her."

"I already went there," Giselle stated with more of that sorrow in her voice. She did seem genuinely upset about the whole situation. She'd been in survival mode and would be for the rest of her life if she always stayed tangled up in a relationship with criminals. "She's gone. The box is open."

"Box?" Quint had to pretend he didn't already know what had happened. His years of undercover work made it impossible to detect he was lying, and yet Ree would know if she looked in his eyes. They had a special bond, a connection like she'd never felt before in a relationship.

"Lindy did it. He forced her into a coffin to scare her and keep her from fighting," Giselle explained. It was half-way true. But then, could Ree really expect someone like Giselle to come completely clean?

"And then what?" More of that thunder rumbled in his voice.

"He started shoveling dirt on top of her," Giselle said in a helpless tone. "I stopped him, though. I put my foot down and got him to listen to me. I convinced him to walk away and go back to get her today. But he's going to flip out when he realizes she isn't there."

"And what exactly does that mean to you?" Quint asked.

Now they were getting to the real truth of why Giselle had shown today since she'd known it wasn't purely out of concern for Ree.

"He'll take away my baby, Quint. My son will never be safe again. Lindy is already suspicious of me, but then, he's paranoid of everyone," she continued. The voice stopped moving, which meant she'd planted her feet. It took all of Ree's willpower not to come out of that closet, because she had a sneaky suspicion Giselle was about to hit on Ree's man.

"There's nothing I can do about that," Quint said. Based on the volume of his voice, he'd moved into the kitchen. Was he putting a barrier between him and Giselle?

Ree's muscles coiled as she hunkered down. It seemed like a good time to remind herself this was a case. Giselle's actions weren't anything personal. Besides, how could anyone be trusted who hit on the first person she saw? Okay, the statement wasn't exactly true. Giselle seemed picky about who she spent time with, but hitting on Quint was her in pure survival mode. It must be awful to be at everyone else's mercy. Ree couldn't understand people like Giselle. Wasn't it so much harder to worry about where her next meal was going to come from or who she had to please over getting a job and taking care of herself and her son?

Granted, she might have to give up the penthouse party life, but what was that giving her? Status?

To Ree's thinking, status didn't put food on the table every night for a kid. It would do Giselle a world of good to kick off those stilettos and put on a pair of sneakers. Plenty of people were hiring. The woman might have to start at the bottom, but she could build a life from there. It would be honest work that Giselle could feel good about at the end of the day. Ree thought of Zoey, a young woman from a previous case who Ree had helped get into an abused women's shelter in Austin after the that case came to a close.

Zoey had adopted a dog and was working. She had plans for the future. The changes in her since getting the help she needed were astounding. Ree had so much respect for Zoey. All she'd needed was a little push in the right direction. Now she was thriving and building a life from the ground up.

Did Giselle think she was too good to start at the bottom? Because Ree had news for the woman: she wasn't doing very well on the party circuit. Give it a couple more years and she would age out. Or worse, end up working for the crime ring. She would be pulled deeper into a life that would chew her up and spit her out. But that was her choice to make.

"Please help me," Giselle begged.

"Take a couple of steps away from me and toward the door or I'll pick you up and throw you out myself," Quint practically growled.

"Sorry," Giselle said. "Don't you think I'm pretty enough?"

"Not the point," he quipped.

"I know that I'm not her, but she might never come back again, Quint. You have to face facts, and we could be a powerful team," Giselle said.

Ree's blood boiled at hearing those words, and it was taking everything inside her not to remove herself from that closet immediately.

QUINT SHOULDN'T HAVE been surprised at the offer from Giselle. And yet there he was, dumbfounded by the fact she thought it was acceptable to walk right into the home he shared with Ree and hit on him.

"Out," was all he said, all he could say without losing it. He'd gotten everything from this conversation he wanted to know. And now she needed to go before Ree climbed out of that closet and dragged Giselle out of the apartment in a body bag.

Giselle didn't put up much of a fight. She seemed to know when she'd lost a battle. Quint figured Ree had even more reasons to throat-punch her betrayer after this visit. Quint shook his head as he heard the elevator ding, and then the doors open and close, but he checked the peephole anyway just to be certain Giselle was gone.

The second Ree must've heard the front door close, she sprang from the closet. She also must have remembered how easily sound echoed from the hallway, because she held her tongue even though it was easy to see from the tension lines on her face she had a lot on her mind.

He shot her a look that he hoped would help calm her down, then checked the peephole again to be one hundred percent certain Giselle had left the floor.

"She's gone," he said to Ree before walking over and pulling her into his arms. She buried her face in his chest.

"I don't know what it is about the sound of her voice that had me wanting to climb out of my skin. I must still be associating her with that box," Ree said. "It took all my willpower not to strangle her."

"No one would blame you if you had," Quint reassured her, holding her as she trembled. The experience from yesterday must have impacted her a whole lot more than he realized, because she was the strongest person he knew.

"And then she hit on you," Ree stated.

"The move reeks of desperation," he explained.

"She is clearly good at saving her own hide," Ree continued. "Although, I must say, she wasn't lying when she said that she convinced Lindy not to bury the box. She will probably go down for my escape because of it."

"You could have suffocated otherwise," Quint said. "That couldn't have been what he wanted. He had to know I would come after him like a pit bull locked onto a side of beef."

"She fought hard for me. I heard it. And he could be just that arrogant," Ree pointed out.

"True. It's like the frog in the pot when the temperature is only turned up one degree at a time. The frog doesn't even feel it until it's too late," he agreed. In truth, it was the same with most criminals. They got away with something small before moving on to bigger crimes, better takes. Over time, their confidence grew. Many ended up getting cocky and thinking they were untouchable. That was when mistakes happened. Without those mistakes, the smartest criminals would end up doing a whole lot more damage. On the side of the law, strict rules had to be followed so no one's rights were violated during the evidence gathering process. While Quint cursed having to go about things the right way from time to time, he realized how important it was to follow protocol.

As far as those who were guilty as sin, they never got away with it for long on Quint's watch.

"It's going to be my pleasure to slap cuffs on Lindy, lock him up, and throw away the key," Ree said, and the fierceness in her eyes showed she meant every word.

An uneasy feeling settled over Quint. Cases took time to develop. They just didn't have it to give, and he had no idea when the sand was going to run through the hourglass.

Chapter Eight

It has gone down.

The text indicating Vadik's fake murder came an hour after breakfast. Quint set his phone on the counter and locked gazes with Ree. He took in a deep breath with the full knowledge the bubble they'd been in this morning was about to burst. The real world and the case were about to take over their lives until arrests were made. The few hours of quiet they'd shared had to be enough to hold them over.

Quint had an "in" with Lindy now. Another adventure was about to begin.

"What do we know about Lindy?" he asked, figuring he needed to be briefed as much as possible before heading over to Lindy's place. The penthouse where Vadik used to live would be off limits now.

"Rolph Lindberg has been Dumitru's right-hand man for the past two and a half years," Ree supplied as she hunkered over the laptop, studying the screen. "There isn't a whole lot known about him other than he kind of appeared on the scene and was directly tied to Dumitru. Lindy is from the same village in Romania as Dumitru, and the two are believed to have known each other long before they came to America."

"I'm guessing Lindy hasn't been fingerprinted, and

there's no information about him in the Integrated Automated Fingerprint Identification System IAFIS database," Quint said.

"You would be right. There's no birth record that can be traced to his name, so it could be an alias," Ree stated. "I wouldn't be surprised one bit if that was the case, actually."

"A new identity for a new country," Quint said. It was an old trick and how the same criminals were able to go back and forth easily. A new identity, a new passport was only a forgery away.

"Other countries also don't keep the same kinds of records we're used to. You already know that," Ree stated.

"So, basically, this guy was a ghost until he came here to work for Dumitru, right?" Quint asked.

"Yes," she responded. "So there isn't much else to say except that he lives four blocks over from Vadik in an even nicer building."

"Are you thinking what I am?" Quint immediately asked.

"Dumitru has to live around here somewhere," she confirmed. It was the only thing that made sense if two of his closest advisors lived locally.

"How have we not seen him yet?" Quint asked.

"We've only been downtown a few weeks," Ree pointed out. "Also, I highly doubt he visits Lindy or visited Vadik." She snapped her fingers a few times. "It might not hurt for me to change my appearance and follow Lindy around for a few days."

"We can get someone else to do that," Quint offered.

Ree shot him a look that made him realize he needed to address his statement.

"Hear me out," he started. "Lindy knows what you look like. It's the only reason for the suggestion. Even with a hair change or dye, you're distinct."

Ree sat there, quietly contemplating what he said. She always sat back in her chair and rounded her shoulders forward a little when she was concentrating. Another telltale sign was the concern line creasing her forehead. It also showed up when she was studying something carefully like the laptop screen or her phone. Speaking of which, they needed to get her a new cell phone.

A man with a ghost of a past wasn't exactly someone Quint liked to go after. They were too slippery.

"Fair point on not being able to change my look so drastically that I could be absolutely certain Lindy wouldn't recognize me," Ree stated.

"I'll contact Bjorn and request more resources on the case," he said.

"Are you sure this has nothing to do with what happened yesterday morning?" Ree asked.

"I'd be lying if I said I wasn't bothered at my very core over what happened," he admitted. All he could do was be one hundred percent honest with her. "Believe me when I say there's no other agent I'd rather be working with on the professional side. On the personal side, I'm a work in progress."

"I'm capable," she began.

"I know," he said. "It's the reason I don't want to work with anyone else. But I can't ignore my personal feelings for you either. Can you honestly say that being in love hasn't changed the way you feel about me going out to do my job?"

"It has," she stated. "This whole relationship caught me off guard, and it's all new territory. I respect what you do, and I know you're the best. But there's this piece of me that remembers the look in my mother's eyes after my dad stopped coming home. The way she left his clothes in his closet for years like he was going to walk through the door any second and reclaim them. In fact, I didn't even want to acknowledge these emotions were still there until we started talking about it just now. Is that weird?"

"Not to me, it isn't," he said.

"I'll bring up a map of the city, and we can see if Grappell can get a floor plan for Lindy's building, as well," Ree said, changing the subject before he could say anything else. It was probably the stress of the case that had her thoughts all over the place.

He walked over to her and planted a tender kiss on her lips.

"Are we okay?" he asked, feeling like she'd just shut down and shut him out.

"Of course," she said, kissing him back despite the fact there was no conviction in those words.

"Good." This didn't seem like the appropriate time to dig into why a wall seemed to have just come up between them. Their personal life needed to be put on hold a little while longer until he could finish what he'd started with the case. They were close. He could feel it.

Lindy would be the ticket in to Dumitru. Everything else could be dealt with when this case was behind them.

Quint picked up his cell phone and sent a text to Lindy confirming the murder had taken place.

Proof?

Quint issued a sharp sigh. Then he fired off a text to Grappell, who immediately sent a picture of a bloodied Vadik. His gaze was fixed and his skin pale. Quint forwarded the pic, and then asked, Where is my wife?

The response came quickly.

Complication. Meet me. Lindy gave an address that Quint recognized as Lindy's building.

"He wants to meet," Quint said to Ree.

"That's good," she said a little too quickly. She put on a smile he instantly recognized as forced. Instinct said he should stop what he was doing and make her a priority. He should stop right there and ask her what was really wrong and, better yet, what he could do to make it better. They'd covered a lot of topics lately, and emotions had been running high since her kidnapping yesterday.

Quint needed to clear his head before he tackled more serious subjects with Ree. The only way to do that was to put all this behind them.

"Looks like he wants me to come to him," he said, staring at his screen instead of watching her try to hide her disappointment.

"Be careful," she warned. "He has a few tricks up his sleeve."

Quint didn't respond with anything other than another kiss. He didn't know what to say to make things better between them. "I'll be back as soon as I can."

"Text me," she said, and then it seemed to dawn on her that she'd lost her phone.

He walked over to the closet where he kept the locked tackle box. He produced a key and then opened the lid. The lock kept their personal identities secure in the event prying eyes found it. There was a backup cell phone inside. He pulled it out for her.

"Here you go," he said after locking, then replacing the box. He held a new phone on the flat of his palm.

He probably should have been concerned when she didn't look up at him. Instead, she took the cell and turned around to face the laptop screen.

"How do you plan to go inside? Hot or cool?" she asked, and he knew exactly what she was talking about.

"Hot," he admitted. Any person worth their salt in a relationship would be blindly angry over what had happened to Ree. "I can buy a couple of days for you. Tell him that you called from a gas station today after walking all night. I'll say you're so angry at me for allowing this to happen that I don't know when you'll be back."

"Sounds good," she said without argument, and the knot in his gut tightened.

"I'll text when I can," he offered.

"Okay," she said. "Quint, don't let them trick you like they did me."

"I'll see what I can do." He touched her hand before securing a gun in his ankle holster and then walking out the door. At least she could lay low for a few days and catch her breath while he did some of the heavy lifting on the case. Besides, he was getting closer to Dumitru. Quint could feel it. And what needed to happen was between the two of them.

Quint scanned the street as he exited their building. It was midmorning by this point, closer to lunch than breakfast. With every step closer to Lindy, Quint's mood intensified. The non-fight he'd had with Ree had set him on edge. How was he supposed to know what to do with their relationship? He didn't exactly have all the answers. All he knew was that she was the one. He loved her more than anything in this world. The rest would work itself out. It had to. He couldn't imagine a life without her now that he'd found her.

She'd brought up her mother and the fact her father had been killed on the job in law enforcement. Was she getting cold feet in their relationship? Figuring history was repeating itself?

Hell if he knew what was on her mind. She didn't seem to have it all figured out either, which didn't help.

Quint had to push those thoughts aside as best he could

to get his mind in the right space for the meetup with Lindy. This was exactly the reason it was a bad idea to mix personal with business. Falling in love was a distraction. Being overly protective was a distraction. Thinking about a future and kids was a distraction.

Quint hit the crosswalk to the sound of a horn blaring. He sidestepped the sedan that almost rammed him in the leg. He muttered a curse as he brought his hand up to wave. The driver flipped him off. Great.

For the rest of the walk, Quint kept his eyes on the road. When this case was over, he would have time to sit down and talk to her about how he felt. Right now, his one hundred percent focus needed to stay on getting to Dumitru.

Walking into the lobby of Lindy's building, Quint noticed the nothingness of the expansive space. The floors were some kind of fancy white marble tile. They were shiny, like walking on glass. A pair of flat wooden benches sat across from each other and on opposite sides of a white fur rug. Other than a few plants placed here and there, and a fireplace, there wasn't much else to the lobby. It gave minimalism a whole new meaning.

There were two men wearing almost all black standing near the elevator bank to the right. Quint didn't recognize them but would bet money they were connected to Lindy. Almost as soon as Quint had the thought, Lindy came around the corner. He flicked his gaze over to Quint before motioning toward the elevators with a nod.

Summoning all the frustration over the case and anger at this man kidnapping Ree to force Quint's hand, he made his way toward Lindy. The guy was all thick bushy eyebrows and facial hair. His dark eyes practically glared at Quint. He'd be damned if he let Lindy get away with pushing Ree around.

"You should have just come after me instead," Quint

said as he charged into the two younger Romanians. They closed ranks. One of the men tried to push Quint back a couple of steps. His attempt was unsuccessful. Quint threw a shoulder into the man on his right and the guy backed to regain his balance.

Lindy's gaze widened. Did he seriously think Quint was going to lie down and allow a creep like this to walk all over him? It would strip any street cred he'd built throughout the case and basically invite others to treat him the same. It couldn't be allowed.

Guy number two reached behind his back. Quint knew exactly what was about to happen, and he didn't want this to escalate while it was still three against one.

He threw his hands in the air.

"All right," he said. "I'm good. There's no reason to whip out a gun."

The guy froze, keeping his hand back as though he might change his mind at any moment. He glanced over at Lindy, who gave a slight nod.

Quint wasn't finished with Lindy, but this wasn't the time or place to exact revenge. He reminded himself it wouldn't be too much longer, though.

"If you can control yourself," Lindy started, looking more shaken than he probably wanted to, "we can go upstairs now."

"Fine by me," Quint stated. "But let me know if you need to be reminded the wives and girlfriends stay out of this. Whatever happens is between you and me, and I expect it to stay that way. *Comprende?* Or should I turn around and walk right back out of the front door?"

Lindy offered what seemed like a reluctant nod.

"If anything had happened to her because of you, I would hunt you down and personally slit your throat. Do you understand?" Quint ground out as the elevator doors closed behind them. There were rules about respect and family that were followed even with the criminal element. In fact, those rules were etched in stone, and a person's family was off limits even if a relationship hadn't been made official by marriage.

Quint's hands fisted at his sides as he stared at Lindy.

"My mistake," Lindy acquiesced. His words sure sounded good, but Quint doubted the man would pull back even after the confrontation.

Lindy lived on the ninth floor of a twelve-story building. There were six apartments on his floor. Quint was surprised Lindy's apartment wasn't as expensive or flashy as Vadik's. Lindy's easily looked like a family might live here.

In fact, the door to the kitchen was closed, and Quint was certain he heard a female in there humming. Was Lindy a family man? He was a far cry from the bachelor Vadik.

The decor was the complete opposite of the lobby's. The sofa was a leather sectional that looked expensive but also gently worn. It faced a flat-screen that took up almost half the wall. The corner fireplace anchored the room. Paintings on the wall were from the Renaissance era, expensive and possibly original. This place reeked of old money and, Quint had to admit, good taste.

"Step outside?" Quint asked Lindy, motioning toward the balcony that was bricked halfway up. The structure looked solid.

Lindy's thugs started to go with them.

"Alone," Quint said.

With a look of reluctance, Lindy finally waved off his buddies.

Quint led the way outside, walked straight to the edge and listened for the sliding glass door to close. The second it did, he whirled around on Lindy, grabbing him by the throat before spinning him around. Quint walked Lindy until his back was against the bricks. He was bent over in a backbend.

One hand on the man's throat and the other on his jaw, Quint dug his fingers into meaty flesh. He heard the door open behind him.

"Take one more step and he goes over," Quint said without looking back. It was the first evening this month he could tell a break in the relentless Texas heat wasn't far away. He locked gazes with Lindy. "Tell them!"

Lindy made a couple of grunting noises as he tried to speak while Quint's hand was clamped around his throat. Quint eased his grip enough for the man to get out one word.

"Stop!" Lindy coughed. His eyes looked like they might bulge out of their sockets. A vein in his neck pulsed and throbbed. He had a face hardened by a life of crime, but none of that showed through right now.

"Babe?" a female voice said from much closer than Quint expected. "Everything okay out here?"

Chapter Nine

Lindy's gaze pleaded with Quint, who wasn't ready to budge. He had half a mind to throw the sonofabitch over the brick half wall right in front of the woman Quint assumed was Lindy's wife.

"C'mon," Lindy managed to say despite Quint tightening his grip. It would be so easy to cross the line right now and eradicate this filth from the earth forever. Blood rushed to Lindy's head, causing his face to turn beet red.

For more than a few seconds, Quint contemplated doing just that—ending this jerk's crime spree. But then he was reminded of the oath he'd taken to serve and protect. He recalled the real reason he was here in the first place. Tessa's face came to mind, and so did Ree's. He couldn't bring his best friend back, and he couldn't risk losing the only woman he'd ever truly loved by going to jail himself. Squeezing the life out of Lindy might feel good in the moment, but Quint didn't want to live with any more regret. And he would have remorse. First, for taking a life. Second, for ruining the investigation. Third, and most important, for losing Ree.

With a sharp sigh, Quint grabbed a fistful of Lindy's shirt and yanked him upright. He shot the man a murderous look.

"Go back in the kitchen," Lindy said through heaves. "Everything is fine out here. Just a misunderstanding."

Quint had had to make sure Lindy knew he wasn't the only one who could strike at what was important. Lindy's home should be sacred and respected. Since Lindy crossed a boundary with Quint, Quint was forced to reciprocate or appear weak. Being weak in a crew like this meant certain death.

"I did what you asked. Vadik is dead," Quint said, not budging an inch, standing toe-to-toe with Lindy. "Now, back off."

Lindy put his hands up, palms out, in the surrender position, but the sneer remained on his face. He didn't like being shown up in his own home and in front of his wife. There were probably kids inside somewhere too.

"You did everything I asked," Lindy said. "There's no reason to fight amongst ourselves. My orders came from someone else anyway."

Quint highly doubted Lindy would be ordered to kidnap Ree, but this wasn't the time to argue the point.

"You doubted Vadik's loyalty," Quint stated. "What's to say you won't turn on me?"

Lindy's sneer grew wider.

"It goes both ways," he said.

"Yes, it does. Try to remember that," Quint stated with more than a hint of threat in his voice. "Tread carefully, Lindy. If we're going to work together, you're going to have to find a way to trust me and not put my back against the wall."

"Point taken," Lindy said, his dark eyes boring holes through Quint.

"Where is she?" Quint demanded.

"I'm not allowed to give you that information," Lindy stated. "This meeting is over."

"That's where you're wrong. We haven't even begun," Quint practically growled.

"Walk out now or you'll never work for Dumitru," Lindy threatened.

"Who were you taking orders from?" Quint pressed. "I want to see him."

"You'll get your chance," Lindy stated. His gaze fixed on someone or something behind them.

The temptation to turn around and see who or what was back there was too great to pass up. Quint craned his neck around in time to see the backside of a male figure as he walked out the door into the hallway. The creepy-crawly feeling people referred to as a cat walking over their grave struck as the guy turned his head to the side and Quint got a glimpse of his profile. Dumitru?

From this distance and at a glance, it was impossible to be certain. Quint had to fight every instinct inside of him that wanted to bolt after the person who could be Dumitru and confront him. Keeping his cool, he reminded himself that he was here for the long game, the arrest, the evidence that would lock this man away for the rest of his life so he couldn't hurt anyone else.

"Was that your boss?" Quint turned his attention back to Lindy.

He was met with an eerie smile.

"Like I said, you'll find out soon enough," came Lindy's response. The man was a little too overconfident now. Quint didn't like the change in demeanor.

Taking a step back, he released his grip on Lindy.

"I'm all in with whatever you want or need me to do," Quint said. "But if you ever touch my woman again…"

Lindy swatted empty air.

"You already said," he responded. "The same goes for

you if you ever walk into my house and pull anything like this."

"Turnabout is fair play," Quint stated.

"We're done here," Lindy ground out.

"You know how to reach me," Quint said before turning around and walking out the door. He half expected a bullet in his back and was pleasantly surprised when none came. He'd stood his ground and gave Lindy something to chew on in the process. Quint laid down the law and showed that he wouldn't be pushed around. Since the move hadn't killed him, he'd most likely earned a serious amount of street cred.

He missed the elevator Dumitru had disappeared onto by a solid couple of minutes. It had been necessary and, he hoped, his patience would bring him into the fold faster.

Quint didn't truly exhale until he was out in the fresh air. He wanted to check on Ree to see how she was doing or if she'd discovered anything while he was gone. She had probably dug into the case files, and he wanted her take on the information.

The walk home felt longer than it took. The closer he got to their building, an unsettled feeling took hold. He was up the elevator and back inside their apartment in a matter of minutes, but it sure felt like an hour. The way he'd left things earlier sat like hot lead in his gut.

Talking about their relationship and their future had to be put on hold. He only hoped Ree understood and could forgive him.

The minute he opened the door, she came around the corner to the foyer. Her gaze skimmed his body with urgency, and he realized she was looking for injuries or bullet holes.

"I'm okay. See?" He held his hands high in the air and performed a quick spin to accentuate the point.

Ree practically launched herself at him. He caught her and kissed her, hard and unyielding. Her lips were the equivalent of heaven on earth, and her body pressed to his was the way he wanted to stay for a solid week when this was all said and done. Breakfasts in bed. A wedding. A honeymoon. The works.

When she finally pulled away, she caught his gaze.

"How did it go?" she asked. "Tell me everything."

He linked their fingers and walked over to the couch before spilling all the details of what had gone down.

"Good move on your part," she said when he told her about his attack on Lindy.

"Anything less would have placed an even bigger target on my back," he said.

She nodded agreement. The tension lines in her forehead eased but not enough to go away.

"What did you learn?" she asked.

"I now know where Lindy lives and that he has a wife. I believe he has kids, but I didn't get a look at them. His place is the opposite of Vadik's in pretty much every sense. And he is successful. I saw paintings on the walls that probably belonged in museums and not some random person's home," he explained. Then added, "I'm almost certain Dumitru was there too."

Ree gasped.

"Why don't you know for certain?" she asked, and he could already tell what she was thinking. If she'd been there, she could have followed Dumitru.

"I only saw his profile from a distance, and there were others in my line of sight. Now, those folks wanted to take my head off," he said with a chuckle that failed miserably at lightening the mood.

"I've been doing a little research myself," she said with a glint in her eyes that said she found something useful.

REE HAD DUG into case files rather than go crazy while waiting for Quint. The worst part about working with the man she loved was how losing him would shatter her. The death of any partner would be tragic and traumatic. Losing someone she respected, worked with, and intended to spend the rest of her life with would destroy her world.

"Dumitru has ties to a woman by the name of Lizanne Vega," Ree informed him. "She owns a 'toys' and lingerie shop on Central Expressway and Arapaho."

"I know the area. It would be an easy place to stake out, considering there's always a lot of traffic and noise in the shops in the area," Quint stated.

"Of course, I want to barge right in and lean on her, but the bull in a china shop method probably isn't the best course of action," Ree admitted. "The worst thing about being undercover is not being able to use a badge and a gun. Makes it hard to push people into talking."

"We could always send in a colleague. See who Bjorn or Grappell recommends," Quint stated.

"Could make her nervous, and then she'd tell him not to come around," she reasoned.

"I did get the sense from Lindy and his guys that everyone in the organization is on edge right now," Quint said.

"The fact they want anyone who gets arrested to be erased almost instantly is another giveaway," she pointed out.

"Is there a romantic tie between Lizanne and Dumitru?" Quint asked.

"Let me show you her pictures." Ree retrieved the laptop and pulled up a photo of the store. It had Lizanne pictured in sexy lingerie. "I'm guessing she supplies clothes to the local exotic dancers."

Dallas was well known for its topless bars.

"It's possible she has a few friends in the clubs, then," he said. "Or could be friends with the owners."

"I was surprised to find Dumitru linked to anyone in a business that could shed light on his operation. Topless clubs in Dallas are heavily monitored by local police as they do tend to attract a seedy element," Ree stated.

Quint pulled out his wallet and the crinkled piece of paper with the tree drawing on it. He'd been carrying it around so long the edges were tattered. He smoothed it out on the coffee table. Dumitru's name sat at the top with two long branches below. One was marked "Lindy." The other was marked "Vadik." Quint retrieved a pen and crossed off Vadik's name. He added a smaller branch and added Lizanne's name.

"We can always drop a surveillance camera in the parking lot. It's a public lot, so we wouldn't need to obtain permission first," Ree offered.

Quint nodded and smiled.

"We could drop a listening device in the shrubbery if there is any," he added.

Ree looked up the shop online, pulling up the location on Google Maps. "The name of her place isn't exactly creative."

She pointed to the name, Adult Lingerie, written in cursive. The sign on the strip mall center was in red.

"No one is going to mistake the place for a family pajama store," Quint mused with a chuckle.

"You got that right," she agreed, looking at the street view and seeing mannequins in the window that were wearing garter belts and fishnet stockings. She didn't even want to know if that was allowed or against code in a state that didn't allow alcohol sales before 10 a.m. on Sundays.

Ree gave a mental headshake.

"Ready to take a ride over?" she asked.

"You're not too tired?" he asked. It was getting late.

"I'll sleep better if I feel like I've accomplished something today," she admitted.

"Let's do this," came the response.

"I'll drive," she said, figuring he'd done enough for one night.

They filed down to the waiting SUV after locating a couple of devices to drop near Adult Lingerie. The Chevy was sitting in the exact spot where they'd left it. Ree walked the perimeter anyway, checking for bombs or tracking devices. When she deemed it safe, she gave the go-ahead to Quint, who had just finished walking his side.

She climbed in the driver's seat as Quint rummaged around in the back seat. He produced a pair of baseball caps.

"These are better than nothing," he stated, handing one over after placing the other on top of his head. Ree put hers on, lowering the bill as far as she could.

There wasn't a whole lot of traffic on 35E heading toward Central Expressway at this hour of the evening, so it didn't take long to reach Adult Lingerie. Ree drove past the strip shopping center, sticking to the service road and slowing down enough to get a good look at the area.

"Why would there be a light on in the back of the store at this late hour?" Ree asked as they drove past.

"You got me," he said. "Except there's a motorcycle parked on this side of the lot."

Part of the lot was obscured by shrubs that reached high enough to shroud vehicles parked close to the service road. Ree figured that was done on purpose to protect clients who didn't want to be caught parking in the lot. The other establishments were a CBD oil shop, a smoke shop and a deli.

And then it dawned on her.

"Didn't you say there was a motorcycle at the bust where Tessa…" Ree didn't finish the sentence, and she didn't need to.

"I sure as hell did," Quint responded. His gaze locked onto the parking lot as they passed.

"I'll swing back around. Give me a minute." She hit the gas and made a U underneath the highway, then another to get back on the proper side of the service road.

Since there were no cars on the road, she slowed to a crawl rather than go into the near-empty parking lot and possibly get unwanted attention.

"It's not the only vehicle in the lot," she said as she realized a small black sports car was parked alongside the motorcycle.

"It has been a while since the bust, and my mind could be playing tricks on me," Quint admitted. "I'm going to be real honest, though, and say that looks like Dumitru's bike."

Chapter Ten

Twice in one day.

Quint didn't want to push his luck, but the idea of being this close to Dumitru caused his danger radar to skyrocket.

"What do you want to do about it?" she asked. They couldn't legally track his movements without filing the proper paperwork first. He technically wasn't a suspect and hadn't been tied to a crime. There'd been no finger-prints of his on the scene, only a trail leading straight to the man. No one so far had been willing to testify against him, and the people who could seemed to turn up dead a little too regularly.

"Speed up." He slid down low in the seat as movement inside the shop caught his eye. "Did you see that?"

"No. What happened?" Ree asked.

"Someone is coming outside," he stated.

"I'll whip back around but can't promise I'll get back in time," she said. "Anything else and we'd be too obvious."

"A guy like Dumitru will be looking over his shoulder," Quint agreed. He just hoped she could make the circle fast enough to see which way he was going. This might just lead them to his home address. Since he didn't own any-thing in his name, there were no property records tied to him. In fact, Grappell had run Dumitru through the motor vehicle database and came up empty as well. It was a common trick for a career criminal not to have any property tied back to his or her own name. Except for Lizanne here.

"Does Lizanne have a record?" he asked, realizing he hadn't before.

"Nothing recent," Ree said. "She was brought up on charges of check fraud years ago, but it looks like she's been running a clean business for the past decade."

"He could be laundering money through her storefront," Quint said.

"We already know how easy it is for some of these store owners to have 'extra' merchandise in the backroom," she said.

Vadik had kept the kids he'd planned to traffic in his own store for safekeeping. It was easy considering shipments came in through the back. Large trucks parked as close to the rear door as they could get, making it difficult for anyone who happened to be nearby to see what was coming in and out. There were regulations that had to be followed, but it was easy to stay unseen in the back of a place like this one. Considering there was a smoke shop and a CBD oil shop, these weren't exactly neighbors who would be too nosy about what was going on in Lizanne's place other than to possibly ogle the customers as they came through.

There were a few vehicles zipping around on the highway. If the motorcycle rider hopped on Central Expressway, it would be a lot easier for Ree and Quint to follow without being too conspicuous.

"What do we have on Dumitru so far?" Ree asked. "Other than our suspicion he's the ringleader of A-12?"

"We have more than suspicion. There's Axel, for one. And Vadik," he said.

"Is that him?" she asked as the motorcycle pulled out of the parking lot and drove towards the on-ramp.

Ree followed far back enough they could keep watch but hopefully not far enough to lose him. To be fair, there was a smattering of vehicles on Central and no other motorcycles.

"Yes," Quint confirmed.

"What's he doing now?" Ree asked as the motorcycle exited on Belt Line Road. He'd been heading south and, Quint assumed, back home.

"I have no idea why this joker would get on the highway and then hop back off unless for evasive measures," Quint stated.

"Have you ever seen any of his top guys without security around?" she asked as she followed the motorcycle off the expressway.

"As a matter of fact, no, I haven't," he said. She was right. He'd never seen Vadik without an entourage. Maybe he was seeing what he wanted to with Dumitru instead of what was actually there. Plenty of folks rode motorcycles in the Dallas area. All the times Quint had been in the city for cases proved it to be true. He would never know why anyone would want to be on a motorcycle during rush hour, but he'd seen it.

"Hold on," she said as they both watched the man take the U-turn underneath the expressway. "Are you kidding me?"

"Drive a block or two up," Quint stated, but he had a hunch she already planned to do just that. "If we lose him, we lose him. It can't be helped." It might not even be Dumitru.

Ree issued a sigh, watching helplessly as the motorcycle disappeared from both of their views.

"It's hard to be this close and have to hold back," she said, stopping at the light. She smacked the flat of her palm against the steering wheel. "And now we'll really be behind the eight ball."

"I'd rather lose him tonight than be made because we got too anxious," he said.

"I would never jeopardize the case by being overeager," she protested as the light finally changed and she hit the gas pedal.

"I know you wouldn't, and I'm normally the definition of patience," he said. "This case gets to me. Throws me off my game."

Ree didn't immediately respond. She drove to the next light and made the turnaround. The sound of a motorcycle gunning it and heading south on the highway in the direction she was heading gave Quint hope this night wasn't a total loss.

"He's just trying to throw anyone who might be following him off the trail. He literally must have made a circle and then hopped back on the expressway," he said.

"Oh, I don't know, Quint," she said. "How do you know it's not just a person on a motorcycle? That does happen on our wide-open roads, especially at night."

"Hop on the expressway in the direction we were originally headed and we'll see," he said.

"If we can catch him," she said as she took the next on-ramp. She floored the Chevy's gas pedal.

There was a decent dotting of cars out at half past midnight. This seemed to be the time folks really decided to go for it, racing by like the Chevy was a go-kart as it got up to speed with the flow.

"There's no way we're going to find him again," she said under her breath.

"His helmet was distinct. There was an orange glow-in-the-dark all-seeing eye on the back," Quint mentioned.

"That should give us a direction," she said.

Quint was just about to call it when he heard a noise up ahead. "Do you hear that?"

"I sure do," Ree stated, getting the Chevy up to speed as fast as it could go.

"It's him," Quint stated. The sticker was unmistakable.

Ree slowed enough to blend in behind a Dodge Ram truck. "If we stay back here, we should be okay."

"He should be making the turnoff," Quint said. "He's about to pass the last exit for downtown."

"Is it possible he lives south of Dallas?" she asked.

"Anything is possible," he said, even though he'd pegged Dumitru for someone who would live close to Lindy and Vadik.

"He could be delivering something," Ree hedged. "Never mind. We both know he wouldn't be the one doing the dirty work."

"It's what will make him hard to pin down for any of his crimes," Quint agreed. In fact, he needed a more concrete plan to be able to nail him against the wall. The trail would be difficult. At this point, Quint's brain was running around in circles as to how to nail the bastard for the crimes he was committing and directing others to commit.

"Let's just see where this guy is headed, and once we get an address, we can run it through Grappell and see if he comes up with anything," Ree said.

The assumption the guy on the motorcycle would exit was a mistake. He kept going past downtown and stayed on Central Expressway until it turned onto 45.

"What are the odds it's him?" Ree asked.

Basically, they were heading toward Houston.

"No idea," he said. "But if you get tired of driving, we can switch places. There's no need to pull over. We can make it work."

"I'm wide awake," she said. "Although I wouldn't argue against a cup of coffee at this point."

"Looks like we're in this for the long haul tonight," he said. "As soon as it's feasible, we'll stop off and get a cup."

Ree glanced in the rearview as lights brightened behind them. "What's this jerk's problem?"

Someone had on their high beams, and it was annoying. Then it became dangerous as the larger vehicle roared up to the bumper. Quint pulled his weapon from his ankle holster and took aim.

IMPACT SNAPPED REE'S head forward. She muttered a string of curses as she gripped the wheel and swung right to avoid a second tap on her bumper as Quint climbed into the back seat. There were too few vehicles on the road to weave in and out of or provide any sort of protection, and her first thought was keeping innocent bystanders safe.

"Hang on back there," she warned as she cut a hard left. "I guess we weren't as sly as we thought we were."

"Clearly not," Quint stated. "I can't see anything clearly with those high beams on."

"Let me try to get beside him," Ree said. "Are you holding on?"

"Sure am," he confirmed.

Ree slammed on the brakes, grateful for the person who invented seat belts at this point. She was also thankful the tap to her bumper hadn't been hard enough to deploy airbags.

Was this person trying to scare her? Run her off the road? Let her know she and Quint had been seen following the motorcycle? There was no doubt in Ree's mind who the motorcycle belonged to now. And it seemed the turnaround earlier had been meant to shake them off Dumitru's tail. This guy was sophisticated and smart. Those two traits were the reason he sat on top of the organization and not in jail where he should be. Not yet, anyway.

The larger vehicle she assumed was a souped-up SUV mirrored her lane change. There were half a dozen cars dotting the highway on this stretch. The motorcycle had been baiting them. He was long gone. She should have realized he would put the pedal to the metal. He'd hung back to give his security detail a chance to catch up.

Ree mashed the brake. Hard. Quint's hand slammed against her seat as he braced himself. She cut the wheel right in time to miss being hit from behind.

"Sorry," she said.

"No worries," he shot back.

Since the motorcycle wasn't in sight, she figured exiting the highway would be the best course of action. Her training and skills with evasive maneuvers weren't doing much good on a long and flat stretch of highway with citizens on the road.

Ree banked right at the last minute, catching the exit ramp just in time. She glanced in her rearview, hoping she'd been able to shake their tail. No such luck. The SUV seemed to anticipate the move.

She was being too predictable.

The next on-ramp was tempting, considering there wasn't much else around. On the one hand, it was probably good that most citizens were in bed, fast asleep. In this case it worked against her. Open roads were the enemy of evasive tactics.

The SUV came close to nailing her back bumper but pulled away last minute. Why?

"What is going on?" Ree shouted. Adrenaline coursed through her, bringing all her senses to life. Blood thumped through her veins. Her heart pounded against her rib cage.

These rushes were part of the job, a part she used to enjoy. Not so much any longer.

What had happened to her? How did she become the person her mother wanted her to be? A little voice in the back of her mind picked that moment to say she was getting older and was starting to want something different out of life. It didn't mean her mother had gotten into her head and changed her in any way.

"Watch out," Quint stated. "They're coming for us."

The answer to Ree's question about what was going on came when the SUV barreled up to the back of the driver's side and then made a hard right, smacking into her vehicle and sending her into a dangerous spin.

Within seconds, the Chevy flipped and started rolling down a ravine. It registered that Quint wasn't wearing a seat belt and should be flying all over the cab of the vehicle by now. Did he manage to secure himself somehow at the last minute?

The death roll of the Chevy seemed to slow time to a crawl. Her thoughts snapped to the fact they were out in the middle of nowhere, most likely near or on the outskirts of a cattle ranch with nothing and no one for miles except landscape. The ravine would make it impossible for anyone to see them from the highway.

Ree didn't know up from down by the time the Chevy stopped. Airbags had deployed. She felt every jolt and bang. The fact he was quiet sent a cold chill racing down her back.

Trying to get her bearings, she blinked a couple of times and reached for her seat belt.

"Quint?" she managed to get out against a suddenly dry throat. She swallowed in an attempt to ease some of the drought happening.

The fact he didn't respond sent more of those icy chills

circulating through her. Worry seeded deep inside her. What if she lost the only man she'd ever truly loved?

As Ree's eyes began to focus and she started to get her bearings, she realized the Chevy was flipped on its side. Resolve started building within her. She needed to assess the situation and figure out how to get out of the vehicle. Possibly help Quint too.

From what she could tell over the deployed airbags, the windshield appeared to be intact. That was probably a good sign. She craned her neck around, trying to get a glimpse into the back seat.

"Quint," she said a little louder this time, a little bolder.

Through the windshield, she saw flashes of light coming toward them. The SUV?

"Quint," she repeated for the third time as hopelessness threatened to swallow her whole. There was no way she would leave her fiancé in the back seat and take off. Ree scrambled to find her cell phone. The contents of the vehicle had been scattered around like fall leaves in north Texas after a violent thunderstorm.

His non-answer sent her pulse racing as the flashlights picked up the pace.

Chapter Eleven

The sounds of a familiar frantic voice cutting through the fog in Quint's brain registered as Ree. He tried to shake off the confusion, but that only made his head hurt even worse. Her voice had a distant quality, like she was standing inside a tunnel.

But that couldn't be right.

"Come on, Quint. You have to wake up. They're coming," she pleaded.

He wanted to. He also needed to know what had her so twisted up. Then it came back to him. The motorcycle. The chase. The SUV. Then the crash. He'd barely gotten his seat belt clicked when they'd swerved off the road.

There were other voices. Ones he didn't recognize, but they still caused icy fingers to grip his spine.

Quint blinked blurry eyes open. Ree was positioned over him, her gun aimed toward the voices. His head felt like it might crack into a thousand pieces at any moment, but he couldn't give in to the fog rolling over him and through him.

A half-dozen thoughts competed for attention, but there was only one he would allow to surface. They needed to get the hell out of there. The Chevy's front and side airbags had probably saved their lives.

"Ree," he said, and could hear the raspy quality to his

own voice. He coughed a couple of times before he realized the reason for the sudden dryness. "Fire."

"You're awake?" The shocked quality to Ree's tone said he'd been out far longer than she was comfortable with.

"I'm here. Something's on fire," he said.

"Let's climb out the back," she said. "Can you move on your own or do you need me to help?"

Quint stretched his legs out as far as he could given the fact he was on his side in the SUV. He removed his seat belt, releasing the cutting pressure running diagonally across his chest. He was already pressed against the door. His hip dropped, smacking against the armrest. He ignored the shooting pain and scrambled onto all fours.

"Lead the way," he said to Ree before realizing his Sig Sauer was around somewhere.

"The flashlights are getting closer," Ree said. "I'll see what I can do to hold them off."

She disappeared out the back of the vehicle as Quint felt around for his weapon. A few seconds later, the sound of a bullet split the air. A flash of light came from the back of the vehicle before there was shouting. The voices were male, and he was able to detect two distinct tones. It looked like they were evenly matched. He liked those odds, especially with a crackerjack agent like Ree on his team.

Everything outside of the Chevy went quiet, save for the sound of the blaze that was growing by the second. The glow from the fire gave him some light to work with as he crawled around. He needed to get out of there before the fire spread to the gas tank or lines.

He was about to give up and abandon his gun when his fingers touched the cool metal of the barrel. He stretched them around the driver's seat where the gun had ended up on the floor and retrieved the weapon. Their odds of survival just increased dramatically with this find. To be fair, Ree was doing an excellent job of holding off the attackers.

A returned shot had him scooting out of the back of the vehicle at lightning pace. It was pitch black in the area surrounding them, so he had no idea what they were about to run toward. The only thing for certain was he needed to get them away from the burning vehicle and the roadway, which meant heading into the blackness.

Quint checked his back pocket for his cell phone. Relief they'd won the first battle washed over him. They could use the phone to navigate out of wherever they were about to end up. *If* they had cell service, a voice in the back of Quint's mind picked that moment to say.

It was true. Still, he'd take having his cell over losing it any day.

"Do you have your personal belongings?" he asked Ree.

"I have my Glock," she stated. "Having my purse would be nice, but I didn't think to grab it."

She was most likely focused on saving his backside, and that was the reason for the slip. He owed her one for that.

"Looks like we have a little time before this thing blows. I'll grab it," he said. "Hold them off just like you're doing and I'll return before you know it."

Ree opened her mouth to protest, but he was already climbing in the back of the vehicle. There was enough light for him to locate her handbag a whole lot easier than his gun, which had been wedged between the driver's seat and the door.

The fact Dumitru had played them in the worst possible way and then gotten away sat hard in Quint's gut. This was the equivalent of shoving Quint's nose in his mistakes.

This wasn't the time to chide himself for losing the bastard. What was done was done. There was no going back now. Eyes forward, Quint grabbed Ree's handbag and retreated to the back of the SUV in time for another round to be fired.

The gunfire was returned. A bullet pinged off the Chevy not two feet away from Ree. He grabbed her and pulled her out of harm's way in time to shield her from the next one.

They fell into a heap on the hard Texas soil.

"We need to run," she said. "Can you?"

Quint performed a quick mental inventory of his body.

"I'll figure it out," he said. His headache alone was enough to slow him down. There were other ailments that—thankfully—the recent boost of adrenaline would handle.

"Let's go," she said, securing the strap of her handbag over her shoulder. She didn't wait for an answer as they both ducked as low as possible to make them harder targets to hit and took off in the opposite direction of the highway and into the blackness.

The rolling hills were a stark contrast to the flatness of Dallas. The farther they ran from the Chevy, the thicker the underbrush became. The toe of Quint's boot got caught on it, causing him to face-plant. Ree came down with him. Both held on to their weapons. The accidental move was probably where their luck would run out as a pair of bullets whizzed past their heads. Falling had narrowly saved them.

They lay there for a long moment, heaving, trying to quiet their own breathing so they could hear how close the attackers were. Something had been bugging Quint about the motorcycle incident. Had they jumped to a conclusion that Dumitru was the rider?

The sobering thought they'd been led here to be killed nailed Quint. After his exchange with Lindy, anything was possible. Lindy might have decided the organization didn't need Quint. Had he and Ree acted too quickly in spying on Lizanne's place without a solid plan?

Other thoughts raced through his mind, but those had to be shelved for the time being. He'd analyze the situation once they were clear of danger. Considering another set of bullets split the air, they needed to get out of there.

"We're being too predictable," he whispered through labored breaths. "We need to zigzag our way toward safety, heading that way," he said, pointing to what he believed was northeast.

Their eyes had adjusted to the light enough to see objects right in front of them.

"Hold on," Ree said, squeezing his fingers. "Okay. Now, let's go." She hopped to her feet at almost the exact moment the Chevy exploded. Gas and fire weren't exactly the best of friends.

The blaze caused enough of a distraction for the two of them to make it out of the firing line. A couple of wild shots were fired, but Quint could easily see they were out of desperation and not because the shooters had either of them in their sights.

The hills seemed to roll on forever in this area. Quint had hoped they would make it to trees at some point. Those would be useful for cover and would make shooting them a whole lot more difficult. At least they still had weapons and cell phones. That should help with escape and eventual recovery.

Bjorn wasn't going to be thrilled with what had just happened to the Chevy. Quint wouldn't need to quit when this case was over. She would string him up for the cost of the vehicle.

When the only thing they could hear was the whisper of the wind, Ree stopped and plopped down.

"Stay low, just in case," she said, tugging his hand so

he would sit down beside her. She located her cell phone, saw that she had a couple of bars and called 911.

He listened carefully for the sounds of footsteps while trying to catch his breath. He wasn't out of shape, but this case was threatening to do him in. He'd been beaten within an inch of his life and was still recovering. He'd been slapped around more times than he cared to count. The battle scars were racking up. Normally this run wouldn't have winded him to this degree.

Could he keep his strength up long enough to make it through the night and get answers?

A VEHICLE SQUEALED off in the distance, and that was the first time Ree really breathed. Thankfully, this area carried sound. The second exhale came when she heard sirens, which she prayed weren't just ringing in her ears from the crash.

"Do you hear that?" she asked Quint.

"I sure do," he confirmed.

"I'm guessing that's the reason the bastards took off," she said.

"Either way, the blast probably just saved our lives," he pointed out. She couldn't argue there.

"We should make our way back to the Chevy," she said, "or what's left of it."

The red glow had disappeared after they'd climbed and then descended the most recent hill.

Quint pushed up on his elbows as the sirens grew closer. He leaned over and kissed Ree in a manner that was so tender it robbed her of breath.

"What was that for?" she asked when they finally pulled apart.

He shrugged his shoulders.

"It was just something I needed to do," he said.

Ree's heart squeezed in her chest at the sentiment. She'd felt a wall come up between them after their last talk. One that wasn't completely down yet. This was a start.

She urged him to his feet, realizing he'd taken a pretty hard tumble inside the Chevy as it had rolled. He squinted and winced as he pushed to standing.

"Are you okay?" she asked.

"I'll be fine," he reassured her. "This body has been taking a beating on these cases. I'm ready for it to be done."

She couldn't agree more with the sentiment.

She asked the question that had been bugging her. "It wasn't Dumitru. Was it?"

"I don't think so," he confirmed.

"Any ideas who, then?" she asked.

"My mind immediately snaps to Lindy," Quint said, returning his Sig Sauer to his ankle holster. "The way he looked at me earlier was murderous. If Dumitru really was in the apartment, Lindy would have lost face big time. It could cause him to seek revenge. This certainly sent a message to us both."

"He's definitely on the list," Ree remarked, putting the safety on her Glock before tucking it into the compartment in her purse made for an easy concealed carry. "But something in your voice tells me that you're unsure."

"Lizanne might have good security. Our Chevy might be more recognizable than we realize. Anyone at the top of the organization could have us followed," he said. "Here's the thing. Lindy didn't have to let me walk out of the apartment today. I took a risk once I let him up from his vulnerable position on the balcony. He had a couple of guys there who could have followed me outside and done a number on me. They didn't."

"Which could mean he didn't want your killing tied back to him," she reasoned. Quint had made a lot of good points. But their thinking might be too narrow. Like a scientist who came up with a theory, and then all his thinking and evidence afterward built a case to prove it. Consciously or subconsciously. "What else?"

"This could be protection for Lizanne," he stated. "We must have been caught casing the place, and whoever was inside might have believed we were out to rob her or make a hit on someone."

"I was thinking the same thing. Lizanne and her people definitely go on the list," she said. "We can ask Grappell to get any and all information about her background, where she likes to eat and where she lives. That kind of thing. He has plenty of resources in the office at his disposal to help him dig around."

Ree reached inside her purse to check for the replacement cell phone and found it. She fired off a text to Grappell and found out there was no cell service.

Quint scratched his head, wincing the second he made contact.

"How is your vision?" she asked Quint, redirecting the conversation. She didn't want to think about Giselle right now. Not when Ree was still so angry at the woman she could barely see straight.

"It's fine now," he said.

"Do you know what you hit your head on?" she asked.

"It all happened so fast," he said.

"We can ask for a medic once we get back to the Chevy," she offered. They probably should get him cleared medically. Bjorn would ream Ree out otherwise. Not to mention the fact Ree was concerned about how much Quint's body could take. Granted, he was strong and fit. He had muscles and stamina for days, but he wasn't twenty any longer. He'd taken a lot of hits over the course of three cases. Now, they were on their fourth with no break in between.

The speed had been necessary, but that didn't mean it was good for his longevity. In fact, they were in more danger with each passing day. Plus the list of people they'd angered was growing. The fake killing of Vadik should have bought them more time.

A thought niggled at the back of her mind. Was there another player involved? Someone they'd miscalculated or overlooked? Crime organizations weren't exactly known for recruiting decent and honest people.

"With all the arrests, the ranks might be getting itchy to make a name for themselves," she said.

"There could be a power struggle going on," Quint agreed. "It would explain why someone wanted Vadik dead."

"You said 'someone,'" she pointed out. "Does that mean you don't believe the order came down from Dumitru?"

"I have questions," he stated.

Chapter Twelve

Now that the discussion was gaining steam, Quint's mind was going down a very different path. He didn't trust Lindy or Giselle as far as he could throw either one of them. They clearly knew each other, though, because they'd been working together to kidnap and bury Ree.

As they neared the Chevy, a fire truck blasted the area with water. They gave it a wide berth as they linked their fingers.

"We should hold our hands up so no one gets too anxious about us popping up from nowhere," Ree said.

They did just that as a sheriff came around the side of the vehicle with a searchlight.

"That's our vehicle, sir," Quint stated. "We were going a little too fast and took the corner too hard."

He didn't want to give away their identity to the sheriff, and he figured he could play the victim pretty well. They should be done with this and on the road back to Dallas in fifteen minutes.

The sheriff was tall and looked exactly like the cliché one would think of coming from Texas. He was dressed in tan clothing from head to toe. His belly hung over an oversized belt buckle, and his crooked nose was a little too big for his face.

"I'm sorry, sir," Ree picked up when the light burned

their eyes. "I was driving, and I got distracted. My fiancé hit his head."

"Tell me what you two were doing out here alone so far away from your vehicle, and don't leave out any of the details," the sheriff said without introducing himself. Some of the sheriffs in Texas got their jobs through connections and intimidation rather than by popular vote. Quint imagined it happened in every state on some level, but it practically burned him to pieces this was happening here. This sheriff could very well be one of them.

Quint didn't normally like to give himself away, but one glance at Ree said she was already thinking the same thing. Of course, their badges were locked in the tackle box back at the apartment, so they couldn't exactly prove they were law enforcement.

"Sir, I'll tell you what," Quint began. "Since you didn't seem to feel the need to identify yourself or take that blinding light out of our eyes, I'm going to ask you to call my boss instead."

"And who might that be?" The sheriff sounded incredulous, like he couldn't believe they were trying to pull one over on him.

Quint evaluated his options. It was possible someone from the crime organization had ties to the community. Doubtful, but he'd already made an assumption that got them in this position in the first place.

"You know what?" he said. "On second thought, let me tell you what happened from the beginning without leaving anything out."

"Go on," the sheriff said, lowering the searchlight enough for Quint's eyes to stop seeing stars.

"My fiancée and I were getting a little frisky while she was driving," he began. Ree shot a hard look at him, but he continued, "She doesn't like talking about our sex life with strangers."

Ree's fingers tightened around his.

"It was my fault," Quint continued. "I couldn't wait until we got to the hotel room. Our GPS flipped out and kept wanting us to drive in circles." He threw his arm around Ree's shoulders. "And we just got engaged recently."

The sheriff scowled.

"The two of you need to come with me," he said.

This was highly unusual and unprofessional, and there were a few choice words Quint wanted to throw out right about now. Instead, he clamped his mouth shut and nodded.

"Step apart and walk over to the fire engine," he said. "Spread your legs and put your hands on the vehicle."

"Are we under arrest, Sheriff?" Ree asked in an innocent tone.

"Not yet," the sheriff responded.

"Okay, but you should know we're both carrying," she said, raising her hands high in the air. "I have a weapon in my handbag, and my husband has a gun in his ankle holster."

It was legal to carry in the state of Texas, so the sheriff shouldn't have a problem with this.

He cocked an eyebrow.

"Hands against the vehicle," was all he said.

Quint couldn't wait to get this jerk's badge number and report him. If only the sheriff knew he was messing with another law enforcement agency, Quint highly doubted the man would keep the smirk on his face, a smirk Quint wouldn't mind personally erasing.

Bjorn wasn't going to be thrilled with the phone call she was about to get, Quint thought as he complied with the sheriff's request. After being patted down and having his gun confiscated, he was seriously ready to throw a punch.

"I need to make a call," Quint stated, all attempts at courtesy now gone.

"I'm afraid—"

"The last time I checked, unless I'm under arrest, I have a right to make a phone call," Quint stated with a little more anger and frustration seeping in than he'd intended. "Unless you're prepared to deny me my rights."

"No, that won't be necessary," the sheriff said. "Make your call, but keep your hands where I can see 'em. And hand over your IDs first."

"You just confiscated the only weapon I have on me, and, meanwhile, my vehicle has just gone up in flames. So I don't exactly have any means with which to hurt anyone," he quipped. Ree fished her license out of her purse as Quint pulled his out of his wallet. They handed them over, and then the sheriff disappeared into his vehicle after a stern warning that they shouldn't go anywhere.

Where did he think they were going to go in the boondocks without a car?

Ree shot Quint a warning look the second the sheriff's back was turned. She was right, though. His temper was flaring dangerously close to out of control, and he needed to rein it in.

Quint white-knuckled his cell phone. He didn't look forward to the behind-chewing he was going to get from his superior, but Bjorn would lose her cool on the sheriff first and would back Quint to no end. He was confident in that fact. She wouldn't rip him a new one in front of this jerk of a sheriff.

He took a deep breath and faced the music, tapping her number into the cell. Bjorn answered on the second ring. And, yes, she'd been dead asleep.

"What is it?" she asked, voice stern.

"We're in some Podunk town being held by a sheriff

with no cause and he won't properly identify himself or give us a badge number," Quint stated. "We need your help."

"What a jerk," Bjorn said.

"You got that one right," Quint agreed.

"I was talking about you," she quipped, leaving no room for doubt she didn't appreciate the middle-of-the-night interruption. That was fine. Quint wasn't exactly in a cheerful mood either.

"This one is not on me," he stated.

"Where are you?"

"Your guess is as good as mine," he stated. Then whispered, "We were run off the road. This guy is harassing us, full tilt."

Bjorn cursed. She was protective of her agents and wouldn't take this news lightly. He hoped it would soften the other part he was about to tell her. Giving the boss a heads-up was always about delivery more so than the message.

"Are either of you hurt?" she asked.

"We're fine," he said.

Ree moved next to him and said, "Not exactly. Quint's hurt."

"What? You buried the lead, Casey. How bad is it? How many resources do you need?" she asked rapid-fire. He could hear her scrambling to get out of bed. Bjorn's reaction was over the top, especially for her. But then, this case had had a dark cloud hanging over it since day one, and she'd seen him after the last beating.

"You're talking to me, right?" he asked. "So, I'm alive."

"That's a good place to start," she said on a sigh. "Where are you hurt?"

"Head took a blow. Had a little blurry vision. I'm better now," he reassured her.

"So, I'm hearing you had a concussion," Bjorn stated.

"Not this time," he countered. He'd had enough to know the signs.

"Well, that's a relief," she said, and he could hear the release of some of the tension in her voice.

"Chevy didn't fare so well," he stated, figuring it was safe to deliver the news when her guard was down.

The string of curse words she released would have made a sailor blush.

"And I'm hearing that you don't know where you are. Is that true?" she finally asked. "Not even a general idea?"

"We were headed from Dallas to Houston. Hold on," he said as Ree touched his arm. She had her own cell phone out and was using the map feature to figure out where they were.

She gave him the exact coordinates, which he immediately relayed to Bjorn.

"I'll have to take a second to look that up to figure out whose jurisdiction you're in," Bjorn said. Knowing her, she slept with her laptop on her nightstand. It didn't take long for her to identify the county they were in along with the name of the sheriff. "I've had reports on this imbecile before. Not only is he incompetent, but that makes him dangerous."

"Doesn't sound promising," Quint stated.

"Don't worry. I'll take care of him. It's high time he was put in his place." The line got quiet for a stretch of a few minutes while the sheriff sat in his vehicle, calling in their IDs.

"Your friend is about to get a phone call," Bjorn said when she finally came back on the line. "Trust me. He isn't going to like this one bit."

"This is the best news I've heard all day," Quint admitted. And then he sat back and watched with amusement as a startled-looking sheriff took the call.

HOME. SHOWER. BED.

Those were Ree's top priorities despite the momentary distraction of watching the sheriff get his due. The man genuinely paled.

The phone call didn't take long, and he sure didn't waste any time when it ended. He was out of his SUV in a heartbeat.

"Excuse me for coming down hard on the two of you earlier," he said. "We've had a rash of..."

His voice trailed off like he couldn't think of how to finish the sentence, a sure sign he was lying. Ree clenched and released her fingers a few times, trying to work off some of the tension and frustration from the interaction they'd had with him a few minutes ago.

It was amazing what an attitude adjustment could do. The sheriff's smile was ear to ear as he handed both their identification and weapons back to them.

"My apologies about taking those," he said, leaning forward rather than stepping too close.

Ree wasn't certain what he'd been told but he now seemed afraid of them, and she didn't mind the change in demeanor one bit. It also reminded her just how powerful their boss was, considering she could make a call in the middle of the night and have a sheriff change his tune in a heartbeat.

"My name is Sheriff Rex Gunther," he said, offering a handshake.

Quint stared at the man's hand for a long moment before finally giving in and shaking. Ree was next, and she had similar enthusiasm.

"I'm at your disposal," Sheriff Gunther said. "Anything you need, you ask."

"We need a ride back to Dallas," Quint stated. "Preferably now."

"Take my keys," the sheriff said. He dug inside his pocket and tossed over the key fob. "I have a deputy on the way, and I'll be here on the scene taking detailed notes and pictures for quite a while."

"Dallas is a couple of hours from here," Quint said. "Are you sure you want us to take your primary vehicle?"

Ree shook her head.

"We can't." There was no way she was driving up in a sheriff's SUV unless she was in the back seat with handcuffs on or else she would blow her cover.

"I can arrange an unmarked vehicle," he offered before checking his watch. "I can have something here in the next fifteen or twenty minutes if you can hold tight."

"That would be fine," Ree said. "And, Sheriff, do you have an EMT available to take a look at my fiancé's head injury? He took a blow during the crash, and I want to make one hundred percent certain he gets a green light before we leave the scene. You'll probably want to put all this in your report, as well."

"I'll wake Donovan. There's no need for a report on this one. We'll just get you checked out, set up and on your way in a jiffy," he said, holding up a hand as if to say he was on it. He had a whole lot more skip in his step now as he'd made certain an EMT was on the way to the scene. He returned with a couple of bottled waters in hand. "Would you like to wait inside my vehicle? Take a load off?"

"We would, Sheriff. Thank you," Ree said, wondering whose name Bjorn had to have dropped for this turn-around from the sheriff or who their boss said they were.

While she was at it, maybe they could get answers as to who was driving the SUV responsible for this mess.

Chapter Thirteen

"Does it strike you as strange that Giselle was working with Lindy?" Quint asked as he took a seat beside Ree in the sheriff's vehicle. Sheriff Gunther stood a few feet away, talking on his cell.

"Now it does," Ree said. "In all honesty, she has been bothering me in general since the whole 'tricking me outside' scenario, so I'm probably not the best one at being diplomatic when it comes to her."

"No one blames you for wanting to wring her neck," he said.

"She showed up at our apartment, looking for someone to protect her," she stated. "The woman was ready to throw herself at you."

"With Axel in prison, it is more difficult for him to protect her," he said.

"We all thought he arranged for her to be with Vadik after going inside," she stated. "What if she did the same thing with Vadik?"

"Went in and basically threw herself at his mercy while also playing Axel?" Quint asked.

"She would be smart to hedge her bets," Ree pointed out. "The world she lives in could crumble down at any moment."

"We could go have a conversation with Axel about Giselle," Quint stated.

"Yes, but he might tip her off," she pointed out. "We have no idea what he knows about her current life and he is still doing his best to protect her. Even by placing himself in harm's way."

"He might have been the one to instruct her to go see Vadik and ask for help initially," he reasoned.

"But what about Lindy?" she asked. "I just don't see these guys looking out for each other's girlfriends."

"Lindy used you to get to me," Quint said. "With most organizations, girlfriends and wives are off-limits no matter how bad the conflict within becomes."

"We've already seen this one break that boundary with Axel's wife and kid," Ree said. "Maybe I should have seen my kidnapping coming."

"Don't do that," he said. "Don't condemn yourself when I'm just as much to blame as you."

"You weren't the one who ran outside the minute Giselle wanted to meet," she pointed out.

"True, but that doesn't mean I'm without blame," he said. "I should have been there to protect you. I wasn't."

"You can't be everywhere," she whispered as the sheriff walked toward the vehicle.

"Donovan is about three minutes out," Sheriff Gunther informed them. "He'll drive you wherever you need to go. That way there'll be no need to worry about arranging for a pickup. I know him personally. He's a good guy."

"Thank you," Quint said. They could get a ride downtown and have Donovan drop them off a couple blocks from their apartment. It was safer that way. He didn't mind the sheriff's buddy knowing the general area, but there was no need to be dropped off at the front door.

"You should know Donovan won't say a whole lot so as not to make you feel uncomfortable," the sheriff explained.

"Good to know," Quint said. Ree was quiet. He could

almost see the wheels turning in her mind, churning over their conversation about Giselle.

True to the sheriff's word, Donovan arrived exactly three minutes later. All conversation between him and Ree stopped with the sheriff standing within earshot. Donovan looked to be in his late twenties. He had a short, stocky build and gave the impression he'd probably played football during high school. He had a square face and a boxer's nose. He came toward them with his hands out wide, away from his body, carrying a medical bag.

"This here is the patient," the sheriff explained, motioning toward Quint.

Donovan's serious expression never faded as he gave a nod before setting down his bag and then opening it. First he took out his stethoscope. "Are you experiencing any dizziness?"

"No," Quint stated.

"Blurred vision?" Donovan continued in his all-business tone.

"Not since right after the accident," Quint admitted.

"How about your head? Any pain there?" Donovan asked.

"I have one helluva headache," Quint said. "Nothing I haven't dealt with before, though."

"Okay. I'm going to flash a small light in your eyes and take a look. Okay?" Donovan asked.

Quint nodded and blinked the minute the light hit his retinas.

"Sorry about that," Donovan stated.

"The light hurts. I have a minor headache. What are we talking about here? A mild concussion at best?" Quint laid it all out.

"Sounds like you've been down this road before," Donovan said.

"I played sports growing up," Quint explained. "And then there are job hazards."

"Understood." Donovan finished his exam. "I agree with your assessment. You need to rest and drink plenty of fluids. Avoid screens if at all possible."

Compared to the head injury he'd sustained on their last assignment, this was nothing. Still, the damage was piling up.

When they were finished with the lecture, Donovan asked, "Are you ready to go?"

"Yes, we are," Ree answered, and he realized how tired she must be. "And if we can stop off for coffee so I can make it back to Dallas, that would be great."

"I'll see what I can do," Donovan promised. He seemed a little too quick to want to please Ree, and that got underneath Quint's skin. He reached out and took her hand in his, linking their fingers as they walked over to Donovan's dual-cab pickup. It looked comfortable enough inside.

Once Ree was seated in the back, Quint said, "Why don't you rest your head on my shoulder and sleep on the way back to town instead of having coffee?"

"Are you sure?" She blinked up at him with those emerald eyes that shone like rare gemstones. As corny as it might sound, it was easy to get lost in those eyes.

"I got this," he said. Besides, he wanted to think a little more about how Giselle and the others might be connected and, more importantly, Ree needed to rest.

Ree leaned against him and, as it always did when she was this close, the world righted itself for a moment.

"I love you," he whispered, and was rewarded with a smile he couldn't see so much as feel. That was Ree. She had an affect on him no others could touch.

"Where to?" *Donovan* asked.

"Downtown Dallas." Quint rattled off the cross streets

two blocks from their apartment. It was as close as he wanted the EMT to get to their actual address. They could easily walk from there.

Donovan entered the streets into his GPS and navigated onto the highway. The young man kept his eyes on the road in front of him and the vehicles around them.

The steady hum of the road lulled her to sleep a few minutes after they reached the highway. Quint's thoughts rolled back to the start. Who had been on that motorcycle? How was Lizanne involved with Dumitru? Were they business associates or something more?

The motorcycle had been too far away for him to get a picture of the license plate. He could kick himself for not trying when it was in the parking lot. Although, to be fair, if Dumitru had been on the bike, it wouldn't likely register back to him officially.

The rider had been dressed head to toe in white. Who did he think he was? The Milkman? Milkman knew how to ride, that was for certain. At the speeds he'd been going, he would need a handlebar stabilizer on the type of bike commonly referred to as a crotch rocket. Quint's mind was drifting, so he brought his thoughts back into focus.

Milkman was smart. He'd checked to see if they were following him, and then he'd called for backup. But why? Did he recognize Ree and Quint? The thought didn't sit well. It was possible he was used to watching out for a tail, which meant he was involved in illegal activity up to his eyeballs. Then again, that was a given. Did this mean Lizanne was dirty too? She'd been running a legitimate business for years on the surface at the very least. Would she jeopardize her livelihood? Or had she been dirty all along and was just that good at hiding it?

Vadik had cooperated, and he was the reason they'd made it this far. A lot had happened in the past forty-eight hours. Quint generally needed to mentally shut down at some point in a busy day to process everything. Ree had already sent Grappell a text asking him to check into Lizanne's background and business. The agent was a miracle worker, so Quint hoped they would have information about her by lunch tomorrow.

Considering it was almost 2 a.m. and they'd been in a car crash, Quint figured both of them could use a day to sleep in. It wouldn't hurt to take a couple days off in order to gather intel and study the situation. They were moving too quickly and impulsively. Granted, his instincts were normally dead-on, but this case was different, and they'd been under for a long time. Fatigue was an issue, mental and physical.

Jazzy, his mentor, used to tell Quint to rest when he was tired, not quit. Bringing his grades up after goofing around for years had been a challenge. Without Jazzy's guidance, there was no way Quint would have graduated high school let alone be where he was today in his life and career. Jazzy retired from police work and now spent a whole lot of time with a fishing rod in his hand. Quint needed to give him a call.

Since his thoughts were bouncing all over the place on the ride home, he made a mental note to circle back to Axel. The two needed to have a conversation about Giselle without Quint showing his hand. He wanted to get a sense of whether or not Axel believed the woman could survive on her own.

Another thought struck. She'd come to his apartment to offer herself up in exchange for protection. Was she trying to get close to Quint to figure out what had actually happened to Ree? Giselle could have been sent in to cozy up to Quint so she could spy on him and Ree. There were a whole lot of men who would have taken her up on the offer. She'd insinuated sex came with the bargain. That, and subservience. The thought made his stomach churn. He couldn't imagine being with any woman who wasn't an equal partner in every area of their lives. Anything else would make him feel like a creep. The whole idea of using a powerful position to get what someone wanted from the opposite sex was no longer acceptable. A new dawn was on the horizon, and Quint welcomed it. Because it meant having real conversations with a partner. It meant sharing responsibilities. Quint didn't need a mother. He'd had the best, and she'd done everything in her power to ensure he turned out to be a good man. He hoped he would have made her proud if she was still alive.

Once again, his thoughts drifted to how much he wished his mother could have met Ree. The two would have gotten along well. His mother had a heart as big as the Texas sky. His father had broken her spirit, so he'd had a ringside seat to the kind of damage a terrible partner could do. Was it the reason he'd been so careful with his own heart?

For a while there, he'd all but given up on finding someone as special as Ree. Children had never been a consideration for him or for her until she'd gotten pregnant.

Quint exhaled slowly and pinched the bridge of his nose to stem the headache. He'd refused any medication earlier and now was wondering how smart a decision that had been. He'd pulled the tough-guy routine when he probably should have accepted help. Why was it so hard to admit he wasn't indestructible?

He thought back to his childhood, and the tough exterior he'd put on like armor. He'd gotten into his fair share of trouble. Shame still cloaked him over the way he'd treated his single parent mother when she'd needed him to step up.

Going back in his thoughts always filled him with regret. Thankfully, she'd lived long enough to see him turn his life around and get through high school. His mother had died way too young, and he realized now that she'd lost the will to live working odd jobs to keep the family afloat. She'd gotten him through school and not much more. She'd helped him cross the finish line and get started on a better life. There wasn't a day that went by he didn't think about her and her many sacrifices. If she were alive, he would buy her the house she'd never had. His mother didn't talk about her own childhood much, but Quint always had the impression hers wasn't great. His father was supposed to be her ticket out of poverty when, instead, he left her holding the bag with their child and all the expenses that came along with having one.

Speaking of single mothers, he couldn't help but compare the ones he met to his own mother. Giselle was the exact opposite. Rather than be with her kid, she was out partying with a criminal element. Quint's mother had been beautiful by most standards. She could have ditched him and hooked up with another guy after her husband walked out. He'd overheard her on the phone one day explaining her lack of a dating life to one of their distant relatives over the holidays. She'd said there was no way she was bringing home a stranger while she had a young son in the house. Was she afraid all men were like Quint's father? That they'd take what they wanted and leave her?

He couldn't ask those questions now. All the time he'd lost with her while he was out making trouble filled him with more regret. If he'd stayed home, he could have gotten to know her better.

Either way, she'd still been an angel walking on earth in his eyes. Nothing like Giselle, who seemed ready to throw herself at any man. Nothing like this woman who seemed eager to let her sister bring up the boy she claimed to love. Did she even visit him? Did he even know who his mother was? Or was her sister bringing him up as her own child with Giselle out of the picture?

Another thought struck him while he was on the topic. Did Giselle get pregnant in order to trap Axel into support and protection? It seemed possible. Desperate people did desperate things, he thought. And yet, no matter how desperate his mother had been, she'd always walked the line of honesty. At one time, he'd convinced himself that she was living in a fairy-tale world when she told him to keep his nose clean, his eyes open and his heart kind. He'd thought she was one step away from being committed. Honesty and kindness weren't the norm on the streets where he grew up. His mother had been a bright light in the eye of a storm. She had somehow remained calm despite having their electricity shut off on more than one occasion. She had somehow kept her dignity when they only had hand-me-downs to wear. She had somehow managed to keep her chin up, at least around him. He'd overheard her crying into her pillow one too many times. It woke him up and caused him to decide to hold up his end of the bargain.

If Quint could go back, there was so much he would change with regard to how he'd treated his mother during his dark years. Funnily enough, she would have forgiven him in a heartbeat, told him he was just learning what not to do, and then given him a big hug. Why was it so hard to forgive himself?

Chapter Fourteen

"We're here." The voice startled Ree awake. She'd been sleeping so deeply, slobber dribbled down the side of her mouth. There was something about being with Quint that had a way of making her feel safe.

"Are you awake?" Quint whispered, and his voice was a low rumble in his chest.

She lifted her head and wiped her mouth with the back of her hand before nodding. It was probably a good thing there were no mirrors around, because she probably looked like a hot mess. But the couple of hours of shut-eye did make her feel surprisingly rested. Muscle stiffness following the crash was a whole different story but she could cope with it.

"I am now," she said with a smile. Looking up at Quint, she saw the tiredness in his eyes. There'd been no way he would have allowed her stay awake while he slept, so she didn't push the issue. He would have wanted to ensure there was no damage from the concussion, and she'd respected his need to stay awake and focused. "How much does your head hurt?"

"Believe it or not, it's improving," he said.

She studied him as *Donovan* pulled over onto the side of the road.

"Liar," she said.

"I never said you had to believe it," he quipped. He was being a funny guy to distract her from the fact he was actually in pain. Not a good sign. She wouldn't call him out on it. All she wanted to do was get him home and to bed.

"Thank you for the ride," Ree said to *Donovan* after rolling her eyes at Quint.

"You're welcome," he said with a smile and a courteous wave.

Ree climbed out of the back seat and onto the familiar road two streets over from home. She took Quint's arm and wrapped it around her shoulders, partly because she wanted to be close to him and partly because she wanted him to be able to lean on her if he needed to.

Quint thanked *Donovan*, as well. The man made a U-turn and split so fast Ree's head could spin.

"Ever see someone so happy to be rid of two people?" she asked Quint, figuring she needed to keep the topic light. Her fiancé and partner had no doubt been going over details and thinking about the players nonstop, trying to figure out what they were missing.

"Can't say that I have," Quint fired back. He stumbled but regained his composure quickly. Adrenaline had long since faded, and they were at the mercy of their bodies at this point. Between the crash and the long drive home, he had to be exhausted.

"Same here."

The closer they got to the apartment, the more Quint seemed to lean on her. By the time the elevator dinged, indicating they'd arrived on their floor, he was basically sleepwalking.

"Straight to bed with you the minute we walk through that door. Got it?" she said with a stern look before cracking a smile.

"You wanting to take me to bed isn't exactly going to

cause any argument from me," he stated. Good to know his sense of humor was still intact.

"Not tonight, tough guy." She closed and locked the door behind them, half expecting Giselle to jump out from the door to the stairwell before they'd made it inside. Of course, she had to know Ree was back by now. Lindy would have mentioned it. Ree was still trying to wrap her mind around the two of them being in league.

"Since I smell like…" Quint made a show of lifting his arm and making a face.

"You don't stink, but I think you were about to say that you needed to take a shower," she said. "Make it quick, mister."

"Have I told you how much I like it when you boss me around?" Quint teased. He was half-drunk with sleepiness. The tired had officially kicked in, and Quint's brain was leaving the building.

"Hurry up and I'll help you undress," she said with a wink.

A man had never raced to the shower faster.

She could pick his brain in the morning or afternoon, whenever they managed to wake up. Quint wasn't the only one in need of a shower. She could probably use a good night of sleep too, but she wasn't sure if that would happen now that she'd had her power nap. Napping had two outcomes with Ree. It either energized her or made her feel like she was walking around outside of her body for the rest of the day. Normally she didn't risk it because she never could be certain which nap would show up.

Ree joined him in the bathroom, mainly to keep an eye on him. As tired as he was, she couldn't risk him taking a fall in the shower and cracking his head again. He seemed to have skated without a serious head injury from the crash, and she wouldn't tempt fate twice. She was, however, grateful for the person who'd invented seat belts and the person who invented airbags. Both were the reason the two of them had walked away from what should have been a fatal accident.

Quint turned on the spigot and let the water heat up while she helped him undress. The man was perfection if ever there was a perfect body. She noted the scars too. The places he'd been stabbed and where bullet fragments had nicked him. He'd been lucky so far. Her only fear was that the luck would run out before this case could be put to rest.

"I spent the whole ride home thinking," Quint finally said after stepping into the water and closing the glass door to the shower.

"I figured as much," she said. "What did you come up with?" She didn't want to go into it too deeply before they slept, but curiosity was getting to her.

"My mind keeps going back to Giselle and wondering if she is as innocent as she seems," he said.

"Mine too," Ree confirmed.

"And I can't figure out what Lizanne would have to gain by exposing her legitimate business to a criminal," he continued.

"She's either in a relationship with Dumitru or protecting him," she said. "He could also have something on her and be forcing her to cooperate. These bastards take what they want and have no regard for others."

"I was thinking along those same lines too," he stated. "Think we can have a discussion with Axel about Giselle?"

"As long as we're not obvious about it," she reasoned. "Maybe we can have a face-to-face with him and say we're checking on him and his family. We can even pretend to be bringing him information about Giselle. Say we're worried about her and that we're doing everything to keep her safe. He might not tell us the truth, but his reaction will give us some information to go on."

"I agree on all those points," he said.

It was impossible not to watch him in the shower. He made something as simple as washing himself look graceful. No, *graceful* wasn't the right word for Quint. Although he did have an athletic grace about him that was downright sexy.

They talked about mostly mundane topics for the rest of his shower. When Ree was reassured he'd be fine putting himself to bed, she took a turn. There was something nice about washing the day off her before bed. The warmth of the water soothed her aching muscles.

The hard object that smashed into Quint's skull could very easily have nailed her instead. She could have lost Quint if his head had been positioned a little to one side and his temple had been struck instead of the back of his head. She might have been hit just as easily. It was dumb luck that had the object smashing into him and not her.

Her first thought was her mother. What would happen if Ree died? She'd been too young to remember many of the details of when her father passed away but had overhead her mother speaking to Ree's grandfather one night about it. Her mother had been crying, something Ree rarely ever saw her mother do. Her grief had spilled out of her eyes, and she'd talked about the last words she'd had with her husband before he left for work that day.

Regret was powerful. Was that the reason her mother had always kept Ree at arm's length? Was her mother afraid of getting into another argument right before Ree walked out the door? Was that the reason the woman had an almost permanent scowl when she looked at her daughter? Wouldn't she want to hug Ree tightly every day before work instead, just in case? Or could her mother not even go there with something actually happening to Ree?

Seeing regret eat Quint from the inside out helped Ree realize just how powerful remorse was. When this case was over, she needed to talk to her mother. Between now and then, the words would probably come to her. Right?

After her shower, she climbed into bed with Quint. He was already in a deep sleep. She didn't care. All she wanted to do was curl up against his warmth. The thought of how fragile life truly was had stirred a place deep inside her chest. A thought surfaced. Had she ever gotten over the loss of her father? Had she ever given herself a chance to grieve? Or had watching her mother's sadness imprinted on Ree?

Those were the thoughts spinning around in her mind as she gave in to sleep.

They'd been asleep for a solid eight hours when pounding on the door caused her to sit bolt upright. Quint snapped into action, throwing off the covers, stumbling around a couple of steps as he hopped into his jeans. Ree wasn't much better as she managed to slip into yoga pants. The T-shirt she slept in would have to do as she retrieved her Glock and followed her partner to the door.

He checked the peephole, took a step back and then shook his head. He mouthed the name *Lindy.*

Ree reached for the knob, but Quint put a hand on her arm to stop her. Heart beating against her ribs, she held her breath.

"We need to talk," Lindy said through the door.

Was he checking up on them to see if they'd lived after last night's crash? The Chevy wasn't in the garage downstairs. But then, it seemed like he already knew.

"Are you home?" Lindy practically shouted. He was

loud enough to disturb a neighbor who opened their door and asked what the hell was going on out there.

Ree released the breath she'd been holding when she heard Lindy mutter a curse word before stomping away toward the elevator. The man had a temper, which probably shouldn't come as a surprise.

But what was the visit all about?

QUINT DOUBLE-CHECKED to make sure Lindy was gone. He was in no mood to deal with that sonofabitch.

"It's clear," he said to Ree.

She exhaled and secured her weapon back in her holster. He did the same, and then they both placed their guns inside the closet for safekeeping.

"What the hell did he want?" she asked, but the question was rhetorical.

"I'll check my phone in a minute to see if we had a warning before he showed up," he said. The clock on the wall read eleven-thirty. His body cried for more, but he could get by on what he'd gotten.

"You look much better today," Ree said to him before walking over and giving him a kiss.

"I feel it," he said after bringing her into an embrace. "A couple of muscles are screaming at me, but my headache is basically gone."

"That's good news," she said. "I'll freshen up and make some coffee."

He watched as she disappeared into the bathroom, thinking he was the luckiest man on earth. This case would be behind them before they knew it, and she would be making wedding plans. He didn't mind leaving the details up to her. He already had everything he needed once she'd said yes to his proposal. The rest was just paperwork and formality as far as he was concerned. He was still bouncing all around at the idea of children, one minute thinking he could do it and everything would magically be okay and the next wondering if his father would pass down his miserable genes.

Rather than waiting for Ree to make coffee, Quint made himself useful and started brewing a pot. After his turn in the bathroom, they worked side by side in the kitchen, toasting bagels and slathering cream cheese and jelly on top.

By the time they sat at the counter, they had gotten down a couple of bites of their breakfast and a few much-needed sips of caffeine. He could take an over the counter pain reliever once he had enough food in his stomach. That should help with the residual soreness, whiplash and muscle aches.

"How are you feeling, by the way?" he asked Ree.

"Like I got in a car crash last night," she quipped.

"When we're done eating and checking phones and emails, we both need a couple of ibuprofen," he said with a smile.

"No argument from me there," she said, stretching. It looked like her left shoulder caught as she raised her arm. "I'm feeling the creaks and groans hard today."

"We've earned a day off," he said.

"It would be a good idea to take stock of what we already know and try to put some of the puzzle pieces together. At the very least, we can lay everything out and see where we end up," she responded.

"My mind was spinning way too much to be able to sleep until we got home and my head hit the pillow," he admitted. "Now that I have some caffeine inside me, I'll check to see if I have any messages."

It was probably good they didn't respond to the "emergency"-sounding bangs on the door. They'd caught

Ree off guard with the text from Giselle that begged her to meet for lunch. There was no way Quint planned on falling for the same kind of trick again. Slow and methodical would be his mantra from now on. It was too late in the game for mistakes when it was clear someone was willing to kill off anyone who seemed to get in the way or threaten the operation.

He glanced at his screen. There were messages, all right. His gaze landed hard on the last one from Lindy.

"Giselle has gone missing," he said to Ree.

"She was trying to keep me alive and now..."

Had Giselle come to him because she knew something was about to happen?

Chapter Fifteen

"Giselle looked and acted desperate when she came here yesterday to ask for my help. You're not the one to blame for whatever's happened to her." Quint made sense, and yet guilt still ate Ree alive.

Since sitting around stewing over what they could have done differently wouldn't change a thing, she threw aside her regret before it had a chance to take hold.

"I'm guessing Lindy thinks we had something to do with her disappearance," Ree commented.

"His tone does give me that impression," Quint stated.

"This looks bad," she admitted. "At least, to an outsider."

"Or someone in law enforcement," he added.

"Or someone on the inside of a crime ring," she continued.

"She could have gone into hiding of her own volition," he reasoned.

If she truly had been in danger and was down to begging for protection, she might have stepped on more toes than theirs. Since the organization was showing signs of cracking under pressure, the higher-ups might be looking for targets or anyone they deemed as someone who might talk in the case of an arrest.

"After she came here, she might have figured the best

way to stay alive would be to get off the grid for a little while at the very least. Wait until things blow over," Ree said. "It's exactly what I would do if I was in the same situation."

"We were attacked and Giselle has gone missing all within a twenty-four-hour period," Quint pointed out.

"Hold on," he said. He pulled up a contact on his phone and made a call. "Ree is here with me. Mind if I put the call on speaker?"

There was a short pause before Grappell's voice was on the line.

"Ree?" he said.

"I'm here," she confirmed.

"We've been worried about the two of you," Grappell scolded, his voice the equivalent of her fifth-grade schoolteacher's. It made a cold chill race down her back.

"Sorry," she said. "I just saw your texts. Sounds like you have information about Lizanne."

"That's correct," Grappell stated, a little less schoolteacher and a little more agent-like. "Her real name is Loraine Ridden. She started out as a stripper in a club near White Rock Lake fifteen years ago, and that seems to be where she met several members of Dumitru's organization. Although the ties are murky like pretty much everyone else we try to investigate in this case. At least we know Lizanne's birth name and age. She's now thirty-eight and considered attractive by most standards. I sent over another picture of her back then and now."

Ree checked her phone and then held up the photos so Quint could see them too.

"She looks a whole lot like a young Anna Nicole Smith in the early years," Quint pointed out.

"And probably more like the famous ex-stripper than she should in her older years," Ree said. Lizanne had breast implants that made hers too large for her frame and bleached blond hair styled similarly to Anna Nicole's. The resemblance probably helped Lizanne become very popular in the Dallas strip club scene, where big boobs and bigger blond hair meant raking in the cash.

"Lizanne had made enough money by age twenty-five to start her lingerie business," Grappell mentioned. "She has to have some business savvy in order to achieve a successful enterprise."

"Or, like in many cases, a very wealthy backer," Quint said.

"She hails from Blum, Texas," Grappell continued after agreeing to Quint's statement.

"Now, there's a small town," Ree said.

"Population of less than five hundred residents," Grappell informed them.

"How is that even possible?" Ree asked, thinking there should be a minimum number of residents before a place could call itself a town.

"I grew up in a small, boring town outside of San Antonio," Agent Grappell said. "It wasn't right for me. There was nothing to do unless you enjoyed bonfires out by the lake, underage drinking, and the big highlight of your night was cow tipping."

"Sounds awful," Ree said. "Don't get me wrong, I love a good small town, but there needs to be shopping nearby, restaurants and things to do on the occasional night out."

"Same, except for the shopping bit," Agent Grappell said.

"Well then, it's possible she had stars in her eyes from a young age and would have probably been bored to death in a small town with so few distractions," Ree said. She laughed. "My family would have taken up half the population."

"Wouldn't the entire town be related?" Quint quipped.

"Scary thought and probably not too far off base," Ree confirmed. It might be a nice town to grow up in, but young people would have to move if they wanted to go to college or work in most professions after high school other than ranching. The latter wasn't a bad life, but it wasn't the one she'd signed up to live.

"Lizanne's connections to Dumitru must go back a long way," Quint stated after a thoughtful pause.

"Or she could have gotten her seed money from someone else," Ree said. "An older gentleman who likes to frequent those types of establishments. Someone with money like the oil guy Anna Nicole married."

"We could be looking at this the wrong way. What if Lizanne was the one to help Dumitru?" Quint reasoned.

"It's good to pick this apart from all angles," Ree agreed. Divergent thinking had helped solve many cases in a world where the norm didn't seem to exist any longer. Despite her observing the men in A-12 to be chauvinistic, it could be a mistake to paint them inside a box and leave them there. Who knew what the true boundaries were anymore?

"I'm afraid public records aren't a huge help there. Not without a subpoena," Grappell stated. "We'll keep digging until we've checked every last resource to see what we can find."

"Your efforts are much appreciated," Quint confirmed.

"We couldn't do what we do without your expertise," Ree stated, adding her two cents for good measure. It wasn't a huge shock the two of them agreed on almost everything. What had been a surprise was just how much they'd clashed on their first case together. Their chemistry or whatever it was called had been white-hot. Combined with the fact she'd been a bundle of nerves over working with a legendary agent despite being fully capable herself, and there'd been sparks between them from the get-go. Sparks that had led to a slow-burning flame she prayed would never go out.

Being with Quint she'd experienced the hottest kisses, the absolute best sex and, yes, the best conversations in her life.

The image of him naked in the shower from last night put a smile on the corners of her lips despite the serious focus on the case. It was impossible not to grin a little bit when she thought about how well the two of them fit together in bed and out.

There was only one thing standing between the two of them heading into their future with open arms and making their life plan...this case.

"I think that is about all I have to contribute for now," Agent Grappell said. "I'll let you know when I come up with anything else."

"Thank you," Ree said at the same time as Quint.

"Lindy thinks we're involved with Giselle's disappearance," Quint stated.

"He said that?" Grappell asked.

"In so many words, yes," Quint said.

"Be careful," Grappell warned.

"Always," he said. Now it was time to put their heads together and figure out their next step. "Can you dig up Giselle's sister's address? We need to swing by and see if the kid is still around."

"Will do," Grappell said before he promised to text as soon as he had it.

"Shouldn't take him and the team long to find that," Ree said. "We probably have time for another cup of coffee."

They also needed a vehicle if they were going anywhere, but the look on Quint's voice said her other thoughts could wait.

QUINT POURED A second cup of coffee for Ree before refilling his own mug. He grabbed a couple of ibuprofen for her, then filled a glass of water. Once Ree had downed hers, he followed suit. Twenty minutes was all it would take for the pain relievers to kick in. His body felt rough on a good day after the beatings it had taken over the years.

"Hey," he said. "I know we're focused on the case right now."

"Sometimes changing the subject and *not* thinking about it brings the best results," she reasoned.

He couldn't argue with that logic considering he was about to say the same thing.

"I do realize I've been going back and forth on a topic that I think has become important to you, and it could impact your happiness in a future with someone like me," he began. This probably wasn't the time or place to think about starting a family, but he was still on the fence about it, and he needed to know if his position was a deal breaker for her.

"Are you referring to having children?" she asked.

"Thinking about Giselle's relationship with her son—" he paused "—or should I say non-relationship, had me going down a bad path." He needed to get this out, and then they could swing by Giselle's sister's house to see if the boy was still there or if Giselle had ditched town with the kid. The thought of either didn't sit well because if she took the kid, then she was in real trouble. This wasn't the topic at hand, and he was letting his mind wander because he didn't know how to approach talking about what had been on his mind. "I'm not sure how I feel about reproducing or extending my genetic line."

Ree sat perfectly still, hands in her lap, a look of compassion on her face. It wasn't anger, so he'd take it.

"Here's the thing. I want you to have everything you

want," he continued when she didn't immediately respond. What could she say? He'd just dropped a bomb in her lap. He hadn't seen the kid thing coming, which was stupid on his part. He should have realized someone with a big family might want to have kids of her own.

"I already do," she said after a thoughtful pause.

"What if I'm not enough?" he asked, his pulse racing like he was asking out the prom queen.

"You are," she confirmed, and he really believed she meant it.

"That might be true now, Ree. But what about in the future?" he asked, but it was a rhetorical question.

She sat there, perched on the stool. Her lips were compressed like when she was thinking hard about a topic or searching for an answer she knew was there if she concentrated hard enough. He loved knowing these little things about her.

"Let me ask you a question," she began after a long pause. "Last week, did you know you were going to be in a car crash yesterday?"

"No, of course not," he stated, not sure where this was heading.

"Me neither," she continued like her thoughts were the most logical things. "Do you know what last night taught me?"

He shook his head.

"That not everything can be planned for. I mean, you do your best in life, and then there's just this whole big piece that no one can predict and no one can plan for. You know?" Her forehead wrinkled, and she pursed her lips.

"Life is unpredictable," he conceded. "I'm not sure what that has to do with me denying you children if you want to become a mother, and I can't get there in my mind.

That's a big topic that some would definitely view as a deal breaker."

"It is a big deal, and it surprised me when the thought basically attacked me," she admitted. "I never considered children before I met you, and now that's changed. Some might say it's wholly unfair to you to do an about-face like that."

"How could you have known how you felt before it hit you?" he asked, and then her point smacked him square in the chest with the force of a bomb detonating.

"I know two things for certain in life right now. The first is that I want to marry you. You're the one for me, Quint. It's just you. That's all I need. The other is that I need to find a way to forgive my mother and let her know that we're okay. After worrying about you, she was the first person I thought about after last night's crash," she said on a sigh. "I have to make that relationship right or I'll never be able to forgive myself if something happens to her."

Quint walked over to his bride-to-be and brought her into an embrace.

"I know that I love you more than life itself," he said, wishing this could somehow be easier and that he could just promise her the moon. He *wanted* to give her the stars and the whole sky. And yet he knew himself, and he was having doubts about the whole family bit. "I've never said that to another person, and I know I'll never find someone like you again if you walk out of my life."

"That can't be what you want, Quint," she said, and he could hear the hurt in her voice. Hurt *he* put there. Hurt he couldn't erase.

"It's not. There's no question in my mind that you're exactly the right person for me. You're all I need," he said. "I feel complete. But you don't, and that's where the complication comes in."

"I didn't know it would happen," she said, and when she looked up at him, her emerald eyes were shining with tears. He hated to be the one to put them there. "And I never said you weren't enough."

"No, you didn't." He didn't put up an argument. There was no use. He could tell by the resignation in those eyes that she knew they'd hit a wall in their relationship too.

"What we have is better than anything I've ever experienced," she continued. "And I might want kids right now, but who knows if that will change by tomorrow?"

They both knew it wouldn't.

"I don't want to lose what we have, Quint," she said. Those words nearly broke his heart.

How could he stay with her and force her into a life she might not want? And how could he leave her and shatter both of their hearts?

Chapter Sixteen

Ree could live without kids. Right?

Before she could get too involved in the thought, her cell buzzed. She picked it up and checked the screen.

"We have an address," she said to Quint. "Now all we need is transportation."

Quint retrieved his cell phone as the conversation they'd been having came to a standstill.

"It looks like we have a Jeep downstairs. Keys are inside underneath the driver's seat," he said. Then he stopped and looked at her like he was looking through her. He was the only person who she would swear knew what she was thinking. "Are we okay?"

"I told you that I love you and my future is with you," she said. "I needed you to know that I was at the very least thinking about what it would be like to have a family with you and whether or not that seemed like something I would want. Turns out, it is. But we don't have to have all the answers right now."

The look in his eyes and the way his jaw muscle ticked planted a seed of fear deep inside her that they didn't see their futures in the same light.

"You deserve the world, Ree," he said, locking gazes with her. There was a storm brewing behind those gorgeous sapphire blues.

They had to be able to work this out. She couldn't allow herself to believe this would be a showstopper for either one of them.

"And so do you," she pointed out before standing up, pressing to her tiptoes and kissing him.

He teased his tongue inside her mouth, and a thousand campfires lit inside her, warming her, drawing her toward their light. She could stay like this forever. Quint was enough. Kids, in this moment, were optional. However, he had made a good point. Would she regret not having them?

It didn't matter, she thought as they broke apart. She loved this man. She planned to make a life with him. And, besides, who really knew if kids were in the cards anyway? She could want them until the cows came home, but what if she physically couldn't? She'd been in relationships. Granted, she'd been careful. There hadn't been any surprises over the years despite no method of birth control being absolutely foolproof.

Ree was getting older too. At this point, she didn't even know if she could have children. Her eggs were, like, ancient in egg terms. So he could be concerned about something that might not even be possible.

The only things she knew for certain were that life could be unfair and unkind. It never made a promise that tomorrow would come or the next day. It didn't promise a rose garden. And it didn't promise that all anyone's wants would be met. People lived happily with far less than what she and Quint had between them. Besides, she had a niece and a nephew. Her other brothers would have kids at some point. Men weren't bound to the same biological clock as women anyway. Her brothers could have kids well into their forties. For women, the statistics weren't so great.

"I'm pouring a to-go cup of coffee after I get dressed

since I didn't finish my second one and now it's cold," she said to Quint. "Do you want one for the road?"

"No, I'm good with this one." He picked up his cup and polished off the contents. He made a face that told her just how cold the coffee had become.

Ree wasn't an iced latte type, and neither was Quint. Despite the heavy mood, his reaction was priceless.

After retrieving their weapons and getting dressed for the day, they headed downstairs to the garage and the waiting Jeep. When something like this happened, there was always the fear one of the folks they were after would question them having a replacement turn up so quickly. But then, it seemed like pretty much everything could be ordered and delivered in twenty-four hours or less from the internet. However, their cover story of Quint coming out of prison and them staying in a borrowed apartment only went so far. They were supposed to be broke. The SUV was long gone, and they could always say they sold it for the Jeep if push came to shove, she guessed.

"How far away is the address?" she asked as they climbed inside the Jeep. The ibuprofen was doing its job at least. She was in considerably less pain than earlier unless emotional scars counted, and those were racking up today. She hadn't meant for the "having a kid someday" conversation to turn into the possibility of a breakup. Life could deal some really interesting twists.

Rather than stew over it, she realized Quint would have to come to his own decision about moving forward with their relationship. There wasn't anything she could do to stop him if he wanted to throw what they had away. And she understood on some level that what she'd been asking might rattle him. Given his past, the thought of kids wasn't on his radar.

Then there was Tessa and her baby. Was he still blaming himself for their deaths? It would be just like Quint to convince himself that he didn't deserve a real family after Tessa's death. Logic flew out the window in times like these, even with intelligent people, people like Quint.

The thought she might have just destroyed an entire relationship over kids she didn't even know were physically possible struck hard.

Ree shelved the thought as Quint pulled up the address on his cell phone.

"It's an address in Frisco, so looks like we'll take a straight shot down the tollway and exit on Eldorado Parkway," he said. "Considering it's the afternoon, we should avoid any heavy traffic. I'd say we'll be at their door in half an hour or less."

Ree checked his phone. He wasn't kidding about the residence being a straight shot. Once they got off the tollway and onto Eldorado, they needed to hang a left and then drive a couple of blocks to the neighborhood on the right before Teel Avenue. Easy peasy.

They sat in silence on the ride to the suburbs. A few cloud rolled by, and the sun was buried behind the swaths of gray. While a population of less than five hundred was definitely too small for Ree, the suburban sprawl seemed worse. There might be pizza delivery and more restaurants than any one person could feasibly cover in a lifetime around this area, but the utter lack of space in between houses made her feel claustrophobic.

Exiting the highway, they made a left and then a few minutes later pulled into the neighborhood of newish houses that all pretty much looked the same to Ree. Small front yards. Manicured landscaping. Cookie-cutter houses. Definitely not her taste, although she liked the fact they were new. The neighborhood lacked the tall trees she was used to on her own property—a property she'd seen far too little of in the past couple of months. She was beginning to miss home from a place deep in her soul.

The only thing that would make her home better was having Quint there full-time.

"What's our cover?" she asked as Quint turned onto Giselle's sister's street. She'd been so caught up in her own thoughts, she'd forgotten to ask the family's names.

"I think we go to the door as a sales team," he said.

"What exactly are we selling?" she asked, wondering if people went door-to-door to sell anything these days considering everything was a click away on the internet.

"Educational services," he said after scanning the homes. "These look like people who would spend their money to help their kids get ahead in life, so I'm thinking we pretend we have a new business and are trying to let local folks know about it."

"What kind of educational services?" she asked, thinking the man was a genius and could read a room like nobody's business.

"SAT prep or math tutoring," he said after a thoughtful pause.

She shivered.

"No one wants to learn math from me," she said, making a sour pickle face. "Plus, won't we need a flyer or something?"

"We can ask if anyone in the home is getting ready for high school," he said. "This seems like a neighborly community. I'd bet they would be willing to hear about a neighborhood business opening. All we have to say is that we're having mailers printed and will be sending those out but wanted to stop by and meet as many folks as we can on a personal level. That will be our marketing ploy. We are different from the competition because we get to know the family and we care."

"Wow. Remind me to ask you for help when I develop the next big thing and need to get the word out," she said in appreciation. He could actually make a living at this whole marketing business.

His smile caused more of those campfires to light inside her chest.

"I used to sell stuff in my youth," he admitted.

"Drugs?" she asked, shocked.

"Baseball cards," he countered. "And shame on you for thinking I was a druggy."

"I never said you were," she shot back. "I only mentioned that you might have sold them. There's a huge difference. In fact, one of my friends went into the police academy. He flunked out, or so everyone believed, and then he was back on the street working a normal job. He was also selling pot, but it turned out that he was actually undercover, had graduated first in our class, and he couldn't tell me until six months later when the busts had been made. As it so happened, he sold drugs in his youth without ever touching them for himself."

"How close are you with this 'guy'?" Quint made air quotes around the word *guy*, suspicion obvious in his tone.

"What? It was a million years ago," she said defensively. It was impossible to be mad, because it was adorable when he was jealous. "And I can be friends with guys, you know."

He seemed to catch himself when he smiled.

"Yes, you can," he said. "I just hope this guy knows his place with you."

"You're missing the point of the story," she quipped.

"Oh, right," he said. "And that was?"

She playfully slapped his arm. "The point is that you don't have to be a 'druggy' to sell drugs. Some people see it as a business transaction or a way to make easy money if they are reasonably smart or have fallen on hard times."

"Or they could sell baseball cards," he said.

"True enough. But is there the same demand?" she asked.

"That's what develops the sales skills," he said. "When you have a product not everyone realizes they need yet."

"Good to know that you're not just arm candy," she teased, appreciating the lighter conversation. They needed to switch gears and get back into work mode. The whole baby and family conversation had thrown her completely off track. "Ready?"

Quint pulled in front of the home that looked more like a mini-mansion. Ree wondered who needed this much space. She preferred cozy over what had to be room after empty room. No matter how many kids she and Quint might have, she wanted to live in her place even if it meant crawling over each other at times. And if there were no kids, the place was also perfect for her and Quint. Not too big and not too small. Not an inch of wasted space or money. It warmed the practical side of her that knew what it was like to grow up without a whole lot of extras. Her family wasn't broke, but her mother had worked hard to support them after losing her husband.

"You should talk if Giselle's sister answers," Ree said. She figured there weren't many women who would even listen to what was coming out of Quint's mouth, as gorgeous as he was.

"And what if her husband answers?" he asked.

"I'll take that one," she offered. "But what if Giselle is here, hiding?"

It was a possibility, however slight.

"I don't think she is," he began. "And here's why. This is the first place anyone who knows her would come. In fact, we'll have to be careful because of it. She might warn her sister that if anyone or anything seems weird, the woman should call 911 immediately. I'd prefer not to have another scrape with the law on this case if at all possible."

"Same here. In fact, I'm still trying to figure out whose name Bjorn dropped to get that sheriff to stop giving us a hard time and instead practically volunteer to fix us tea and fluff our pillows at night," she said.

"Fluffing the pillows is a little dramatic," he said on a chuckle. Joking around eased some of the tension that came right before facing an unknown event or outcome in a case. It was good to calm the nerves.

"I'll give you that one," she said. "So, what are we walking into here? What's Giselle's sister's name? I get that she's married with kids of her own. How many? And do we know what ages?"

Quint studied his cell phone.

"Her sister's name is Nicole, and she's married to a guy by the name of Terrence." Quint scrolled down with a flick of a thumb. "They have two kids who are both school-age. The boy is in fifth grade, and the daughter is in third. Nicole married up the social scale and into a little bit of money."

Ree glanced at the clock.

"Looks like the kids will be getting out of school in the next hour," she said.

"Let's hope Nicole is home," he stated.

"We already know Giselle's son's name is Axel," Ree supplied.

"That's right," Quint said. "Now, let's go see if the little guy still lives here."

"She might have taken him with her," Ree said.

"I'm thinking Giselle most likely took off in a big hurry if it was her choice to disappear," he stated. "I doubt she had time to fill her sister in on who might show up at the door looking for Axel. She might tell her to be careful or not to open the door to strangers."

"Right," Ree said.

"Which brings up another good point. Someone might have already been here," he said.

"And they could still be watching the house," Ree stated.

"Then we probably shouldn't sit here for long," he said before exiting the Jeep. He came around to her side and held out a hand as she exited.

Ree took the offering, hoping they weren't walking into a trap.

Chapter Seventeen

Ree kept her head down as she walked up the sidewalk to the two-story mini-castle. She glanced over at Quint as he brought his fist up to knock.

"Promise me you'll never want to live in one of these," she whispered.

He chuckled, but the enthusiasm about their future was gone from his eyes, and that scared her more than anything else they might face today.

Quint knocked on the door, then rang the bell for good measure.

"Who is it?" a female voice Ree assumed belonged to Nicole asked through the door. A shadow passed behind the peephole.

Ree nudged Quint into the woman's view. He had a way of getting doors to open once women got a good look at him. She also reached for his hand once she saw Nicole's reaction to his face in her portal.

"Hello, my name is Quint, and I'm here with my wife, Ree. We are opening a new business next month at the corner of Teel and Main, and we'd love to come in and tell you about it if you have a moment," he said.

Nicole's eyes widened for a split second before she seemed to pull it together enough to smile.

Ree moved into view and returned the smile. The snick of the lock coincided with the word, "Sure."

The solid mahogany door opened enough for them to get a good look at Nicole.

"Come on in and tell me about your new business," she said.

A TV blared in the background as she led them to the kitchen and closer to the noise. A little boy with a thick black head of hair sat in the middle of the floor, entranced by the TV. There was a smattering of toys scattered around him that looked like someone had overturned a box and let the contents fall where they might. The toys were all manner of bright colors, covering the rainbow.

She surveyed the area to see if there were any remnants of Giselle around like an extra purse lying on the floor. If she was there, she would most likely have hidden before her sister answered the door.

Nothing jumped out at Ree as odd.

"Your son is adorable," Quint stated as they followed Nicole to a table, each taking a seat.

"Thank you," she said with a warm smile and a wistful look. "He's not mine, though. He belongs to my..." She seemed to catch herself before adding, "...neighbor. I'm just babysitting while she works."

"Oh, that's really kind of you," Ree stated. "He is a cutie."

Nicole looked over at Axel with a mix of pride and trepidation. The contrast between sisters was striking. Nicole married money, plays tennis and has a family life. Giselle was a partier. Her hair was in a ponytail, and she had on a tennis skirt. Her nails were perfectly manicured, so they had that in common. And that seemed about it. Nicole lived a suburban wife's life while Giselle partied and spent time with criminals.

"Tell me what kind of business you're starting," Nicole stated after asking if they wanted a cup of coffee. They both declined. "And please tell me it's not another nail shop or day spa. We have too many of those as it is."

Nicole was what Ree would describe as chesty with a little too overly tanned skin. To the point it had an orange glow. She had long fake lashes shading light blue eyes. All in all, she would be considered attractive by many people's standards. Ree was more the flannel shirt and jeans type of person. What nature gave her, she was stuck with because she had no plans to go under the knife for a bigger bra size or to change her appearance in any way. Even her tiny early wrinkles were badges to her. She'd smiled a whole lot to earn those babies.

"No, nothing like that," Quint started, taking the lead. It was for the best since Nicole seemed distracted by his good looks. "We're offering SAT prep for high schoolers and tutoring for anyone who needs a little help."

"Oh, that sounds wonderful," Nicole piped up. She seemed to sit up a little straighter as he spoke, causing her ample chest to thrust toward him.

Ree had to stop herself from making a snarky comment and refocus. She used the time to look around as though she was admiring the decor. One entire wall was covered with an array of crosses in different shapes and sizes. There were professional quality photos of her two children over the fireplace mantel along with another one of the whole family together. Everyone wore jeans and a white shirt.

There didn't seem to be any pictures of the sisters together or of the bigger family. The little boy was still focused on the TV. It didn't appear that his mother had been in the room a few moments ago. And there was no immediate evidence Giselle was hiding out here. Again, the odds of her doing that were probably slim.

Should Ree and Quint be concerned that the woman didn't seem to have spoken to her sister? If she had, Nicole would likely have been far more suspicious of her and Quint showing up randomly at the door. She most definitely wouldn't have invited them in. So, no, Giselle didn't seem to have warned her sister.

Then again, she might not have wanted her sister to worry. It was possible Giselle got herself into something she couldn't easily get out of and decided to disappear for a couple of days to let it blow over. At this point, they'd only ruled out her being here.

As angry as Ree was with the woman, she genuinely hoped Giselle hadn't been taken or disposed of. The thought caused a cold shiver to race down her back. In this world, anything was possible. Plus, these guys didn't seem to hold women as sacred as some other criminal organizations did.

Quint finished his sales pitch about their fake business while Ree stared at the little boy in the family room. Something funny happened on TV, because his face broke into a wide smile.

"You two planning on starting a family soon?" Nicole asked, breaking into the moment.

"How do you know we don't already?" Ree asked.

"Oh, I just saw the way you were looking at my...at my neighbor's little boy. I recognized that look." Nicole practically beamed when she referenced Axel despite the almost-admission he was her nephew. Ree couldn't help but wonder if Nicole knew who his father was and what kind of life her sister truly led. Then again, maybe it was best not to ask too many questions when it came to family.

"He's adorable, but, no, we aren't planning our family right now," Ree said. "We're just now planning the wedding."

"I call her my wife because we've been together for a long time and, in my heart where it counts, she already is," Quint explained, and Ree realized her slip.

"And we hope you'll visit our business when your kids are old enough to benefit," Ree continued, trying to draw attention away from her mistake. "We consider our customers family and would love to help your children meet their college goals."

"Sounds good," Nicole said with a big smile plastered across her face. "College is so competitive these days. These guys will probably need all the help they can get in a couple of years." She waved her arms in the air and blew out an exasperated breath.

Ree had no idea what the college scene was like. It felt like a hundred years since she'd gone. The admissions requirements must have gotten out of control, though. She'd heard about all the entrance scandals that had come to light with famous folks and company CEOs trying to buy the way in for their children.

"That's what we're here for," Quint said. "Since we're not opening for another month, we haven't received our business cards yet. Would you mind helping us spread the word around the neighborhood in the meantime?"

"Not a problem at all," Nicole said. "My dry cleaner is over there, and I know exactly the area you're talking about. That's a great location, by the way."

"We hope so," Quint said. "We're planning on putting our heart and soul into this business, and we hope to be able to serve the community."

"That's so sweet of you," Nicole said, and Ree was certain the woman blushed. Not that she could blame her.

Quint had that effect on the opposite sex. He was good-looking beyond words and had that rugged sex appeal that was so magnetic, it had its own orbit. "Do you live around here?"

"We're building a place off of Legacy," Quint stated. His comment received a nod.

"It doesn't surprise me. Although I thought they'd found every nook and cranny to put a house out that way by now," she quipped. Nicole stood up, so Ree and Quint followed her lead. "Welcome to the community."

"Thank you," Ree and Quint said in unison.

"Anything I can get for you guys before you leave? A bottle of water?" Nicole asked, glancing at the time. She gasped, but the little boy was too entranced in the TV to notice. "I need to give little Ax his snack before I put him down for a nap."

"Thank you for your time," Quint stated, extending a hand Nicole seemed all too eager to shake. "You've been very helpful."

"Anytime," she said with a smile. The woman blushed.

Ree would have to get used to it. She couldn't believe the two of them wouldn't be able to work out the differences over whether or not to have kids. But Quint's kids, if he decided to have them, would hit the genetic lotto as far as she was concerned. It would be a shame if he didn't change his mind about having them.

QUINT WALKED BEHIND Ree with his hand on the small of her back. He missed the contact the minute she climbed inside the vehicle. He waited until they got settled in the Jeep and were safely on the road before thinking about speaking.

"It doesn't look like anyone is following us," Ree reported, checking the side-view mirror for the third time since leaving the small neighborhood. It was good to be diligent and cautious when it came to dealing with A-12.

"I didn't see any sign of Giselle inside the house and no signs of stress on her sister's face," he said.

"Which could mean Giselle didn't contact her sister before her disappearance," Ree said.

"I'm concerned about it, if I'm honest. Why wouldn't she let her sister know that she was about to go MIA, especially when the sister is caring for little Axel?" he asked.

"We haven't really established how often the two are in communication," Ree stated. "Giselle doesn't strike me as the type who would keep to a routine like clockwork as far as visitation goes."

"That's a fair point, and now that you bring it up, I agree with you one hundred percent," he said. "It would have been nice if we could have just flashed our badges and gotten right to the point on that visit."

"Agreed." Ree leaned back in her seat and pinched the bridge of her nose.

"Everything okay?" he asked, his concern level hitting the roof as he navigated onto the tollway.

"Yes," she said. "Fine. Just a bit of a headache working up."

"It's been a while since you had ibuprofen," he realized. "Maybe the last dose is wearing off."

"Might be a good idea to take more once we get back to the apartment," she said, leaning her chair back to more of a reclined position. "I know we just ate breakfast, but I'm hungry too."

"We had mostly carbs," he said. "They run through the body pretty fast. Quick energy hit but not enough protein to last the day."

Her skin looked a little paler, but then, he didn't exactly have time to really look at her while he was driving on the tollway. It could be the lighting or the clouds that were gathering steam. Cars and trucks zipped about and treated the road like it was a raceway. He had no idea why this was, but the threat of rain in Texas caused drivers to lose their minds. Why? Driving in rain wasn't all that drastically different than any other weather condition. The main requirement was to go a little slower and be a little more careful. Why was that so difficult?

"I'm kind of nauseous, actually," Ree stated.

"Do you need something?" he asked, realizing there wasn't much inside the Jeep to work with if she needed to empty the contents of her stomach.

"Maybe we could pull over?" she asked. "Get off the road for a second."

"Yes, sure. We have time," he said, immediately navigating off the tollway and to the nearest parking lot.

"Do you feel sick at all?" she asked.

"Me? No, I'm fine. Why?" he asked.

"I was just wondering if maybe something we ate this morning was bad or past the date," she said as he hooked a right into the closest lot. He pulled into a spot as fast as he could. One look at Ree and he wondered if it was fast enough. She practically bolted out of the vehicle and to the nearest trash can.

Quint rushed to her side, rubbing her back as she emptied the contents of her stomach. A flashback to doing a similar thing to Tessa before she'd announced her pregnancy news suddenly hit him.

Tessa had made an excuse, something like bad food, as well. Was there any chance Ree could be pregnant? She would have told him. Wouldn't she? There was no way she would hide the information from him and try to pass this off as a stomach virus or bad food if she didn't get her period.

A knot tied in Quint's gut. Could this be the reason Ree had been mentioning kids out of the blue? Was she testing the waters to see what his reaction would be?

For a split second, Quint thought he might actually join her in getting sick. There was no way he was ready to be a father. He was, however, ready to be Ree's husband, as long as she didn't want kids. Quint could admit that wasn't exactly fair. They hadn't really talked about having a family together before the engagement but, again, wouldn't it be the next logical step for any couple?

All thoughts of the case flew out the window as he watched Ree retch. He felt helpless as he stood there, rubbing her back, wishing he could somehow make her feel better.

"What can I do?" he asked.

She shook her head and continued until there couldn't possibly be any bagel left inside her. She'd probably thrown up all the coffee too.

"Water?" she asked.

"There's none in the Jeep. Will you be all right if I run over to the convenience store real quick?" he asked. There was one anchoring the parking lot.

"Go ahead," she said, but he hated to leave her out in the open like this, vulnerable.

"You're sure you'll be okay?" he asked.

"I'm good. I'm done. I'll just wait inside the Jeep while you go inside," she said.

"I promise to be right back." With that, he took off running toward the store. The pregnancy thoughts cycled through his mind. For the second time he wondered if Ree would have said something if she was pregnant.

A thought struck.

Did she even realize it herself? Or was it so early in the process she hadn't figured it out?

Quint bought the largest bottle of water he could find and made the jog back to the Jeep in record time, his heart battering the inside of his ribcage. Ree was in the seat, leaning back with her arm over her eyes.

"Here you go," he said as he slipped into the driver's side.

Ree took the offering, then opened her door after washing out her mouth. She ran over to the bin and spit.

Quint's chest squeezed as panic gripped him. All the shame and regret for letting Tessa take a bullet nearly crippled him. The memories caused the air inside the Jeep to thin. Air. He needed to be able to breathe. The simple act that he'd taken for granted every minute of the day locked up his chest. Anger and a deep sense of loss flooded him, bringing up too many painful memories from the past. With great effort, he did his best to shove those thoughts aside. Would they impact his actions in a critical moment if this case blew up?

The answer came almost immediately. They most certainly would. What the hell was he supposed to do now?

Chapter Eighteen

Ree's stomach roiled. She had no idea why. At first, she thought the food was bad. Maybe the jelly or the cream cheese she'd so generously slathered onto her bagel a little while ago. But wouldn't Quint be sick as well? He'd eaten the same things.

"The coffee from earlier just sat in my stomach," she said. "I thought I got it all out."

"I asked the clerk for a bag. He looked at me like I was losing it but handed this over." Quint produced a plastic bag.

"Thank you," she said, taking the offering. "I seriously don't know what could be wrong with me."

"Let's get you home," he said. "Think you'll make it okay?"

"I will with this," she said, motioning toward the bag before buckling herself in. She'd better not have a virus. Yes, they'd been running on empty lately, pushing themselves beyond normal physical limitations. Yes, they'd been going without proper sleep. Yes, they'd been at this for weeks on end with no real break in between.

The ride back to the building was like being seasick with no port in sight. She had the fleeting thought they should get in contact with Nicole to let her know she had likely been exposed to a virus. But without knowing what exactly was wrong, that seemed premature.

The stress of this case wore on her like no other in the past. She never would have survived as an agent this long if the cases were always so intense. The one tiny moment she'd had in between cases two and three, she'd stopped off for Sunday supper and gotten into an argument with her mother. *Fight* wasn't the right term for the standoff between the two of them.

Ree's mother had gotten in a few jabs, noting her disapproval at Ree's lack of domestic skills. Well, Ree might be getting married—at least she hoped it was still on—but there was no one, repeat, no one, who could force her into the kitchen every day. She wouldn't bake homemade pies for their Sundays either. Ree could forgive her mother for their past differences, realizing it was just a mother concerned about her only daughter and filled with regret about the husband she'd lost.

It was truly a sad situation when Ree thought about it from her mother's perspective. Unlike Quint's upbringing, Ree's had been filled with people and love.

Who did he have? He'd mentioned Officer Jazz. Then there was Quint's mother, who Ree already marked as a saint. She only wished she could have met the woman who'd brought up such an amazing human being. Quint had told Ree about his childhood struggles and the difficult time he'd had after his father had abandoned the family. Ree's heart went out to him for being an only child.

Was that the reason it was so hard for him to depend on others? Was that the reason it was so difficult for him to think about having a child? Did it have to do with his father? He'd mentioned something about the gene pool. Was he concerned his child would end up like Quint's father?

Ree could make the argument that environment was

more important than having money or a pre-programmed genetic code. It probably didn't help that Quint spent his career locking away bad guys. It did have a way of tainting a person when they only ever saw the dark side of humanity. Without her family, Ree had no idea how she would stay so grounded. But there was something about being home on Sundays and surrounded by her brothers and Shane's kids that helped her stay focused, kept her eye on the prize so to speak. The whole reason she did the job in law enforcement was to lock bad guys away and keep them off the streets. As corny as it sounded, and she heard the words rolling around in her own thoughts, she really did get into this business to make a difference, as so many law enforcement officers and agents did.

Was she also there to carry on her father's legacy?

There was probably some truth to the idea. She couldn't deny that she'd never felt closer to her father than in her early days on the job. There'd been something about following in his footsteps that made her feel like he was there with her. The connection had worn off years ago, but the work was interesting and kept her challenged. She'd set goal after goal, determined to climb the ladder and be successful.

The risks were easier to take year after year. Ree rarely thought about them anymore. She'd long ago realized no one at home would miss her if something happened to her on the job. She had no kids or husband depending on her. Her mother, grandfather, and brothers would care, but it wasn't the same as starting her own family. No wonder her mother freaked out about Ree going into law enforcement. Ree had never really considered the risks from a mother's perspective. Now that she had, there was no going back.

Ree was so lost in her thoughts on the way home that she hardly noticed Quint hadn't said a word.

"I'll be okay," she reassured him, thinking he was probably just worried about her coming down with something.

She got little more than a grunt in response. The look on his face, the worry lines etching deep grooves in his forehead, tipped her off as to his stress level. Quint had a habit of getting quiet during intense times. As an agent, he was all about communication. In his personal life, not so much.

Quint parked the Jeep and exited almost immediately. He came around to her side of the vehicle before she could get her seat belt unbuckled. Ree was grateful she hadn't felt the need to purge any more of her stomach contents for the rest of the ride home.

"Do you need help walking?" Quint's concern was endearing but also unnecessary. Nothing she hadn't experienced before and gotten over relatively quickly.

Was he worried she would be down for the rest of the case? Or maybe that she wouldn't be able to perform at peak level?

"No, thanks," she said. "I'm feeling much better now anyway."

He studied her as they stepped inside the elevator. Based on his frown, he also realized she wasn't being completely honest.

"You can tell me the truth," he said. "How are you really feeling?"

"Another wave of sickness is striking. I might be coming down with a stomach bug," she admitted. The elevator dinged, letting them know they'd reached their floor. "In fact, I need to get inside the apartment fast or this elevator will forever be tainted."

Quint wasted no time dashing across the hallway and jamming the key in the lock. He easily opened the door in time for her to bolt through and straight to the bathroom. Somewhere along the way, she dropped her purse and didn't care.

Would this day ever end?

QUINT STARED AT his phone while Ree was in the bathroom. He'd already knocked and found out there wasn't anything he could do to help. *Run to the store and get a pregnancy test,* he thought. But that would be more for him than her. She seemed oblivious to the fact she might be pregnant. He wasn't.

What he needed to do was figure out a response to Lindy. The texts from him came across as desperate before. The man could truly be that clueless, or he might know exactly where Giselle was, and this was his way of trying to draw suspicion away from him. Quint had no idea what to say to Lindy at this point. Plus, he was distracted by the Ree situation.

They also needed to speak to Axel, the sooner the better.

He fired off a text to Agent Grappell, asking him to arrange a meeting. This wasn't news Quint wanted to deliver on the phone. He needed to see Axel's reaction to what was happening with Giselle when they told him. He also needed to see if, by chance, Giselle had been in contact with Axel.

The thought occurred to Quint there was some kind of turf war considering all the chaos going on in A-12 right now. The arrests seemed to be making everyone jumpy. Did they believe Dumitru had lost his touch? Or was being targeted by law enforcement? It would explain a whole lot about what had been happening in recent weeks.

Quint's cell buzzed in his hand.

There's been an incident with Axel.

The message from Grappell shocked Quint. He jumped to his feet and raced to the bathroom door. While standing there, he made the call.

"What kind of incident?" Quint immediately asked the second Grappell answered.

"He's been moved to the infirmary," Grappell said. "At this point, I'm not certain about how bad the attack was. There seemed to be a lot of confusion about what happened, and I can't get a straight answer out of the warden."

"We're heading over there," he said. "Get us inside."

"I'm not so sure that I can," Grappell said.

"Well, then use the name Bjorn dropped last night to open doors, because that seemed to work miracles," Quint insisted.

"I'll see what I can do, but there's a strict order in place for no visitors in the building after the fight," Grappell informed him.

"Do whatever you have to," Quint stated. "Just get those doors open."

"Give me ten minutes," Grappell said before ending the call.

"What is happening?" Ree asked through the door. He heard the spigot turn on, and it sounded like Ree was washing her hands.

"It's Axel," he said. "Someone made a move on him at the new facility."

"We should have known," Ree said. "We should have anticipated this after Giselle went missing."

"We don't know that the two are related," Quint said as the door opened and a flush-faced Ree stood there.

He led them back to the kitchen, unsure if it was safe for her to take anything for her stomach. They might have something in the medical emergency kit he kept in the tackle box that would help. Since Tessa had kept her early pregnancy quiet, and he hadn't exactly been around a whole lot of pregnant women, he had no idea what was allowed and what might hurt a fetus.

Bringing up the topic to Ree if she wasn't prepared for the possibility could cause her to spiral. Even if she knew on a subconscious level, she might be blocking it out. None of the scenarios were good right now. So he shelved the topic.

"He could have warned her to go into hiding. It's possible he knew someone would come after him or at the very least suspected it," she reasoned. "What about his wife and daughter? Are they still in protective custody? Are they okay?"

Quint grabbed his cell phone and started firing off questions to Grappell by text.

"We'll know soon," he said to Ree. "In the meantime, what can I get for you?"

"I wish I had some crackers," she said. "Oatmeal would be nice. I think I got the worst of it out of me."

Her skin paled, and he wondered if that was going to be the case.

"We need to speak to Axel," Ree said. "There's no way he told us everything he knew before."

"Agreed," Quint stated. "I have no idea how bad of a shape he's in."

"Then we need to get him out of there," she said with conviction.

"I don't think you can go anywhere in your condition," he said.

"I'll bring a box of trash bags if I have to," she insisted. "We have to talk to him face-to-face."

"I'm on it," Quint stated. "But I need you to feel better and not push yourself."

She chewed on the inside of her cheek for a few seconds.

"All I need is to be able to keep something down and I'll be fine," she countered. "This is just a passing bug or bad food or something. It'll be over before it gets started."

The last thing he wanted to do was upset Ree before they headed out.

"How about this…you stay here while Grappell works his magic and I run out to grab a few supplies. It can't hurt to get some chicken broth in you, and it'll take a while for Grappell to be able to arrange everything, and—"

"Oh no," Ree gasped. "We have to get him out of there. A lockdown means no one in or out. It will give anyone on the inside a chance to get to him in an infirmary, and I'm guessing that's where he is."

Quint bit out a few choice words before bringing Grappell on the line.

"Mind if I put the call on speaker?" he asked the second Grappell picked up.

"Not at all," Grappell responded.

"We need to get Axel out of prison and into WITSEC," Quint immediately started.

"I'm working on it," Grappell said.

"Do you need escorts?" Ree asked. "Because we're here, and we need to speak to him. This way, we could kill two birds with one stone."

She seemed to realize the impact of her word choice when she made eye contact with Quint.

"I didn't exactly mean it to come out that way," she explained with a frown, wishing she could go back and reel in the word, "kill."

"We know," Quint stated. Ree could be hard on herself. He recognized the trait because he possessed the same one.

Despite making progress on the case, he couldn't get the pregnancy question out of his mind. This was the worst time to ask, but he wasn't sure how much longer he could hold it in, either. A flashback of being in a similar position with Tessa assaulted him.

When this phone call was over, he needed to ask Ree about the possible pregnancy.

Chapter Nineteen

"As far as an escort goes, I don't know if I can get Axel out of the building, let alone have the warden trust the prisoner he's responsible for to strangers," Grappell stated.

"Could we risk telling him that we're ATF?" she asked.

"Possibly," Grappell said.

"I know we'd rather not play that card while we're undercover. It's just a thought," she said.

"How about Bjorn?" Ree asked. "She worked miracles last night. Is it possible to have her wave the magic wand to get the doors opened?"

"Not with the lockdown." Grappell issued a sharp sigh. "The US marshal in charge of his wife and daughter has just confirmed there was a security breach. He is on his way to pick up and relocate those witnesses."

"How can this be happening?" Ree asked, but the question was rhetorical, and they were all on the same page.

Frustration gave her something to focus on besides the urge to vomit that was currently taking hold. Again?

How on earth?

Ree excused herself and headed for the bathroom, hoping nothing too interesting happened while she was out of the room. She sat on the edge of the bathtub, ready for the onslaught should it come. There was literally nothing in her stomach right now, so there couldn't possibly be anything to throw up. The voices had gone quiet in the next room, but they were probably just waiting to see if she was okay. After a few minutes, the nausea eased, and she felt able to return to the living room again.

Ree checked the kitchen. Nothing. There was no one in the living room. Quint was gone.

Her cell was sitting on the counter. She picked it up, ready to call Quint and give him a piece of her mind. Anger welled up along with frustration that he would exclude her from something…

Wait. She read the text on the screen. Be right back with crackers.

Well, now she really felt bad. She'd jumped to conclusions about Quint taking off and excluding her from the case "for her own good," and he hadn't done anything of the kind. It wasn't like her to be flooded with so many emotions over something that hadn't even happened. Ree really was off her game.

This sickness or whatever it was needed to move on out of her, because she didn't like feeling this way, and she really had no patience for being sick in the first place. It made her cranky because it felt like a colossal waste of time. She'd never been the type to lie in bed all day or groan and complain about a little cough.

Of course, vomiting was an entirely different story, and she'd sworn to do that as little as possible for the rest of her life after a particularly awful experience in fifth grade. She'd mostly held to the promise and rarely ever got threw up.

By the time the apartment door opened, she felt like she'd gotten her sea legs again.

"Saltines," Quint said as he held up a box that looked a whole lot like heaven. "And a few other things I thought might help."

"You really are a beautiful man," she said.

"Hot," he corrected her with a smile that would melt ice during a Siberian winter.

"That too," she quipped, returning his smile.

"You look better," he said as he set the pair of paper bags down on the counter.

"I am," she said. "It's weird because I felt awful before you left. Must've gotten it all out before because nothing came up the last time and I started feeling half human again. A little mouthwash and toothpaste have gone a long way."

Quint pulled out a couple cans of chicken soup.

"There isn't anything we can do until we hear back from Grappell. Even with Bjorn's considerable network and resources, it might take a couple of hours before we can go anywhere. I didn't respond to Lindy yet because I can't figure out what I'm going to ask or say until we speak to Axel. So now you're caught up," he said, and she could have sworn his chest puffed out just a little bit. "Figured I might as well nurse you back to health in the meantime. I need my partner up and running, and at full capacity."

"Well, food sounds good right now. Broth and saltines are calling my name," she said, enjoying the lightness in the conversation.

Quint started pulling out supplies one by one from the brown paper grocery bag. He grabbed a bowl as he handed over the crackers.

"You might want to get started on those," he said.

"I wasn't kidding a few seconds ago. You really are beautiful," she teased. He didn't seem impressed, but she could see the small, satisfied smirk upturning the corners of his lips.

Ree couldn't wait to tear the box open and get started. The crisp crackers with just enough salt were her idea of perfection. Within minutes a can of chicken noodle soup had been heated, poured into a bowl and delivered by the man who seemed to be in a competition for sexiest man alive. She wished all her exes had realized being competent in the kitchen was so erotic. Throw in a load of laundry and she wouldn't be able to hold herself back.

This probably wasn't the right time to mention she wouldn't be against having another round of incredible sex. Quint wouldn't want to kiss her on the mouth after she'd been throwing up despite the fact she'd rinsed and brushed. The image of her bent over a random trash can earlier probably wasn't the sexiest thing he'd ever seen. So she scratched the idea of turning him on while those images might still be fresh in his mind.

Besides, the call from Grappell could come at any moment, and they would need to be ready to bolt out the door. Their window of time to get to Axel and possibly be part of his transport team might be small.

The bowl of chicken noodle soup went down great. The crackers made her feel like she might have kicked this virus or whatever.

"Has Lindy reached out to you since earlier today?" she asked.

"No," he admitted, finishing off a sandwich he'd made for himself. The thing was layered with turkey meat, ham, cheese and half a salad in between two thick pieces of bread. The only thing that could make the sandwich any better was bacon and an iron stomach. He polished off the bowl of soup he'd made for himself and brewed fresh coffee. Seeing him move around the kitchen with athletic grace, the way the cotton of his shirt stretched and released on top of his back muscles had her staring.

When he turned around, his expression sent a shockwave rippling through her. There was an uncertainty in his eyes, which were almost always sure. There was a pensiveness to his expression that warned of trouble.

"Here's the thing," he began. She was rooted to her chair in some mild form of shock with the realization he was about to say something serious. "I don't want you to panic at what I'm about to ask you."

"It's hard to agree to something when I have no idea what's about to go down," she said, very uncomfortable with where this might be heading. Her mind snapped to too many scary places—places that were permanent and involved words like *this won't work*. Just the possibility shredded her.

"I think it's important for us to be totally honest with each other," he hedged. "I've been in relationships and friendships in the past where secrets were kept, and the damage done can be irreparable."

Ree's chest squeezed, and her heart sank to her toes.

"Okay," she conceded. "I agree that lack of honesty destroys bonds. What is it, Quint?"

"I'm not trying to be evasive," he said. "I just don't know how you're going to take what I have to say, and—"

"Just spit it out," she said, her heart hammering the inside her ribs. "When it's out there, we can decide what to do."

He issued a sharp sigh before setting his soup bowl in the sink. Then he reached into one of the bags and pulled out a box before placing it on the counter in front of her.

Once Ree read the label, she almost lost her stomach again. Not a whole lot threw her off her game. But this?

"A pregnancy test?" she asked, dumbfounded.

"Based on your reaction, I'm guessing you haven't considered pregnancy as a possibility." Quint hadn't been certain about the decision to put his cards on the table. But he was being serious a few minutes ago. If they were going to make a go at long term, he needed to be able to talk about everything, including the subjects he wanted to avoid.

"No, I haven't," she stated with a little more shock and indignation than he'd expected.

"Then we would just be dotting every *i* and crossing every *t*," he said. "If the possibility exists. But I haven't seen you use any products or mention anything about your cycle in a long time."

Ree hopped off the stool and retrieved her cell phone. "Hold on. I have a tracker in here because it's generally the last thing on my mind until it happens."

Quint hoped the possibility of a pregnancy didn't exist. There was no way he was ready to make the call to be a father right this minute. Not while he was still trying to figure out if he wanted children at some point later. Much later.

"Oh no," Ree stated, and her skin paled again. "That can't be."

He stood there, rooted to his spot, waiting for confirmation a pregnancy couldn't be in the cards.

"This tracker is dependent on me putting in the dates of my cycle, and we've been so busy with back-to-back cases that I probably just forgot to log it. That's all," she said, but the terror in her voice said she wasn't exactly convinced the statement was pure fact. She glanced up at Quint with the most pitiful eyes. "My recent talk about wanting children came out of the blue. I promise. I didn't have a plan for this possibility. I didn't even know it was…"

The way she stammered and seemed to search for words combined with the utter shock on her face made him feel like a jerk for bringing it up. If she was pregnant, though, they needed to know. There was no way she could continue on this case.

More of those flashbacks nailed him. Tessa smiling and touching her stomach when she came to terms with being pregnant and finally told him the news. She'd also been nervous and scared, certain there was no way she could bring this child into the world and raise it alone.

Quint had promised to step up to be a surrogate father. He'd planned to be the best godfather there had ever been. He'd told Tessa that she was going to be fine and everything would end up working out for the best.

Now? All he could think was how much of a hypocrite he was for saying those things to her and then freaking out about the possibility of Ree being pregnant.

"Man," he began. "Have I been a class-A jerk."

Ree's face wrinkled as if she'd just sucked on a sour pickle. Her eyebrows drew together like she had no idea where he was going with this.

"When Tessa finally admitted to me that she was pregnant, I bent over backwards trying to reassure her that everything would be okay and she would be an amazing mother," he started as the pieces clicked together in his mind of what a true jerk he'd been in this situation. "I said everything would work out because she had me in the wings and that I wanted to help."

Ree tucked her chin to her chest in the move she did when she was getting emotional and didn't want him to see her eyes tearing up.

"I was so ready to jump in and save the day for my friend," he said.

"Best friend," Ree corrected him.

"Yes, but that's the thing," he said, coming to a realization. "You are so much more to me than that. You are my best friend, my partner, the one I want to spend the rest of my life with, and what did I say to you when you told me you wanted to have kids?"

"The situations aren't the same," she countered. "You're comparing apples to oranges."

"How so?" He was curious as to her explanation, because in his book, he'd let her down in the worst possible way.

"Tessa was already pregnant and scared," Ree reasoned. "I was talking about planning for a child. My brother Shane has two kids, and now I remember how freaked out he was when he found out his wife was pregnant with their first. He said it was impossible for him to 'plan' to have a baby, because who could willingly take on that much responsibility?"

"You thought about it and decided it might be a good idea," he pointed out.

"Not before I met you," she said. Those words were like daggers to the heart.

"Believe me when I say that I never would have asked for a family," he began, trying to find the right words. "With you, anything feels possible. If you're pregnant now, I don't want that to be a bad or scary thing, because I will always be here for you. You are so much more than my best friend and life partner. You are the great love of my life."

A tear spilled from Ree's eye and rolled down her cheek.

"I love you too," she said. "And I'd like to face whatever life hands us together."

Quint walked around the counter and to his future bride. They could do anything as long as they had each other to lean on. He kissed her, tender and slow.

When they pulled apart, Ree reached across the counter and picked up the test.

"I'll be right back," she said before heading to the bathroom.

She returned a few minutes later with the test resting

on top of the box. She set it down. "Three minutes is all we have to wait now."

A whole range of thoughts went through Quint's mind, not the least of which caused a wave of panic at the thought he might actually bring a child into the world.

Quint's cell buzzed. He checked the screen.

"It's Grappell. We have to go. Now," he said.

Chapter Twenty

"What do we do about the test?" Ree figured this was how timing usually worked. The answer to the most important test of her life was minutes away and she had to leave.

"It'll still be here when we get back," Quint said as he secured his ankle holster. She followed suit, grabbing her own weapon and hiding it as they raced out the door. Not that long ago, he was concerned she'd have to get off the case if she was pregnant. The thought he could lose two pregnant partners should this investigation go south practically gutted him. Losing a pregnant best friend had nearly destroyed him. He couldn't even go there with Ree. He couldn't go to a place where she was suddenly gone along with their child.

It barely took a minute for them to hit the elevator button. The temptation to run back inside the apartment was overrun by reason. The results weren't ready, and she would be wasting valuable time. At least this way she would have time to digest the possibility of a pregnancy.

"The address is on my phone," Quint said, handing over his cell after he hopped in the driver's seat. He paused for a second. "You look better. I should have asked you before, but are you up to this?"

"I'm surprisingly good," she said, figuring that probably

gave a point to "pregnant" as much as she wasn't ready to acknowledge it.

"Okay, then," he said, but his voice was anything but reassured. "Let's do this."

Ree nodded and smiled before turning her attention back to the cell phone. She clicked on the address in the text from Grappell. A map filled the screen. An address on Horton Road in Forest Hill came up. "They're keeping him in a federal facility not too far from here."

"I know that one," Quint stated. "He'll be at the medical center on Horton. Same street, but the medical building is considered Fort Worth," Quint stated.

"Axel could be recognized in this area," she said. "It was stupid to keep him anywhere near the DFW area."

"We need to have a conversation with the marshal in charge of taking care of him and his family," Quint stated. "His current location might be related to being closer to his wife and kid."

"They shouldn't be anywhere in the area either," Ree pointed out. "His teenage daughter seemed more concerned with having to leave her boyfriend than the scary people who were after her father. Besides, their brains aren't fully developed yet, and teens make all kinds of bad decisions. I'll never understand why, at the height of when their brains seek thrills, we put a driver's license in their hands."

"Our kid won't drive until he or she is twenty at the very least," Quint said. The words just rolled off his tongue like he didn't even have to think about them or their impact. Had he decided she must be pregnant? She still wasn't so sure, and they'd had to skip out on the test before the results came back. There were plenty of reasons she could be late with her cycle, not least of which was the amount of stress they'd been under from recent cases and the fact she hadn't taken a break from work yet. Her diet had been off. Her sleeping habits had been off. Her exercise routine had been off. Any one of these excuses could cause a delay. Combined, she was more and more convinced there was nothing to panic about.

They arrived in front of the medical center gates and, after a quick conversation and an ID check, were allowed inside. Aside from the tall security fences, the building and grounds looked more like a community college with its large green lawn and Spanish-style architecture.

After checking in, they were taken back almost immediately to visit Axel.

"Am I the only one who thinks it's a bad sign Axel isn't being wheeled out to greet us?" Ree whispered to Quint as they moved down the hallway.

He shot her a look that said he agreed.

They were taken to the infirmary, where Axel was lying down. Thankfully, there weren't any machines hooked up to him.

"I'll be at the door if you need me," their escort said before circling back, and waiting.

Axel was on his side. His face was swollen, bruised and cut. He groaned when he saw them, and she was pretty sure he was trying to say hello.

Quint moved to his side and squatted down next to Axel's face. Ree sat on the foot of the bed, where she could keep an eye on their surroundings and still see and hear everything happening between Quint and Axel.

"I'd ask how you're doing, but I can see for myself," Quint stated.

Axel tried to speak and coughed instead.

"Do you want water?" Quin asked.

Axel nodded.

There was a bottle of water next to the bed on the nightstand. Quint grabbed it and handed it over. "Do you want to sit up?"

He nodded. Quint went to work figuring out how to raise the bed so Axel could sip water without too much discomfort.

Ree had no idea how they were going to transport Axel in this condition. He didn't look like he could move and probably needed a nurse or doctor around just in case. But if he got a medical release, she and Quint would have to figure out how to care for him while they transported him.

Shouldn't the marshal in charge be here? She pulled out her cell phone and texted Grappell the question. His response came quickly. They'd beat the marshal to the facility.

"Listen," Axel finally said. "I have evidence against Dumitru. It's everything you want and need to convict him, lock the bastard away for the rest of his life. I kept records. There are pictures. I have evidence linking him to personally killing two of the men who used to work for me."

"Why are you telling us this now?" Ree asked. This information would have been helpful on the last case. And could have ended this whole ordeal.

"I was framed before," Axel stated. "As you both know. He was trying to shut me up. I thought if I cooperated that I'd eventually get out while protecting my family and kids, and this was my leverage against Dumitru to keep him honest. This was going to be how I got back into the money and forced him to set me up with some cash and a new crew."

Ree shook her head. Yes, she was grateful for the information. But damn, she really wished they'd known all this sooner.

"It's obvious he's going to stay at me until he kills me," Axel said. "I just want my family and Giselle to be kept out of this. Dumitru crossed a line when he started going after wives and kids."

"What do you get out of giving us this information?" Quint said.

"Safety for my family," Axel stated. "At least, I hope they can be protected. They didn't ask for any of this. They didn't know what kind of business I was in."

Ree had her doubts about his last statement.

"Where is all this evidence?" Quint asked.

Axel's gaze shifted from Quint to Ree. "It might be time to spice up your wardrobe."

Ree glanced down at the jeans and cotton shirt she was wearing, confused as to what he could be talking about.

"Not for daytime," Axel stated, and then it clicked.

"Is she involved? Lizanne?" Quint asked.

"She's been trying to shake Dumitru for the past few years, but he isn't having any of it." Axel coughed again, and this time, it sounded like a lung might come up. "He's threatening her business, and she's done. He helped her early on when she needed to get started, and he never forgot about it or let her off the hook. She runs a legitimate business and has a kid she's trying to protect."

"Does the kid belong to Dumitru?" Quint asked as Ree's gaze flew to her stomach.

"No. Nothing like that," Axel said after a few more coughs that sounded like he was hacking up another lung. "This boy is a teenager now. Him and his mother are close. She keeps him out of the family business and far away from her old life, including Dumitru."

"Why doesn't she turn Dumitru in?" Quint asked.

"Are you crazy? Go up against Dumitru? No way can she afford the backlash," Axel said. "He would send his people, like he's doing with me. I'm not even safe in protective custody." Axel coughed a couple more times. They couldn't argue with his logic.

"Where is this evidence against him?" Quint asked again.

"I already said," Axel claimed.

"Then let me be more specific. Where *exactly* is this evidence?" Quint continued.

"In the ceiling of her shop," Axel stated. "I put it there myself. She doesn't know."

"Smart," Quint said. "That way it's there if you need her to get it for you. You already know she'll help."

"True, but I didn't want to put her in the middle of this thing," Axel admitted.

"What about Giselle?" Quint asked. "How much does she know?"

"She shouldn't know anything," Axel said. "Why?"

"Because she's disappeared," Quint stated. "I thought maybe you had something to do with it."

"Oh no," Axel said, and the sadness in his voice was palpable. "How about little Ax?"

"He's fine," Quint said. "We saw him with our own eyes. Nicole has no idea what's going on based on our visit."

"Giselle can be…flaky," Axel said. "But I doubt she would take off on her own like that."

"What about Lindy?" Quint asked.

"The organization is uneasy. Folks are trying to push their way to the top. He's just as bad as the others, but he seems loyal to Dumitru," Axel said before another coughing jag. He took a sip of water.

"Where will you be safe?" Quint asked. "Is there such a place?"

Axel shrugged. He winced with the movement.

"It might be too late for me," he said. "Unless Dumitru

ends up in jail. Then I've got a shot. Lindy likes me, or he used to, and he's the next in line from all I can tell in here."

"We need to get you to safety," Quint said. "Then go find the evidence."

"There's a chance it's not still there," Axel said. Those weren't the words Quint and Ree wanted to hear.

"We'll find out," Quint said. "But I need you to call Lizanne and tell her to let us in."

"Can't you just go get it?" Axel said.

"Not if we want to use any of the evidence in court," Quint pointed out.

"Right." Axel nodded, glancing at them with a look that said it must be a pain to have to follow the letter of the law. But it was the right way to go about it. Ree never took for granted taking away someone's rights by arresting them. She had to take the bad with the good.

Quint asked the guard for a cell phone. He produced one a few moments later.

"Do you remember her number, by chance?" Quint asked Axel.

"As a matter of fact, I do," Axel stated with more than a hint of pride in his voice.

"How?" Ree hadn't meant to ask the question out loud. She was truly that shocked.

"Simple. I've known Lizanne for years, and she's on my emergency call list when I get arrested," he said. "I had to memorize her number in case my cell...disappeared."

His hesitation had caused Ree to fill in the blank with a whole different line of thought. Or should she say a whole bevy of reasons his cell might "disappear"? She could spend days coming up with ideas.

Axel punched in Lizanne's number.

"Put the call on speaker for me, okay?" Quint asked.

Axel nodded and complied.

"Hey, gorgeous," he started the minute Lizanne answered the phone.

"Axel?" There was a whole lot of excitement in her brandy-soaked voice. "Is that you?"

"It is," he confirmed. "I've got you on speaker because I'm locked up, and I have friends in the room. Okay?"

"Sure," she said, drawing out the word. "What can I do for you?"

"Give my friends a private tour of the shop," he said.

"Oh." There was a long pause. Then came, "Do I want to know what this is about?"

"It's better if you don't ask questions," Axel confirmed.

"How will I know if it's your friends?" she asked.

"They're a couple, for one," he said. "And they'll give you the code word…" Axel glanced around the room. His gaze settled on a piece of fruit on a plate on the nightstand. "Apple."

"Apple," she said. "Got it."

"Good. I'll owe you one," he said.

"No, you won't," she quickly countered. Based on their exchange, it was easy to realize the two were friends who went way back. "But I'll collect anyway."

Axel laughed, and it caused him to bend forward to cough. When he finally composed himself, he said, "Sorry about that."

"You don't sound so good," she stated.

"I look better than I sound. How about that?" Axel asked.

"I'll wait for them," Lizanne said. "And don't be a stranger when you get out."

"I won't," Axel promised. He ended the call and handed over the cell, looking a little at a loss.

"We'll get you transported and then head over," Quint said.

Axel was shaking his head before Quint could finish

his sentence. "No, sir. You have to go as soon as possible. I have no idea how long they'll leave her alone or if Dumitru has spies in here listening to everything I say. Get the evidence and arrest the sonofabitch."

All Ree could think was *easier said than done.*

Chapter Twenty-One

Quint stood at the door of Axel's room until the marshal's team arrived ten minutes later. He couldn't risk leaving Axel alone, and it gave him and Ree a chance to talk about their next steps. If Axel's claims were true and there was enough evidence to bring Dumitru down, they still had to find the man in order to arrest him. Quint caught himself glancing at Ree's stomach more than once during their conversation, wonder creeping in no matter how much he tried to keep the question at bay.

They would know soon enough, and there wasn't anything either could do to change the outcome. Worry would do no good. And Quint could tell himself the fact all day, and it still wouldn't stop the thoughts from looping. Even if Ree was pregnant, this was different. They were about to get married, and a family wasn't the worst thing that could happen to them. The thought surprised him.

Back in the Jeep, they pushed the speed limit until they reached Central Expressway and the lingerie shop.

The sun was winding down by the time they parked in front of a restaurant so their vehicle wouldn't be recognized and then made the walk over to the lingerie store in the strip shopping center. There were no cars parked out front. Quint had a feeling Lizanne had rushed out any customers who wandered inside or denied them entrance altogether.

Quint exchanged a look with Ree before opening the door.

"We're about to close," the familiar brandy-soaked voice said. The attractive woman in her late thirties came out of the backroom.

"Apple," Quint stated.

Her blue eyes widened for a split second as she took in Quint and then Ree. Keys jingled from a ring as she walked to the door. She locked it.

"I'll be in the storeroom if you need anything," she said. "My only request is that you don't trash the place while you look for whatever Axel told you to pick up."

Quint examined her posture; tension radiated from her. She was putting herself on the line for a friend, and seemed very aware of the fact.

"We'll be careful," Ree reassured her in the way only she seemed to know how. There was something about her presence that calmed others. He'd noticed it more than once over the course of their cases. She'd the same effect on him once they'd gotten over the hump of their first meeting, which had been every shade of awful possible. It was almost funny now, but hadn't been at the time.

"I'd appreciate it if you hurried," Lizanne said.

"We understand," Ree stated.

Her gaze narrowed on Ree, and then she studied Quint.

"Sorry about last night," she said. "I've learned that you can't be too careful, and there's been a lot of drama around Dumitru lately."

"That was *you* on the motorcycle?" Ree asked.

"I'm afraid so, and I called the guys to eliminate the threat. If I'd known you were friends of Axel's, I wouldn't have tried to get rid of you," Lizanne said. She carefully scanned outside the front window into the parking lot before disappearing into the back.

Ree climbed on top of the counter with the cash register and started pushing up the white ceiling tiles. Dust floated down like snow. She waved her hand in front of her face and turned away. She sneezed.

Quint grabbed the stool behind the counter and got to work on the computer.

"Found something," Ree said when he was still on his third attempt to get into the computer system. She pulled out a boot box. "This must be it."

He hurried over to her and grabbed her around the waist to help her down. She eased to sitting on the counter and set the boot box beside her, wiping the dust off.

"Wow, Axel wasn't kidding," she said after opening the box.

Quint released the breath he'd been holding. There were flash drives and Ziploc bags with what they could only assume was evidence inside them. "Everything he promised seems to be here."

"He was thorough," Ree stated. "All we have to do is verify the contents, and we should be able to get approval to make the arrest before the night is over."

"Ready to head back to the apartment?" he asked.

"As ready as I'll ever be," she said, and he realized exactly what that statement covered.

"Once we get the arrest warrant, we have another hill to climb," Quint stated as Lizanne emerged from the backroom.

"I know where Dumitru will be tonight," she said. She seemed as eager as they were to get Dumitru off the streets.

"Where is that?" Quint asked.

"The Dallas World Aquarium," she supplied. "It's a private party meant to reassure his people that everything is okay, and that's going to be the venue."

"It's a bold move," Quint said.

"He is in damage-control mode, showing his people that he is still in charge and can get one over on us," she explained.

"Makes sense in his twisted world." Quint realized she was holding something in her hand, a folded piece of paper. No, an invitation.

"This should get you through the door," she stated, handing it over. "I'd appreciate if you would leave my name out of it."

"No need to drag you into the middle of our fight," Quint reassured her.

"He's slippery, so he'll have a couple of exit plans," Lizanne said.

"Good to know," Quint said.

"Make sure you cover all the exits," she said. "And he'll always have an escape vehicle nearby. His favorite is a motorcycle. If you see one within a block of the place, it most likely belongs to him. But you can tell for certain if it has an all-seeing eye sticker on the helmet strapped to the back."

"Thank you for the information," Quint said.

"Just do us all a favor," she said, and she sounded exhausted. "Lock the sonofabitch up and throw away the key. We'll be better off."

"That's the plan," Quint stated.

"Before you head out," Lizanne started, twisting her fingers together. "Will Axel be okay?"

"He's in good hands," Quint promised.

"Thanks," she said.

Then she unceremoniously walked over to the door and unlocked it before heading to the backroom.

"We got what we needed," Quint said to Ree as they made their way back to the Jeep, arms full.

"All we need now is to secure the evidence and get the warrant," she said.

"We need to update Grappell as soon as we get out of this parking lot," he said. "I have a feeling hanging around here isn't good for our longevity."

Ree made eyes at him. Neither said another word until they were on the expressway again.

"I'll make the call," Ree said.

Grappell's voice came on the line after the second ring.

"What's happening?" he asked, and there was more than a hint of worry in his voice.

"We have everything we need to lock Dumitru up for the rest of his life if all the evidence checks out," Quint stated. "And we have a location. If we can get an arrest warrant in the next hour, I know where he'll be."

"On it," Grappell said. "Where are you now?"

"Heading back to the apartment, loaded with evidence," Quint stated.

"I'll have someone meet you in the parking garage," Grappell said. "Wait there."

The line went dead, but they both knew he would text or call back with the information about which agent and what kind of vehicle would meet them.

There was only one problem with the plan. The pregnancy test results waited upstairs, and they were both eager to check the stick.

"We go upstairs together," he said, hoping she agreed. This was their future, and they needed to face it together. Period. He wanted to be there for her no matter what the result turned out to be.

"TOGETHER." REE LIKED THE sound of that word. When he put it like that, she wasn't nearly as scared of the results.

As long as they dealt with the news together, she could face this.

The text from Grappell came when they were halfway home. A banana-yellow Camaro would be arriving close to the same time as them. The driver would park behind them in the garage and be ready to flash his badge.

They were home within eight minutes of receiving the text, and the Camaro pulled in right behind them, as promised. Thankfully, there was no waiting around. They handed over the evidence, and then all they had to do was wait for the green light to raid the aquarium.

Oh, and one more thing, find out if they were going to be parents.

"Are you ready for this?" Quint asked, linking their fingers.

"As ready as I'll ever be," she confirmed. Her heart rate increased with every step toward the apartment. The elevator ride took her stomach away, and she could literally hear her heart racing in her ears as she walked the few steps to the front door.

Quint put the key in to unlock the door, and she noticed a slight tremble to his hand. Was he just as nervous as she was?

Quint held the door open a solid thirty seconds before Ree had the courage to walk through. She took in a deep breath and glanced down at her stomach. There was no way she was ready right now. Didn't mean she would never be or that she wouldn't pull it together if the answer came back pregnant.

Quint linked their fingers as they walked to the counter. One line. Not pregnant.

"Wow. That's good," Ree said as a whole host of emotions washed over her and through her. Relief flooded her. "We're not ready for a—"

She glanced over at Quint, and his expression stopped her from continuing. There was a haunted look in his eyes, and she wondered if he was thinking about Tessa and the baby his friend lost.

"I'm sorry, Quint," she said, tugging him over.

He took the cue and brought her into an embrace.

"I thought you would be happy about the result," she whispered. "I'm confused."

"So am I," he stated. "I *should* be happy. I didn't think I wanted kids at all. Especially now, when it wasn't planned."

"Is it Tessa?" she asked. "Does this remind you of her and what she went through?"

"No," he said. "I can honestly say that I'm ready to move on and marry you. And, much to my own surprise, I'm ready to start a family whenever you are."

"It'll happen when the timing is right," she reassured him.

"All I have to do now is put the bastard behind bars who is responsible for Tessa's death," he said, clenching his back teeth as he finished his sentence.

And what if that didn't happen tonight? Would it ever be over? Would they ever be able to move on with their lives if the bust fell apart?

Chapter Twenty-Two

The map of the Dallas World Aquarium on Griffin Street in downtown Dallas had been studied. The blocks surrounding the place had been memorized. The plan to get in and get Dumitru was set. Best laid plans. Quint, of all people, knew how quickly everything could turn on a dime.

Having an idea of how they wanted this to go down helped with the nerves.

"Just the two of us are going in," Quint said, reviewing their notes while noticing how beautiful his future wife looked in a shimmering green minidress that brought out the emerald of her eyes. They were both dressed, wired and ready to go.

"But a team of five will be waiting on the outside. We'll have a pair of agents in a minivan parked across the street, Tex and Stanley. We'll have a jogger circling the area, Ben. And we'll have a couple strolling, Lisa and Evan. Tex and Stanley will be in full gear, ready and waiting. There'll be no mistaking them," Ree said. "We've both worked with the others or at the very least crossed paths with them."

"I could pick all our agents out of a lineup," he said, studying their photos in the database. They were pictured in several disguises to make it easier to spot them.

Quint kept his nose in the file as long as possible, doing his best to block out all the surprising feelings about the non-pregnancy. He should have been happy about the test result. After losing Tessa, had he blocked out any possibility of kids in his life? He still wondered if he'd be father material. And yet Ree's confidence in him had opened his heart to the possibility of a family.

Strange how losing something he never had in the first place caused an ache in his chest the size of Palo Duro Canyon. Life was confusing and strange. One thing was certain. He wanted to spend the rest of his life with Ree. It was the only thing he was one hundred percent sure about.

"I'll have my weapon, and you'll have yours," she said. "Once we spot Dumitru, we'll close in."

"No one will be too shocked about the two of us being there since we're known quantities," he said, circling back to the case.

"Once we get him in our sights, we'll make the call to the others for the raid," she said. "The other agents will grab as many folks as they can."

"We'll take down Dumitru," he said.

"Which should be easy since we'll already be standing within five feet of him," she said.

"Easy in theory," was all Quint said in response.

Ree's face said she agreed. "Let's go over the layout of the aquarium one more time."

"We should eat too," he said. "Who knows when we'll get the chance once this starts rolling?"

"Good point," she said. "I'm feeling a whole lot better. Should we order in?"

"I can probably pull together a meal based on leftovers," he said. "It'll be faster and will give me something to do."

"Waiting is the worst part," she said. He couldn't agree more.

Ten minutes later, they had a feast of two tacos, half a pizza and a salad. When this case was over, he was going to take a week off. The first couple of days, all he wanted to do was order in, be with Ree and sleep. He didn't care if they went to her place or his. On second thought, her mattress was far more comfortable than his. *Hers.*

It was good to make plans for what he intended to do after a bust. It was part of the process of envisioning how he wanted it to go down. It was a ritual he and Tessa had skipped that fateful day.

As he sat down to eat with Ree, he asked, "What's the first thing you're going to do when this is all over?"

"Kiss my fiancé before we start planning our honeymoon," she said with a smile that caused his chest to squeeze.

"I like the sound of that," he said, returning the smile and knowing it fell short of hers. "Our next mission will be our honeymoon. Count me in."

Ree practically beamed.

"I'd like to make peace with my mom too," she said after a thoughtful pause.

"That's another great idea," he stated. "There isn't a day that goes by I don't wish my mom was still here. Especially now. She would have loved you."

"I would have liked to spend time with her too," Ree said. "If we have a girl someday, I'd like to honor your mother by giving our daughter her name."

The sentence would have had the old Quint bolting out of the room to get fresh air. Now?

"I can't think of a better way to acknowledge her memory," he said. Kids? Who knew he'd be all in so fast after thinking he would never be fit for the responsibility?

That was the power of love, he thought.

"If we wrap this up tonight, we can make Sunday supper tomorrow," he pointed out.

"We could," she said. Again, the warmth in her smile could defrost a freezer in a matter of minutes.

"It's a date," he said. Ree reconciling with her mother would be huge. There was no reason to wait, either. It would only give her a chance to talk herself out of the decision. But the time had come for forward motion. No more being stuck in the past or letting the present dictate the future. The time had come for healing.

Quint's cell buzzed as they cleared the dishes. He checked the screen.

"It's go time," he said to Ree.

For what felt like a long moment, she stood there. Then came, "We're ready for this. Let's finish what we started."

An ominous feeling settled over Quint. Past mistakes tried to edge their way in and break down his confidence. He shoved them aside and secured his weapon inside his ankle holster. Time to saddle up for the ride.

The first thing he noticed was the Jeep's flat tire, driver's side. Quint muttered a curse and prayed it wasn't a sign.

"I can help with that," Ree said, moving to the back of the vehicle where the spare was kept. Her high heels brought out the muscles in her calves.

"Normally, I'd be all for it, but you probably shouldn't get dirt all over you in that dress," he said. "You look incredible, by the way."

"Thanks," she said with another one of those smiles. "So do you."

"I'm wearing all black," he said with a laugh. "But, hey, I'll take the compliment."

He made the change in what had to be record time, and they were back on track within minutes. Ree sat in the passenger seat, not sulking exactly, but he could tell she wasn't thrilled with not being able to pitch in.

"Sorry," she mumbled, arms crossed.

"No worries," he reassured her. "You're already being tortured enough in those things strapped to your feet."

"That's true," she said with a half smile.

"Believe me when I say they look amazing on you, but no one should have to wear stilts to walk around in," he said as he cranked the engine. The Check Engine light came on. "You have to be kidding me, right?"

"What is it?" she asked, probably distracted from the torture devices on her feet and her inability to throw her hair in a ponytail, roll up her sleeves and get a job done.

He pointed to the irritation.

"Ignore it," she said. "The dealer probably just wants to make money off us somehow."

"True. That light used to mean something," he agreed as he headed toward the aquarium.

"Yes, it meant pull your buns off the road as fast as you can and park this sucker until a tow truck arrives," she quipped.

"Not so much anymore," he stated.

"Funny how much has changed since my dad was alive. He taught me that long before I was old enough to drive," she said, and there was a hint of sadness to her tone. "I have a few vivid memories of him and not much else. I wish I'd known him better."

Quint reached over and covered her hand with his briefly. There were no words that could soothe the loss of a parent, so he didn't try. All he could do was sit there with her in her moment of sadness and not try to offer hollow words to make it better.

"Looks like we're there already," she said, turning her face to the window and, he guessed, wiping away a stray tear.

She cleared her throat.

"I'll park in the adjacent lot like the others," he said, pulling in and finding an open spot. He memorized the number, opened the parking app, and paid.

"Looks like the party is in full swing," she said, glancing around at the near-full parking lot.

"It does," he said, noting how much easier it would be on them if there were only a few people here. A crowd could turn to chaos in a heartbeat. They could get lost in throngs of people.

"We can walk around the building to check for the motorcycle," Ree said after they'd parked and paid.

He nodded before reaching for her hand. Apparently she had the same idea. They ended up meeting in the middle. A quick smile and nod later, and they were making the rounds. The motorcycle was parked directly behind a dumpster at the back exit of the building. How convenient. And, yes, the sticker was on the helmet that was strapped to the seat.

Quint pulled out a blade and slashed both tires.

"That will slow him down," he said as they casually walked the rest of the building. All he could think was that someone should have put a security detail on the bike, but he was glad they hadn't.

The aquarium layout was a labyrinth. The journey started at the front door and then wound through the building, leading Ree and Quint through various rooms that had a distinct look and feel as well as a different type of habitat for exotic birds, mammals and fish.

As they walked through the maze that was the aquarium, he scanned the faces. From the looks of it, the entire place had been rented. Ree was beside him, doing the same thing. The sound of a waterfall filled the air. Between that and the low hum of conversation, it would be impossible to pick out a particular voice. They were shoulder to shoulder as they looked for Dumitru.

Ree squeezed Quint's hand the moment she got confirmation everyone was in place. The cavalry had arrived. All was ready to go. Now all they needed was to find Dumitru. Quint searched face after face, looking for blond-haired, blue-eyed bastard. The man seemed more ghost than real at this point to Quint. Many had seen him from his inner circle. No one outside of it. He had a knack for disappearing at critical moments. Was he even here?

Waiters moved through the crowd with trays hoisted above the fray. They somehow managed to serve drinks.

At some point during the walk through the rain forest, Quint was handed a drink as they made their way to the immersive shark tunnel. If Quint was a betting man, he'd put money on Dumitru being there. What was it about criminals and sharks? Both opportunists? Kindred spirits?

There were more people at the mouth of the tunnel than seemed like there was space to fit them. Quint's adrenaline spiked and the hairs on the back of his neck pricked as they neared the crowd. The tunnel itself was impressive.

From behind them, someone was pushing through the crowd. Quint turned in time to see Lindy coming straight at them. Quint instinctively stepped in between Lindy and Ree, using his body to block the man from coming at her.

Quint cursed underneath his breath. This wasn't the time for a confrontation. Lindy could blow the whole night if he spooked Dumitru. Quint dropped Ree's hand as a furious Lindy came right at them.

He shoved Quint back a step, causing his drink to go flying. Arresting this jerk was going to be a pleasure when this night was all said and done. There was enough evidence against Lindy to lock him up for a very long time. But he wasn't the one Quint was after tonight.

"What the hell?" Quint asked, shoving Lindy right back.

Afterward he stood there with this arms folded across his chest, just daring Lindy to make another move.

"Where is she?" Lindy demanded.

"I have no idea," Quint shot back. He held his hands high in the air and glanced around, making a show of not hiding anything. "Why don't you tell us?"

Lindy reared his hand back in a flash, but Quint saw the punch coming from a mile away. He caught Lindy's fist as the man tried to punch Quint in the face. Then he squeezed, putting enough pressure on Lindy to come close to cracking a bone.

"You want it to go down like this?" Quint asked. He didn't dare remove his gaze from Lindy, but he could feel the tension in the area ratchet up. Since there were no metal detectors in use at the doors, Quint realized it was possible that most everyone in the room would be packing. The last thing he wanted was a bloodbath.

"What's going on over here?" an unfamiliar voice asked from the dark tunnel behind them.

"Nothing," Lindy said, seeming to backpedal a little too fast.

"What does that mean?" the voice continued. "I heard something. Explain to me what it is."

"It's fine, Dumitru," one of the others consoled him, and there was a nervous note to his voice.

Since Lindy backed off, Quint risked turning around to get a good look. The crowd had parted like Moses was about to cross the Red Sea. The man Quint had been hunting for months stood there in the center of the tunnel, arms folded, in a show of dominance as a large shark swam overhead. Dumitru looked to be in his early forties, older than Quint expected, although he wasn't certain why. It made sense. He had sun-worn skin and tattoos peeking out of his expensive, tailored, silk button-down shirt. Quint guessed the man's height to be around five feet ten inches, and he had tree trunks for arms.

Ree had disappeared into the crowd forming around Quint. The thought of her being alone in this group sent an icy chill racing down Quint's back. But this was not the same situation as with Tessa.

Had she given the signal to the others to descend on the building? An earpiece would be a dead giveaway, so neither had one, but they were wired. Quint glanced around. Where was Ree?

Chapter Twenty-Three

Chaos could be good. It also could be deadly.

Ree used the moment of chaos created by Lindy coming at Quint to circle the crowd and position herself behind Dumitru. There were several folks in her line of sight, blocking a straightforward view of the happenings. She'd taken advantage of the opportunity presented. All she waited for now was to make eye contact with Quint so she could give the signal. If she got close enough to Dumitru, she would go ahead make the call for the team to come inside for an arrest.

This seemed like a good time to slip out of those high heels in case she needed to run. Ree sat on the wall, blocking visitors from getting too close to the glass in the tunnel. She quickly slipped out of her shoes, brandishing one to use as a weapon should the need arise. The heel was essentially a spike.

The crowd around her was on edge. She could feel the tension rising. It wouldn't take much to stir up mob mentality. Since everyone was most likely armed, this situation could get out of hand real quick if they weren't careful.

Standing up, she pushed up to her tiptoes, trying to get a look at Quint. She saw him just in time to watch two guys jump him, one on each side. The men started dragging him toward her and where she figured they were about to teach him a lesson.

"Move," one of the men said as Quint struggled, trying to break their grip.

Was he waiting for her?

"You never answered my question," Lindy said to Quint. He was one of the few people in the room who could identify Ree. She let her loose curls fall around her face, trying to use her hair as a shield.

Anger welled up inside her at the sight of him, standing there sneering as Quint was dragged past her.

"Take him to my office," Dumitru said, turning to follow Quint.

It was then that Quint glanced over at her and gave the slightest nod. She knew exactly what it meant. Go time.

Ree reached around behind her and pressed the button sewn into her dress's lining. The cavalry would arrive in a matter of minutes. She followed, being elbowed by the crowd as she made her way toward the back against the grain.

"Go back to the party," Dumitru announced, giving a quick wave of his hand.

Most stopped following, but there was no way she was letting Dumitru out of sight. In fact, she ended up a little too close to him because there was nowhere to go when he stopped and turned around. She nearly bumped right into him. Her clutch had a secret compartment that contained her badge and a pair of zip cuffs.

They belonged on Dumitru's wrists.

"Hey there, beautiful," he said, snatching her by the arm. His fingers dug into her forearm as he yanked her toward him.

She lost her balance and ended up smacking against him.

"That hurts," she said, glancing down at his grip.

"Good," he practically sneered. "It'll only get better later."

A literal shiver rocked her at the thought of being forced to do anything with this man other than place him under arrest.

"I have a message for you," she said, leaning toward him.

"Oh, yeah?" he asked. A smile that was probably meant to look sexy but ended up creepy split his face. "Is it what you're going to let me do to you later?"

"How about what I'm going to do to you right now," she said through half-clenched teeth. In the background, she caught a glimpse of two faces coming right at them, Grappell and Bjorn. The desk agent was average height and build, not exactly someone who spent his days at the gym but not heavyset either. He had red hair and blue eyes, and she was thrilled to see him heading toward her. Their boss was a couple steps in front of Grappell. Bjorn had on navy slacks and a white blouse. Blond hair with brown eyes, she was tall, fit, and could best be described as fierce.

"Good." Dumitru brought his hand up around the base of her neck and forced her face within an inch of his. "Because I can hardly wait to get started."

"I should start by telling you that you're under arrest," Ree stated.

The shocked look on Dumitru's face was priceless as she continued reading his Miranda rights.

His shock didn't last long. In fact, he threw an elbow into Ree's rib cage and tried to break free from the grip she now had on his wrist.

In the next couple of moments, Quint twisted free from the men holding him, and all hell broke loose as Bjorn and Grappell arrived on the scene.

Quint came at Dumitru like a linebacker going in for a sack. He ran him up against the wall, causing Dumitru to trip backwards. Ree drew her weapon and pointed it toward the gathering crowd as Ben bolted in.

"Hands where I can see them," Bjorn said to the group to no avail.

A voice came through loud and clear from a megaphone outside, though.

"You're surrounded by law enforcement. The best thing each of you can do is cooperate," the voice she recognized as belonging to Tex said.

The crowd scattered, but Quint was all over Dumitru. The next time he was standing upright, he was in cuffs, and his face was pressed against the wall.

"Where is Giselle?" Quint asked Dumitru. It took a couple of threats, but Dumitru finally said she was in the office. Stanley came out with her a few minutes later. Her eyes were red-rimmed and her face anguished.

"I didn't want anything to do with this," she said. "He threatened my boy and Axel isn't here to protect us. I'm so sorry for everything."

Ree wasn't a mother but she could imagine how powerful the need to protect a kid might be. After all, she'd watched her own mother try to keep Ree out of any possible danger.

Lisa and Evan rounded up as many folks as they could until the walls were literally lined with people, hands up.

The first thing Ree did when Dumitru was safely being led away was kiss her future husband. Then she excused herself and walked outside to get some fresh air.

Ree pulled out her cell phone and punched in her mother's number. The number would come through as unidentified, so she wasn't sure if her mom would answer. What she had to say couldn't wait.

Thankfully, her mother answered on the second ring.

"Mom, it's me, Ree," she started.

"Oh, Ree. I didn't recognize the number," her mother said, sounding concerned.

"I have a second phone for work and what I have to say to you couldn't wait," Ree continued. She needed to keep talking before she lost her nerve. "Mom, before you say anything else, I just want to tell you that I'm sorry I turned out to be a disappointment to you."

"What?" Her mother sounded confused now. "You're not a disappointment."

"It's okay, Mom. I know that I am. I don't bake things from scratch, and I'm sorry I never wore bows in my hair. How hard would it have been for me to let you put a bow in my hair?" she said.

"I'm the one who is sorry, Ree," her mother said. "You've always been strong-willed, and true, you were never the kind of girl who would let me dress you up in bows, but that doesn't mean you're a disappointment. I'm the one who should be sorry if that's how I've made you feel, because you gave me an even greater gift."

"I did?" Ree was the one confused now.

"That's right. I never had to worry about anyone taking advantage of you," her mother said. "You knew your own mind and how to stand up for yourself. That's far more useful than being able to bake a pie."

"But you love pie," Ree countered, still trying to process what her mother had just said.

"I love my stubborn daughter more," her mother said. "And I'm certain you came by your stubbornness honestly."

"Dad?" Ree asked.

"Oh, he could be stubborn when he wanted to be," her mother said. "But it's the women in the family who hold the record."

Ree laughed at that.

"I love you, Mom," she said.

"I love you too," her mother said. "And I wouldn't have had you any other way."

Tears streamed down Ree's cheeks as she turned back toward the building.

"Can you set a place at Sunday supper for me and my fiancé?" Ree asked.

"I'd love to," her mother said. She didn't ask who the man in Ree's life was. She had to know it was Quint, though.

"Then, we'll see you tomorrow," Ree said before ending the call. As she did, Quint came out the back door, his gaze searching for her.

"Over here," she said to her man, her future, her version of home.

He made a beeline toward her and immediately brought her into an embrace. There she stood for a long moment in the arms of the only man she could ever love.

"He's going away for a very long time," Quint said while he held her as though he hung on for dear life.

"Yes, he is," she agreed.

"Bjorn said Vadik will get visitation with his mother, who will stay in the facility where she is being well cared for," he continued.

"Good. That seems fair," she said before adding, "justice will be served with Dumitru. He didn't get away with it. Tessa didn't die in vain."

"No, she didn't," he said. "I will never forget her or her child."

"Good. Because I want you to tell me your stories. Tessa was a big part of your life. She was your best friend long before I met you. I want to hear all about your friendship and why it was special," she said to him.

"Okay," he said with a warmth that wrapped around her, soothed her. "Someday. I'll tell you all about our friendship. Right now, I'm ready to put the past behind me and think about the future. Dumitru will spend the rest of his life behind bars but that won't bring back Tessa or the baby. I've come to realize that obsessing over past mistakes won't make them any easier to get over."

"All that is true and I agree. But I want to get to know Tessa better. I hope that part of your past can move ahead with us," she said.

Quint brushed the backs of his fingers against her cheek.

"I've never met anyone like you, Ree," he said, catching her gaze and holding onto it. "And I could live a hundred years without finding another person who could hold a candle to you. I'm ready to put the past behind us, and step into our future. Together. I only want to take the good memories of Tessa with me from here on out."

"I think that's a wonderful plan," Ree said as she gazed into his eyes. Quint Casey. Her man. Her love. Her home.

Quint dipped his head down and kissed her, leaving no room for doubt they belonged together. And now, it was time to look to tomorrow instead of wishing the past could be different. It was time to embrace the life that lay ahead of them. Together forever.

Epilogue

Ree checked her reflection in the mirror one last time. She took in a deep breath as she stared at herself.

"Ready?" her mother asked, beaming with what looked a whole lot like pride.

"To marry Quint? Yes," Ree said, thinking she'd never seen a more beautiful dress than the one her mother had helped her pick out. "And thank you."

"For what?" mother asked.

"Everything," Ree said. "But mostly accepting me for who I am and being here to support me on this day."

"That was easy once I pushed aside my own stubbornness," her mother said with a sly smile and a wink. She really was the greatest person and Ree's older brother Shane had been right about Ree needing to lighten up when it came to their mother. But she had no intention of telling him that. There was no reason to give him a big head. "You really are beautiful. And I don't just mean in the dress."

"Love you, Mom," Ree said. "P.S., you're not supposed to make the bride cry on her wedding day. You'll ruin my makeup."

Her mother's warm smile brightened the moment.

A knock sounded at the door before her brother stuck his head inside.

"The reverend is here," he said, his gaze moving from their mother to Ree. "Wow. Sis. You look..."

He seemed to choke up on the last words. She couldn't have him getting too sentimental this early in the day.

"Like someone who could use a drink," she said with a smile.

"Nervous?" Shane asked, stepping inside and leaving the door open.

"Surprisingly, no," she said. She wasn't. Marrying Quint was the best thing she could imagine doing. "But I am ready."

Mother smiled before wiping a stray tear.

"Your grandfather is going to lose it when he sees how beautiful you look," Mother said, covering her own emotions with a cough. She took in a deep breath before placing her hands on Ree's shoulders. "This day will go by in a blur. Make sure to pay attention to the little moments and spend a few minutes with each person who cared enough to show up for you."

"I will," Ree said before embracing her mother one last time before walking down the aisle.

"The music is starting, Mom," Shane said. "You should go so you can be seated."

"Okay," Mother said before adding, "I love you both so much."

After another round of hugs, Shane held out his arm toward Ree.

"I refuse to give you away," he whispered as they exited the bride's room. "But I'm happy to bring Quint into the family."

Her brother's words had a calming effect on Ree.

"Thank you," she said to him. "For being the best big brother a person could ask for."

"Back at you, sis," he said as he walked her to the sanctuary of the church.

Everyone stood as they entered the room. Bjorn and Grappell were there, smiling from ear to ear. The aisle wasn't too long. Zoe, her maid of honor stood to the left. Angie stood next to Zoe. These two women were a critical part of Ree and Quint's love story. It only seemed right to include them in the ceremony.

To the right, Quint stood there with his hands clasped looking sexier than any groom had a right to. Next to him stood his best man and the person responsible for helping Quint become the human being he was today. Jazzy's look of pride nearly caused Ree's heart to burst. Jazzy held a puppy in his arms that seemed determined to wiggle out.

She looked at Quint, confused.

All he did was smile and nod in response, which confused her even more. Quint's best man had a little explaining to do, but she'd learned to expect pretty much anything when it came to her and Quint. Their relationship had its own pulse and she was learning to roll with it.

"Take good care of each other," was all Shane said as he joined Ree and Quint's hands.

After, Shane gave his sister a peck on the cheek before taking a seat with the family.

"The puppy is a wedding gift for you, by the way," Quint leaned forward and whispered. "I want you to have everything your heart desires and then some."

"I do," she said.

"The reverend hasn't asked us any questions yet," he said with a warm smile.

"Doesn't matter," she said. "I already do."

"Then I do too," he said.

There was a short ceremony that was immediately followed by a bone melting kiss. When Ree turned around, she skimmed the faces of those she loved and all the people who were important in their lives.

There was so much love and happiness in one room. She was ready to get started on forever. But first…cake.

* * * * *

LAKESIDE MYSTERY

CAROL ERICSON

Chapter One

A shiver snaked through Ashlynn's body, even though the sun streamed through the branches of the trees, creating a dappled pattern on the ground. She hugged herself, clutching her pepper spray in one hand against her upper arm. Her brother, Sean, had agreed to meet someone near a lake…and it hadn't ended well for him.

Of course, she wasn't exactly meeting someone, and Sean had traipsed out in the dead of night. Unlike her foolish brother, she'd ventured out in the middle of the day with hikers panting along the trail and mountain bikers kicking up dirt as they trundled up the hill. Her nose tingled with tears and she wiped her sleeve across it. Nobody could tell Sean anything.

He had been a successful true crime blogger because he'd embraced danger, taken those necessary risks. She'd have to remold herself in his image if she hoped to keep his blog going strong. She didn't want *LA Confidential* to die with her brother.

She puffed out her cheeks and trudged onward. She'd venture as far as the lake, have a look around, maybe take a few pictures, and wait for the next message—if there was a next message. If her anonymous contact didn't send her another communication after the first one about a submerged car in Lake Kawayu, she'd look for another story to feature on the blog.

Stopping under a tree, she tapped her phone to bring up the trail map and had to lunge out of the way of on-coming runners. She called into their dust. "Where's the turnoff for the lake?"

One of them yelled something unintelligible but pointed to his right. Another several yards and Ashlynn spotted the weathered sign pointing toward Lake Kawayu. How could a car possibly make its way down a trail like this to plunge into a lake?

She veered to the right between two oaks, their leaves dripping water from the rain the day before.

Ashlynn shuffled downhill through the debris of leaves, twigs and pebbles that littered the trail. Any minute she expected to see the lake through the branches of the trees, but spring had done its job and the forest bloomed and flourished around her so that she could barely see beyond the next bend.

When the foliage thinned, and a couple toting a fiberglass canoe squeezed past her, she knew she was close.

She rounded the next corner and caught her breath as a dark blue ripple appeared below. She had to scrabble down a small incline to reach the shore of the lake, and she placed her hands on her hips and took a deep breath of the pine and earthy muddy scent that assailed her.

She scanned the perimeter of the body of water, her gaze lingering on the north shore where a dirt parking lot boasted several cars belonging to people who knew they didn't need to hike a mile and a half to reach the lake. She also realized that if a car were going to plunge into the water, that parking lot had to be its origination point.

Shading her eyes, she judged the distance to the parking lot to be another half mile. She glanced at the sturdy sneakers on her feet and pulled a bottle of water from her small daypack. She took a long gulp of water and watched the couple launch their canoe into the lake with a splash. She'd come prepared—and she needed a new story for the blog.

Her shoes crunched the coarse sand lakeside as she started walking the semicircle to the parking lot. She didn't know why her anonymous tipster had contacted her—probably because *LA Confidential* still sported the sheen of her brother's success—but she didn't want to dismiss it. Sean had told her some of his best stories started as anonymous bits of information.

If this were just a submerged car, she'd blow it off, but the tipster had claimed there was a dead body in the car. The least she could do was check it out. It's not like she had a lot on her plate. She'd quit her job at the magazine when Sean was…killed. She couldn't go back to it now, and she didn't want to. Sean had died just when his blog had hit peak popularity, and she felt an obligation to carry on with it. She'd had a modicum of success with her first story—an exposé of Reed Dufrain, addiction recovery guru turned drug dealer—but she couldn't rest on her laurels.

A few families frolicked in the water, and Ashlynn shivered. Must be out-of-towners, because it was definitely too cold for thin-blooded Angelenos to take a dip. Summer was still a season away, and the sun starting to make its appearance every day lacked the wattage of an August or September in LA.

Still, Ashlynn had a one-piece on under her clothes and a towel rolled up in her pack. How else could she spot a submerged car? Maybe one of these swimmers would discover it first and save her the trouble of a chilly dip.

When she reached the parking lot, she downed more

water from her bottle. She nodded at a group stoking the flames in a hibachi, paper plates of bratwurst and burgers standing by. She was pretty sure the city didn't allow an open fire like that in Angeles Crest, but she wasn't here to be Smokey the Bear's helper.

She wandered to the edge of the dirt lot, facing the water. No barrier or lip separated the lot from the lakeshore, and plenty of tire tracks indicated that people drove right up to the water's edge. Into the water?

She scuffed through the sand and rocks up to the dark, oily water lapping the banks. No swimmers had ventured into the lake from the parking area. They most likely preferred the cleaner-looking water down from the trees, but that probably explained why nobody had found the car yet.

Sighing, Ashlynn swung the pack off her back and dropped it in the dirt. She fished out her towel, shook it and set it next to her daypack. Then she toed off her shoes and wriggled free of her clothes, quickly, kicking both onto the towel.

She waded into the water, her arms folded over her chest, goose bumps crawling across her bare flesh. When the water reached her hips, she pushed off the rocky bottom with her feet and paddled into the murky lake. The parking lot wasn't that wide and a car launched from the banks couldn't go that far. She did a breaststroke in a line horizontal to the shore, kicking her legs in a wide circle and peering into the water. She moved a little farther into the water and repeated her course back the other way.

A few people from the barbecuing bunch in the parking lot stood at its edge, staring at her. She supposed she must look a little crazy to people watching, but as she took another stroke, she muttered, "I'll never see them again."

The lake had gotten deep fast, and her toes no longer even skimmed the bottom. A whole car could definitely be submerged under the water and nobody would notice it from the shore.

As she circled into another wide turn, her fluttering feet made contact with something hard and smooth...and big. Holding her breath, she ducked beneath the water and opened her eyes. She flipped and swam downward for a few feet. Her hands met solid metal before she saw its glint.

Her lungs bursting, she propelled herself to the surface and gasped in a long breath. She'd found the car. Was there a body inside?

DETECTIVE DENVER HOLT STARED over his clenched hands on the steering wheel at a knot of people gathered at the edge of the murky lake. The hoist to lift the car from the cloudy depths was already in place, and he could imagine the divers below hooking up the winches. His captain had sent him on another thrilling adventure to assist the traffic division with an accident or possible stolen while his name languished on the list for Robbery-Homicide.

He smacked the steering wheel with the heels of his hands. He'd sworn to protect and serve—even victims of auto theft. He exited his sedan and strode toward the commotion, his wing tips crunching the sand and gravel on the shore of the lake.

"Detective Holt." Flashing his badge at the uniform, he asked, "Have the divers indicated yet if there's anyone in the car?"

"Officer Brooks." Brooks tapped his nametag and shrugged. "If they found anything, they haven't told me about it. I'm here for crowd control."

Denver scanned the smattering of people and smirked. Some crowd. "Who discovered the car?"

Brooks jerked his thumb over his shoulder. "The woman with the towel and the wet hair—Ashlynn Hughes."

Denver lifted his sunglasses and squinted at a redhead wearing jeans, a wet T-shirt sticking to her body. She'd draped a striped towel over her shoulders.

He snorted. "What did she do, jump off her canoe to get a closer look?"

"She wasn't in a canoe. She saw it while she was swimming." The cop rolled his eyes and held up one hand. "I know, I know. Don't ask me."

"How close are they to hauling it out?" Denver dropped his sunglasses back over his eyes and fished his notebook from his jacket pocket.

"They've been at it for a while. Should be anytime now."

"Thanks, man." Denver picked his way across the rocky shoreline to the woman fluffing the towel through her red locks that glinted with fire every time they caught the sun.

"Ms. Hughes?" He thrust out his hand. Even in bare feet, this tall drink of water almost stood nose to nose with him. "I'm Detective Denver Holt. I understand you're the one who spotted the car and called 9-1-1."

She grasped his hand with a firm slightly damp grip. "I am. I mean it's weird, right? A car in the lake? I wasn't just going to swim on by without telling someone."

His pulse jumped and his gaze behind his dark lenses sharpened. That was a lot of words for a simple yes. "Weird. Definitely weird. Could be an accident, stolen car, insurance fraud. Thanks for calling it in, Ms. Hughes."

Her shoulders beneath the towel slumped as she nodded. "Yeah, I thought so. You can call me Ashlynn."

"Okay… Ashlynn." He flipped open his notebook. "What were you doing in the lake?"

Her blue eyes widened. "What?"

"The lake." He leveled a finger at the body of water. "What were you doing?"

"Swimming." She plucked her soggy T-shirt from her chest, revealing the outline of a one-piece suit beneath. "I went for a swim."

Denver tipped his head back to take in the sky with a few clouds scudding across the sun and hunched into his suit jacket against the sudden breeze. "Not exactly swimming weather."

She flapped her hand toward a few kids paddling and splashing in the water beyond the parking lot. "Tell *them* that. Some of us aren't as…sensitive as you are, Detective."

He cracked a smile. He should've expected feisty with that hair. "So, you decided to drive down to Lake Kawayu and head straight from the parking lot to the water for a swim, and while paddling through the…crystal-clear water you notice a car below you?"

She jutted out one slim hip and wedged a fist on the curve. "Don't put words in my mouth, Detective Holt. I hiked down the trail to get here and jumped in the lake to cool off. While I was swimming, I went vertical to make sure I wasn't going too far out, and my feet skimmed a slab of metal—not what you'd expect to find in a lake."

"Not what I'd expect." He tapped his pen against the notebook. "You ducked down to see what you could see?"

"Yes, and even though the water was cloudy, it was evident that I was floating above a car. I swam back to the shore and called 9-1-1."

"Did you see anything inside the car?" He glanced

over his shoulder at the beeping sound from the tow truck. They'd find out soon enough anyway.

She clasped her hands in front of her, knotting her fingers, her sassy demeanor fading as fast as the sun overhead. "I—I didn't get a good look. I didn't want to dive down any deeper, and it was dark and murky."

"Good decision. Did anyone else go into the water after you to take a look?" He made a half-turn to watch the progress of the car as the roof broke the surface of the lake and the water sluiced over the metal.

"I didn't tell anyone what I'd found. I called 9-1-1 and waited for the police. These other people started gathering when the cop car showed up, and then the officer wouldn't let anyone in the water after that." She bit her bottom lip as the dark sedan cleared the water and swung from the pulleys like a bloated fish on the line.

Denver shaded his eyes against the sun glinting off the lake. "Doesn't look like it's been sitting there too long."

She shivered and rubbed her arms. "No, it doesn't."

"Thanks for the information, Ms. Hughes." He stuffed his notebook into his pocket. As he turned, she covered her mouth with both hands.

He stopped. "You don't recognize the car, do you?"

"No, no, of course not."

He strode toward the tow truck, grabbing his cell phone from his pocket. He took several pictures of the car as it dangled above the lake.

He stood back as the winch settled the vehicle on the shore with a groan, water pouring from its orifices. He borrowed a flashlight from Brooks and crept toward the waterlogged car, which was still hissing and weeping. He leaned toward the windows and aimed the beam of light inside. It illuminated the empty front seat He shifted the focus to the back seat and saw nothing.

He let out a breath and called to one of the divers emerging from the lake, removing his mask. "Anything or…anyone around the car down there?"

"Nope, but the doors were closed and no broken windows, as you can see, so it doesn't look like anyone escaped from the vehicle, either."

"But the water pressure could've closed an open door, right?"

"Could happen."

"Key fob's in the cup holder." Denver pulled on a pair of gloves and tugged on the door handle. The door opened with a whooshing sound. More water gushed from the car, soaking his shoes. He leaned inside and snatched the key fob from the cup holder.

He almost bumped into Ashlynn Hughes as he backed out of the vehicle. She'd followed him beyond the yellow tape.

"Nothing in the car?" Her breathless voice matched her wide eyes and wayward hair.

It was like the shock of finding a submerged car was just hitting her.

"Nothing." He cupped her elbow. "You can move back, Ms. Hughes."

She shuffled back a few steps as he raised his phone to take pictures of the California license plate and the interior. He'd call it in. They still might be able to read the vehicle registration if it hadn't gotten too soggy. The car looked new. Maybe someone had stolen it or abandoned it for insurance fraud. Different scenarios popped into his head as he took pictures. They'd have to get into that trunk, too.

"Are you going to check the trunk?"

The redhead was still hovering, and he swung around,

phone in hand. "You really need to step away, Ms. Hughes."

"Ashlynn, and don't you usually open the trunk?" Her shirt had dried, but her teeth chattered, and she pulled the towel tighter around her body.

Officer Brooks huddled close to the rear of the car with a crowbar in his hand. "Do you want me to do the honors?"

"The key fob was in the cup holder." Denver dangled it from his finger. His thumb trembled slightly as he smoothed it across the trunk button on the fob. Then he stabbed it.

The lock clicked and one of the divers, who was standing behind Brooks, let out a sigh. Denver held his breath as he nudged up the trunk with two gloved fingers.

The lid swung high, and Denver's heart slammed against his chest. Looked like he'd got his homicide, after all.

Chapter Two

Ashlynn gagged and stumbled backward, covering her nose and mouth with one hand to ward off the smell emanating from the trunk—part rotting meat, part swamp creature.

Detective Holt turned on her and shouted in her face. "I told you to get back."

And I told you to check the trunk.

She clamped her lips shut and gritted her teeth, which helped keep the nausea at bay, anyway. She ducked under the yellow tape and pressed a fist against her stomach.

Her anonymous tipster had been right. How much of her story should she reveal to Holt, now speaking into his phone?

"Homicide, it's Holt. I went to investigate a car submerged in Lake Kawayu and found a body in the trunk."

Ashlynn narrowed her eyes. The hot detective didn't even work in homicide. As Holt continued to yammer on about license plates and registration, Ashlynn scanned the crowd that had grown bigger when the tow truck hauled the car to the surface.

Had one of those spectators already known there'd be a car in the lake? Had he or she already known about the body? Was someone watching her? Now that the tipster had proved to be accurate, Ashlynn needed to contact him or her—ask for more.

Sean would know what to do at this point. She'd look through his old exchanges with other informants to see how he'd handled it. This could be her chance to revive *LA Confidential* to its former glory under her brother.

She glanced at the pale flesh in the trunk of the car and her stomach turned. Sean had started the blog to get justice for victims after someone had murdered his friend AJ, and the case had gone cold. She couldn't lose sight of that mission. Sean would want her to get justice for that woman in the car.

And her brother didn't always play by the rules.

She squared her shoulders as Detective Holt marched toward her, his suit jacket flapping in the breeze, revealing a broad chest and flat belly beneath his dress shirt. He stopped on the other side of the tape from her, and she could see herself reflected in his dark glasses.

"Why were you so anxious for me to open the trunk? What were you really doing out here... Ashlynn?"

He'd finally used her first name, and it sounded like a sneer on his lips. She cleared her throat. "I wasn't anxious. I figured you'd be opening the trunk anyway. Right?"

His face reddened. "Of course. I don't need you to tell me how to do my job, but I still don't understand why you were swimming in Lake Kawayu, a body of water more suited to boaters and kids splashing on the shore than serious swimmers."

"Serious? Who said I was a serious swimmer? I hiked almost two miles and fancied a dip in the water to cool off." She clamped her teeth together to stop the tremble rolling through her body. "It's not against the law to swim in this lake. Then my foot hit the submerged car, and I called the police. Why am I in the wrong here? You should be thanking me."

Detective Holt opened his mouth and then snapped it shut with the arrival of a dark sedan, similar to the one the tow truck had just hauled from the lake. Holt held up his index finger instead and said, "Don't go anywhere."

She had no intention of leaving. As he strode toward a tall woman getting out of the car, Ashlynn aimed her phone at the people clustered beyond the yellow tape and started taking pictures. Her tipster could be one of them.

Thirty minutes later, after consulting with the woman from the unmarked police sedan and bagging items from the car, Holt returned to her with a decided spring to his step. How anyone could be in a chipper mood after hovering around that trunk was beyond her, but cops had a different sensibility from civilians. Sean had always had a love-hate relationship with them.

Detective Holt stuffed a hand in his pocket and pulled out a business card. "Here's my card. Don't hesitate to call me if you remember anything else about the discovery of the car…or why you were swimming in a dirty lake on a day that reached sixty-six degrees tops."

Snatching the card from his fingers, she said, "I gave you all I got, Detective. D-did you identify the victim yet?"

"No." He tipped his sunglasses down to the end of his nose and tagged her with a stare over the top of his lenses. "Fingerprints were hard to get, license plates came back to a different vehicle, so we know they were swapped out, no registration in the glove compartment, and a filed-down VIN."

Her mind got stuck on the image of the victim's fingertips, and she shook her head as if to clear it. He'd surprised her with the details he'd provided—and seemed to surprise himself, as well.

His jaw hardened and he shoved his glasses back into place. "I may be calling you to follow up."

I should be so lucky. She watched his broad shoulders encased by his suit jacket as he returned to the car. While they had been speaking, a coroner's van had shown up at the scene and a few officers had tented the car with a pop-up, blocking the view of the onlookers.

She didn't want to watch the guys in biohazard suits load that body in a bag, anyway. She crouched to pick up her daypack and slung it over one shoulder. Her T-shirt had mostly dried, but the seat of her jeans was still damp. She twisted her hair into a bun and started the trek back down the trail.

Her contact had proved to be accurate about the car and the body. What else did her anonymous source know...and how?

DENVER SPENT ANOTHER HOUR at the crime scene before packing it in and heading back to the Northeast Division. His anger and disgust at discovering that poor woman in the truck of the car tempered his satisfaction with his temporary assignment to Robbery-Homicide to work this case. He'd been on loan to Homicide as a floater before, and had been itching for another opportunity. Too bad the death of that woman had landed him his chance.

On the other hand, he'd do his damnedest to find out who'd killed her and deliver justice to her family. Justice the Portland PD had failed to deliver to his own family when his father was murdered.

Someone had gone to a lot of trouble to disguise the car—swapped out the plates, removed the registration, and filed down the VIN. But all those efforts would prove to be fruitless, as most car manufacturers placed the VIN in a couple of places—some not readily apparent. LAPD's auto theft should be able to figure it out soon enough.

When he got back to the station, he checked in with Captain Fields and then got down to business. Identifying the victim took precedence over everything else right now. He pulled up the database for missing persons in Los Angeles County and narrowed the search based on gender, age and race. Date range would be tricky, as the medical examiner at the scene couldn't pin down anything specific due to the condition of the corpse in the water that had flooded the trunk.

As Denver clicked through the photos and details of the missing women, a hand clamped on his shoulder and he jumped.

Detective Billy Crouch nodded toward the computer. "Heard you're working the case of the woman found in the trunk at Lake Kawayu. What race is she?"

"I'm helping out. It's Detective Marino's case." Denver flicked his fingers at the waifish blond, one of the missing women, peering at them from the monitor. "Caucasian."

Crouch snorted. "If Marino caught the case, that means you'll have a lot of work to do. Anything yet?"

"Not yet and no viable prints from the victim."

"Let me know if you need any help navigating that database… I'm an expert." Crouch twisted his mouth into a grimace before heading out the door.

Crouch obsessively homed in on any case involving a dead woman, as his own sister had been missing for years. If the woman in the trunk had been African American, Crouch would've demanded to see her, no doubt.

Denver could understand that kind of fixation. His father's murder had galvanized his own determination to work Homicide. He didn't need a therapist to figure that one out.

After more than an hour staring at the computer monitor, his eyes began to glaze over. The missing woman on his screen had been gone for three years already. He massaged his temples. How did the families cope with that?

His phone rang and he grabbed it, grateful for the interruption. "Holt."

"Detective Holt, this is Dr. Saleh with the ME Coroner's department. We haven't done an autopsy yet on the victim in the lake, but we do have a preliminary cause of death."

"Go ahead." Denver brought up the file on his computer that contained the details from the case.

"Gunshot wound to the head."

The breath Denver had been holding escaped in a noisy rush. "So, not drowning."

"I did say *preliminary*. Of course, seeing the wound leads us to believe death by firearm, but we can't yet rule out the possibility that someone shot her first, shut her in the trunk and let her drown."

Denver's gut lurched. "All right. Thanks for the call, Dr. Saleh. You'll let me or Detective Marino know when you have the full autopsy?"

The doctor clicked his tongue. "Yes, I just tried calling Detective Marino, but he didn't pick up, and your name was second on the list."

"I'll be sure to let him know. Thanks, again."

When he ended the call with the ME, Denver drummed his fingers on the edge of the keyboard. Crouch had been right about Marino. He had a reputation for laziness, and Denver planned to take advantage of that fact. If he could solve this case without much input from Marino, he might be on the fast track to Robbery-Homicide.

As he thumbed through his notebook to make sure he'd transferred all his information from its pages to his file online, he stopped at Ashlynn Hughes's name. What had she really been doing in that lake? No sensible adult would be swimming laps in Lake Kawayu.

Maybe she'd witnessed the car going into the lake…or something worse, and hadn't wanted to get too involved. But finding the car itself had put her smack in the middle of the investigation. He'd give her a call, have her come into the station. Sitting in an interrogation room seemed to prompt people's memories.

He reached for the phone and stopped when he heard a wail from down the hall. That didn't sound good. He jumped to his feet and followed the sound of the commotion—jagged crying and soothing voices—right into the Robbery-Homicide division.

Clinging to the doorjamb, his gaze swept the room, landing on Crouch sitting on the edge of his desk in front of a red-faced woman flailing her arms in the air.

In contrast to Crouch's low voice, which Denver couldn't hear, the woman cried out, "I know it's her. She's been missing for three days. I've checked everywhere."

Denver's pulse picked up speed and he took a few steps into the room, raising his eyebrows at Crouch.

"Here's the detective working the case, Mrs. Edmunds." Crouch cupped his hand and gestured him forward. "I'll let you talk to him."

Denver squared his shoulders. Nobody liked this part of Homicide. On his way to Billy and the woman, he pulled out a chair next to an empty desk. "Mrs. Edmunds, I'm Detective Holt. Why don't you take a seat, and we can talk?"

He did have photos of the dead girl in the trunk, but

he'd never show those to a mother—whether the picture was of her daughter or not.

Mopping her face with a handful of tissues he was sure she'd gotten from Billy, Mrs. Edmunds walked toward him with a jerky gait. When she sat, he wiped his own hands on the thighs of his slacks. If he could be half as good as Billy at this, he'd ace this encounter.

"Start at the beginning, Mrs. Edmunds. What's your daughter's name?"

"Tiana Fuller. H-her father and I are divorced, and I remarried."

"You say she's been missing for three days? Did you report her disappearance before this?" He hadn't seen a Tiana Fuller or Edmunds in the database this afternoon.

"I'm reporting it now." Her gazed shifted to Billy, now logging off his computer, his head cocked, listening to their conversation. "My husband and I were out of town. We drove down to San Diego to visit his aunt, who'd had a fall. Tiana is twenty-one. S-she lives in Long Beach, near campus. She's just home for spring break and to housesit for us, so we left her on her own. We didn't re-alize she was missing until we came home this afternoon and couldn't reach her. I thought at first she might've gone back to her place in Long Beach."

"Were you in touch with her while you were in San Diego?"

"We exchanged a few texts the first day. She didn't answer later texts, but Tiana's been living on her own for two years at school. We didn't want to…hover." She dropped her head and balled the wad of tissues in her fist. "We should've. We should've come home sooner."

"And you're here now because you heard about the woman found at Lake Kawayu?"

She nodded without lifting her head.

"What makes you think this is Tiana? Did she frequent that area?"

Her head shot up and she pinned him with her wild, red-rimmed eyes. "I just know it. I have a feeling."

Denver massaged his stiff neck. Any parent of a missing child would feel the same after learning of the discovery of a dead woman. "Do you have a picture of Tiana, Mrs. Edmunds?"

Sniffling, she dug into her purse, eager to be doing something at last. With a trembling hand, she held out a picture of a young woman with light brown hair and a turned-up nose.

Denver swallowed. The woman in the trunk had brownish-blond hair and a slender build like Tiana's—but so did a lot of young women. He took the photo from her and studied the face, keeping his own impassive as Mrs. Edmund's gaze probed him.

She croaked. "Is it her? Is she the girl in the trunk?"

"I can't say right now, Mrs. Edmunds. Do you have any idea what she was wearing when she last went out? What car she'd be driving?"

"Her car's at home." She shredded the tissues. "I don't understand why you can't tell me if she's the one in that trunk."

His gaze darted to Billy, who was taking his sweet time logging off and packing up his stuff.

Billy cleared his throat. "We can't make a positive ID based on just a picture, Mrs. Edmunds. Leave the photo of your daughter with Detective Holt. The next step is to provide us with your daughter's DNA—hair from her brush, toothbrush—something like that."

She bit her bottom lip. "You can't show me pictures of the dead girl? I'd know Tiana anywhere."

"That's not advisable at this time, Mrs. Edmunds."

Denver shifted forward to meet her gaze. She had to know what he meant. "As Detective Crouch said, we want to wait for a positive ID through DNA first."

"Okay." She slumped in her chair.

She obviously hadn't been looking forward to the task of collecting her daughter's DNA. What made her think she could look at a picture of a dead body that had been submerged in water?

Once Denver got more information from her and gave her his card, he walked her to the exit and then jogged upstairs to talk to Billy.

Denver leaned against a desk and crossed his arms. "Thanks for rescuing me."

"You would've figured it out." Billy hitched his bag over his shoulder. "Who found the car, anyway? Doesn't seem like a boater would run into it or hit it with an oar. You can't see anything in that lake from the air."

"It was a swimmer. She went vertical, and her foot brushed the top of the car."

Billy's jaw dropped. "A swimmer in *that* lake? I mean, I know little kids like to splash around the shore, but swim?"

"That was my reaction. I was just going to call the witness to invite her in tomorrow and grill her a little more. She seemed…vague."

"Same age as the victim?"

"Older, but not by much. Different last name, of course, so no link there. Hughes. Ashlynn Hughes is her name."

Billy whistled through his teeth. "Oh, boy."

"What?" Denver pushed off the desk, his heart pounding. "Do you know her?"

"Not personally, but I know who she is, and I knew who her brother was."

"What?" Denver shook his head, pain lancing the back of his neck. "Her brother? What are you talking about?"

"You know the true crime blog, *LA Confidential*? Her brother, Sean Hughes, wrote that blog until he was murdered, and his sister's picked up where he left off."

Denver clenched his jaw. Know it? He not only knew about *LA Confidential*, that blog and Sean Hughes had made his life a living hell.

Chapter Three

Ashlynn wedged her feet against the edge of the coffee table and flipped open the computer in her lap. Holding her breath, she navigated to the private message area connected to the blog. If readers didn't want to post something publicly to the comments section, they could message her directly. That's how her anonymous tipster had sent her the first message about a car in Lake Kawayu—with a body in the trunk.

She scanned the direct messages, skimming over the ones asking her to take on a case, tearing up over the ones with condolences on Sean's death, and deleting the marriage pitches and indecent proposals. Had Sean gotten those?

She slumped against the couch and took a sip of green tea, lolling the mellow flavor on her tongue. Nothing new from her source. He or she must've seen the discovery of the car and the body in the lake. It had been all over the news. Detective Denver Holt's face had been all over the news. A girl could get lost in those chocolate-brown eyes.

She took a quick gulp of tea that went down the wrong way, and she hacked and wiped her eyes. That's what she got for straying from her purpose.

Neither Holt nor the news reports had mentioned her name, so maybe her tipster didn't realize she'd been the one to report the car. She scooped in a breath and poised her hand over the keyboard. She'd have to remedy that and keep those tips coming. The more firsthand knowledge she had of the case, the more she could engage her readers—and take them with her on to her next adventure.

At the time of Sean's death, he'd been working on morphing his blog into a podcast. She'd been helping him with the project, never imagining she'd have to go it alone.

She flexed her fingers and typed in a response to the initial message, thanking her source for the tip and letting him—her?—know that she'd been responsible for finding the car and reporting it.

She hit the return key with a flourish and watched the blank space below her message. Sighing, she wrapped her hands around her mug. Sean had been so much better at this than she was proving to be. Sean had been so much better at most things.

She slid her laptop onto the couch and took her cup to the kitchen. As she rinsed it under the faucet, her cell phone buzzed. She hightailed it back to the living room and swooped down on the phone as it vibrated on the coffee table.

She screwed up one side of her face. She usually didn't answer calls from unknown numbers, but she was operating in a different world now. She answered, willing the trepidation from her voice. "Hello?"

The man on the other end dispensed with the niceties. "You are a liar and a fraud. What do you think you're playing at?"

Ashlynn pressed a palm against her skittering heart. "What? Who is this?"

"You know damned well this is Detective Holt, and

I know who you are. *LA Confidential.*" He spat out the words so forcefully, she twitched.

The edges of the phone dug into her hand as she gripped it. She'd been expecting this. Sooner or later, Holt would've become aware that she was featuring this case on the blog. She'd just hoped it would've been later.

"I didn't lie." Not really. She sank to the couch, her knees hitting the coffee table. "I was swimming in the lake and I discovered the car."

He gave her something like a growl over the phone. "That's a lie. You pretended like you were there by chance when you went in that water specifically to look for that car."

She needed Sean's bravado about now. "It doesn't matter why I was in the water, does it? I found the car and did the right thing."

"Who told you about the car? How'd you know it was there? Why didn't you call the cops when you got the tip?"

"Well, I'm just not going to answer those questions. This was confidential, anonymous, information."

"You're not a psychiatrist or an attorney." The sneer in his voice slid through the phone and slithered under her skin.

"I'm a journalist." She enunciated each syllable.

"Is that what you call it? Encouraging online sleuths to launch their own investigations. Hampering the police. Smearing people's names." He stopped the tirade and took a big breath.

She could picture his dark, narrowed eyes, flushed cheeks, thin line of his lips. She shivered, glad they were on the phone and not across from each other.

"Whatever your opinion of journalists, we need to protect our sources." She sawed at her bottom lip with her teeth. "Besides, I couldn't tell you, anyway. The tip was anonymous. I don't know who this person is."

"You got the tip on your computer?"

"I'm not answering that."

"We can trace activity on your computer."

She muttered a curse. It hadn't taken him long to trick her. "You could trace it if you had my computer. You don't."

He lowered his voice and almost purred in her ear. "Don't you want justice for this young woman?"

She blinked. He didn't fight fair. "O-of course, I do. Look, I don't have any information that's going to help you find her killer..."

He heard the pause. "Yet. Is that what you mean? You don't have anything yet, but you hope to solve this case—you and your wannabe detective minions. Butt out, Hughes."

He elongated the *S* at the end of her name, sounding like a snake.

"You do your job, Detective Holt, and I'll do mine. Maybe the twain will meet at some point, and we can help each other."

"Don't count on it."

He ended the call before she could form a retort. Instead, she said it to the empty room. "Whew, someone woke up on the wrong side of the cage."

She'd known Detective Holt wouldn't be thrilled that she planned to feature this case on *LA Confidential*, but she hadn't expected him to get so mad about it.

From what she understood about him, he didn't typically work Robbery-Homicide. If he were on loan for this case, an arrest would make him look good—better than he already did. Maybe she could help him. Maybe they could help each other. She'd have to get past that wall first.

Ashlynn tucked a leg beneath her and dragged the computer into her lap. She entered his name in a search engine and her eyes popped at the number of entries. This had to be him. Who named their kid Denver?

She clicked on a promising link and read the article with a sick feeling in her belly. Denver's father had been murdered in Oregon years ago. They'd never found his father's killer.

She clicked on a more recent link and smacked her hand to her forehead. *LA Confidential*, her brother, had done an investigation into the murder of Denver's father and had insinuated that his mother was the killer.

"Oh, Sean." She covered her face with her hands. Denver Holt didn't just hate blogs—he hated *her* blog and her dead brother. Could she blame him?

She accessed Sean's archives for the blog. Why had her brother even dug into the Holt family tragedy in Portland? *LA Confidential* usually stayed true to its name and focused on crimes in Los Angeles. It's not like this city had a shortage.

As she scrolled through the archives, her computer dinged, indicating a new private message on the blog. She navigated to the in-box and her hand trembled just a little when she clicked on the message.

She read it aloud. "'Knew I could count on you. Have more but don't want to be traced through these messages. Meet me tonight.'"

The blood pounded in her temples. This is exactly how Sean had lost his life. He'd gone to meet a source... and wound up dead.

She massaged the back of her neck. That was different. Sean had made contact with a serial killer. He was acting as the conduit between a murderer and the cops who were trying to stop him. This was a concerned citizen, afraid to go to the police, trying to get justice for a murder victim. Wasn't it?

Sean's voice echoed in her head, warning her that she'd never succeed if she weren't willing to take risks. Her parents' voices chimed in, predicting she'd never continue the blog's popularity without Sean.

She pushed her hair from her face and asked for a name. A message popped up immediately: Angel.

Did her silent partner mean to put her at ease with that? Angel could be a man or a woman, or could stand for guardian angel. Ashlynn asked for the meeting details, already more than half sure she'd be going through with this.

Angel suggested Venice, the slice of Washington Boulevard near the pier, loaded with bars and restaurants. She'd walk along the sidewalk and Angel would approach her with the phrase *Try the mai tai at Tahiti Nui*. Tahiti Nui was a bar in the area, so that made sense, but not something a complete stranger would say to someone.

Ashlynn ended the exchange with a description of the clothing she'd be wearing, but when Angel assured her she knew what Ashlynn looked like, a whisper of fear tickled the back of her neck.

She sat for a few minutes staring at the screen. Could she trust Angel? Why not? There was no reason for Angel or anyone else to want to harm her. She didn't know anything about the case of the woman in the trunk...not yet. Angel wouldn't be probing her for information, as Angel was the one providing all the tips. Ashlynn was just a mouthpiece. Wasn't that what Sean always maintained?

Until he'd become the mouthpiece for a serial killer and lost his life.

Ashlynn bounded from the couch and snagged a denim jacket from the closet by the front door of the duplex she rented in Culver City. She didn't live far from Venice, but she didn't want to be late. If Angel didn't see her right away, she might think she'd gotten cold feet. Ashlynn didn't think she could muster up her courage again for this meeting.

She slung her purse across her body and tucked a canister of pepper spray in the outside pocket—just in case Angel was no angel.

As she closed her door, she waved to her duplex neighbors just pulling their car into the spot next to hers. Niles was a software engineer, and his girlfriend, whose name she'd forgotten, had just moved in with him a few months ago. They clambered from their car, weighed down with bags of food from the local Chinese place and waved back.

They knew what she did. Knew about *LA Confidential* and what had happened to Sean. They didn't hold it against her—of course, the blog had never accused their parents of murder. She'd tried to dismiss Denver from her mind, but she hadn't been successful. Even without the blog stuff, she'd have a hard time forgetting Denver Holt—tall, dark, handsome and...ornery. She couldn't help herself. She'd always had a weakness for guys who were hard to get—or at least played hard to get.

She'd make a more concerted effort to block him from her mind, as he was probably married with a few kids and, well, he hated her. There was hard to get and then there was near impossible. She'd slot him into the latter category and forget about him.

She cruised west into Venice and the indigo sky that hung above the ocean, soaking up the last of the sun's rays that still floated on the water.

Parking was no picnic in Venice, and Ashlynn circled twice before waiting for a couple getting into their car. When they vacated the spot, she wheeled in.

She stepped out onto the sidewalk and adjusted her purse. She'd arrived fifteen minutes before the appointed meeting time and could squeeze in a stroll to the pier and back before expecting Angel to approach her.

She strode down Washington to the pier, looking straight ahead. She didn't want it to seem as if she were looking for someone, and she didn't want to catch the eye of any of the homeless people who mingled with the rest of crowd scooting in and out of the bars and restaurants that lined the street.

At least Angel had suggested a populated location, although Angel must've been wary of any cameras catching them inside one of the businesses. It sort of made sense to Ashlynn, which was one of the reasons she'd agreed to pounding the sidewalk aimlessly until Angel approached her with the code phrase.

Her gaze flicked toward Tahiti Nui, patrons with drinks in their hands crowding the patio in the front. Angel knew this area, unless she'd just looked it up on the internet. You could discover anything on the internet—including why the hot cop you'd immediately crushed on hated you.

She sauntered to the beginning of the old pier and inhaled the salty air. A few fishermen in silhouette packed up their gear, and an old man carefully navigated the wooden slats. She gulped in a few more breaths and turned to face the boulevard where someone calling herself Angel awaited.

She crossed the parking lot and started walking down the north side of the street. When she reached Pacific, she crossed to the other side of the street and headed back toward the pier. Before the parking lot as she crossed back over, a homeless woman approached her with her dirt-encrusted hand held out.

"Spare change?"

"Sorry, not today." Ashlynn moved past her and, out of the corner of her eye, saw the homeless woman turn in her direction to follow her. Great. She should probably just slip her a dollar to get rid of her.

As Ashlynn plunged her hand in her purse, the woman whispered, "You should try the mai tai at Tahiti Nui."

Ashlynn spun around. "What did you say?"

The woman opened her mouth in a toothless grin and crooked her finger. "Try the mai tai at Tahiti Nui."

Stumbling after the shambling woman, Ashlynn asked, "Who are you?"

This couldn't be Angel, could it? Where would a woman like this get a computer? The library? It made sense. A transient might be more likely to witness a crime without someone noticing her. A transient might be less likely to contact the police for fear of being dismissed, or worse. Did homeless people read *LA Confidential*? Again, they could have access to computers at the library. Anyone could get access to technology today.

The homeless woman didn't turn right onto the sidewalk. She crossed the parking lot and started down Speedway.

Ashlynn hesitated. She didn't want to go this way. They were supposed to stay in a well-lit, crowded area. She licked her lips. "Hold on."

Sand scuffled on the ground to her right and a shadow loomed over her. She clawed for the pepper spray from the side of her purse and as her fingers curled around the canister, something whacked the back of her head.

She dropped to her knees. Dizzy and nauseous, she waited for the next blow that would end her life—just like Sean's.

Chapter Four

With adrenaline coursing through his veins, Denver broke into a jog and rounded the corner of Speedway, slipping and sliding on the loose sand. Ashlynn lay crumpled on the ground and a dark figure sprinted into the night.

"Hey!" Denver took a few steps toward the fleeing person but heard Ashlynn moan behind him. He cranked his head over his shoulder and skidded to a stop on the gritty pavement as a transient poked Ashlynn with an umbrella.

Denver roared. "Stop that, unless you want to wind up behind bars."

The homeless guy backed off and melted into the shadows.

Denver crouched beside Ashlynn. "Are you all right? What happened?"

Her long eyelashes fluttered and she opened one eye. "What are you doing here?"

"I'll get to that later." He wound an arm beneath her and hoisted her to a sitting position, propping her up against the dirty wall of the building. He hoped she wouldn't notice the stains. "Are you injured?"

She rubbed the back of her head, her fingers showing traces of blood. "Someone hit me on the head."

"That homeless woman you were following?" His gaze darted left and right, but he didn't see any sign of the female transient.

"How do you know...?" She shook her head. "Not her. Someone came at me from between the two buildings. Hit me with something."

"An umbrella?"

"Umbrella?" She wrinkled her nose and he noticed a few freckles scattered across her skin. "Heavier than an umbrella. Felt like a brick. Is it bleeding badly?"

Leaning over her, he parted some strands of her hair, sticky with blood. His fingers traced a small bump. "You have a lump on your head, but it's not gushing blood. I'll call the paramedics."

"No." She grabbed his arm as he reached for the phone in his pocket. "I don't need any medical attention. Just some ice and maybe a drink—no mai tais at Tahiti Nui."

He cocked his head. She must still be confused and dizzy. "You sure you don't want to get treated?"

"I'm sure." She flattened a hand against the stucco wall and then snatched it away. "God, this is gross. Can we get out of here?"

He helped her up and she staggered against him. Tucking an arm around her waist, he led her back to the street, the lights and the people. What the hell had she been thinking, following that woman onto Speedway in the dark?

He walked her past Tahiti Nui and steered her across the street to Venice Whaler. They bypassed the hostess and he settled Ashlynn in a booth at the edge of the bar. "Do you want to use the restroom to clean that wound? It looks like it stopped bleeding. I'll get some ice from the waitress and a plastic bag. What do you want to drink? Anything but a mai tai?"

"Get me an Irish whiskey—Jameson, neat."

He raised his brows as she scooted out of the booth. Not what he'd expected, but she did look like an Irish lass with all that red hair. He kept his eyes on the dark recess where Ashlynn had disappeared—just in case someone followed her.

A waitress flicked a couple of napkins onto the table. "What can I get you?"

"Jameson, neat, and whatever light beer you have. Can you also get me a small plastic bag with ice?"

When the waitress quirked her eyebrow, he explained. "My friend bumped her head."

"Oh, is she okay?"

Denver tipped his head at Ashlynn making her way back to the table. "She's fine."

The waitress touched Ashlynn's arm. "I'll bring you that ice. Do you need anything else?"

"He ordered the whiskey?"

"He did."

"Thanks, I'm good." She slid into the booth across from Denver. "Now that my head is somewhat clear, you can start talking."

"Me?" He jabbed a finger into his chest. "Why don't you start by telling me what you were doing down here?"

"You obviously followed me or—" she narrowed her eyes "—whatever. You go first."

He held up his hands in surrender. "You got me. That's all there is to my story. I followed you here."

"From my house? You know where I live?" She winced and squeezed her eyes closed briefly.

"I'm a cop." He tapped the side of his head. "Is that wound giving you trouble?"

"Hurts, but I'm fine. You looked me up after you

yelled at me on the phone and then drove out to my house to…what? What did you hope to see?"

"Exactly what I did see." He splayed his hands on the table, touching his thumbs. "You, out on some fool's errand. Just like—"

The waitress appeared just in time to stop him from blurting out something insensitive. A serial killer had murdered her brother. He didn't need anyone to remind him what it felt like to lose a family member to murder.

He took a gulp of beer and toyed with the corner of a napkin. "You need to be careful."

Ashlynn took a tentative sip of her whiskey, and she still sniffed. "I know what happened to your father, and I know my brother covered his case in *LA Confidential*. I'm sorry."

His hand jerked and his beer frothed over the side. "Are you? Isn't that what you bloggers and podcasters do? Go after cold cases and find a killer—even if you're ruining people's lives?"

"I'm not sorry that he featured the case on his blog." She traced her fingertip along the rim of her glass. "I'm sorry you lost your father that way."

He clenched his teeth. Can't accuse this woman of soft-pedaling anything. He usually liked that, didn't he? He took a deep breath and another deep drink.

"I'm sorry about your brother, too. Losing a family member like that messes with your mind. I know it's no consolation to you, but at least you know who killed him. My father's case is still cold—despite your brother's efforts to implicate my mom."

"I had assumed it was the copycat who killed my brother after tempting him with being his contact with the LAPD, but it was really The Player, who'd objected to his copycat working with a true crime blogger. That was a shock." She hugged herself. "Gave me the creeps."

"And this doesn't?" He flicked a finger at the window that looked out over the beach. "Is someone giving you a heads-up about this case? How do you know it's not the killer of that girl in the trunk? How do you know he's not just toying with you? Hoping for some publicity?"

The skin around Ashlynn's luscious mouth turned white and she took another sip of whiskey—not so tentative this time. Her blue eyes watered, and she dabbed her nose with a napkin.

"Who said I was meeting anyone here about the case? I came out to Venice for a walk and a drink." She lifted her glass and the light caught the amber liquid as it sloshed up the sides. "Someone decided to conk me on the head and mug me."

He narrowed his eyes. "That's the way you want to play it? Clicks or whatever you're after are more important than finding the killer of this girl?"

She swirled her drink. "I don't have anything to give you, Detective—no evidence, no clues. I can't solve this case for you."

"You got that right." He smacked his hand on the table, rattling the glasses. "So don't even try."

AFTER ESCAPING DETECTIVE HOLT'S dark stare and smoldering anger, Ashlynn slumped in the seat of her car, wedging the bag of ice against her bump with the headrest. She'd been annoyed that Denver had followed her, but he'd probably saved her life. Had she thanked him for that?

She'd been too busy trying to dismiss his suspicions that her contact was just some weirdo looking for publicity...or worse. She couldn't deny that her tipster had just led her into a very dangerous situation.

She tapped her phone and navigated to the blog, which still displayed her wrap-up to the Reed Dufrain case. Her lips turned down at the number of blog visits. You were only as good as your current case—and now she had one. She still had to write and post her first entry for the girl in the lake, but at least she had a name for the case: "The Girl in the Lake."

Now, if only her person of contact wasn't trying to kill her.

She glanced at the empty message in-box and then sighed and started the car. Sean had made it look so easy. But then, he'd made everything look easy.

As she pulled out of her metered parking space, she glanced in her rearview mirror. She'd made it laughably easy for Denver to follow her here. She hadn't once checked for a tail on the way over.

And when had Detective Holt become Denver in her mind? Probably when she was mooning over his dark, liquid eyes across a couple of drinks. She still didn't know if he was married, but a surreptitious glance at his left hand said no, or maybe he didn't like rings.

Would he be chasing after witnesses on his off hours if he had a wife at home? If he were hers, she wouldn't let him out of her sight. She huffed through her nose. That's why her previous relationship had ended—too needy, too clingy. Who wouldn't be with parents like hers?

At least she had both of her parents. Denver's eyes had shimmered with loss when he'd talked about his father's murder—and her brother had added to his pain by suggesting Denver's mother had had something to do with the death.

She cruised up Venice Boulevard, back to her duplex,

her eyes darting between her rearview and side mirrors. It had occurred to her there might be others who could be following her; others who meant her more harm than Denver—not that he posed any threat to her. He just wanted his case back, and whatever info she could give him. She could use that to her advantage. He wasn't a detective in LAPD's Robbery-Homicide division—but oh, he wanted to be.

Ashlynn swung into the driveway next to Niles's car. As she exited her vehicle, she grabbed the bag of ice.

She fumbled with her key and, once inside, made a beeline for her kitchen. Dumping out the half-melted ice in the sink, she refilled the bag from her freezer. She downed an ibuprofen with some water and scooped up her laptop with one hand.

Let's see how her tipster wriggled out of this one. She brought up the blog messages and asked Angel what the hell had just happened.

Sipping her water, Ashlynn clicked back and forth between Sean's archives and the blog messages until a ding indicated a new message. She read the explanation from Angel, with a hand at her throat.

Angel insisted she'd been followed and hadn't wanted to put Ashlynn in danger, so she'd melted away without approaching her. They went back and forth, as Ashlynn described what had happened to her, including the code words the homeless woman had uttered—leaving out the part about Denver coming to her rescue.

The fact that the transient had known the phrase freaked out Angel. She couldn't understand how that had happened, unless someone had hacked into her computer. As soon as Angel expressed that thought, she signed off.

Ashlynn nestled her fingers in her hair to trace the small bump on her head. Could she trust Angel? If someone had followed Angel, or had hacked into her computer, that someone knew she had information about the woman in the trunk, and she'd already put herself in danger. Now Angel had put Ashlynn in danger, too. She and Angel had never made contact in Venice, so the person who'd attacked her must've recognized her. Ashlynn had told Angel what she'd be wearing. She must've been easy enough to spot. If Angel were telling the truth, she had been hacked. How could Ashlynn hope to get anything more from her?

Maybe Denver was right. She should give up the whole thing. Who was she kidding? She didn't have Sean's talent, his drive, his courage.

She shoved the computer from her lap and put the glass in the dishwasher. She'd hang on to the bag of ice and give it another ten minutes before she went to bed.

She toed off her running shoes in the bedroom and crossed the floor to the master bath in her stockinged feet. She pushed open the door and blinked in the bright light.

As if in slow motion, her gaze tracked from the lipstick cap on the floor, to the open tube on the vanity, to the letters in red scarlet slashed across her mirror.

Find Another Case.

Chapter Five

After receiving Ashlynn's frantic call about a warning on her mirror, Denver swore as he gunned it on the freeway. He should've followed her home. It's not like she would've known. He'd followed her to Venice tonight on a hunch, and she hadn't noticed him.

He'd had a hunch when she'd set off for her place tonight, too, but he hadn't followed through. After that attack in Venice, he'd known she'd put herself in a sticky situation—and now someone had broken into her house and scribbled a message on her bathroom mirror. Gutsy.

He careered down the off-ramp and ran a few red lights to reach her. When he rolled up her street, he saw the dome light in her car parked in the driveway. She'd been home for almost an hour before she'd discovered the message in the bathroom. The perpetrator would be long gone by now, but he could understand her reluctance to wait inside like a sitting duck.

As he pulled to the curb across the street, Ashlynn shot out of her car and waited on the sidewalk, practically hopping from foot to foot. She started talking before he was halfway across the road.

"Someone broke into my place. I don't know how they got in because as soon as I saw the message on my bathroom mirror, I fled. I don't know if they're still there, hiding."

"Good idea." His forehead creased. "Why didn't you call the police?"

"I did. I called you." She tipped her head at him, making him feel ten feet tall that he'd been her go-to guy.

He had an idea why she hadn't called 9-1-1. When he reached her, she spun around, leading the way to her house. He put a hand on her shoulder. "You can wait out here, if you want."

Her red hair flicked as she glanced over her shoulder. "I feel safe now that you're here."

Did she actually bat her eyelashes? And what was with all the compliments when, two hours ago, she couldn't even thank him for rescuing her from a street attack?

He kept a few paces behind her, not intentionally to watch her hips sway, but that was an added bonus. When she reached the door and unlocked it, he nudged her to the side and withdrew his weapon. "Let me go in first."

Her eyes widened for a second and she held up a canister of pepper spray. "I was going to use this, but that's much more effective."

He eased open the door and stepped into a small entryway, the kitchen branching off in one direction, a hallway in the other, and the living room spread before him.

"I'll check the windows." He tugged on the two snug windows in the kitchen, and studied the one in the living room. She'd locked up tight.

"Do you ever leave this unlocked?" As he walked up to the sliding-glass door that led to a small patio and grassy area, he noticed the drapes puckering inward. He whipped them aside. "Hello."

"What?" She'd been right on his heels and bumped into his back when he stopped.

With his fingertip in the air, he traced the square of glass cut from her door, right next to the handle and the lock. "He got in this way. I take it you don't have a lock on the track of the slider."

Clutching his arm, she bent forward to inspect the intruder's handiwork. "He used some sort of glasscutter to cut and lift that square out, and then reached in to unlock the door."

"Doesn't even have to be that fancy. Someone can just smash through the glass and unlock it if it's the only lock on the door." He jerked his thumb at what must be the wall she shared with her neighbors. "Probably didn't want to make that much noise."

"Damn." She kicked the metal door track with her bare foot. "I had a little screw-on device on here at one point."

"Weren't you in the living room before you discovered the note in the bathroom? You didn't notice the air coming in through this door?"

"The drapes were already closed, and I was sitting on the couch with my back to that door. Never even noticed it." She folded her arms and hunched her shoulders. "I guess I should've checked all the windows and doors myself after what happened tonight. I didn't think… I mean I didn't see anyone following me from Venice. Whoever this is, knows where I live."

"Unless he's followed you before…maybe home from the lake that day."

"So, now that we know how he gained entrance to my house—" she crooked her finger at him "—I'll show you the scary part."

As she led him through her bedroom, he skirted the king-size bed with one corner of the blue floral bedspread turned down, and his gaze flicked toward a pile of clothes on a chair, a lacy bra dangling off the arm.

She pushed open the bathroom door with a flourish. "He used my lipstick and didn't bother to put it away when he was finished. I actually noticed the lipstick before the words on my mirror."

The red warning leaped out at him immediately—block letters, no misspellings, intentional or otherwise, and no regard for Ashlynn's lipstick.

"I hope that wasn't your favorite color." He nudged the cap on the floor with the toe of his shoe. "Do you have a plastic bag?"

She loosened her grip on the doorjamb and ran a hand through her wavy hair that curled at the ends. "You mean like to bag this up as evidence?"

"I doubt we'll find any prints but yours, but it's worth a try." He met her eyes in the mirror. Two chips of ice stared back.

"I'm not reporting this." She folded her arms at her chest, crossing one leg over the other. She looked like a pretzel.

"You sort of did report it." He spread out his arms. "As you pointed out earlier, I am a cop."

Her gaze dropped to his backside, and he felt a coiling response in his belly. "You're not wearing your cop clothes and, besides, you're LAPD. The last time I looked out my window, I lived in Culver City. We have our own police force."

He turned to face her. "We work with Culver City all the time. I'm sure they'd be more than happy to help out with a homicide in LA."

"Who said anything about a homicide in LA?" She gave him a bug-eyed stare and an exaggerated shrug, like a cartoon character. "I got scared because someone broke into my place and scrawled a message on my bathroom mirror. I did what any girl would do who had the phone number of a hunky cop at her fingertips—called him."

She thought he was hunky? Did women even say hunky anymore? He stiffened his back and just managed to avoid puffing out his chest. "You're telling me you called me so you could check out my ass?"

"I was not…" Her cheeks matched her hair, and she knew it. She took a deep breath. "I called you because your number was handy and I was scared…and you already saved me once tonight."

He rubbed the back of his neck. "Let's start over. You are planning to feature this case on *LA Confidential*, and someone is already warning you off. I checked the blog, and you haven't posted anything about this case. How did your intruder know to warn you off? I think we can agree that the attack in Venice was another warning. How did that person know you were going to be down on Washington tonight?"

She drummed her fingers against the door. "Let's get out of the bathroom. Coffee? Water? Beer?"

"Did this turn into a social call?"

"Friendly business." She backed away from the bathroom. "I'll even get the baggie for the lipstick."

He had no choice but to follow her. Hell, even if he had a choice, he'd follow her.

She gestured toward the couch. "Have a seat, or help yourself to something to drink first. I'll bag the lipstick and cap, and don't worry, I won't touch either one."

She rummaged in a kitchen drawer and hustled back to the bedroom, a small plastic bag stuck to her fingertips.

Denver took her place in the kitchen and opened the fridge. He grabbed a soda from the top shelf. He could use a little caffeine right now but couldn't face coffee.

He didn't want to be too wired for this friendly business meeting, but he needed to be on his toes.

Ashlynn sashayed back into the living room, swinging the baggie with the lipstick tube and cap. "Here you go. Just don't do anything official with it because I'm not reporting this break-in."

Cocking his head, Denver asked, "Why not?"

"What happens in the blogging world, stays in the blogging world. I don't want any official record of what I'm up to." She pretended to turn a key at her lips.

He supposed this was what he'd signed up for when he agreed to work with her. He circled his finger in the air. "Did you ever check to see if anything was missing?"

"Just made sure my laptop was still here—that's it. I don't have any expensive jewelry stashed away, no bundles of cash, no fancy electronic devices, and no guns—yet."

Denver rolled his eyes. "God, help us. I got a soda for myself. Did you want one?"

"I'm good." She dropped the baggie on the coffee table next to where he was perching on the arm of the couch. "What can you do with that…unofficially?"

"I can get someone to run prints…unofficially." He answered her raised eyebrows. "I know people."

"I'll bet you do." She took the other end of the sofa, bracing her back against the arm and stretching out her long legs toward him.

He glanced at her toes wiggling in her socks and slid down the arm so that he landed on a cushion of the couch, her feet inches from his lap. "What business could we possibly have together?"

She pulled her knees to her chest, wrapping one arm around them. "I need a case…and you need a case. This could be it for both of us."

His nostrils flared as some emotion thumped in his chest. Anger? Shame? Excitement? He couldn't even ID it, himself.

He ran his hands across his face, his day-old beard scratching his palms. "You're suggesting we help each other—I keep you apprised of the investigation and you give me what you're getting from the readers of your blog."

She nodded, blue eyes sparkling. Anyone looking in at her might think they were discussing wedding plans instead of murder.

He held up one finger and growled more fiercely than he'd intended. "I see one problem with that."

She flashed him her pearly whites. "Only one?"

"One major problem." He cleared his throat and took a sip of soda, the bubbles rushing to his nose. "The information I'd be giving you would be accurate. The stuff you'd be passing off to me…garbage."

She tipped her feet back on her heels and tapped them together. "Did I find garbage in Lake Kawayu? No. I found a car with a body in the trunk. Would you have found that body without me? Doubt it."

"Which brings us back to the beginning." He jabbed his finger into the couch at the edge of her toes, where the gesture lost all effectiveness as his finger sank into the cushion. "How did you know where to find the car? Why did you go to Venice tonight?"

"If I tell you, can you keep it to yourself? It's all garbage, anyway, right? Lunatics out in cyber land who want to play detective. If word gets around in law enforcement circles that I'm cooperating with a cop, I might not get any more information. If we keep this hush-hush between us, I might still get the info, I can feed it to you and you only, you can give me a little inside story and—" she clapped her hands "—I've got a blog worth reading and you're the hotshot detective who solved the case. That's what we both want, isn't it? Justice for that woman in the trunk?"

Denver circled his fingers around the can of soda and squeezed in one side of the aluminum. How pathetic and obvious he must've come across. Playing at being a homicide detective without really being a homicide detective. Ashlynn had spotted his desperation a mile off, must've smelled it coming from him in waves.

What did he have to lose?

He thrust out his hand. "Justice for the girl in the trunk."

A LITTLE THRILL fluttered through her veins as she clasped Denver's warm, strong hand. "It's a deal, Detective."

"If we're going to be working with each other, you can start calling me Denver." He squeezed her hand before releasing it.

She settled back against the arm of the couch, failing to mention she'd already been calling him Denver in her head. "I'll try."

His eyebrows knitted. "Start now. How did you know that car was going to be in the lake with a body inside?"

He wanted to get right down to business. She took a deep breath. "I got a tip on my blog."

"I figured that. How?" He hunched forward, elbows on knees. "Someone posted on the blog for everyone else to see?"

"I—Sean had a private message feature on the blog. People can hit the message icon and contact me directly, without anyone else seeing it."

He rubbed his knuckles against his stubble. "More

private than emailing you because the person can mask his or her email address."

"Exactly. Sean thought that method would encourage more tips—and it has."

Nodding toward the laptop on the table, he asked, "Can you show me the message?"

"Yes." She swung her legs off the couch and flipped open her computer. She accessed the blog, clicked on her private messages, and scrolled back to her first contact with Angel.

She jabbed her finger at the screen. "That's the first time she contacted me."

"'She'?" He pulled the computer into his lap, forcing her to scoot closer to him if she wanted to see what he was reading.

"She has since identified herself as Angel."

"Angel. *Angel.*" He pronounced the name the second time in Spanish. "Could be a Latino dude."

"Could be, but I have a feeling this is a woman."

He squinted at the screen. "She tipped you off to a car in Lake Kawayu and indicated you'd find a body in it, but she didn't mention the trunk."

"If she didn't know the body was in the trunk, that rules out Angel as an eyewitness or accomplice, right?"

The corner of Denver's mouth twitched, and she braced herself for sarcasm.

"Maybe, unless Angel saw this at night, knew there was a body somehow, but didn't know where the perpetrator had left it."

No sarcasm detected.

"Yeah, I see how that could happen. Same for an accomplice. She could've left the woman in the car with the killer at the lake and not watched or known what he'd done with the body."

He flicked his finger at the message. "Not much here. You got the message and hightailed it to the lake the next day to look for the car."

"That's how this works. True crime bloggers take a lot on faith. We're not like cops—we don't have to verify, we don't have any rules."

"And that's what gets you in trouble." He brushed his thumb against the mouse. "Angel must've sent you something else to send you on your way to Venice tonight."

She waved her hand in the air. "Keep scrolling. She saw the news and knew I had acted on her tip. She wanted to meet me in person to give me more information. I was supposed to walk along Washington and wait for someone to approach me with a code phrase. That's why I followed the homeless woman—she had the code phrase."

Denver whistled. "Unless Angel is the culprit, somebody learned that code to preempt your meeting."

"I don't think Angel is playing me. Read on. She contacted me after the meeting went south. She thinks someone might be hacking into her computer, and that's how he knew our code phrase."

"That's not good." Denver tapped the keyboard to view the rest of the messages. "Someone reading this knows that Angel tipped you off. Angel put a target on your back...or two targets. Looks like they double-teamed you tonight. One person went to Venice to disrupt the meeting and, while they knew you were out, someone else came here to scribble a warning on your mirror—just in case getting whacked on the head didn't do the trick."

"It didn't." She rubbed the knot on the back of her head.

"Sounds like Angel isn't going to contact you via computer anymore, but that doesn't matter. We have a guy at the station who can track this IP address. We can talk to Angel in person."

"Wait a minute." She pulled the computer from his lap to hers and snapped it shut. "That's not our deal."

"Our deal—" he crunched his soda can in one hand "—is to find the killer of some poor woman stuffed in the trunk of a car."

"My contact is going to help us do it—on her own terms. If she'd wanted to call the cops, she would've done so. If she suspects I'm working with the LAPD, that'll be the end of the flow of information."

"That might be over now."

Denver's cell phone rang and he held up one finger.

"Holt." His dark eyes widened and his fingers tightened on the phone. "Well, isn't that something? I'll pay them a visit first thing tomorrow morning."

The call ended with nothing more than a few grunts on Denver's side. A crease formed between his eyebrows as he tapped the phone against his chin.

The call had something to do with the case...and it was big. She cleared her throat. "I gave you what I had. It's your turn now."

He smacked the phone against his palm, and she jumped. "That car you found in the lake?"

"Yeah?" She twisted her fingers into messy knots.

"It's part of a fleet that belongs to the Campaign to Re-Elect Mayor Wexler."

Chapter Six

The following day, Denver dipped into the parking structure beneath the sleek glass-and-steel structure that housed the offices for the Campaign to Re-Elect Mayor Wexler. Or, as Wexler's staff liked to call it, CREW.

Marino had thrown this case his way, as the detective was busy wrapping up another homicide. Denver was flying solo on this interview, but he had the weight of Chief Sterling behind him. The chief had already given the mayor's office a heads-up- –hell, the two men were golfing buddies. As long as their tee time didn't interfere with his investigation, he'd use all the help the chief offered.

Twisting around, Denver grabbed his jacket from the back seat. He'd opted for his most expensive suit for this interview, courtesy of Cool Breeze himself, Detective Billy Crouch. Billy had hooked him up with his personal tailor, and Denver needed as much confidence as he could muster to go charging into the mayor's campaign headquarters asking questions about a dead body in the trunk of one of the campaign's official cars.

He stepped into the elevator, smoothing the lapels of his jacket and using the same motion on the sides of his hair. Either the chief trusted him with this case, or Sterling knew he could manipulate the sap. But this sap had a secret weapon—a redheaded blogger with a burning desire to prove herself.

He'd read some of the stories Ashlynn had written for that magazine she'd worked for, and he had no clue why she was so hell-bent on picking up where her brother had left off. Her brother had a reputation of being anti-police, and the department hadn't been a big fan. Detective Jake McAllister had only agreed to work with Sean Hughes because the guy had opened a channel of communication with one of The Player's copycats. But in the end, Hughes had gotten burned by that fire when The Player himself had killed him for interference.

He hoped like hell Ashlynn wasn't traveling down the same path as her brother. He hoped like hell he wasn't leading her down that path.

The elevator dinged on the ninth floor of the building, and Denver gave his tie a tug and exited onto a slick tiled floor. He swiveled his head in search of a reception desk or receptionist, but the floorplan stretched into a large, light open space with cubbies here and there, exercise balls in front of desks in lieu of chairs and a few glass-walled offices hugging the perimeter of the room.

As his gaze tracked among the busy worker bees, he cleared his throat. Not one of them looked up or even broke stride. If nobody was going to play nice, he'd be as intrusive as possible.

Making a beeline for one of those offices, he squared his shoulders and plunged into the melee, skirting desks and charging past the exercise balls, sending them skittering sideways. That earned him a few quick glances and openmouthed stares.

Out of the corner of his eye, he saw a man scurrying toward him, a laptop clutched to his chest. "Excuse me. Excuse me, Detective Holt?"

Ah, so they *were* expecting him. Denver halted in midstride and swung around on the guy, causing him to stumble to a stop. A second minion careened through the desks to intercept them, her oversized glasses giving her a startled, bug-eyed look—or maybe she was startled.

Denver stuck out his hand to the man with the laptop. "Detective Denver Holt. You must be Christian Bushnell."

Bushnell juggled the laptop in his arms and shook Denver's hand, his mouth twisting up at the corner as Denver went in for the hard squeeze. "Nice to meet you, Detective Holt. This is my coworker, Amalia Fernandez."

Denver finally released Bushnell's hand and turned to Amalia, who was much better at navigating the handshake and the laptop, which was tucked under her left arm.

Did these people walk around with laptops and tablets attached to their bodies?

"Good morning, Detective Holt. I'm the mayor's campaign director and Christian is my assistant." She sure wanted to set the record straight. She swept an arm to the side. "We'll be talking in one of the offices for privacy."

"Looks like that's in short supply here."

Amalia drew back her shoulders and flicked her neat dark ponytail. "Mayor Wexler prides himself on transparency."

Always campaigning, this bunch. Must be exhausting. Denver gave a tight smile. "That's what I'm counting on."

He followed the two of them to an office with glass walls that looked out onto the controlled chaos of the rest of the room. If the Northwest Division had interview rooms like these, the cops wouldn't garner half the confessions they got.

He pulled out the chair Amalia indicated with a nod

of her head and tried to perch on the edge. The slant and cushioning of the seat made that difficult. The cops would have even more trouble getting confessions out of anyone sitting in these chairs.

He grabbed the edge of the table to keep from sliding back into the black leather, and plucked a notebook from the front pocket of his shirt. He smacked it on the table, and Amalia and Christian both flinched.

Not as calm and collected as they appeared.

"You both know why I'm here. A body was found in the trunk of a car that belongs to this office, and the car was sitting at the bottom of Lake Kawayu."

Christian shook his head. "I had no idea that lake was so deep."

Amalia shot him a look and may have even kicked him under the table because Christian clamped his mouth shut and reddened up to his eyeballs.

"I—I mean, we were shocked when we found out."

"We heard the news, Detective Holt." Amalia folded her hands in her lap. "We, and that includes the mayor, were so distressed. What can we do to help? Mayor Wexler has instructed us to cooperate fully, of course, and has assured his good friend, Chief Sterling, that we're here to help."

"That's good to know." Denver held his pen poised above a clean sheet on his notepad. "Why did you tamper with the license plate and VIN on that car?"

Christian swallowed a big lump in his throat and Amalia's smile froze on her face. "Excuse me. We don't tamper with license plates or destroy the VINs on our cars, and didn't do so to that car. Whoever stole the car from our garage must've done that."

"That car was stolen?"

"Of course." Amalia spread her hands on the table. "This is LA, Detective, the car theft capital of the world."

Denver opened his eyes wide. "Even with Mayor Wexler at the helm?"

The smile stayed plastered on Amalia's lipsticked mouth, but had dropped completely from her eyes. "One of the many issues he's going to address in his second term."

Hunching forward, Denver placed the tip of his pen on the paper in front of him. "When did you report the car stolen?"

"We didn't." Amalia pursed her lips and jutted her chin out aggressively.

He knew they hadn't reported it stolen, and she knew he knew. He let his pen drop to the table, and Christian's reaction would've made you think he'd fired a shot instead of dropped a pen.

Denver screwed up his face. "Oh, I'm sorry. I misunderstood. I thought you said the car had been stolen from your lot."

Crossing her arms, Amalia said, "You didn't misunderstand, Detective Holt. You knew we hadn't reported it stolen, or you would've already had that report in your hand. We have a lot of cars in our fleet here at CREW. We don't always keep track of them as well as we should. We didn't notice this car was gone, but I can assure you, somebody stole that car out of our garage."

"You might've just solved the crime, Ms. Fernandez. You have cameras at the garage?" He scribbled some gibberish in his notebook. They were both too far away to read it anyway.

"We do have cameras, and I'm a step ahead of you, Detective. I've already ordered the security footage. Unfortunately, we keep it for seven days only, so if the car was stolen before that…" Amalia shrugged her shoulders.

Denver mumbled under his breath. "That's convenient."

"Excuse me?" Amalia narrowed her eyes.

"I said, how inconvenient, but we'll work with what we have." He rapped on the desk just because he liked seeing Christian jump. "I'm going to need a list of everyone who works on the campaign."

"What?" Christian had finally found his voice, and it had a decided squeak that had been missing before. "We have hundreds of people working on CREW."

"I hope you can print out all those names from a database. That'll make it easy." Denver snapped his fingers. "I'll do you one better. Get me the list of people who worked on the campaign *and* had access to the fleet of vehicles. I'll take that breakdown first, and then you can supply the names of all the campaign workers."

Amalia drummed a sharp set of talons on the table. "Waste of time, Detective Holt. I already told you the car was stolen."

She'd gone too far even for Christian, who shot her a worried look from beneath a creased brow.

Denver clapped a hand over his heart. "Thanks for your concern and, uh, expertise, Ms. Fernandez, but you let me worry about what's a waste of time and what's not." He picked up his pen again. "What do staffers use the cars for?"

To make up for Amalia's misstep, Christian launched in helpfully. "All sorts of things—delivering items to campaign stops, doing door-to-doors, providing transportation for the mayor's guests for speeches and events, e-even picking up lunch for the CREW."

"Do all these perks come from the city budget?"

Christian opened his mouth but Amalia cut him off with a slicing motion. "Absolutely not. That would be a campaign violation. The cars, the lunches, everything you see here is funded by the Campaign to Re-Elect Mayor Wexler."

Denver held up his hands in surrender. "Hey, sounds good to me. I'm here to investigate a homicide, not the mayor's finances."

Sitting perpendicular to the office door, Denver spotted a man in a cap with the parking service logo on the front approaching the office.

Amalia jumped up before the guy finished knocking. "Thank you, Gerardo."

She took something from his hand and started to close the door, but Denver pushed back his chair and lunged forward, putting his foot against the doorjamb. "Gerardo, can I ask you a couple of questions? I'm Detective Holt with the LAPD."

Gerardo slid a glance to Amalia before saying, "Yes, sir."

Denver pointed to the thumb drive swinging from a ribbon wrapped around Amalia's index finger. "That contains the footage from the garage for the past seven days?"

"Yes, it does. It covers both exits, so it catches any cars that left the parking garage by either exit in the last week."

"No way to get footage from more than seven days ago."

"I'm afraid not, Detective. It's taped over."

Denver felt in his front pocket and pulled out a card. He extended it to Gerardo. "Call me if you remember anything about the cars in Mayor Wexler's fleet, or anything unusual in the garage the past few weeks."

"I'll do that." Gerardo murmured something in Spanish to Amalia, and she gave a quick shake of her head.

Denver didn't know if he would've understood it even if he spoke fluent Spanish—which he didn't.

When Amalia closed the door after Gerardo, she dangled the thumb drive in front of Denver. "Here you go, Detective. I thought it would be easier for you to review the footage at the station. If you have any questions about it, you can call Gerardo."

He pocketed the thumb drive. "Thanks, Ms. Fernandez. Did, uh, Gerardo have something to add at the end there?"

She blinked her eyes, rapidly. "He just asked if he could use the restroom here on his way out."

"Oh, you didn't let him?"

She opened her mouth once and snapped it closed.

"I mean, you shook your head like no."

"We don't allow anyone but staffers to use the restrooms on this floor." She gave him a tight smile. "I think Gerardo understood. Now, is there anything else, Detective Holt?"

"One more thing." He held up a finger. "Do either of you know the name Tiana Fuller?"

Denver shifted his gaze to Christian, the weak link. The boy didn't disappoint. Christian's Adam's apple bobbed as if he'd just swallowed a golf ball.

Amalia didn't give Christian the chance to step in it, though. "Never heard that name before. Is she the…victim? A suspect?"

"Can't say right now." He tipped his head toward Christian. "You?"

"Wh-what?" The color rushed from Christian's throat to his cheeks. He'd never make it as a poker player.

"Have you ever heard the name Tiana Fuller or know who she is?"

Christian rolled his eyes to the ceiling. If he'd had a thinking cap, he'd have slapped it on his head. "No. No, I haven't."

"That's all I have—for now." He tapped his finger next to the card Amalia had left on the desk. "Give me a call if you think of anything else. I'll review the footage from the garage while waiting for you to send over the list of campaign workers. I expect that today, right?"

"Of course. I'll have Christian get right on that for you. Shouldn't take long." Amalia opened the door. "Mayor Wexler is anxious to clear this up, and his office will be sending condolences to the family—once we know the identity of the victim. Will you let us know, Detective Holt, or do we find out from the TV news like everyone else?"

"I'll let you know as soon as we get an ID— just in case."

"In case?" She narrowed her dark eyes.

"In case she's connected to the campaign…or Mayor Wexler."

Chapter Seven

After he'd mentioned Tiana's name in connection to Mayor Wexler, Amalia escorted him out of the CREW office so fast he could hear the wind whistling past his ears. When he reached his car, he shrugged out of his jacket and smoothed it out carefully in the back seat.

He'd like to get Christian alone, but Amalia had probably already schooled him in the proper responses to this investigation—we know nothing, the mayor knows nothing.

Denver checked his phone and his heart pounded as he listened to a voice mail from Captain Fields. Mrs. Edmunds had delivered her daughter's DNA to the station, and if he hurried, he might be back in time to learn whether or not Tiana Fuller was their victim.

He positioned his phone on the console for the Bluetooth and tamped down the disappointment he felt over the absence of a message from Ashlynn. Maybe she didn't want to step on his toes and expected him to take the lead. They had a business relationship, not a romantic one.

He tapped in her number and her phone rang through the speakers. She answered after the second ring, out of breath, as if she'd just jogged a mile or two.

Before he could even get through the niceties, she asked, "Did you read the blog post?"

"I did. It was good. You're a good writer."

She coughed. "Does that mean it grabbed you by the throat and left you wanting more?"

She left him wanting more.

He cranked up the AC. "Yeah, it was like a story, a mystery. Have you gotten any more tips? Hear from Angel?"

"I've gotten tons of public comments, and a few weird private ones that I'm still sorting through." She paused, taking a sip of something. "Do you have anything for me yet? Has she been ID'd?"

"Not yet. We're working on it." Denver glanced in his rearview and accelerated onto the freeway. "Weird tips? Do you feel safe?"

"Yeah. I had a locksmith come out and install a proper lock on the sliding door and got the glass replaced. I'm submitting everything to my insurance company. I mean renter's insurance has to cover something, right?"

At her breezy tone, he loosened his grip on the steering wheel. He hadn't cared about anyone's safety for a long time. He'd made sure he never cared about anyone enough to worry about them. After his father's murder, he'd driven himself, and everyone around him, crazy with his hovering and double-checking. Had given himself an ulcer, too—at least, that's what the department-mandated shrink, Kyra Chase, had told him.

He licked his lips. "Wouldn't hurt to get a security system, maybe a camera. Lots of people have them these days."

"I'll look into it. If that lipstick message and the assault at Venice Beach meant to warn me off, I'm not heeding it. Who knows what this person will try next?"

Denver's palms broke out in a sweat and he wiped them, one by one, on his slacks.

He needed to back off. If she wanted to put herself in danger, that was her business. He had a job protecting people—strangers. Mom had a new husband, and his sister had married a guy with hundreds of relatives practically living on top of them. He'd relinquished the reins of their protection to others, and he had no intention of picking up another set. "Okay, keep me posted, and let me know if you hear from Angel again. I'll tell you what I can."

He ended the call abruptly and sped back to the station.

When he got there, he bypassed his new desk in Robbery-Homicide and went straight to the lab. The remodel of the Northeast Division had included a state-of-the-art lab where the techs could do DNA matching.

He sidled up next to Lori Del Valle, one of the fingerprint techs. "DNA match done yet?"

"No, it isn't." She shoved at his arm. "Watching the techs isn't going to make it go any faster, but nobody has located Tiana Fuller yet."

He sucked in his lower lip. "It's not looking too good for Tiana. Her mother tentatively identified the top our victim was wearing as Tiana's."

"We know you're lead on this case, Denver. We're going to tell you first." The nudge at his arm turned into a pat.

"Too eager, huh?"

"Understandable." She tossed him a baggie. "But, hey, I processed the tube of lipstick and there are no prints at all—none. That means it was probably wiped."

"I figured." He put his finger to his lips. "Just between us, right?"

"Discretion is my middle name."

"Don't wanna get you in trouble again." He meandered

back to the Robbery-Homicide room with a little less spring in his step and dropped his bag next to his desk.

Detective Falco nodded as she walked past him. "How'd it go at the mayor's re-election office?"

"As you'd expect—closemouthed groupies doing their best to protect their guy."

"You know the chief's going to want you to back off as soon as the CREW is cleared of any association with this woman."

"I'm aware, and I plan to back off when no more arrows point in that direction."

"Good answer."

When she dove to answer a phone, Denver inserted the thumb drive from the garage into his computer. Detective Falco obviously didn't envy him this assignment. The chief could've assigned this to the golden boys—McAllister and Crouch—but there's no way he could control those two. Could the chief control him? Denver could think of a few ways Sterling might try.

He queued up the footage to the very first minute that was available and hunched forward to watch the flickering images on his monitor. He had the gate to Santa Monica Boulevard on the top of his screen, and the one to the side street on the bottom. Seemed like most of the CREW's cars used the side street. The sedans all looked the same, and he kept his eyes on the license plates. Although the plates on the car in the lake had been swapped, he knew the real plate number from the VIN and doubted someone had spent time in the garage removing the plates before driving it out of the garage. And if someone had done that? He'd locate the car without the plates.

When he made it through day one without a hit, he snatched a bag of chips from his desk drawer and popped it open. He rubbed his eyes, and then stuffed several chips in his mouth, crunching as he watched the first car of the next day roll under the parking arm.

He jumped when someone clamped his shoulder. "Boy does not live by chips alone. That footage isn't going anywhere while you get some lunch."

Denver twisted his head around, glancing at Billy's smiling face. Easy for him to say. "One day down, six to go."

"My guess?" Billy circled his finger in the air over the monitor. "You're not going to see that car on camera. The person who took it had to know that it was going to be ID'd sooner or later, even without the correct plates, registration and a scratched-up VIN. He either knew about the footage being taped over every week, or he did something to the cameras."

Denver clicked the mouse to stop the footage and licked salt from his lips. "Tell me something, Cool Breeze. How come you and McAllister aren't on this case? A murder of a young woman, found in a public place, in a car belonging to the Campaign to Re-Elect Mayor Wexler? Sounds right up the alley of the dynamic duo."

Billy brushed his knuckles down his tie, as if worried some of the salt from Denver's chips had attached themselves to the silk. "If you don't know the answer to that, my man, you're probably never going to make permanent detective in Robbery-Homicide."

Denver nodded. The chief couldn't pressure J-Mac and Crouch like he could the new guy. Denver crumpled a napkin in his left hand. "Any advice?"

"Just do your job, Rocky."

"Rocky?" Denver lifted an eyebrow. Like all squads in the LAPD, Robbery-Homicide was notorious for assigning nicknames to the detectives.

"You know—Denver? Rocky Mountain High?"

Denver groaned and shot the balled-up napkin at the sharp crease in Billy's impeccable slacks.

He spent the next two hours speeding through the remaining days, too. As he watched the last car on the footage roll beneath the parking arm, he slumped in his chair. Billy had nailed it. The killer hadn't made this easy. He'd either taken the car in advance, without reporting it, or he'd tampered with the camera or footage. Denver had been watching the counter on the footage and hadn't noticed anything hinky.

Someone had taken the car in advance of the murder—either planning the murder or planning something else he or she hadn't wanted tracked. Or maybe it was dumb luck. Someone took the car without planning anything at all.

Denver pinched the bridge of his nose as his stomach rumbled. A bag of potato chips didn't cut it for lunch.

His desk phone rang and he grabbed it. "Holt."

Lance from the lab said, "We have the DNA match to Tiana Fuller. She is the victim in the trunk of the car."

"Thanks, Lance." Denver's eye twitched.

The ID of a victim always cut both ways. Knowing the victim allowed the investigation to progress in a valuable way, but it also meant ripping apart another family. He'd personally notify Mrs. Edmunds. In most of the homicide investigations he'd worked, he'd become the go-to guy for family notifications, given his own background.

He almost felt it his duty to take on the notifications to protect the other detectives from sinking into the grief pit with the families. He'd already visited that pit, had already been scarred by it.

Taking a deep breath, he swiveled his chair toward the wall and stared at a spot near the ceiling. Then he called Mrs. Edmunds.

She answered after the first ring. She'd been waiting for his call. "Hello? Detective Holt?"

"It is, Mrs. Edmonds. We identified the victim in the trunk of the submerged car as your daughter, Tiana. There is no doubt. The DNA matches the sample you submitted." He held his breath.

Other cops might dance around, might try to couch the news in soft, pretty words. The families of victims didn't want or need that.

Mrs. Edmonds let out a sob. "I knew it."

His chest tightened, and he loosened his collar. "I'm sorry for your loss. I'm going to need to talk to you and your husband. Get a list of Tiana's friends, boyfriends, roommates—but not now. Tomorrow okay?"

She sniffled. "Tomorrow is fine, Detective."

She ended the call before he could respond, but he really had no response. There were no words, and sometimes words made it all worse.

He studied the spot on the wall and flicked the pad of his thumb beneath his eye. Then he spun his chair back to his computer. The garage footage had held his attention all afternoon, although from the corner of his eye he could see emails popping up every so often at the bottom of his screen. Now, he scanned through them, the last of the bunch from Lance with the DNA report, and cursed under his breath.

Christian at the CREW had failed to send the database of campaign workers. As he grabbed his jacket, he tapped Christian's number on his phone. He left the guy a not-so-civil voice mail reminding him what he owed him.

After he left the message, he listened to one from Ashlynn on his way out of the station, inviting him for dinner tonight. Probably wanted to pick his brain some more, find out if he'd learned the identity of the victim.

He'd promised to play ball with her and, as long as Tiana's family knew first, he didn't have a problem releasing Tiana's name to Ashlynn. Her identity would be all over the news and social media by tomorrow morning anyway.

And his rumbling stomach told him the invitation couldn't have come at a better time. He texted her Tiana's name and accepted the invite to dinner, asking if she wanted him to bring anything. Picked brain or no, he never went to anyone's house empty-handed.

A half hour later, as the freeway spit him out onto one of the boulevards bordering Culver City, he stooped over his steering wheel, looking for a liquor store. Ashlynn had promised stir-fried beef and veggies, so he picked up a Pinot Grigio. He also grabbed a bag of trail mix just in case he had to wait for dinner.

He pulled up to the curb across the street from her duplex, opened his door and dusted the salt from the peanuts from his hands and slacks. He still had on his good suit and didn't want to spoil the effect. To top it off, he reached for his jacket in the back seat and slid his arms into the sleeves. Might as well maintain the appearance of a business meeting—with stir-fry.

He knocked on her door, and he heard a chain slide and a dead bolt click. When she opened it, he said, "I'm glad to hear you're taking your security seriously."

She stepped back to let him over the threshold. "When the guy from the lock and key shop came out to install the contraption on the sliding door, I asked him to install a new dead bolt and a chain—just in case."

He sniffed the air and while the smell of ginger didn't do anything for him, he knew it heralded more savory tastes. He held up the bottle in the bag. "Pinot Grigio?"

"Sounds good." She took the bag from him and peeked inside. "Is it cold by any chance?"

"No, sorry. The liquor store had only the cheap stuff refrigerated."

"That's okay. I'll stick it in the freezer and it should at least be chilled by the time we eat."

He nodded, grateful for the trail mix rattling around in his empty stomach. "Have you already released the news about Tiana Fuller on your blog?"

"I have, thanks." She sidestepped into the kitchen and ducked into the refrigerator. "Terrible news for her family."

He clasped the back of his neck. "Yeah, it was."

Waving a hand over his clothes, she said, "Straight from work. I'll take your jacket, and you can lose the tie. You can even lose the shoes, if you like."

"I can just hang it over a chair." He shrugged out of the jacket and made a move toward a kitchen chair pulled up to the small table, already set for two.

She snatched it from him and held it up, giving it the once-over. "It looks expensive. I used to write about fashion. I know, it's hard to believe."

"It's my one really good suit." His gaze swept across her skinny jeans that hit right above her ankles, a pair of gleaming white tennis shoes and light green top that dipped into a V on her chest. She'd swept her red hair into a half up, half down ponytail. She looked neat and crisp, and good enough to eat.

He swallowed. Man, he really was hungry.

She rested her cheek against the material of his jacket and ran one hand down the sleeve. The gesture twisted his stomach into knots. He had a hunger for more than just food.

"It's nice. I'll hang it up." She crossed back over to the hallway and opened a door to the closet. "Don't forget it."

"Do you need some help?" He jerked his thumb at the wok on the counter, next to a cutting board filled with a colorful array of veggies.

She snapped her fingers. "You can warm up the lumpia and eat it."

"Lumpia?" His mouth instantly watered.

"I know I'm sort of crossing cultures here, but my friend Mercy made the lumpia and dropped some off today. It's in the fridge and just needs some heat. Microwave will do."

He opened the fridge and slid a plastic container from the shelf. He popped the lid. "Homemade and everything, huh? My buddy's mom was from the Philippines and always whipped up homemade lumpia when I went to his house. My favorite deep-fried snack. Looked just like this."

She pointed to the microwave. "Not too long. Maybe a minute. You can start eating that while I'm cooking this."

As he put the container in the microwave, Ashlynn peeled the foil from a bowl of beef strips, marinating in some sauce that made his eyes sting. "You were planning this dinner for a while?"

She cranked up the heat under the wok, and her cheeks sported two red spots. "I was planning to cook this for myself tonight after Mercy dropped off the lumpia. Some of us single people still eat more than takeout and pizza."

"We do?" The microwave beeped and he punched the button with his knuckle to open the door. "I know every pizza delivery place within a five-mile radius of my place in the Marina."

"You live in Marina del Rey? Apartment?"

"Condo."

"Must be nice." She jumped back as the meat sizzled and popped in the pan. "I figured you might live closer to the police station up north."

He'd bought the condo with the proceeds from his dad's rental property in Oregon. Dad had left that property to him and his sister, with his mom's blessing.

"I, uh—" he carefully removed the container from the microwave with the tips of his fingers and dropped it on the counter "—used to work Pacific Division. Transferred to Northeast a few years ago for Vice. The commute's not that bad."

"I have chopsticks on the table, and Mercy included some spicy red chili sauce for dipping. Why don't you dig in while I finish this?" She prodded the vegetables in the wok and they hissed back at her.

She didn't have to tell him twice. He backed up to the table, grabbed a pair of chopsticks and fished the red sauce from the fridge. He maneuvered a piece of lumpia between his chopsticks and dipped it into the sauce. He closed his eyes while he chewed.

Ashlynn laughed and nudged him with her elbow. "That good, huh?"

"It would be nirvana even if I weren't starving."

"I knew it. You had that rangy, feral look about you." She puffed a lock of hair from her face. "You wanna give me one of those? I'm a little busy here."

He plucked up another lumpia, dunked it in the sauce, and held it out toward her puckered lips, almost as red as the sauce. She took the snack with her teeth and sucked it into her mouth.

Rolling her eyes at the ceiling, she said, "Yummy."

He devoured two more while she finished the stir-fry and the rice cooker clicked off.

Ashlynn grabbed two plates, piled both high with

sticky white rice, and ladled the beef and veggies on top. "There's more, if you want seconds."

"I probably will." He brought the wine and the lumpia to the table while she set down the plates.

She collapsed in a chair and then hopped up again. "A corkscrew would be nice—I mean, since you said it wasn't the cheap stuff. The bottle probably doesn't have a screw top."

"It does not." He took the corkscrew from her and did the honors. "Only slightly chilled."

She held the glass to her lips and the reflection of the wine rippled in her eyes as she gazed at him over the edge. "You seem more...human tonight."

He took a swig of the wine and felt the warmth flow through his veins. "I had to tell Mrs. Edmonds today that we'd ID'd Tiana as the body in the vehicle. That kind of conversation tends to awaken your humanity, no matter how far you've buried it."

She cocked her head and ran a finger around the rim of her glass where she'd left a sticky print from her lips. "Why is yours buried?"

He concentrated on scooping up some rice and meat with his chopsticks. "What's the internet saying about Tiana? I'm sure you've already taken a peek in between marinating meat and chopping veggies."

She blinked at his abrupt change of subject and tapped the side of her plate with her chopsticks. "Just the usual speculation—sex worker, trafficking, drugs, online dating gone wrong. Nobody knows about the car yet."

"I'm glad you didn't release that information on your blog. I'm sure it'll get out soon enough, though. Everyone at CREW must know it now, and everyone in parking services at that building."

She raised her eyebrows. "You told me not to release

it. I'm still trying to gain your trust, here. It seems like an important detail to withhold, doesn't it? I may be just a blogger, but I have my protocols, as well. If you spew out too much information, you can't discern the crackpots from the people who really know something."

"That's exactly how *we* operate. I figured the more crackpots, the better for you."

She crossed her chopsticks on the edge of her plate. "We really do want to help, you know. It's not all about the clicks. My brother's proudest moments as a true crime blogger were when he actually got to help an investigation."

"Like he thought he was doing with The Player."

"Exactly, even though it cost him his life."

He toyed with a grain of rice on his plate. "That guy I talked to at the mayor's campaign office was supposed to send me a list of campaign workers, highlighting the ones who had access to the vehicles."

"He didn't do it?" She widened her blue eyes, and the smattering of freckles stood out on her nose.

"Nope. I left him a strongly worded voice mail. Now, I'm wondering if they're cleansing the records."

"To protect their own? Why would they want to protect a killer?"

He shrugged. "Their job is to re-elect Wexler. They don't want him to look bad."

"Once it becomes common knowledge that a CREW campaign car is connected to Tiana's death, it's not gonna help. They'll have to go into ultra-spin mode."

"I think they're in that mode right now. Maybe Tiana even worked for the campaign. She was old enough to vote." He dangled a piece of meat over his plate. "This is really good, by the way."

"Thanks. I'm glad you accepted my invitation, though

I have a feeling you did so because I caught you at the right moment. No time for lunch today?"

"Busted." He stuffed the meat into his mouth.

They, or rather he, finished the rest of the food, and he washed it down with another half glass of wine. He poured her another glass and volunteered to clean up the kitchen.

As he rinsed the plates at the sink, Ashlynn settled on the couch with her laptop. He said, "I'm assuming you didn't get anything from Angel since I talked to you today."

"Angel has been mum." The keyboard clicked as her fingers raced across it. "Denver?"

"Yeah?" The tone of her voice caused a dish to slip through his soapy fingers and fall into the sink with a clatter. "Angel?"

"I don't think so, but an important bit of evidence just the same—if it can be believed."

He shut off the water. "What is it?"

"You're not going to find Tiana on the rolls of the campaign workers for Wexler."

"Why is that?"

"Because she worked for his opposition—the Campaign to Elect Veronica Escalante."

Chapter Eight

Ashlynn watched Denver through narrowed eyes, not moving a muscle, her hand hovering over the keyboard. Would he discount her information? Ridicule her sources?

He turned from the sink and wiped his hands on the dishtowel, his eyebrows creating a vee between his eyes. "You're sure it's not from Angel?"

"Funny how you trust Angel all of a sudden. This is from my blog post where I released Tiana's name. It's among the responses." She squinted at the screen. "It already has over a hundred up-votes and a few theories attached to it."

He balled up the towel in his hands and tossed it onto the counter. "Theories but not corroborating proof. Who is this person who posted the link between Tiana and Escalante's campaign?"

"You really wanna know?" She wedged the soles of her sneakers against the edge of the coffee table and expelled a breath. "It was Lil' Snoop."

Denver snorted and cranked on the water to finish the dishes. "We're supposed to believe a statement from someone called Lil' Snoop?"

"It's more than anything coming from someone called LAPD Detective."

"Ouch."

"Think about it, Denver. The LAPD didn't release the information that the car in the lake belonged to the CREW. That's a hell of a coincidence that Lil' Snoop knows Tiana worked for the opposition campaign without knowing she was found in a CREW car."

He retrieved the dishtowel and carefully dried the wok as if it were made of priceless crystal. "The LAPD didn't release that information, but like I said, someone else could have."

Ashlynn's blood boiled and she smacked her palm against her chest. "Me? Is that what you're saying? You think I released that info?"

He waved the dishtowel like a white flag. "I didn't say that."

"You didn't have to. I got the message." She shoved off the couch, clutching the sides of her laptop. "Do you want to see? You read my blog today. I didn't mention the connection to Mayor Wexler."

"I believe you, but there are others who knew. The CREW knew—at least, Amalia and Christian."

"You said they wanted to hush it up. That's not something they're going to voluntarily release." She perched on the arm of her couch, balancing her laptop on her knees, her temper cooling. "Even if that information did get out, it doesn't mean Lil' Snoop is wrong."

"Okay, what cred does this... Snoop have? Is he or she a regular poster on the blog?" Denver shook out the towel and hung it over the oven door handle.

"He is a regular poster and seems to have inside information. He won't tell us his profession, but he has connections in the city. He's usually right. He posts publicly, but he's never messaged me privately." She slid onto a cushion of the couch and crooked her finger at Denver.

"Come here. I'll show you how it looks, and you can read the theories with me."

He joined her on the couch, the sleeves of his dress shirt rolled up, exposing strong forearms corded with veins and muscle. He looked as if he were capable of doing a lot more than the dishes.

He hunched over her shoulder, smelling of dish soap and hot chilies. "Okay, let me see what Snoop has."

She scooted the laptop closer to his legs and jabbed a finger at the screen. "This is his first post—a comment to my blog update naming the victim as Tiana Fuller."

Denver's shoulder pressed against hers as he bent forward for a closer look. "He made that comment less than an hour after your post. That's fast work. I'm still waiting to get the list of names from the CREW."

"Looks legit, right? He doesn't mention the car from Wexler's campaign because he doesn't know about it."

Denver rubbed his knuckles across his sexy stubble. "If this guy's so plugged in, why doesn't he know about the car?"

"That's the beauty of the citizen sleuth." She drew a circle in the air over the screen. "It's small pieces coming together. One person knows one thing. Someone else knows something else. There are people from all walks of life chiming in."

"What I want to know is why these people aren't coming to the police. Why didn't this Lil' Whoever call the LAPD with this information?" He sat back against the couch and shoved a hand through his dark hair.

"There are lots of reasons, Denver. In Lil' Snoop's case, it could be that he'd get in trouble for releasing information. Some people don't want to go on record. Some people don't want the cops sniffing around."

"Great." He slumped, kicking out one leg, resting his

shoe on her coffee table. "I'm going to have to make a visit to the Escalante campaign tomorrow to check this out, after I talk to Tiana's parents. I need to get a list of her friends, boyfriends, her phone carrier—that is, unless you can get all that from your blog."

"Silly." She slugged his hard bicep. "Even I know this stuff isn't admissible evidence for a search warrant."

He raised an eyebrow. "Ever hear of anonymous sources? I'm not going to serve a search warrant on Councilwoman Escalante's campaign headquarters, anyway. I'll just drop by for a friendly visit."

"Weird, isn't it?"

"That Tiana worked for one campaign and was found dead in the car of another? Yeah, weird." He tipped his head toward the computer. "What's the theory online?"

"That someone from Wexler's campaign murdered her to make Escalante look bad."

"And stuffed her in a Wexler car? How's that gonna work out for them?"

"The posters don't know she was found in a CREW car, though, do they?"

"But we do." Denver chewed on his bottom lip, his dark eyes unreadable.

Did the *we* mean him and her, or the LAPD?

She asked, "Do you have a theory of your own?"

"Not yet. I want to talk to her parents first. I want to get to know Tiana."

"Sadly, it's too late for that." Her bottom lip trembled as she thought about that poor young woman in the trunk of the car.

Denver sat up sharply. "I can't save her now, but I can find her killer and get her and her family some justice. That's the thing with being a homicide detective. We come in after the damage has already been done. We're not expected to save anyone, except by getting a killer off the streets."

His vehemence had startled her, as if he were defending his role in the criminal justice process.

"That's huge. You are saving countless, nameless, faceless others by tracking down a killer. Look at The Player copycats. Each time the task force apprehended one of the copycats, it saved the lives of others in their murderous paths."

"That's the idea. Even if Tiana's killer has no intention of striking again, he needs to be brought to justice. I'll get him."

His jaw hardened, and she believed him. She just hoped he'd let her help.

THE FOLLOWING MORNING, Ashlynn rolled onto her side and opened one eye. She stretched her arm across the other side of the bed and smoothed her hand over the undisturbed bedspread. She slept in a king-sized bed, but she barely moved in her sleep. Making the bed consisted of flipping up the covers and tucking in the side of the sheet.

It had been a long time since someone had messed up that other side of the bed. Her ex-boyfriend had been a cheater, and she hadn't felt like venturing into the dating world since. Then Sean had been murdered, and dating had slipped further down her list of priorities.

Her hand bunched the smooth sheets next to her. Didn't mean she didn't miss a body next to hers—especially a body like Detective Denver Holt's.

Despite the sexual tension between them last night, Denver had kept things professional. Or maybe the tension was hers alone.

Sighing, she scooted from the bed and flicked up the

corner. Before she even hit the bathroom, she pulled her laptop onto the bed and accessed her blog.

People had gone crazy over the "The Girl in the Lake" story. Her scoop on the victim's name last night had resulted in an overload of comments. The LAPD had sent a news release to the mainstream media, and Tiana's name and picture were all over the internet now...but she'd been first with it.

She owed Denver, big-time, and she had to deliver more than dinner if she hoped to keep the flow of information coming. She sent a private message to Angel, asking if she was okay and if she'd known Tiana. Ashlynn didn't expect a response, but she wanted Angel to know she still trusted her even after the debacle in Venice.

One idea of how she could help Denver had come to her as she'd drifted off to sleep last night. The plan looked even better in the light of day, and she'd put it into action as soon as she could.

She showered and dressed young—jeans, T-shirt, tennis shoes—pretty much how she usually dressed, leaving off the makeup and scooping her hair into a high ponytail. The sun had come through early this morning, and one of those warm, So Cal spring days called out to everyone to abandon the office and stick their toes in the sand.

Her office didn't resemble most nine-to-five joints, but she couldn't ditch work anyway.

As she nibbled on the edge of a piece of toast spread with crunchy peanut butter, her cell phone buzzed. She wiped her fingers on a napkin and studied the display. Sean always said unknown numbers were the best kind.

She answered with a cautious note to her voice. "Hello?"

"Ashlynn Hughes?" The woman on the line didn't wait for confirmation before launching ahead. "This is

Megan Wright with KTOP. Your blog, *LA Confidential*, published Tiana Fuller's name as the victim in the submerged car in Lake Kawayu before the LAPD released its news item to the press. How did you get that information?"

Ashlynn swallowed. As a news reporter, Megan should know all about confidential sources, and Detective Denver Holt was the most confidential source she'd ever had.

She took a small sip of orange juice. "Hi, Megan. I have my sources, just like you do, and they are every bit as confidential. I'm not at liberty to release the name of my source."

"Got a live one, huh?" Megan chuckled. "Good for you. I, and everyone else, am going to be keeping my eye on the blog. You also found the body. Did that come from this source, as well?"

"No comment." Ashlynn dabbed at a few crumbs on her plate and sucked them into her mouth.

"Are the cops all over you on this yet?"

"No comment."

"Okay, okay. Just keep me in mind for…anything." Megan coughed and lowered her voice. "And I want to tell you how sorry I was about Sean's death. I almost feel responsible."

Ashlynn's hand moved up to her throat. "You? How? The Player killed Sean for working with one of his copycats."

"I knew your brother, had collaborated with him on a few things. I'm the one who suggested his blog as a means of communication between the copycat killer and Detective McAllister." The polished reporter sucked in a breath and her voice wavered. "I wish I had never done it."

"Don't blame yourself. Sean would've killed for that

opportunity. You knew that, and gave it to him. Instead, *he* got killed, but you couldn't have predicted that. Nobody could."

She sniffed. "Just know I considered your brother a friend, and if there's anything I can do for you, just ask."

Sounded like she could do a lot more for Megan than the reporter could do for her. "I'll keep it in mind, and thanks for your condolences."

Ashlynn dumped her plate in the sink, checked her locks and grabbed her keys.

Wouldn't Megan Wright like to know where she was headed right now? Wouldn't Detective Denver Holt? She had no intention of telling either one.

Forty-five minutes later, she breezed through the double glass doors of Veronica Escalante's campaign headquarters. She surveyed the room, bustling with phones and computer activity, but that lasted only a few seconds as a man emerged from one of the offices with a view of the room. He barreled toward her, a used-car-salesman smile on his lips and suspicious beady eyes drilling into her.

"Can I help you?"

She cocked her head, her ponytail swinging behind her. "I hope I can help you. I'm Jenny Cochrane. I'm a poli-sci major at UCLA, and I'd love to volunteer for Councilwoman Escalante's campaign for mayor."

"Excellent. I'm Jed Gordon, Veronica's campaign manager." He snapped his fingers in the air. "You can fill out a form with a few details about yourself, and we'll put you to work."

"Sweet." Ashlynn clasped her hands in front of her. "I have some time now before my classes start. Is there something I can help out with?"

Jed's snaps had produced a decidedly less enthusiastic

campaign volunteer, who shuffled toward them, brushing long, black hair from her face and pouting with a pair of collagen-injected lips.

Jed spared the volunteer a quick glance and said, "How are your envelope-stuffing skills?"

Ashlynn held her hands up and wiggled her fingers. "Top-notch."

The dark-haired woman snickered and asked, "What do you want?"

Jed's lips stretched into a smile. "Lulu, this is Jenny. She's a new volunteer. Can you get a form for her to fill out and show her what we're doing with the envelopes?"

Lulu grunted and turned on her heel.

Jed rolled his eyes at Ashlynn. "Follow Lulu. She'll show you what to do."

Ashlynn nodded and joined Lulu at a table where two other people were stuffing a folded sheet of paper into a preprinted envelope.

Lulu sat and shoved a chair toward Ashlynn with her foot. "Sit down. I don't know why Jed thinks someone needs to learn how to stuff envelopes, but if I sit here for a while with you, he'll stay off my back."

Ashlynn took the chair next to Lulu's. The longer she kept the surly campaign worker at the table, the longer she could avoid filling out any form.

Picking up a sheet of paper and an envelope, Ashlynn asked, "Don't you want to be here? I'm so excited about Councilwoman Escalante's chances. I think she'd be great for this city."

Lulu dug her elbows into the table and propped up her chin with her hands. "I'd rather be anywhere else, but my last name is Escalante. Veronica's my sister, so I sort of have to be here."

Ashlynn's pulse ticked up. Lulu could be a great

source of information about the campaign and her sister. She shoved the paper into the envelope and raised her eyebrows. "Escalante? I thought the councilwoman was married."

"She's married to Kent Meadows. Can't get more Anglo than that." Lulu tapped her long, purple nails on the table. "But she keeps her maiden name to pretend she still cares about *la raza*. As if anyone from the old neighborhood is fooled. She's married to a freakin' billionaire."

Veronica's husband must be the same Meadows as Meadows Developments, who had signs and projects all over the city.

Lulu couldn't be a worse ambassador for her sister—and a better source of dirt. "What do you do when you're not helping your sister run for political office?"

"Mostly get into trouble." Lulu flipped her hair over her shoulder and laughed. "That's why she wants to keep me busy, but I don't think old Jed likes me here."

Ashlynn couldn't imagine why. "Oh, really?"

Lulu wasn't listening. Her gaze had traveled over Ashlynn's shoulder and her dark eyes sparkled. "*Hay, papi.* He's fine."

Ashlynn twisted her head to the side and froze as her gaze collided with Denver's stormy eyes.

Chapter Nine

Denver almost tripped over his own feet as he walked into Escalante's campaign headquarters and saw Ashlynn sitting there stuffing envelopes and chatting with a woman who looked like an escapee from the Kardashian compound.

But he didn't break his stride as he followed Jed Gordon to an office in the back of the room. What the hell was Ashlynn doing here? He hoped she'd planned on telling him about this little undercover stint—they had a deal.

"Please, have a seat, Detective. What can I do for you?" Gordon pointed to a chair across from a desk piled high with papers and folders.

Escalante's campaign headquarters buzzed but had nowhere near the activity of Mayor Wexler's office, and it didn't warrant his good suit. He fished his notebook from his pocket. "We have reason to believe Tiana Fuller, the victim of a homicide, worked for Councilwoman Escalante's campaign."

Gordon's black eyes flickered. Then he skimmed a hand over his shaved head. "That's terrible. Is this the same young woman who was found in the trunk of that car in the lake?"

"It is." Denver dropped his chin to his chest but didn't break eye contact with Gordon. "Did you know Tiana?"

"No." Gordon steepled his fingers and peered at Denver over the point. "We have a lot of volunteers, Detective. Some just wander in and out of this office, happy to do what they can to ensure a victory for Veronica."

Denver winced as he recognized one of Escalante's campaign slogans—Victory for Veronica. These political types never took a break.

"Maybe you'd recognize her face?" He slid the picture of Tiana her mother had provided from his pocket and positioned it on the desk, facing Gordon. "Does she look familiar?"

Gordon squinted at the picture as if bringing it into focus. "Pretty girl, but she doesn't look familiar to me. Like I said, we have a lot of volunteers coming off the streets to help out. Can I ask who gave you the information that this young woman worked for Veronica's campaign?"

"You can ask, but I can't tell you." Denver snatched the picture back. "Maybe some of the volunteers might recognize her."

Gordon blinked but not before his gaze shifted to the window on the busy room. "Sure. You can leave her picture here, and I'll ask around."

Denver pressed the picture to his chest. "I just got this from her mother, and I have only one. I'll do the asking."

"Of course." Gordon pushed back his chair, all feigned eagerness.

"Before we go out there, can you provide me with a list of people who work for Councilwoman Escalante's campaign? Do you have a database of names or something?"

"We do." He brushed his fingers across his computer's keyboard. "I can have someone provide that for you."

"It must be a small list." Denver rested his hand on the doorknob and made a half turn.

"Small?" Gordon rubbed his hands together. "I assure you, we have a lot of volunteers on our team. We're much more grassroots than Mayor Wexler's campaign."

Denver wrinkled his brow, practicing his best dumb cop look. "Oh, you were so sure Tiana didn't work for Escalante's campaign, I thought you must know the names of all the volunteers."

Gordon's lips tightened for a second. "I'm sorry if I gave you the impression that Ms. Fuller never worked here. I just meant I'd never heard of her, nor seen her around the office."

"Okay. Maybe someone else has, or maybe her name will be on your list." Denver stepped out of the office and ignored Ashlynn.

He started on the other side of the room and flashed Tiana's picture to the volunteers, as Gordon stayed close, breathing down his neck.

He saved Ashlynn's station for last. He placed Tiana's photo in the middle of the table. "Have any of you ever seen this woman working here or at any events for Councilwoman Escalante?"

As they all shook their heads and murmured, a chair scraped against the floor. The woman Ashlynn had been talking to earlier, bumped against the table, shifting it.

She covered her mouth with her hand. "Oops, sorry."

Denver asked, "Have you seen her?"

"Me?" She flicked a long fingernail against what had to be fake eyelashes. "No."

Denver stepped back. "Okay. Thanks for your cooperation."

Gordon walked him to the door. "I'll email you that list of volunteers as soon as I get it, Detective Holt."

"Thank you for your cooperation." Denver shook the other man's hand.

As soon as he slid into his sedan, he texted Ashlynn to meet him for lunch someplace far far away from Escalante's campaign headquarters and the beady eyes of Jed Gordon. She had some explaining to do.

A half hour later, when he got to the almost-empty Mexican restaurant, he had the luxury of selecting a booth in the back. The waitress approached the table with a basket of chips and salsa. "Water?"

"Two, please, and I'll take a coffee."

By the time Ashlynn showed up, peering at him through the dark restaurant, he'd munched through half the chips and downed his black coffee.

She paused at the table and studied the picture of Pancho Villa over their table. "Out of all the Mexican restaurants in LA, you picked this one?"

"Serves our purposes—big, dark, and nowhere near Escalante's headquarters." He pointed a chip at the seat across from him. "You wanna tell me what you were doing there?"

She plopped onto the vinyl banquette and gulped down some ice water. "Thought I'd do a little undercover investigation work."

"You're not afraid of getting recognized?"

"Did you see my picture anywhere on *LA Confidential*? It's not there for a reason. I don't do social media. Or, at least, I don't post any pictures of myself on my accounts." She grabbed a chip and dipped it in the salsa. "I'm not visible like a Megan Wright. Nobody there recognized Jenny Cochrane, or I'm sure Jed wouldn't have allowed me to stick around stuffing envelopes."

"He didn't ask you for ID or anything?"

"In case you didn't notice, that room wasn't exactly

a beehive of activity, was it? Looks like they're a little short on volunteers." She waved her second chip in the air. "I was supposed to fill out some form with my name, address—that kind of thing—but I avoided it, and I'll keep on avoiding it."

"Keep on?" He stopped when the waitress hovered, asking if they were ready to order. He'd already studied the plastic menu and ordered a chicken burrito and a refill on his coffee.

Ashlynn ran her finger down the lunch specials. "I'll have the two chicken tacos, but can I get a side salad instead of rice and beans? And a diet whatever."

He leaned forward once the waitress left. "You plan to go back there?"

"I'm going to work the sister."

His hand holding the water glass jerked and the ice tinkled against the sides. "Sister?"

"Lourdes Escalante, goes by Lulu—black hair, long nails, eyelash extensions—total Kardashian vibe."

"That woman is Veronica Escalante's sister?"

"Sort of the black sheep, from what I can gather. No fan of her sister's." Ashlynn tilted her head and her ponytail swung over her shoulder. "Didn't you see what happened when you showed her the picture of Tiana?"

"The business with the chair?"

"That wasn't Lulu. That was Jed kicking the leg of her chair. I guess you couldn't see it because you were on the other side of the table. He was obviously warning her off talking about Tiana."

Denver wiped his hands on the napkin and dropped it back in his lap. "It didn't seem like the others knew Tiana because Jed didn't have to warn any of them."

"I don't know." She shrugged. "Lulu's going to be

closer to the inner workings of the campaign, whether she likes it or not—and she doesn't. She hates working there."

Denver chewed on his bottom lip. "They might be hiding the fact that Tiana worked there to distance themselves from her murder, but wouldn't Tiana have told someone about working for the campaign? I'm meeting with her parents this afternoon. I'll ask them about it."

The waitress returned with their food, sliding his burrito in front of him and refilling his coffee.

As Ashlynn fluffed up her salad with her fork, she wrinkled her nose. "That's a huge burrito, and it's almost too early for lunch."

"Tell me about it, but I figured it would be less crowded here at eleven, and I wanted to talk to you before I met with Mr. and Mrs. Edmonds." He sliced the end off his burrito and steam rose, warning him to back off. "I'm glad I did. I didn't even notice Jed nudging Lulu's chair. She complied, though, didn't she? Kept mum about Tiana."

"Not for long." She poked her chest with the end of her fork. "I'm going to get it out of her."

"How do you plan to do that? Especially if Jed is hovering in the background."

"He's busy in the office, on the phone. He doesn't have time to watch Lulu, and he has no reason to suspect I'm after anything but the thrill of working on a political campaign."

He smirked at her fresh face. "Laid it on thick, huh?"

"I did, and I know just how to get Lulu to open up. I pretended to be slightly shocked by every little thing she said today, and she enjoyed the effect her words had on me. I'll keep that up. Keep supplying the drama for her and she'll keep opening up more and more. Lulu doesn't much like her brother-in-law, either, Kent Meadows. *The* Kent Meadows."

Denver whistled. "His name is plastered all over the city. You'd think Veronica would want to use it for name recognition alone."

"Not sure about that, but according to Lulu, Kent is backing his wife's political aspirations."

"You *did* get a lot out of Lulu. Maybe you missed your calling. Instead of a journalist, you should've been a therapist."

The corner of her eye twitched. "No, thanks. I've had enough of those."

He avoided her gaze and sawed off another piece of his burrito. She seemed too well adjusted to require the services of a therapist. But what did he know? The department had been telling him for years to see a shrink, and he thought he was pretty balanced, too. At least once he stopped caring about anyone enough to obsessively worry, he'd been fine.

"Nothing more on your blog? Anyone talking about Lil' Snoop's claim that Tiana worked for the Escalante campaign?"

"Just more political intrigue theories. Wait until they find out about the CREW car. Are you releasing that information?"

"We are. It's going to get out anyway. The parking attendant in the building where the CREW is located already knows something is up. And once the mainstream media—no offense—pick up the story about Tiana possibly working for Escalante, things are going to heat up in the mayor's race."

She held up her taco, which dripped onto her plate. "No offense taken. If the LAPD can't verify that Tiana worked there, though, they may drop the story. If Jed doesn't have a record of Tiana being a volunteer or her parents don't confirm she worked there, it may be a non-story."

"Or people will confuse the campaigns when they find out the car was from Wexler's. They might think she volunteered for Wexler."

She crunched into her taco and a shower of shredded lettuce fell to her plate. "It is a coincidence, though, isn't it? I mean, maybe her death has nothing to do with the campaigns."

"Maybe." He lifted his shoulders. "But even if another campaign worker murdered her for personal reasons, it ain't gonna look good for the candidate."

"Politics is a dirty business." She dabbed her mouth with a napkin, leaving a string of lettuce in the wisps of hair framing her face.

He reached forward and plucked it free. Holding it up on his finger, he said, "Lettuce in your hair."

"Yikes, can't take me anywhere."

He'd take her anywhere and everywhere. Maybe he needed to take a step back and evaluate why he'd agreed to cooperate with her. Was it because of Tiana and the case, or because he just wanted to be close to her?

He didn't need to be close to her—or anyone.

"Almost done?" He pushed away his plate with the half-eaten burrito.

She had just crunched into her second taco and waved her hand in front of her mouth as she chewed. She swallowed and took a sip of her soda. "You're done already? I'd like to finish this taco."

"You were right. It is too early to eat lunch. I'll take this with me and finish it at my desk." He checked his phone. "I gotta go back to the station right now and write up a few things before meeting with Tiana's mom and stepdad."

Ashlynn's face blanched and her lush lips tightened into a frown. "You go ahead. I'm going to finish my lunch."

As he tossed his napkin on the table and reached for his wallet, she held out her hand. "That's okay. I'll take care of the bill."

He plucked out a twenty and a ten and dropped them on the table. "I got it. You paid for dinner last night, and you gave me some good info today."

She dragged her napkin from her lap and pressed it against her chest. "You don't have to pay me for information."

"I didn't mean it like that. I'll touch base later, if I have anything else to share." He stood and raised his hand. "Take care, Ashlynn."

He spun around and walked blindly toward the exit as Ashlynn called after him. "You forgot your burrito."

He'd forgotten more than his burrito. He'd forgotten his vow never to care for anyone ever again—at least, nobody alive.

Chapter Ten

Ashlynn's nose stung as she dabbed the tip of her finger on a drop of hot sauce in her plate. "Jerk."

The guy had done a one-eighty on her—one minute scarfing down chips and salsa and discussing the case with her, the next throwing down his napkin and practically running for the exit.

She sighed and poked her fork at her unfinished taco. He'd probably prefer to work with Sean, too. She'd had no business taking over *LA Confidential*. She would never reach the heights Sean had reached.

She dropped the fork and squared her shoulders. *Stop doing this to yourself, Ashlynn...and eat.* Detective Holt wasn't anything special—arrogant, hostile—and she could see through it all to the part of him that desperately wanted to be a full-fledged homicide detective.

She scooped up her taco and took a big bite with a smile on her face. She'd uncovered a lot more about this case than he had. What had he given her? The pleasure of his company, that's it. And that hadn't turned out to be much.

Shoving the rest of the taco in her mouth, she waved to the waitress. "Can you please bring me a box for this burrito?"

"Sure." She pointed at the money on the table. "Do you want me to take this?"

"Yes." Ashlynn leaned back against the banquette and patted her full stomach. He'd just paid for her lunch *and* her dinner.

BY THE TIME she'd made it home after running a few errands, proofreading her freelance article on public art spaces in LA, and having an online meeting with her web designer, Denver's burrito had turned into a soggy mess. She'd dumped the whole thing in her sink and run the disposal with gusto.

He hadn't contacted her the rest of the day, so she didn't know how his meeting with Tiana's parents had lasted—not that he owed her anything. In fact, it seemed as if he didn't think he owed her anything at all.

This relationship had been a one-way street—in many ways.

She swung open the fridge door and surveyed the packed shelves. After she'd recovered from her eating disorder, her therapist had recommended that she keep food in her kitchen—healthy stuff. She just figured she'd have some of that stir-fry left, so she wouldn't have to cook again tonight. But Denver Holt had gobbled up everything in sight last night—everything but her. She slammed the fridge door shut.

One night of In-N-Out with animal fries wasn't going to make her relapse. As she grabbed her keys, her cell phone buzzed.

Her heart flip-flopped in her chest when she saw Lulu's name. The two of them had exchanged numbers while working together today. She'd given Lulu her real number, as she didn't mention *LA Confidential* on her voicemail greeting for this phone. She kept a separate phone for the blog.

She pitched her voice higher with an excitement she didn't have to fake. "Hi, Lulu. Wassup?"

"Girl, you left the building so fast, I didn't get a chance to tell you about the fundraiser tonight."

"Fundraiser?" Her voice positively squeaked.

"It's the best part of working for this stupid campaign—the only good part. All the volunteers are always invited to the fundraisers. I'm not saying we don't have to run around like gofers sometimes, but the food's usually good, there's valet parking, and the booze is first rate…and free. Can't get better than that."

"Perfect. I'm always down for free booze. Where and when? And are you sure it's okay if I'm there? I just started today. For all you know, I might never come back."

"I don't care about that, and Jed's not gonna notice you one way or the other—not with my sister in the room." Lulu huffed out a breath. "The fundraiser is at my sister's house in Sherman Oaks. It's up in the hills, off Beverly Glen with all the other mansions. I'll text you the address. It starts at seven, but show up closer to eight when it'll be more crowded."

"So I can sneak in? Are you sure it's okay?" she asked again, unsure.

"You're not sneaking. You're a volunteer. Grassroots and all that. It's just that the food will be circulating by then, and it's easier to snag drinks without certain people watching you."

All of a sudden, Ashlynn was starving. "Sounds dank. What should I wear?"

"If you're looking for a sugar daddy, you can go slinky cocktail. If you wanna come off as the dedicated kiss-ass, dress down from there."

"Thanks for thinking of me, Lulu. I can squeeze in a little more studying by eight. You'll be there by then?"

"I'm already here. I live in this hellhole known as my sister's house."

As soon as they ended the call, Lulu texted her Veronica's address. Lulu had just presented her with the perfect opportunity to get close to the Escalante campaign. Nobody there would know her face.

She scanned through her contacts for Denver's personal cell. Her finger hovered over his name for a second, and then she tossed the phone onto the kitchen counter. If he wanted to cool things down, she could be ice cold.

In the end, she dressed somewhere between sugar baby and earnest young volunteer. She straightened the hem of her little black dress and stepped into the black sandals, waiting in front of the mirror. She released her hair from her ponytail and fluffed it around her shoulders.

When she slid behind the wheel of her car, she tapped in the address for Veronica Escalante's house. If the GPS took her by way of the Valley, she'd force it to change. Even at this time of night, she didn't want to chance traffic out to the Valley. She'd go up the back way and take Mulholland.

Forty-five minutes later, Ashlynn negotiated the hairpin turns on Mulholland to reach Escalante's house in the hills. She rolled to a stop behind a line of cars waiting for the valet parking attendants.

How much money would Escalante raise to ultimately lose to Mayor Wexler? What would her campaign do to make sure she didn't lose?

An attendant in a white shirt and red vest jogged up to her car and she popped the locks. He opened her door. "Good evening, miss."

That was a nice touch. "Hello. Just leave the keys in the ignition?"

"Yes, miss. We'll take care of your car."

She surveyed the gleaming luxury vehicles ahead and behind her in the line. She had a lot less to worry about with her VW than the rest of these well-heeled donors. "I'm sure you will. Thanks."

As she exited the car, she hitched her small black purse across her body. Her heels crunched the gravel as she made her way toward the gates of the house until she hit the pavers on the circular driveway.

The double doors stood open and lights bathed the beautiful garden in front. Ashlynn inhaled the heady scent of jasmine and ducked behind a couple approaching the broad steps fronting the Tudor-style mansion.

Who knew sitting on the LA city council paid so well? But then, Veronica had her own, private wealthy donor.

As soon as she and the couple made it over the threshold, a waiter appeared, bearing a tray of champagne flutes glimmering with the golden liquid. Ashlynn lifted a glass and took a small sip while sidling against a wall to take in the spectacle.

She'd never moved in political circles and neither had her parents, despite their wealth, but these folks knew how to live it up. She snatched a little pastry puff of something from a tray that floated by and stuffed it into her mouth. Shrimp. She hadn't eaten since she'd forced herself to finish that taco from her early lunch with Denver.

She zigzagged her way through the crowd to reach the pretty display of food and lifted a small plate from the stack.

"Told you." Lulu appeared next to her, dressed to kill in a slinky red number with cutouts along the sides and a deep V, clinging to all of Lulu's dangerous curves. "The food is worth the boredom."

"You don't look like you're planning on boredom." Ashlynn piled a few shrimp puffs on her plate, some bacon-wrapped scallops, a couple of tiny ribs and a piece of bruschetta.

Lulu winked. "Sometimes you get lucky."

"Does your sister know you troll for—" Ashlynn waved the bread in the air "—luck at her fundraisers?"

"How do you think she snagged her rich husband? He's gotta have at least twenty years on her. So, as long as I keep it hush-hush, she doesn't care what I do." Lulu narrowed her heavily made-up eyes. "She hates publicity—the bad kind."

Like a campaign volunteer showing up dead in the trunk of a submerged car.

"Who doesn't?" Ashlynn licked some barbecue sauce from her finger and grabbed a napkin. "You don't have to babysit me. I'm gonna make my way through this food, grab a few more glasses of champagne, and flirt with that bartender."

"Don't sell yourself short. You're cute in a wholesome kind of way. These older guys vibe on that." Lulu smoothed her dress over her hips and shimmied her shoulders. "I got a line on one now."

Ashlynn watched Lulu sashay across the room toward a huddle of men old enough to be her father. At least Lulu's game plan would leave her alone long enough to snoop around.

As she stood with her plate, shoveling enough little appetizers in her mouth to make up a three-course meal, Ashlynn sized up the room. She could distinguish the donors from the hangers-on or charity cases by their clothing, and Veronica Escalante was no slouch as a clotheshorse. Ashlynn could spot the councilwoman's designer shoes with the red soles, as she worked her way through the crowd schmoozing.

Ashlynn hadn't been lying to Denver when she'd told him she'd written fashion articles for an e-magazine, but she hadn't told him she knew clothes inside and out because her mother had been a model. Her mother had lived and breathed fashion, and had tried to make it the center of Ashlynn's life, too.

She'd fallen short, literally by one inch, of her mom's willowy five-foot-ten-inch frame, which had only increased her mother's pressure on her to stay thin.

She'd showed her. Ashlynn had become a pro at staying thin.

Ashlynn had left her champagne glass at the end of the table where she'd started, but had no desire to finish the drink. She stashed her empty plate on a tray by the door and asked the cute bartender for a Coke with a lime on the side.

She'd already spotted the other volunteers and made her way to where they stood in a clump by the patio door, which led to a sparkling pool. She hung on the edge of the group, her hand curled around the highball glass.

A lull in their conversation offered her an in. She cleared her throat. "What did you all think about that cop flashing that girl's picture around this afternoon?"

One of the guys glanced her way, and a spark of recognition lit his dark eyes. "Oh, you just started today, huh?"

"Yeah, that's me." She raised her hand as if she were sitting in a classroom. "The new girl."

The man patted his chest. "I'm Andre. This is Sydney, Bryant, and Karis."

"I'm Jenny." Ashlynn nodded to the group, raising her glass.

Sydney, a young woman with a sleek, blond ponytail, definitely dressed for eager political asset, asked. "You work fast. Your first day and you made it to a gala."

"Lulu invited me today."

Sydney's eyes widened. "Lulu invited you here?"

"Y-yeah. Should I not be here?"

"No, we're always invited. It's just that Lulu isn't the friendliest person in the office." Sydney cupped a hand around her mouth. "You know she's Veronica's sister, right?"

"I do. She was friendly to me." Ashlynn plucked the lime from the edge of her glass and squeezed it into the Coke. "I guess nobody knew the girl in that picture."

Andre patted the side of his short Afro. "We didn't know her, but we knew who she was—that murdered girl. We still can't figure out why the po-po came around asking questions."

Ashlynn tipped her head and wrinkled her nose. "I think I heard the cop say something to Jed about that girl working for Veronica's campaign."

Karis, the petite Latina, grabbed Sydney's arm "No way. She worked for Veronica? I never saw her in the office."

"That's crap." Bryant finally spoke, pushing his hipster black-rimmed glasses up on his nose. "None of us ever saw her. She didn't work for the campaign. Maybe she was one of those wannabes who get all excited and then lose interest after they make one phone call. They come and go. How about you, Jenny? You a wannabe?"

"Me?" Ashlynn put her hand over her heart. "I'm all-in."

She jiggled the ice in her drink and took a sip. No Jed here to coach them. They honestly didn't know Tiana, had never seen her at the office, but that didn't mean

Lulu didn't know the dead woman. She hadn't imagined Jed's nudge to the chair when Denver showed Lulu Tiana's picture.

"If you are sticking around, here's a pro tip." Karis tapped her finger against her head. "Stay away from Kent."

Ashlynn widened her eyes as her pulse jumped. "Kent Meadows, Veronica's husband."

"Yeah, he's a creeper." Karis hugged herself. "Right, Sydney?"

The blonde nodded solemnly. "Total manther."

"'Manther'?" Ashlynn had to show her ignorance if she wanted the answer.

Karis giggled and tossed her dark curls. "You know. Instead of a cougar, an older woman going after young guys, he's a manther. Cougar…panther…manther."

Ashlynn wrinkled her nose. "Yuck."

Sydney waved her drink toward the patio. "I see someone lighting up on the other side of the pool. Anyone want to keep me company?"

Bryant answered, "Only if you let me bum a ciggie off you."

As the two of them wandered off, Ashlynn jerked her thumb over her shoulder. "I'm going to get some more free booze before they cut us off."

If Lulu was the one who knew about Tiana, then she should be talking to Lulu. She propped up the wall next to the bar and scanned the room, her gaze meeting Jed's for a split second.

His ankle-length slacks and no-socks ensemble screamed, *I'm trying hard to look fresh*. But at least he glanced away, not recognizing her, and she turned her head so he wouldn't catch her on the double-take—not that she didn't have every right to be there. The other volunteers had showed up, and she'd been personally invited by Lulu, although there didn't seem to be any love lost between Lulu and Jed.

She spied Lulu chatting up an older man in a pair of nice slacks, a black T and a mustard-colored jacket. It worked. He looked put together with a personal twist. He stroked his salt-and-pepper beard, while leaning toward Lulu and her cleavage.

Ashlynn gripped her glass and threaded her way through the crowd to reach Lulu and her conquest.

Attaching herself to the duo, she said, "Great turnout."

Lulu's seductive stance changed in a second as she gave Ashlynn a pointed look. "Yeah, great. Jenny, this is Syngin Parish. Syngin, one of our volunteers."

"Nice to meet you, Jenny." Syngin gave her hand the briefest of squeezes before dropping it. He wanted her gone as much as Lulu did.

"You, too. Thanks for supporting Councilwoman Escalante. She'll do great things for the city."

Syngin's blue eyes sparkled with amusement. "I've known Veronica's husband, Kent Meadows, for years. I'm afraid I'm not very political."

"Everyone needs the support of friends." She winked.

Lulu drilled a knuckle into Ashlynn's back. "You should go find Jed and show him your face for a few brownie points."

"Oh, I will." She put a finger on her chin. "Speaking of the office, did Lulu tell you that a LAPD detective came to the campaign headquarters today asking if we knew that murdered girl, Tiana Fuller?"

Syngin's face didn't register any change at all, but Lulu stiffened beside her.

"I didn't hear that. I heard about the body in the lake, but I didn't know she was connected to the campaign."

"Because she's not." Lulu squeezed Ashlynn's upper arm, her long nails digging into her flesh. "If you actually want to help the campaign, Jenny, you won't talk about murders."

Ashlynn covered her mouth with her hand. "I'm so sorry. I just thought it was weird he was there. Nobody knew her, so he must've been wrong."

Syngin flashed his very white teeth. "You don't have to worry about me. As I said, I'm apolitical. I'm just here to support Kent and Veronica—and because I have lots of money."

"I knew there was something I liked about you." Lulu tugged on the sleeve of the mustard jacket, fluttering her lash extensions.

Ashlynn had never felt more like a third wheel. "I'm going to find Jed, grab some more food and head out. Thanks for the invite, Lulu."

Syngin and Lulu barely noticed her departure as she slipped back into the crowd. She didn't want to draw Jed's attention to her, but it sounded like Lulu would tell him she was at the party, anyway. She might as well touch base.

She studied each knot of people and those wandering in and out of the house. Was Jed a smoker? She stepped outside onto the patio and stood at the water's edge, squinting at the smokers across the pool.

A leaf drifted from one of the trees, which must create a natural umbrella for the patio, and landed in the water. Ashlynn meandered around the curve of the pool and ducked down, scooping the leaf from the lapping water with her hand.

Before she rose from her crouch, she heard whispers from the clump of trees. Holding her breath, she stayed down and strained to hear the voices. A man and a woman went back and forth in heated conversation, but she couldn't make out the words.

Twisting her head, she peered to the side, just getting a glimpse of two pairs of legs. She made out a man in high-cut black slacks, no socks and brown loafers, and a woman in a dress or skirt, long bare legs, her feet in a pair of expensive stilettos. Ashlynn could see the red soles in the dark.

She crawled a few feet away from the trees and rose to a standing position, brushing off her knees. She didn't want to get caught eavesdropping on Jed and Veronica.

Why were they arguing in secret? Better than arguing in public, but why would those two be arguing? Jed was her campaign manager. Veronica's word should be law.

She heard the bushes rustle behind her but she didn't turn around. Instead, she adjusted her purse across her body and dug inside for her valet ticket and a five-dollar bill.

She cruised through the house, giving a quick wave to Lulu and then landing on the front porch. Clutching her ticket and cash, she approached the valet attendants.

"Hey, can I get my car, please?"

One of the young men sprang forward with his hand held out, and she placed the ticket in his palm. His shoes crunched against the road as he scurried off to find her car.

This neighborhood in the hills south of Ventura Boulevard didn't need sidewalks. These streets were for residents only, not scraggly pedestrians who didn't have any business in this hood. Apparently, they didn't need streetlamps, either.

Ashlynn rubbed her arms as she waited for her car,

Ranchera music thumping from a speaker where the valets huddled.

She stepped forward as the attendant pulled her car up in front of her. He left the engine running and the door open.

"Thanks." She slipped him the five and got behind the wheel. Hopefully, the parking attendants would be getting better tips from the likes of Syngin, but she knew rich people. They could be cheaper than anyone. She hoped, for Lulu's sake, Syngin wasn't one of those stingy ones.

She pulled onto the road and turned toward Mulholland Drive again. Even with the twists and turns on this part of the road, she preferred it to going through the Valley. And she'd had only two sips of champagne and a boatload of food. She'd be fine.

She negotiated the first few turns with ease before noticing the headlights behind her. Damn. She was more comfortable driving these kinds of roads if nobody was behind her. She tapped her rearview mirror and said, "You're gonna have to relax, buddy. I'm not whizzing around these curves."

She eased off the accelerator at the next bend but instead of backing off, the car behind her got right on her tail. There were no immediate turnouts for her to allow him to pass. She muttered, "Moron."

She came out of the turn and sped up a little, but the next curve greeted her all too soon. She slowed again, and the guy behind her was not having it.

His headlights flooded her car as he rode her bumper.

"What is your problem?" She hugged the shoulder on the right in case he wanted to risk passing her. Sure enough, he moved into the opposing lane of traffic, but instead of roaring ahead like she'd expected, his car bumped the back of hers.

She grabbed the wheel but her tires were already on gravel and they spun to gain purchase on the shifting surface.

The last thing she saw before rolling down the canyon was the other car's taillights as it sped away.

Chapter Eleven

Denver slid down further in his seat and shielded his eyes against the oncoming headlights of Ashlynn's car. Either she'd found what she'd needed or realized she wasn't going to get anything out of Escalante's donors—and she hadn't even told him about her plans.

He didn't deserve to know after the way he'd treated her at lunch. His scheme had worked the way he'd intended: give her the cold shoulder, make her dismiss him as a jerk and throw cold water on whatever they had going on.

Another vehicle crawled out from a shallow turnout, its parking lights barely illuminating the road. Had the valet attendants been using that space for the guests' cars?

His senses percolated as he watched the low-key car roll past the valet stand and Escalante's house. Why was the driver creeping around? Taking license numbers?

He flicked his rearview and watched the car make the same turn toward Mulholland as Ashlynn had made. He swallowed against his dry throat. Was someone tailing her?

He cranked on his engine and made a tight U-turn in the road, waving out the window at the valets who'd let him park across the street after he'd flashed his badge and given each of them a twenty. He made the turn onto Mulholland just in time to see the taillights of the sedan, which had taken off after Ashlynn's, disappear around the first bend of a winding section of the boulevard.

He sped up, but the car was keeping well ahead of his. Crazy driving.

Coming out of the next curve, Denver blinked his eyes. The reverse lights of the black sedan he'd been following glowed as the driver backed up on the road. Beyond the trunk, Ashlynn's car poked over the edge of the canyon at a forty-five-degree angle.

The stealth car switched into Drive and started rolling toward Ashlynn's precariously situated vehicle. Denver flashed his headlights and flicked on his blue and red revolvers.

The driver of the sedan jerked to the right and, with a squeal of tires, shot off down the road.

Denver had gotten a partial plate, but he couldn't leave Ashlynn's vehicle at the precipice of the canyon. He hadn't seen any movement from the VW, and his heart pounded as he parked his own vehicle, killing the lights, and clambered out of it.

He rushed to the edge of the road where Ashlynn's car pointed toward the canyon, his shoes slipping on the gravel, almost carrying him past the car and into the trees.

Grabbing on to her door handle, he peered inside the window. Her head turned toward him, her eyes wide and glassy, her hands still gripping her steering wheel.

All four of her wheels were still on solid ground— just—and he yanked open her door. "Are you hurt?"

"I—I don't think so."

"Turn off your engine. Put the car in Park. Can you

do that?" He reached across her body and unhitched her seat belt.

She shoved the gearshift into Park and switched off the ignition. Then she placed her hands back on the wheel.

He touched her wrist gently. "You can get out of the car, Ashlynn. It's okay. It's not gonna go over or shift if you move."

She released the steering wheel as if it burned her hands and whipped her head around to face him, her hair dancing at her shoulders like flames. "A car forced me off the road and took off."

"I figured that. I saw the tail end of the accident." He didn't tell her he thought the car was getting ready to push her into the canyon. "The sedan took off."

"Bastard." Her anger broke through her shock and she scrambled out of her car, landing on her knees.

"Steady." He took her arm and helped her to her feet. He glanced at her high-heeled, strappy sandals and swept her into his arms to carry her up to the road.

"I can walk." She kicked her legs.

He set her down on the side of the road. "I know that, but that's some rocky ground. I slipped myself, and I'm not wearing sexy sandals."

Her chin dropped and she stared at her black dress, as if she'd forgotten what she was wearing.

"Are you all right?" He fished into his pocket for his phone. "I'm calling 9-1-1."

"Don't!" She grabbed his arm. "If you make a fuss here, the people from the party might find out about this. I attended that fundraiser as Jenny, ingenue college student and starry-eyed political volunteer. I'd have to give the police my real name."

"You can't leave your car there. You can't back it out

of there without risking it tumbling down the canyon—with you in it."

She covered her mouth. "That's what he wanted. He pushed me off the road. He just didn't push hard enough."

"What happened in there?" He jerked his thumb back toward Escalante's house.

"Wait." She ran a pair of unsteady hands through her hair. "What are you doing here? Did you follow me again?"

"I didn't follow you. I didn't even know you were going to be here." He waved at a car slowing toward them to go ahead. Ashlynn was right. They didn't need a collection of cars and people up here. "I knew about the fundraiser and thought I'd do a little surveillance to see who showed up. I saw you arrive, and figured you were here as your alter ego. Then when I saw you leave, I noticed a suspicious car hot on your tail. I'm glad my instincts kicked in."

"Me, too." She folded her arms and kicked some pebbles with her toe.

She still thought he was a jerk, and that was okay.

"But we need to make sure you're okay…and get your car out of here."

"Don't I look okay?" She spread her arms wide, and his gaze swept over her body in her short black dress, long, slim legs up to there.

He dragged his eyes to her face. "You look fine. Why didn't your airbags deploy?"

"No clue. Maybe because I didn't hit anything? It was like a roll down the hill." She rubbed the back of her neck. "Just noticing a little soreness back here, maybe whiplash."

"Probably. You need to a see a doctor."

"I'll see my own doctor, in my own time. Are you gonna help me get my car out of here?"

"What? Push it up the hill with my bare hands?"

"You know…people, don't you? Can't we do this on the hush-hush? If the cops come out here with their lights and sirens and tow trucks and ambulances, it's going to cause a scene. People leaving the party are bound to stop. I'll have to tell the cops where I was. They might even give me a breathalyzer."

He cut her off. "Have you been drinking?"

"Do two sips of champagne count? No, I haven't been drinking, but the cops might want to check out the party. I can't afford that, Denver. I can't afford to blow my cover."

"You already did." He clenched his teeth. He'd like to get his hands on the person driving that sedan.

Ashlynn caught her bottom lip between her teeth. "You're right about that. Either someone followed me to Escalante's, or someone made me there."

Another two cars wound down the road, and Denver waved them past. "We need to get out of here before more people leave the party. My guess is the majority won't take Mulholland, but enough will."

"So, you agree we shouldn't create a scene here."

"Do you promise me you'll see a doctor about your neck?"

"Promise." She drew a cross over her heart.

"Okay, hop in my car, and I'll get you home, as long as you tell me what you discovered at the fundraiser." He took her arm to guide her to his vehicle tucked into a small outlet.

She slipped from his grasp when she reached the car. "So, now there are two conditions? I go to the doctor and give up what I discovered? When do I get something out of this relationship besides a ride home?"

Opening the passenger door, he held up two fingers. "If we're keeping track here, I've rescued you twice now—three times if we're counting the break-in at your house and the message on your mirror."

"That wasn't a rescue. That was moral support." She dropped onto the seat and slammed the door.

He blew out a breath and circled to the driver's side. When he got in behind the wheel, he slid a gaze to the side. Ashlynn had her eyes closed.

"You're sure you're okay?"

"I probably could use some ibuprofen." She massaged her temples.

"You're in luck." He flipped up the console and felt around for the small bottle every detective kept in every car. His fingers closed around it and he shook it before handing the bottle to Ashlynn. "You can take it down with my lukewarm coffee, if you like."

"Thanks." She popped the lid, shook a green gel cap into her palm and slapped her hand against her mouth. She plucked his cup from the holder and took a small sip, leaving a semicircle of red lipstick on the lid.

He maneuvered his car back onto the road. "I'll call the tow service we use tonight. I don't think anyone's going to see your car off the road in the meantime. I only knew it was there because I saw you roll over the edge and your lights were still on."

"I hope nobody calls it in." She settled into the seat and tucked her hands between her knees. "You wanna know what I discovered at the party?"

"If you're ready." His muscles tensed. Had she been asking too many questions at the fundraiser?

She held up her hand and ticked off each item on her fingers. "I don't think any of the volunteers know about Tiana Fuller. I think Lulu does know something about

Tiana, and so does Jed. Jed and Veronica seem to have something more going on than candidate and campaign manager."

"How'd you determine that last bit?"

"I heard them in a heated discussion out by the pool, under cover."

A muscle twitched in his jaw. "Did you hear what they said?"

"Nope. Whispers, and I didn't want to get too close."

He released a breath. "They didn't see you?"

"Not sure about that."

"That's all you got?"

"That and the definition of manther."

He snorted. "Enlighten me."

"A manther is like a male cougar—an older man who hits on younger women. The volunteers said Kent Meadows was a manther." She slugged his arm. "Don't ever become a manther."

"Don't worry about that. I prefer women to girls." He cleared his throat. "Anything else?"

She pulled her skirt over her thighs. "That and a closer relationship with Lulu. She's the one who invited me to the party. She called me."

"Do you think you can get more out of her?"

"Maybe." She gathered her hair in one hand, dragging it over her shoulder. "But I'd kind of like to get more out of you."

His head jerked to the side. "What do you mean?"

"Don't get excited." She patted his forearm. "I don't mean more warmth or humanity. I'm talking about your meeting with Tiana's parents. You met with them after lunch and didn't bother to fill me in at all. This is beginning to feel like a one-way street."

Should he tell her he'd changed his mind about their

deal? Or at least he had until he'd seen her glide up Escalante's driveway like she owned the place. He couldn't deny having a source like Ashlynn might help him solve Tiana's murder.

He cleared his throat. "I'll tell you about it when we get back to your place."

Closing her eyes, she nodded. "Deal."

And just like that, Ashlynn Hughes was back in his life.

BY THE TIME Ashlynn pushed open the door to her place, she could barely move her head on her stiff neck. She'd taken an ibuprofen in the car, but she needed another.

"Do you want something to drink? I'm going to pop another pill and put some ice on my neck." She hung on to the freezer door. "Ice or heat?"

"I'd start with ice, but I'm no expert." He sidled up next to her at the fridge and said, "Bottled water or tap?"

"I use the water from the refrigerator. I figure it's filtered, and I haven't grown any horns yet."

He brushed past her and lifted two glasses from her cupboard. "Ice to go with your ice?"

"No, thanks." She crouched next to the fridge and pulled a plastic bag from a drawer. "I'm going to fill this with ice and deposit it against the back of my neck. I guess it could've been worse, huh?"

"Are you going to tell me what happened at that fundraiser to make someone come after you and try to run you off the road?"

"I told you everything that happened. I did not draw attention to myself." She punched the button on the ice maker to release the ice and fill her bag.

"Someone noticed you, or someone recognized you. You run one of the most popular blogs in the city. Why do you think you can run around incognito?" He took her place in front of the fridge and filled up two glasses with water.

"*LA Confidential* is not really my blog. I didn't make it popular. That was Sean's doing."

He cocked his head at her. "Take credit where credit is due. Your brother is gone, and you've done a helluva job in his place. That series you did on Reed Dufrain and the shenanigans at the Brighter Day Recovery Center was top-notch. That drug lab sounded like something from a TV show. You did that, Ashlynn. Why are you selling yourself short?"

She shrugged and her bag of ice crackled against her neck. "Just feels like it's Sean's baby, like it'll never be mine."

"Make it your own, or do something else. I thought you said something about a podcast?"

"Yeah, Sean intended to turn *LA Confidential* into a podcast. I had started helping him."

"Take the idea and run with it." He placed his hand on the small of her back and steered her toward the couch. "Sit down, and I'll tell you what I found out from Tiana's parents."

She lowered herself to the cushion on the end, positioning the bag on her neck. "Was it hard talking to them?"

"Hard for me?" His eyebrows shot up to his hairline and the dark lock of hair that had a habit of falling across his forehead. "What I feel is nothing compared to what they're going through."

She nodded. "I remember when the detective came to tell me about my brother's murder. He was so uncomfortable, I almost felt like I was supposed to comfort him. I didn't want to break down too much because I was afraid of what it would do to him."

"It shouldn't be that way. As difficult as it is for us, it's not our tragedy, not our story." He coughed and gulped back some water. "Tiana's parents couldn't tell me much, but I got the impression that she *was* working for the Escalante campaign."

"Just an impression?" The ice slipped to her shoulder and she left it. "They couldn't tell you for sure?"

"They didn't know for sure, but Tiana was a political science major at Cal State Long Beach. She was very interested in local politics, and was looking forward to applying for an internship with the city of Long Beach her senior year. It would make sense that she'd volunteer for a campaign like Escalante's."

"But she never specifically told her parents she was working for Escalante?"

"Nope." Denver scratched his jaw. "I wonder why. If she were so excited about politics, you'd think she'd tell her parents about her volunteer work."

"She was keeping it a secret for some reason." She snapped her fingers. "What about Wexler's campaign? Did they ever get back to you with a list of their volunteers?"

"They did, but her name wasn't on the list. I wasn't anticipating it. If she'd been working for them, I would expect them to scrub her name from the database. Tiana is already connected to one of their cars, they don't want to compound the problem by linking her to the campaign."

Ashley wrinkled her nose. "Tiana is working for Escalante and winds up dead in a vehicle tied to the Wexler campaign."

"Doesn't make any sense." Denver massaged his temples. "Oh, and her mother said Tiana had a boy-

friend up here, or maybe just a guy who was a friend—
Tony Fuentes."

"He hasn't contacted you?"

"No, but I'm going to run him down and find out why."
He pointed to her plastic bag. "That's slipping down your
arm. I thought you had whiplash."

"It's too cold." She snatched the bag from her shoulder, cupping it in her palms.

"That's kind of the point." He took the ice from her
hands and said, "Turn around."

She presented her back to him, tucking one leg beneath her and tugging her dress over her thighs.

Denver swept her hair over her shoulder, his fingers
trailing along her bare back.

A warm flush suffused her body. If he put that ice
against her skin now, it would melt in a matter of seconds.

The ice clacked as he positioned it on the back of her
neck. He kept his hand on the bag, pressing it against all
the stiff spots. She closed her eyes as a chilling numb-
ness seemed to freeze her twitching muscles.

"Okay, yeah. I see the point here." She lifted her shoulders and shivered. "It hurts so good. I mean I kind of
can't stand it, but the ice is definitely numbing the area."

"I think we were right to ice instead of heat." He blew
out a warm breath that tickled her flesh. "I was relieved
to see you weren't hurt—at least not seriously. When I
saw that car take off after yours, I didn't think he was
going to run you off the road. Follow you, maybe, but he
could've killed you."

Ashlynn jerked her head to the side and clamped her
neck with a wince. "Do you think whoever is threatening me graduated to violence?"

He dropped the bag of ice to the coffee table. "I think
he already did that in Venice."

"I'm talking about mortal violence. You think some-one wants to kill me?"

His hand skimmed down her back. "He pushed you into a shallow dip, not off the edge of a canyon. He could've picked a more dangerous spot on Mulholland to start playing bumper cars with you. I think you're still in the warning stage. It's not like you've discovered anything about Tiana yet. Neither have we."

He'd been rubbing a circle on her back, and her eyelashes fluttered when he stopped. "Could you keep doing that?"

She felt his warmth behind her as he gathered her hair in her hand and lifted it from her neck. He pressed his lips against her cool flesh and she could almost feel the sizzle.

"Yeah, like that." She dipped her head and his lips trailed to her collarbone.

Turning to face him, she grabbed the lapels of his denim jacket. "You always seem to be in the right place at the right time to rescue me."

"Right place, but always two beats late." His lips crooked into a smile and the unexpectedness of it took her breath away.

She smoothed her hands against the front of his T-shirt, and his heart thumped beneath her palms, matching the pulse in her fingertips. She raised her eyes to his face and whispered, "Why'd you blow me off at lunch?"

"I realized I had stuff to do." His dark eyes shifted to the hand he was running through her hair.

You didn't have to be a homicide detective to spot that tell. The lie was so obvious, Denver didn't even try to cover it.

She didn't need honesty right now. She'd never demanded that much from the men in her life anyway. Stroking his cheek, she said, "Kiss me."

The fingers sifting through her hair wove around the strands and he pulled her closer. When their lips met, she tasted peppermint and possibilities.

His hand slid to the back of her head and he broke their connection. "I don't want you hurting your neck— even for a kiss."

"If you can't risk it all for a hot kiss, there's something missing in your soul." She touched his bottom lip with the pad of her thumb. "I forgot all about my whiplash for a minute."

"Let me help you forget some more." He wrapped his hands around her waist and pulled her into his lap. Her dress rode up her thigh, and he ran his rough palm across its curve.

"I don't know how you could've believed you were flying beneath the radar at that party in this dress."

She burrowed into his lap and hung an arm around his neck. "I was a moth among butterflies. Believe me. The flash and glitz in that room could've blinded you."

"That's why you probably stood out. You don't need flash and glitz. You have something more indefinable than that—style, sexiness without hitting people in the face with it."

She must be her mother's daughter after all. "Can we stop talking now? I thought you were the strong, silent type."

He gently took her face between his hands and kissed her mouth, his tongue slipping between her lips. She'd wanted him from the moment she'd seen him at the lake, but she always did go after the unattainable ones.

As she peeled herself from his chest, she whispered against his lips, "Let's take this to my bedroom."

His dark eyes searched her face. "Are you sure?"

"My neck is fine."

"I wasn't talking about your neck, I—"

She knew exactly what he meant, but the ring from her phone cut him off. She held up her finger. "Normally, I wouldn't take a call at a moment like this, but under the circumstances…"

Rolling from his lap, she grabbed her phone from the coffee table. She held it in front of him. "It's Lulu."

"Take it."

"Hi, Lulu." She carefully pressed the button for the speaker.

"Girl, are you all right?"

"Why wouldn't I be all right?" The blood thumped in her ears.

"You bounced out of here so fast I thought maybe someone recognized you."

"Recognized me? I thought you said it was okay for me to be there."

"Cut the crap, Ashlynn. I know who you are and, if anyone else does, you could be in big trouble."

Chapter Twelve

Ashlynn licked her lips and flicked a quick glance at Denver, who avoided giving her the *I told you so* look. "Do you think anyone else knows?"

"I'm not sure, but that's not the point. I've been reading the blog, so I know what you're after. I don't know who killed Tiana Fuller, but I do know for a fact that she was working for my sister's campaign. That cop will never find her name on any paperwork here, but I've got proof…if you want it."

"I do want it." Ashlynn rubbed the back of her neck. "Can you email or text it to me?"

Lulu paused. "I wouldn't chance it. Meet me tonight and I'll hand over the proof."

Denver jabbed her hip and shook his head.

She rolled her eyes at him. "How about tomorrow?"

"I want to unload this as soon as possible. I stole it, and I don't want it in my possession anymore. Come get it tonight, or I'm tossing it."

"Wait, wait. I'll meet you. Tell me where." She pointed to Denver and then herself. He could come along. In fact, she wanted him at least in the vicinity.

Lulu said, "There's a dog park at Mulholland and Laurel Canyon. I'll meet you in the parking lot in an hour."

Ashlynn ignored Denver's furious slicing motions in

the air and answered Lulu. "I'll be there. It's going to be safe, right?"

"You don't have to worry about me. I want to help you, but nobody can know what I'm doing. I didn't make you fill out that paperwork today, did I? That's because I recognized you right away. I just wanna be part of the blog."

"I'm not going to call you out."

"God, no. Don't do that, but I'd still know I was part of the blog."

"Okay. I'll see you in an hour."

When she ended the call, she held up her hand against Denver's protests. "She's right. She kept quiet about me today at the campaign headquarters when she could've outed me, and she invited me to the fundraiser, knowing who I was."

"You don't even know if she's telling the truth. Maybe she had no idea who you were earlier. She just found out at the fundraiser because someone told her, and now she'd luring you out with promises of proof that Tiana worked for the campaign." He sat forward and grabbed her hands. "Someone just tried to bulldoze you off Mulholland and now you're returning to… Mulholland. Not a great idea."

"You're coming with me." She drilled her finger into his chest, regretting she'd never even gotten to take off his shirt.

He captured her finger. "This time. I can't be protecting you twenty-four seven, Ashlynn. I do have a job."

"I don't need protection all day, every day. This is one situation that might be a little sketchy, and this *is* your job."

He squeezed his eyes closed and pinched the bridge of his nose. "If Lulu has this proof that Tiana worked for her sister, why not just call me?"

"You're kidding, right? If Veronica Escalante or her

top dog, Jed, knew Lulu even had this information, never mind turning it over to the cops, they'd go ballistic."

"Why? Why the secrecy?" He slammed his fist into his palm. "If they didn't have anything to hide, why would it matter that Tiana worked for the campaign? They must be involved in her death or know something about it."

"Or they just don't want the campaign to be associated with a murder." She pushed up from the couch, tugging on the hem of her dress. "I'm going to change for this meeting. It's probably better if she doesn't see you. She'd recognize you, anyway."

"You think?" He pinched the material of his cotton T-shirt between his fingers. "I'm not wearing my suit, and I have a baseball cap in the car."

"Oh, she noticed you today. I doubt she's going to forget what you look like, regardless of your clothes." She headed for her bedroom and spun around. "Dodgers, Angels or Padres?"

"What?" He glanced up from his phone, his brows knitted over his nose.

"The baseball cap—Dodgers, Angels or Padres?"

"Are you serious? The Dodgers, of course."

She nodded and slipped into her bedroom.

"LULU HAD BETTER not be here early. One look at me and she'll probably bolt—if what you said was true and she'd recognize me." The knots in Denver's gut tightened as he took the last curve toward the dog park.

"Lulu thought you were hot. She's not going to forget." Ashlynn glanced at the phone in her hand. "Besides, we got here in thirty-five minutes. There's no way she'd be this early."

"If Lulu's not alone, take off."

"And leave you out in the park?"

"You can swing by and pick me up later. Get out of here if something feels off." His hands gripping the steering wheel, Denver turned into the lot for the park.

It was really a playground for kids, with equipment and everything, but it was also an off-leash dog park for part of the day. The edge of the common area rushed downhill in a tangle of bushes and undergrowth. He didn't want to hide that far away from the car. He didn't want to be here at all. When people had to meet in secret to give up information they shouldn't have, it all screamed danger.

He let out a long breath as he scanned the empty parking lot. A few lights beamed down on the asphalt, and Denver pulled in under one of them.

He cracked open the driver's-side door. "You could leave the engine running, just in case you need to make a quick getaway. If you see any other car besides Lulu's BMW pull in, take off. If you see anyone in her passenger seat, take off."

"I got it, Denver." She pushed at his arm. "You'd better find your hiding spot before Lulu gets here. She might take off herself if she sees you."

"I'll be behind that clump of bushes at the edge of the playground. If worse comes to worst, run toward me and I'll have you covered."

"You mean with a gun?"

He patted his hip where he'd clipped his holster back onto his belt at her place. "Yeah."

"And I've got my pepper spray." She pulled her purse into her lap.

"Then we've got all bases covered." He tugged on a lock of her hair. "Be careful, and don't do anything stupid."

"I'll be fine. Go."

He stepped from the car, and Ashlynn didn't even bother getting out on her side. He watched through the window as she crawled over the console and slid into the driver's seat.

He loped toward the swing set and ducked behind the bushes bordering the play area. He crouched on his haunches and played with the branches of the bush to get a clear view of his car and Ashlynn's silhouette.

That phone call from Lulu had saved him from making a big mistake tonight. As much as he wanted Ashlynn, he didn't need the emotional entanglement right now—or ever. Would he be crouching behind a bush in the middle of the night if they hadn't almost wound up in her bed?

He sucked in a breath as a pair of headlights swept into the parking lot. Squinting into the darkness, he made out the BMW logo on the front of the car, but he couldn't tell who was driving or if the driver had company.

The car pulled into a space two down from Ashlynn, and the dome light illuminated the interior as the driver got out of the vehicle. His muscles relaxed a little when he recognized Lulu, tossing her long dark hair over her shoulder. She obviously hadn't changed from the party, and the light from the lamp above caught the sequins on her dress, which shimmered as she approached Ashlynn.

As Ashlynn popped her own door, Denver murmured to himself, "No, no, no. Stay in the car."

The two women met in the parking lot, and he strained to hear their voices, rising and falling in a conversational cadence. He covered his mouth with his hand and said, "Get the proof and get out."

As Denver massaged a cramp in his thigh, he caught sight of a shadow moving into the parking lot from the road. His nostrils flared. Was that an animal? Coyotes and even mountain lions roamed this area. The park had closed for a while a few years ago after a coyote had attacked a few dogs.

He blinked at the spot where he'd noticed the movement. The shadow had taken the shape of a dark figure—a man-sized figure. Denver grabbed his gun from the holster, the muscles in his legs coiled.

People came to this park all the time at night for a variety of reasons, but they usually drove cars. A walk from one of the nearby residences would be a tricky proposition, and it was a bit late for a stroll.

Had Ashlynn and Lulu noticed the man? Denver whistled in what he hoped was an approximation of a night bird's cry. He didn't even care at this point if Lulu made him.

Ashlynn turned her head to the side.

Had she noticed the man yet?

Lulu had. She jerked back and grabbed Ashlynn's arm as the man emerged from the shadows, his arm outstretched as he approached them.

The light glinted on an object in the stranger's hand and his voice carried all the way to the playground. "Hand it over."

Gripping his weapon, Denver lunged from his hiding place. "Get down, get down, get down."

The adrenaline coursing through his veins propelled him into the parking lot.

Ashlynn dropped to the ground and grabbed Lulu's hand, dragging her down with her.

The man spun around and ran for the edge of the park, speeding across the grass flattened by countless dogs over the years.

Denver gave chase, shouting over his shoulder, "Get in the car and leave—now."

He slammed into the side of a picnic table that had

come out of nowhere, his knees hitting the attached bench, his palms slapping the top of the table. Cursing, he pushed off and scanned the edge of the canyon that dipped away from the park.

The man had disappeared into the foliage. Had probably rolled down the hill. Denver didn't want to play hide-and-seek in the canyon, even if he had the superior weapon.

He gave up the chase and limped back to the parking lot, the gun still in his hand. This guy could have an accomplice.

He tripped to a stop, his heart thundering in his chest. Lulu's BMW was gone, but his car sat in the same spot... empty. He'd told Ashlynn to get in the car and take off, but maybe someone had prevented her from leaving.

The breath rasped in his throat as he yelled, "Ashlynn! Ashlynn!"

A head popped up on the driver's side of the car, and he stumbled again, his knees weak. He circled around the vehicle and yanked on the handle of the passenger side. The locks clicked and he tried again, swinging the door open so hard it almost closed again.

He dropped onto the seat and asked, "Are you okay?"

"I'm fine. What happened out there?"

"Move." He smacked the dashboard with his hand. "Move."

She cranked on the engine and peeled out of the parking lot, the back tires fishtailing on the loose dirt.

When she steadied the car, he smoothed a hand over her arm. "What happened? Is Lulu all right?"

"She's okay, but she's not happy with me."

"With you? Is she the one who invited the goon with the knife to the meeting?"

"If she was, she's a good actress. She was as surprised and scared as I was when he showed up."

"What did he want? What did he say? I heard 'hand it over' at about the same time I saw the glint of the knife in his hand."

"H-he said he wanted our phones, cash, jewelry."

Denver said, "He was pretending to be a common mugger, but we know better, and Lulu knows better. The whole thing could've been a setup, designed to lure you into another dangerous situation."

"I don't think so, Denver. I don't think Lulu knew about the man with the knife."

"Really? She gets you to meet her at a deserted park in the dead of night on the pretense of giving you proof that Tiana worked for the Escalante campaign and, instead of getting the proof, you almost get knifed. And *she's* mad at *you*?" He plowed a hand through his hair.

"But it didn't play out like that."

"What do you mean? I saw it unfold right in front of me. I chased the guy before he disappeared into the canyon."

"Yeah, that all happened, but I didn't walk away empty-handed." Ashlynn reached into the cup holder and dangled a thumb drive from her fingertips. "Lulu delivered the goods."

Chapter Thirteen

Denver jerked his head to the side, almost giving himself whiplash. He held out his hand and she dropped the thumb drive onto his palm. "Did she say what was on it?"

"Nope." Ashlynn carefully negotiated the last curve and pulled up to a red light at the bottom of the hill. "Just told me it contained proof that Tiana worked for the Escalante campaign."

"How'd she get a copy? They must know she has it."

"Slow down a minute." Ashlynn rubbed the back of her neck. "I can't drive, talk and think at the same time, not when I can't even turn my head."

"Take the turn onto Hollywood Boulevard. We'll get coffee. I have a lot of questions for you."

She slid a gaze to the side. "I have a few for you, too. Why are you limping?"

"I tripped over a picnic bench in the dark. Once that happened, your assailant had disappeared into the canyon that borders the park. I had no chance of finding him." He tapped on the windshield. "Pull into that diner."

Ashlynn signaled a left turn and cruised into the lot of an all-night diner. Patrons for the nearby clubs and bars packed the place, and they grabbed a table in the corner that hadn't been cleared yet.

A busboy swept up the clutter as they sat and ordered two coffees.

Denver, having pocketed the thumb drive, drew it out and dangled it over the table by its ribbon. "This is the proof, huh?"

"That's what Lulu said—before we were rudely interrupted."

"Lulu seemed surprised by the intrusion?"

"Surprised, scared, mad. It was legit. She didn't know." Ashlynn spread her hands on the table, her thumbs touching. "Besides, why would she hand off evidence to me while she was planning to have someone take it right away?"

"To cover herself." He bobbled the drive. "We don't yet know what this contains. It could be garbage."

"One way to find out. Don't know why we're wasting our time here." She circled her finger in the air.

He closed his hand around the device. "Because you— we both just had a scare. The information on this thumb drive isn't going anywhere."

The waitress came to their table and poured coffee into their upturned cups. "Anything else?"

Denver asked, "Do you have blueberry pie?"

"We do, hon. Ice cream with that?"

"Ice cream and two forks." Denver held up two fingers.

Cupping her chin with her hand, Ashlynn tilted her head. "I thought most cops dealt with stress by drinking whiskey. Your poison is blueberry pie à la mode?"

He blew on his coffee before taking a sip. "Don't knock it until you've tried it. A lot of people eat when they're stressed out."

"Or don't."

"Sorry?"

"Never mind." She rubbed her hands together. "I'm ready for your questions. I'm anxious to see what we have here."

"What were you and Lulu talking about for so long? I thought you'd grab whatever she had and we'd get out of there."

"I wanted to ask her how she knew who I was."

"And?"

"She's a big fan of the blog—was a big fan of my brother's."

Denver trapped his sigh in his throat. Couldn't she just once take credit for the blog without bringing her brother into it?

"You said before, your picture's not on the blog and you keep a low profile otherwise. How'd she know you were Ashlynn Hughes?"

"Just my luck, she's kind of obsessive about true crime in general and *LA Confidential* in particular." She folded her hands around her cup and stared into the steam rising from it. "When Sean was murdered, Lulu followed everything about the case and, somewhere in the coverage, my name was mentioned. She looked me up. She saw my picture and recognized me that first day. That's why she didn't follow up with Jed's instructions to have me fill out paperwork, which would've meant a copy of my driver's license."

"You dodged a bullet. Is that why she didn't turn you in to Jed? Because she's a super fan of the blog?"

"That's one reason, or maybe it's the main reason. She invited me to the fundraiser and offered me this info because she wants to be involved in the blog."

"Why didn't she just give you the proof tonight at the party?"

She crinkled her nose. "She wasn't sure she was going

to turn it over. Then when I left so suddenly, she thought I might be in trouble and figured she needed to reveal the truth. She swears neither Jed nor Veronica knows my identity."

"Someone does." He smacked his fist on the table, sending tiny ripples through the coffee.

"Does that mean you want more coffee?" The waitress delivered the pie, two scoops of vanilla ice cream already melting into the crust."

"Sorry, just making a point. This looks great, thanks." Denver aimed a smile at the waitress. He didn't want her to think he and Ashlynn were fighting.

She glanced at Ashlynn's full cup. "Do you want something else, hon?"

"Water would be great."

Denver plucked a couple of paper napkins from the dispenser on the table and dropped them onto his lap. He pointed his fork at Ashlynn. "You'd better eat some of this pie, or that waitress is going to think this is some kind of domestic situation."

"Only a cop would think something like that." She plucked up a fork and ran the tines through the ice cream, scooping up a berry from the plate.

The tart berries exploded in his mouth as the sweet ice cream melted down his throat. He closed his eyes, and Ashlynn nudged his foot under the table.

"Earth to Denver."

"See? Just relaxing." He swiped a napkin across his mouth. "When the stranger approached you, did Lulu seem to recognize him? Did you?"

"He was wearing a ski mask." She asked, "You didn't notice that?"

"I never got a good look at his face He stayed out of the light. How about his voice? Did it sound familiar?"

"No. Didn't jolt any memories for me." She held up her hand. "And before you ask me about race, hair color or anything like that, I couldn't tell you. He had a black turtleneck that met the ski mask, jeans, black gloves. All I can tell you is that he was average height because he was about as tall as me and a little shorter than you."

"Great." He dug his fork into the pie. "And he was a fast runner."

"Are you done with your questions?" She pulled her phone from her purse. "I'm going to check on Lulu."

"Not yet. We need to look at what's on the thumb drive first. If it's junk, she set you up. You need to know that before you communicate with her again." He picked up the other fork, lopped off a piece of pie and held it in front of her lips. "Try it. I can't eat the whole thing."

"Looks like you're doing a great job." She eyed the pie as if it were going to bite her instead of the other way around.

He tipped the fork back and forth. "Going, going…"

Ashlynn opened her mouth and closed her lips around the fork. She chewed for a few seconds and said, "Gone."

He pointed his fork at her phone on the table. "Lulu didn't text you, did she?"

"She didn't. When she heard you shouting, her eyes shot daggers at me. She hadn't expected me to bring company, even if she didn't recognize you as the hot cop from before."

"Even though I could've been saving your lives at that point? What did she think was going to happen? What did you think was going happen?"

"I figured we'd hand over our money, phones, jewelry, and then he'd ask me for the thumb drive, like, 'by the way, give me that, too,' even though we'd all know that's what he'd wanted in the first place."

"He could've hurt you. He had a knife. That's no joke. Yeah, it wasn't a match for my gun, but when someone is that close to you, a knife can do fatal damage."

"I'd transferred my pepper spray from my purse to my pocket. Before you stormed out of your hiding place, I'd planned on using it."

Denver's heart skipped several beats. That could've been a deadly move on Ashlynn's part. He opened his mouth and then nipped it shut. She hadn't had to use the pepper spray—no point in lecturing her.

He pushed away the plate, which had become a swirling mess of purple and white. "We know we weren't followed to the park. I made sure of it on the way over. The only way that guy shows up is if the meeting was a setup, or he followed Lulu."

"He followed Lulu. There's no way that was a setup, or Lulu should stop wasting her time stuffing envelopes and become an actress. She was clearly shocked." Ashlynn ran the tip of her finger through the blueberry swirl and sucked it off.

Denver followed the action and swallowed a gulp of lukewarm coffee. "Why is Lulu being followed? Is it because Jed or her sister don't trust her, or is it because someone saw her talking to you and knows she invited you to the gala?"

"I don't know. Did the pie do its job? Are you done unwinding?" She fingered the thumb drive he'd left on the table. "I'm dying to find out what's on this thing."

"That—" he slipped the drive into his pocket and slapped a ten on the table "—is a bad choice of words."

HE'D TAKEN OVER the driving duty from Ashlynn and forty minutes later, he pulled into the driveway of her duplex.

As they'd turned onto her block, Denver had driven

slowly and studied every car. Maybe they hadn't been followed, but the people after Ashlynn had already proved they knew where she lived. A few new locks might not be enough to keep them out, especially if they believed she had proof that Tiana had volunteered for the campaign in her possession.

When he put the car in Park, he reached for her arm. "Do me a favor and sit in the car until I come around and let you out."

"Is this a sudden spasm of chivalry, or do you think someone's watching us?"

"Chivalry all day, baby."

"Right." She smirked but stayed put as he hustled around to her side, his hand hovering over his gun.

He cracked open the door. "Okay, let's move."

Luckily, Ashlynn's long legs kept up with his stride as he propelled her to the front door. While she unlocked the dead bolt, he did a half turn and blocked her body with his, his gaze scanning the sidewalk and probing the bushes.

He followed her inside and locked up as she headed straight for her laptop.

"You finally ready to see what we have here?"

"Sated with blueberry pie and ready." He pulled the thumb drive from his pocket and handed it to her.

When she woke up her computer, she inserted the drive into the port on the side. A folder opened, containing a video from a phone. Ashlynn double clicked on it.

When the video launched, it displayed a blurry thumbnail of the side of a desk.

"Play it." Denver said the words at the same time Ashlynn clicked the play button.

They both huddled forward to watch, their heads almost touching.

A man's voice came over the computer's speakers as the video showed a table with a couple of cans of soda and a woman's arm, her fingers tapping the table. "So, you're good with that, Tiana?"

Ashlynn sucked in a breath. "That's Jed's voice."

A female voice responded. "Sure. I'll do whatever it takes to stop a second term for Mayor Wexler."

Jed said, "Hold on. I need to answer this text."

The view of the camera shifted upward as Jed held up the phone, pretending to answer a text. As Tiana Fuller came into focus, Denver said, "Stop it."

Ashlynn clicked the mouse. "Tiana doesn't know she's being filmed, does she? Jed was holding the phone in his hand and secretly turned on the video. Now he's pretending to answer a text just so he can hold up the phone and capture Tiana on camera."

"Exactly." Denver's jaw tightened as he looked at Tiana, vibrant and very much alive. "Let's hope Jed reiterates what he just suggested to Tiana, and what she just agreed to do."

When Ashlynn tapped Play, Tiana came to life and tucked a strand of light brown hair behind her ear, presumably waiting for Jed to stop texting.

The camera view shifted to the side, as if Jed were still holding it up but not pointing it directly at Tiana. Jed continued. "It's just a few dirty tricks, right? Nothing too serious, nothing against the law. Campaigns do it all the time. Hell, we might have a Wexler mole in our own office."

Tiana laughed; a high, tinkling sound that made Denver flinch. "You never know, huh? This could be fun. This is the side of politics that interests me—the behind-the-scenes stuff, what makes a campaign tick."

"I'm with you on that. The upside is that Veronica

Escalante is a great leader. You'll be providing a great service to the city if you can help get her elected as the next mayor of LA."

"I can't wait to start. Will you invite me to all the war room meetings? I feel as if I have a lot to learn from you, Mr. Gordon. You're the best." Tiana gave a flirtatious giggle.

Jed coughed. "I think I can teach you a few tricks."

The video ended and Ashlyn turned to face Denver, her eyes wide. "Sounds like Jed recruited Tiana to spy on the Wexler campaign. Why would he lie to you about knowing her, and why'd he take this video?"

"I'm not sure about any of that yet, but after watching that video—" he tapped the laptop's screen "—I'm starting to wonder who was playing who."

Chapter Fourteen

"Something sounded off to me, too." Ashlynn sat back and jabbed a finger at the video still on the screen. "Was Tiana *flirting* with Jed? He sounded all in control, and then she turned on the feminine charm to flatter him when she didn't need to. She'd already gotten the gig, right? Sounds like she'd got it even before the video started."

"I'm glad you heard it, too. I didn't know if I was picking up on her tone because I'm a guy or because I'm a detective. But the dynamic shifted at the end." He shoved that lock of hair from his forehead. "One thing that is clear from this video is that the Escalante campaign was using Tiana to get some dirt on the Wexler campaign."

Ashlynn bit the side of her thumb. "Maybe she got the dirt, someone from the CREW found out and killed her for it."

"Why would the Escalante campaign be hiding that information?" He spread his hands. "If Jed's right and everyone plays these tricks, what's the problem for them? I'd say murder is a little more serious than campaign dirty tricks. You'd think he'd want to point the finger at the Wexler campaign."

"You'd think. I mean that's not a good look for Escalante, either. Set up a young girl to pull a fast one on a political campaign, and then she gets murdered."

"Why?" Denver jumped up from the couch and circled the room. "What exactly did Tiana find out about Wexler? And if she did dig up some serious infraction, why wouldn't Escalante use it? That info should be all over the news by now."

Ashlynn flopped back against the cushions of the couch, suddenly exhausted. "Something's not adding up, but I guess it explains why Tiana never told her parents she was working for Escalante. She must've been there in an undercover capacity. That's why the other volunteers didn't know her—and I believe them."

"Lulu knew about Tiana because Lulu, whether she likes it or not, is in the inner circle. Maybe that's why Lulu gave you the video. She thinks it's going to help her sister's campaign." Denver finally stopped pacing and propped his shoulder against the wall, folding his arms.

"I'm not sure Lulu is all that interested in helping her sister's campaign, but I'm wondering why she decided to color outside the lines and copy this video. Just to be part of *LA Confidential*?"

"And why did Jed make the video?"

"That makes no sense to me, either." She patted the couch next to her. "Have a seat. You're making me nervous, and you're still limping."

"Maybe he made it to have proof that Tiana agreed to the spying, in case things went sideways and she accused the campaign of coercing her." Denver sliced his hand through the air, still standing against the wall. "That doesn't make sense. Jed still looks complicit in that video. He's not doing himself any favors."

"Maybe he didn't make the video for protection but as proof he asked Tiana. Maybe he made the video for Veronica."

Denver shrugged and then crossed the room to perch on the arm of the couch, his leg brushing her arm. "Whatever his motives, Lulu got hold of the video and gave it to you."

"Speaking of Lulu, now that we know her proof was legit, I'm going to text her and make sure she's okay."

Denver warned. "Keep me out of it. Even if she thinks she recognized me, don't cop to it—and tell her to be careful. She has an enemy in the campaign."

Ashlynn snatched up her phone from next to the computer on the coffee table, and typed a message to Lulu. She waved the phone at Denver. "I just told her thanks for the video and asked if she was okay."

"How about you?" He stroked her hair. "Are you okay? The threats seem to be building against you—two in one day. How's your neck?"

She squeezed the back of her neck. "The car wreck seems like it happened days ago. I feel all right. Did you happen to hear from the tow service about my car?"

He patted his pocket. "Forgot to tell you. They towed the car and tested it at the yard. It started just fine. I can take you there tomorrow morning to pick it up. They mentioned a few scratches on the body and sent pictures. I'll send those to you."

"Now I'm feeling even better."

He asked, "Anything from Lulu yet?"

"No. My phone dings when texts come through." She turned over her phone and glanced at the display, just in case. "I hope she's okay, too. She must've risked a lot to get that video and then hand it off to me."

"What is it with Lulu, anyway? Does she hate or love her sister?"

"A little of both, I think." Ashlynn picked up her laptop and carried it to her kitchen table. She plugged in the charger. "She doesn't like the phoniness of politicians, but Veronica basically supports Lulu in a style that she enjoys—mostly from Veronica's husband."

"I looked him up. The dude's a high roller. He's putting up buildings all over downtown LA. Even if Escalante loses, and I think she will, she won't be hurting for money."

Ashlynn ran her fingers through her hair. "I'm glad you were there tonight. I don't know if that guy would've hurt us, but he would've taken the thumb drive for sure."

"I wasn't about to let you meet Lulu on your own, not after what happened on Mulholland." He rubbed his knee. "Even if I missed the guy."

"Maybe *you* need some ice." She tipped her head toward the fridge. "Can I get you some?"

"I'll survive, but you can give me the thumb drive."

She dropped her lashes and wound an errant strand of hair around her finger. "You're leaving already?"

"Already? It's late. I thought you were exhausted." He stretched, and her gaze meandered down his body.

"I thought maybe…before…" She covered her warm face with her hands. "I was hoping you'd stay, and we could finish what we'd started earlier, before Lulu's text."

The silence from across the room rolled over her in waves. She spread open her fingers and peered at him through the narrow spaces.

He rose slowly from the couch, as if in slow motion, his gait halting, which had nothing to do with his knee.

His eyes kindled with a dark seductiveness that she

felt as a tremble through her body. Her toes curled into the floor.

"You're sure?" His voice sounded gruff, as if he hadn't used it in years. Or maybe there was something else he hadn't used in years.

"You don't want me to sign a contract, do you?" Without expending conscious effort in the act, she'd been moving toward him and the invitation in his eyes.

"No, but—" he spread his hands "—I don't have any protection."

She flicked her fingers. "I do."

At the quirk of his eyebrows, she said, "I—I mean they're leftovers. Could even be expired by now."

His lips curled, and they were close enough now that she could see the slight flush on his throat. "I'm willing to take my chances, if you are."

She exhaled, and he took the final step toward her and gathered her into his arms. His kiss burned hotter than it had before, as if he'd been warming up and now it was full-steam ahead.

She wrapped her arms around his neck and sagged against his body. She didn't have the energy to play any games with him. If he could take her right now, she'd gladly face her next brush with death.

As if he sensed she'd never let him go, he swept her up into his arms and murmured against her lips, "Bedroom?"

"Uh-huh." Her place was small enough that he remembered the way, and her body jostled against his as he carried her to her room.

He actually had to kick open the door, which only added to the deliciousness of this moment. His next move had to be tossing her across the bed, but he must've figured her body had endured too much trauma tonight.

He backed up to the bed and sat on the edge, still holding her, folding her into his lap, her long legs awkwardly hanging over his thighs, her toes brushing the carpet.

She ran her hands beneath his shirt, the texture of his warm skin causing her fingertips to buzz. Lulu could keep her smooth sugar daddy. She'd take this slightly tangy, rough-around-the-edges cop any day.

Denver fell back on the bed and toed off his shoes.

Rolling to his side, she yanked open the drawer of her nightstand, feeling around for the foil packets of condoms.

She dragged out a strip and waved them in the air. "I think they're still good."

He unbuckled his belt and unzipped his jeans. "I think they have a shelf life of a hundred years, just in case."

She curled her hand over his as he hooked a thumb in his fly. "Let me undress you a little at a time. I'm not sure my system can withstand the shock of seeing a totally naked man in my bed all at once."

"Watch what you're calling little."

She giggled like a virgin schoolgirl and tugged at his shirt. As it rolled up his body, her hands replaced the material and she caressed his flesh, feeling him shiver beneath her touch.

She planted a kiss at the base of his throat where his pulse throbbed and slid her hand down his belly to his open fly. She peeled back his jeans and he lifted his hips to help her do the honors.

Suddenly, she lost all patience, hooked her thumbs beneath the elastic of his boxers and yanked them down to his muscular thighs along with his jeans.

She sighed and smoothed her hands over him. "Nothing little about it."

He kicked off his pants. "Your turn and, unlike you,

I'm looking forward to seeing a totally naked woman all at once. I'll get over the shock quick enough."

She unbuttoned her shirt and shrugged out of it. Presenting her back to him, she said, "Can you unhook my bra? It sort of hurts my neck when I reach around."

With a twist of his fingers, he unhooked her and didn't even wait for the bra to come off her arms before he reached around and cupped her breasts.

He sucked in a breath. "Pretty and pert, just as I'd imagined them."

She cranked her head over her shoulder despite the pain. "You were imagining my breasts."

"Among other things." He stroked her cheek. "Turn around."

She shimmied around to face him and then lay on the bed next to him. He pulled off her jeans and underwear as she twisted this way and that—anything to facilitate his access to her body.

He trailed his fingers from her neck to her belly, and she arched her back. Placing a finger against her throbbing lips, he said, "Don't hurt your neck. I'll do all the work."

She narrowed her eyes. "Do you think making love to me is going to be work?"

"Some of us love our jobs."

And she approved of the tools of his trade as he used his lips, tongue and fingers to push all the right buttons.

When he had her breathless and panting, he entered her fully.

Her hands clawed through his thick hair and then she dug her fingernails into his shoulders as he moved against her, in her, with her. Her muscles tightened, and she wrapped her arms and legs around his frame, drawing him further inside.

Ashlynn broke apart when she reached her climax, which gave him the signal to release. As she came down from her high, he thrust into her, building to his own peak.

When he came inside her, she felt his pleasure in every shiver and tremble of his body. Spent, he shifted to her side and growled in her ear, "Was that worth all the pain and suffering you've been through?"

Speechless, she nodded and turned toward him, molding her body to his side.

When the lethargy left her body and Denver's breathing no longer sounded like he'd just run a marathon, Ashlynn scooted off the bed. "I'm going to brush my teeth and splash some water on my face."

"I'll dispose of the evidence and put some toothpaste on my finger and run it across my teeth." He gathered up the used condom with a tissue from her nightstand and planted his feet on the floor.

"I may even have an extra toothbrush from my dentist, so you don't need to rough it."

As Denver went to the kitchen to get some water, Ashlynn brushed her teeth, washed her face and found a brand-new toothbrush for him.

He handed her a glass of water and disappeared into the bathroom. By the time he came out, she'd straightened the covers and fluffed the pillows.

"Come join me." She patted the bed. "This is the part where we cuddle. Do you mind?"

"If that means I get to relish the touch of your bare skin against mine and wrap my fingers in your red-gold hair as I drift off to sleep, you can call that anything you like."

The bed dipped as he slid in beside her. He hadn't been kidding about the skin-on-skin contact or the hair, but there was no drifting for Denver. Within minutes of his head hitting the pillow, he was out.

She soaked in the feel of his heavy arm around her waist, his warm breath against the back of her neck. It felt good to have someone on that side of the bed again—she'd even deal with the messed-up covers in the morning.

He took a few shuddering breaths and rolled away from her, onto his other side.

A few minutes later, she hoisted herself up on one elbow and peered over his shoulder. That pesky lock of hair lay plastered against his forehead. Lifting it with one finger, she kissed the skin beneath it, her breasts pressing against his arm.

He stirred and mumbled in his sleep, and she held her breath until he settled again, his breathing slow and steady.

Then she slipped out of the bed. She bent at the waist and picked up his T-shirt from the floor, pinching it between two fingers. Dangling the shirt by her side, she tiptoed from the bedroom. She pulled the door almost closed behind her.

She dragged his T-shirt over her head, thrusting her hands through the sleeves. Her nostrils flared as she inhaled his scent—a mixture of citrus and spicy, his body wash and deodorant at war with each other.

With the T-shirt brushing her thighs, she padded to the kitchen, the cold tile shocking the soles of her bare feet. She settled into a chair at the kitchen table, and flipped open her charging laptop, the thumb drive still jutting out from the side.

She right-clicked the video icon on the screen and made quick work of copying the recording to her laptop. She ejected the drive and tugged it from the computer port. Swinging the thumb drive from its ribbon, she crept to where Denver had left his jacket draped over the back of the chair and tucked it into his pocket—so he wouldn't forget it in the morning.

She returned to the laptop, eyeing it as if it were a dangerous snake ready to strike. Then she plopped down on the chair and brought up *LA Confidential*.

Biting her bottom lip, she glanced down the hallway at the bedroom door behind which Denver lay slumbering like a man with no reason to suspect a betrayal. She shook her head and brushed her hair out of her face. Denver hadn't told her *not* to post this video.

The people of LA had a right to know the dirt about the campaign of one of its mayoral candidates. Her online sleuths had a right to know. Maybe with this video out there, someone else might step forward with more information. As far as Ashlynn could tell, her readers were the ones bringing the heat on this investigation—not the LAPD.

She clicked on the button for a new post and began to type, the words of the blockbuster story pounding against her temples. She read the first few sentences aloud in a harsh whisper. "'Escalante campaign busted. Proof surfaces that murdered student Tiana Fuller had volunteered for the campaign in a covert role.'"

Ashlynn's fingers flew across the keyboard, each click a nail in the coffin of her budding relationship with Detective Denver Holt.

Chapter Fifteen

Denver woke up with a start, his body bolting upright in the bed. For a second, he couldn't remember where he was. Then his fingers smoothed a lock of Ashlynn's bright hair against her pillow. But he sure remembered who he was with.

He eased out of the bed and crept from the room on silent feet. Ashlynn seemed to have a well-stocked fridge, unlike most single women he knew, so maybe he could whip up some breakfast for them before they had to take off.

He couldn't let her sleep much longer. He had to get home and change before work, and drop off Ashlynn at the tow yard to pick up her car. He couldn't exactly go into the station looking like this.

He swept his boxers from the floor and stepped into them. Then he snatched his neatly folded T-shirt from the top of her dresser. He cocked his head as he shook out the shirt. Had he placed it there while in the throes of lust? If so, he'd exercised more self-control than he remembered. He shrugged and pulled it over his head. After tugging up his jeans, he made a beeline for the kitchen.

Ashlynn's laptop sat on the kitchen table, charging. His heart skipped a beat as he brushed his hand across the side of the computer where he'd expected to find the thumb drive sticking out.

Then his heart skipped another beat as Ashlynn stood, framed in the hallway, naked from her head to her toes, a grin lighting up her face. "Good morning."

"Morning, you." He jabbed a finger at the laptop. "I was looking for Lulu's thumb drive."

"I put it in your pocket, so you wouldn't forget it this morning." She stretched her arms over her head, tangling her hair in her fingers, just as he'd done last night. "Are you making breakfast, or what?"

He made a sweeping motion with his hand. "Go do your thing. I'll whip up something."

While Ashlynn showered and dressed, Denver scrambled some eggs and shoved a couple of pieces of bread in the toaster. She'd run out of coffee, but he could always drink the swill at the station.

He glanced at her closed laptop on the table. She was usually glued to that thing first thing in the morning. Shower must've been more important than the blog this morning.

"Smells great." She bustled through the room, her long legs in a pair of dark jeans, her red hair vibrant against an emerald-green sweater. She joined him in the kitchen. "Sorry, I don't have any coffee. Tea?"

"I'll get some coffee at the station." He nodded at her plate on the table and jabbed a fork into his own eggs. "I forgot to tell you yesterday in all the excitement, Tiana's parents mentioned a boy. A young man Tiana was hanging out with ever since the beginning of the new semester. They figured he lived nearby because she saw him when she was home."

"You already told me about him. Tony Fuentes, right?"

"Good memory. I must still be rattled." He shook his

head as if to clear it, but he didn't think he'd ever dismiss the memory of Ashlynn's body beneath his hands. "With any luck, we'll get his number from Tiana's phone records. Weird that he hasn't called us if he was that close to Tiana."

"If he was her boyfriend, it's strange that he hasn't stepped forward." She crunched her toast.

"Not sure it reached that level, but parents are usually the last to know with these new dating rules."

"Are there new rules?" She blinked. "No wonder I can't get lucky."

He cleared his throat. "What would you call last night?"

"Luck had nothing to do with that." She fluttered her eyelashes. "I set my sights on you from the start."

Had she? Instead of feeling flattered, wings of anxiety took flight in his belly. He'd stumbled right into her web by playing the hero to the rescue. She'd been in real danger, though. She hadn't faked any of that.

She nudged him. "I'm joking."

"We'd better get moving." He shoved the last bite of toast in his mouth and chewed. "After I drop you at the tow yard, I have to go home and shower and change." He took his plate to the sink and rinsed it off before putting it in the dishwasher. "The thumb drive is in my pocket, right?"

"Yeah." She bumped his hip with hers in front of the sink. "I'm going to finish these delicious eggs, and then I'll put away the rest of this stuff. You should collect your gun. You don't wanna leave that here."

He tugged at the ends of her hair and kissed the crumbs off her mouth. "I'm glad you're safe. I'm glad Lulu's safe. How's your neck?"

"In need of pain relief. How's your knee?"

Reaching down and squeezing it, he said, "Just another war wound."

He left her in the kitchen and clipped his holster onto his belt. He felt the side pocket of his jacket, his fingers tracing the oblong shape of the thumb drive. Jed would have some explaining to do today and, with any luck, so would Tony Fuentes.

Ashlynn had been unusually quiet on the drive to the tow yard. Had they made a mistake sleeping together? How could a mistake feel so good? But the act had introduced a level of awkwardness between them that hadn't existed before.

Maybe once this case was over, they could date like normal people. He didn't even know what that looked like anymore. Other women he'd gone out with in the past had accused him of being cold and aloof.

He'd tried that with Ashlynn, but she'd poked through his reserve. He huffed out a breath as he pulled onto the freeway. He'd better get a grip. He couldn't be detached when he'd found Ashlynn in danger—and she always seemed to be in danger. The heightened stakes had them colliding together. She'd wanted him last night because he'd rescued her, and he couldn't deny it to himself that he'd wanted her for the same reason.

Coming to the rescue still gave him a charge, but only if he succeeded. If he were to fail…again, he'd wind up in a very dark place.

After showering and changing at home, he drove to the station. He parked and burst inside with purpose driving his steps. He'd call Jed Gordon first thing and ask him about the video. Then he'd circle back to the Wexler campaign and ask them what they knew about Escalante's dirty tricks. Christian had finally sent over the list of volunteers, and it was no surprise that Tiana wasn't among them.

As he jogged upstairs, he passed Detective Marino, who

slapped him on the back. "Good deal when the journos do our work for us, isn't it? I'm glad I let you take lead."

Denver almost tripped on the next step. "What?"

Marino waved his hand without answering, and Denver continued to his desk in Homicide, his steps decidedly slower. Was Marino directing that comment to him?

He yanked out his chair and fished the thumb drive out of his pocket. As he booted up his laptop, Captain Fields poked her head into the room. "Holt, my office."

With his mouth dry, he glanced around the room, but nobody met his eyes. He was being paranoid. He was lead detective on the Tiana Fuller case. Of course, the captain wanted to talk to him.

He tossed the drive in the air and caught it, clenching his hand around it. He had something to show her.

Captain Fields was already behind her desk when he approached the door. "Captain?"

"Have a seat, Holt."

He kicked out the chair in front of her desk and sat back. He didn't want to put his anxiety on display. He waited while she tapped her keyboard.

When he heard Jed Gordon's voice talking to Tiana Fuller, the blood drained from his face and his hands gripped the arms of the chair like claws.

Captain Fields spun her laptop around to face him, but he didn't need to look at the video. "How is it that a blogger is getting more information about the Tiana Fuller case than you are, Holt?"

He relaxed his clenched jaw and tipped his closed fist over, dropping the thumb drive on the blotter in front of her. "I have the same thing. That's Jed Gordon, Councilwoman Escalante's campaign manager, and he's talking to Tiana Fuller."

Her gaze flicked to the thumb drive. "I know that already and so does half of LA. My question to you is, why did half the city know this before I did?"

He lifted a stiff shoulder. "I guess my source delivered this video to me and... *LA Confidential*."

"You say *LA Confidential* as if that's a person. Your source didn't deliver it to *LA Confidential*. He or she delivered it to Ashlynn Hughes—the enemy."

His eyebrows jumped. "Enemy. That's kinda strong. I—I mean, she's not her brother. Her brother was murdered, for God's sake."

Hadn't Ashlynn just become the enemy to him? A person who'd used him, slept with him, to pull a fast one. The captain was right.

"Don't get me wrong." Captain Fields ended the video. "What The Player did to Sean Hughes was despicable. Nobody in this department would say otherwise, but when you play with fire, you can expect to get burned."

He rubbed his knuckles along his jaw, feeling the singe. "I don't think Ashlynn is as bad as her brother."

She just might be worse.

"Nevertheless, I don't like being blindsided, Holt."

"I'm sorry, Captain, but I can't control my sources. If they want to communicate with the press, they have a right to do that." He swept up the thumb drive and rapped his knuckles on the desk. "I was about to get right on this. I interviewed Jed Gordon yesterday, and he told me at the time he'd never heard of or seen Tiana Fuller. He might just be my first suspect."

"Get to it, Holt. I just hope the blogger didn't spook Gordon."

"If he runs now, we have even more reason to suspect him."

"Don't make me regret taking a floater and making

you lead detective on this, Holt." She waved her hand in dismissal.

"No, ma'am." So, he had Captain Field to thank for his position, not Marino.

As he walked back to his desk, he ground his back teeth. Why the hell was he defending Ashlynn to Captain Fields? She'd betrayed him.

Ashlynn hadn't been interested in her laptop this morning because she'd already written her blog and posted the video. When did she have time for that? Between kisses?

He slumped in his chair and brought up *LA Confidential* on his phone. He'd be damned if he'd let the other detectives catch him reading the blog on his laptop.

He didn't need to play the video, but he read the blog, his breath coming in short spurts as he cupped his hand over his cell. Damn, Ashlynn was a good writer.

The post had already garnered hundreds of comments. He'd cull through them for anything useful. What had Marino said...*journos do our work for us*? That might be good enough for Marino, but Denver wasn't about to let it happen on his watch.

He pulled Jed Gordon's card from the file on his desk, flicked the corner and then tucked it into his breast pocket. If Jed had any intention of running, Denver didn't want to give him a head start by calling him first.

Grabbing the keys to his department vehicle, he called out to nobody in particular. "Heading out for an interview."

Billy yelled back at him. "Get there before the blogger."

Denver held up his middle finger as he strode out the door, a chorus of laughter erupting behind him.

Wait until they found out he'd slept with that blogger last night. That wouldn't come from him, but who knows what Ashlynn had planned in her quest for blog world dominance.

When he got to his car, he shrugged off his jacket, feeling warm under the collar already. He smoothed it onto the front seat and took off for the Escalante campaign headquarters. He didn't expect to find Ashlynn there. She'd been made.

He'd better find Jed there.

This time when he burst through the door, heads swiveled and eyes darted. Before he had a chance to open his mouth, demanding to see Jed Gordon, the man himself glided out of his office, hand outstretched.

"Detective, I expected to see you this morning. Please join me for coffee down the street."

Denver gripped the other man's hand and searched his drawn face, the eyes pleading for...something. Was there fear in that look?

Nodding, Denver said, "Just so happened, I missed my morning coffee."

Jed's shoulders sagged in relief before his lips stretched into a smile. "Excellent. We can walk."

Jed barked a few orders to the staff on the way out, and heaved a long breath when they hit the sidewalk.

Denver looked over at him. "Everyone see that video?"

Jed said through gritted teeth, "Yes, and I'd like to know where that...blogger got it."

"Why'd you lie, Gordon?"

Jed put his fingers to his forehead and closed his eyes. "Can we wait until I'm sitting down with some coffee in front of me?"

Denver sealed his lips and walked beside Jed in silence until they reached a coffeehouse on the corner. Jed ordered a complicated concoction while Denver opted for the daily brew—black. He picked up the tab to get on Jed's good side.

When they sat across from each other at a large table, Jed slurped from his coffee cup. A thin layer of foam coated his upper lip, but he didn't seem to notice. "I lied to you yesterday. I knew Tiana Fuller and asked her to spy on the Wexler campaign for us."

"Yeah, I know that now." Denver popped the lid on his cup and blew on the steaming liquid. "The question is why."

"Why do you think?"

"Let me ask the questions, Gordon." Denver drilled his finger into the table, and Jed jerked back, his coffee sloshing over the rim.

"I asked a young woman to put herself at risk by pulling a few dirty tricks on Wexler, and she was found in the trunk of a Wexler car in a grungy lake. That makes me, the campaign and Veronica look bad."

"Yeah, you should've seen how it made Tiana look."

Jed's eyes bulged. "I never meant that young woman to come to any harm—none of us did. These things happen between political opponents. A little mudslinging here, a little defamation there—it's all part of the political landscape. The voters believe what they want to believe anyway."

"Whose idea was it to enlist Tiana Fuller's help?"

"It was hers."

"Sure it was." Denver crumpled a paper napkin in his fist. "She came up with that plan all by herself."

"Not the actual plan, but the suggestion." Jed swirled his coffee, his tongue darting out to capture some foam from the surface of the liquid. "Why do you think I videoed it on my phone?"

Denver leaned forward, spreading his hands on the table. "Explain it to me like I'm real stupid."

"I—I figured if I had Tiana on record agreeing to the plan, if anything happened, I'd have proof that she was a willing participant."

"What did you expect to happen?"

"Not *murder*." Jed's hand trembled so much, he had to set his cup down. "What could Tiana have possibly found out about the Wexler campaign that led them to murder her?"

"'Them'?"

"Wexler's people." Jed waved his hands in the air. "Isn't that obvious? The CREW found out Tiana was spying and took care of her…in one of their own cars."

Denver tented his fingers. "What *did* Tiana find out? Did she report anything to you?"

"She filed a few reports with me, but it was stupid, petty stuff. She discovered some of the Wexler volunteers were ripping down Escalante posters, creating fake social media accounts to bolster Wexler and criticize Escalante —that kind of thing. Do you think anything like that warrants murder?"

"Not one for politics, but I can't imagine it would. Was she working on something? Did she ever indicate to you that she'd discovered something big?" Denver's phone dinged in his pocket, signaling an incoming text, but he ignored it. He wasn't ready to hear Ashlynn's excuses or apologies.

"Never. Like I said before, all minor league stuff."

"Did Councilwoman Escalante know about Tiana's role in the campaign?"

"No!" Jed folded his hands around his cup, his face reddening. "She called me this morning and read me the riot act when she saw that video."

Denver traced a finger around the rim of his cup, his eyes downcast to the dark liquid he'd barely tasted. "Was she mad that you recruited Tiana to spy, or was she mad that you made the video and got caught?"

"Veronica is clean." Jed pounded his fist on the table and the little packets of sugar danced.

Denver held up his hands. "She's a politician. You just said this was common practice."

"Among the campaign workers."

"Oh, okay." Denver nodded slowly. "How did Tiana get all this information for you?"

Shrugging, Jed said, "I don't know. I didn't ask, and she didn't tell."

"What did you mean earlier when you said this spying was Tiana's idea?"

"Just that. She's the one who suggested it. Said she had some contacts in the CREW and she could use them to get some dirt on Wexler."

"That's not on the video." Denver drummed his fingers on the table. He still didn't get why Jed had lied to him about Tiana's role in the campaign if she'd just discovered minor infractions.

"I—I couldn't get my phone in place fast enough to record the beginning of our meeting, but trust me. Tiana came on as a volunteer, bumped into me at a lunch spot down the street and made her case. Of course, I jumped on it."

"How come none of the other volunteers know Tiana, or were they lying, too?"

"Lulu gave Tiana the tour." Jed took a sip of his coffee and choked on it.

Had he just realized who'd stolen the video from his computer?

Jed cleared his throat. "Lulu got her signed up, and

then destroyed Tiana's paperwork on my command. If Tiana got caught Watergate-style, I didn't want it to come back and bite us."

"If that's all that had happened." Denver fished his phone from his pocket after the second insistent ping and glanced at the unknown number, and the beginning of a text with his name.

"Are we finished here?" Jed pointed to Denver's phone. "Looks like you're busy, and I have to get back to it. I'll tell you anything you want, Detective. I don't have anything to hide, and neither does Veronica."

"Good, because I plan to pay her a visit." Denver lifted his cup. "You can leave. I'll stay and finish my coffee."

He watched Jed exit the coffeehouse, already on his phone. Was Jed warning Veronica? He seemed to worship the woman. The two of them had probably been discussing Tiana at the fundraiser last night when Ashlynn had seen them by the pool.

He tapped the insistent text, and adrenaline pumped through his system. Tiana's friend, Tony Fuentes, had finally surfaced and wanted to meet with him. He called the number on the text, but it went straight to a generic voice mail.

Two minutes later, Tony texted him that he couldn't talk on the phone but would meet with him in Venice by the pier. Why did everyone want to meet in Venice all of a sudden?

They arranged a meet location, and Denver took his coffee to keep him company on the long trip to the west side of the city. He could stop by Escalante's place on the way back to the station.

When he slid behind the wheel, he reached for his phone to text Ashlynn to tell her about Tony. He dropped it in the cup holder instead. Ashlynn Hughes could wait.

By the time he reached the Venice Pier, he had the AC blasting. They'd just come off a week of scattered showers, but the sun had been making a stronger appearance ever since and had hit peak Southern California spring beach day.

He parked in the lot next to the strand and left his jacket in the car. He stepped onto the asphalt, the sand crunching beneath his shoes. He couldn't do anything about his wingtips, but he could lose the tie.

He loosened his tie, pulled it over his head and undid the top buttons of his shirt. He dropped his tie on top of his jacket and locked up. He usually didn't leave anything on the seat of his car, especially in an area like this, but he figured the local beach transients wouldn't be interested in stealing his jacket and tie.

As he clumped through the dry sand, he rolled up his sleeves. Tony couldn't have picked a worse location, but Denver didn't want to spook the skittish boyfriend.

He spotted a figure beneath the pier and trudged over the beach toward him. As he drew closer, another person appeared next to the pilings, red hair streaming behind her in the breeze.

Denver's heart rattled his ribs. What the hell was Ashlynn doing here—at his meeting?

He picked up the pace and hit wet sand, veering to his right. "Tony Fuentes?"

The young man with a beard gathered his shoulder-length dark hair with one hand. "That's me. Detective Holt?"

Denver gripped Tony's hand and said, "Now that we've established who we are, can I ask why she's here?"

"Why do you think, Denver?" Ashlynn released her hair to put her hands on her hips, and the red locks caught fire from the sun as they whipped around her face. "This is my source."

Tony raised his hand. "Anthony Angel Fuentes, at your service."

Chapter Sixteen

Ashlynn sucked in her bottom lip. Denver looked ready to explode. She hadn't planned on contacting him today, hadn't even told him about this meeting with Angel, but when she'd seen Denver scuffing through the dry sand and realized Angel had called him, too, she wasn't going to run away. She wanted to hear what Angel had to say.

Denver closed his eyes for a second and wiped the back of his hand over his gleaming forehead. She felt for him. He must be burning up in that suit, or half a suit. He certainly *looked* hot.

"Why did you contact a blogger about Tiana's murder instead of the police, and I mean right from the beginning?"

Tony hunched his thin shoulders, his T-shirt billowing around his gaunt frame. "I was scared, dude. I wasn't sure you'd connect me to T, and I didn't want to expose myself. I don't wanna be next."

Denver held up his phone. "I'm recording this interview."

Not waiting for Tony's approval, Denver recorded the date and time, along with Tony's name. Then he went straight for the jugular. "Do you know who killed Tiana?"

"I don't know who did it." Tony ran his fingers

through his beard. "I—I only know how they disposed of her body."

Ashlynn asked, "How do you know that? How did you know about the car in the lake?"

Denver had turned his back to her, as if he could cut her out of his exchange with Tony. As if Tony hadn't contacted her, too. As if she wasn't a part of this investigation just as much as he was.

She pushed her way into their circle.

"I saw it happen." Tony ducked his head and his long hair curtained his face. When he looked up, he had tears in his eyes. "I knew T was meeting someone. I told her not to go. I warned her. She wouldn't listen to me."

"I know the feeling." Denver's jaw formed a hard line. "Who was she meeting? What did she find out about the Wexler campaign that led to her murder?"

"Dude, I don't know. She wouldn't tell me."

Ashlynn curled her toes into the wet sand. "How did you and Tiana know each other, school?"

"Yeah, we had a few poli-sci classes together." Tony wiped his face and sniffled. "I'm the one who got her to volunteer for the campaigns in the first place. It's my fault she's dead."

"Hold on a minute." Denver unbuttoned another button of his shirt. "Campaigns? How many campaigns did Tiana work for?"

Tony blinked. "Just the two."

"Two? What two? You lost me."

Denver finally glanced at her, a question in his eyes, but she quickly lifted and dropped her shoulders. Tony hadn't told her a thing.

"The Escalante and Wexler campaigns. She worked for both of them."

Denver's wide eyes and open mouth reflected her own

feelings, and she took advantage of his momentary loss for words.

"Tiana wasn't very dedicated to either candidate, was she? Or was she just trying to get as much experience as possible?"

"Oh, no. She was dedicated to re-electing Mayor Wexler. We both were—are."

Denver had recovered and got in the question hovering on her own lips. "If she was pro Wexler, why was she working for the Escalante campaign and in that particular capacity?"

"Dude, I thought you knew." Tony turned his head and spit into the sand. "She was working for the Escalante campaign as a mole. She was team CREW all the way."

Folding his arms, Denver said, "Dude, I didn't know that. How was I supposed to know that with you playing hide-and-seek and slipping tips to a *blogger* instead of the police?"

Ashlynn's blood simmered as Tony's eyes darted between her and Denver. "I figured you already talked to the CREW."

"I did talk to them—Amalia Fernandez and Christian Bushnell, to be precise. Both denied knowledge of Tiana Fuller."

"Dude, that sucks." Shaking his head, Tony covered his face. "I don't know why they're playing that game. Christian knows Tiana. He's the one T told about her plan to infiltrate Escalante's campaign."

Denver ran a hand through his hair. "Was that all Tiana's plan or Christian's?"

"That was all T, man." Tony grinned through his beard. "That girl was fearless. She suggested it to Christian and he gave his stamp of approval, but even if he hadn't, she would've done it, anyway. Then she joined the Escalante campaign and suggested to *them* that she spy on Wexler."

"How do you know she wasn't really working for Escalante and spying on Wexler?" Ashlynn glanced at Denver. "She was found in a Wexler car, not an Escalante car."

"I thought about that, but no way. She was all-in for Wexler. She was especially in favor of his slow-growth policies for the city. You see what Escalante and her husband are planning for downtown?"

"Slow down." Denver drew a line in the sand with the toe of his shoe. "That could've been her plan, but maybe she actually discovered some dirt about Wexler—dirty enough to result in murder."

"I can't believe that." Tony had the ring of the true believer in his voice.

"Let's go back to the car in the lake." Denver wiped the face of his phone on his pant leg. "How did you manage to witness that?"

"T had shared her phone's location with me weeks before her murder. Maybe she forgot, because I did. But when she didn't call me after her meeting, I freaked. Then I remembered she'd shared her location, and I brought it up on my phone. I couldn't figure out why she was heading out toward Angeles Crest, but I had a bad feeling. I followed the phone, and it took me to Lake Kawayu. The phone stopped working at that point, but I got there just in time to see two guys pushing a car into the lake."

Ashlynn covered her mouth. "Why didn't you call 9-1-1? Tiana could've still been alive."

"She wasn't!" Tony grabbed his hair at the roots, looking like a wild man. He turned wide eyes on Denver. "Tell me she wasn't. Tell me she didn't drown in that trunk while I watched from my safe distance."

Denver's voice had a rough edge when he answered the feverish question. "She wasn't. They shot her before they put her in the trunk. The coroner didn't find any water in her lungs. Did you get a good look at the two men?"

"No, but I swear they heard me. They definitely heard my car. I think they might be after me." Tony sank to his knees in the wet sand and sobbed. "I'm such a coward. Maybe I could've saved her."

Denver dropped his hand to the young man's shoulder. "I don't think so, Tony. You're doing the right thing now. We're going to find out who did this, and you're going to do the right thing by T and testify, right?"

"I will, I will." Tony dragged a hand across his runny nose. "Dude, I gotta go now. My ride's coming."

Denver ended the recording on his phone. "I can reach you at the number you used to text me?"

"Yeah, it's a burner, but I'm keeping it." Tony staggered to his feet. "Don't put this in *LA Confidential*. The CREW will know it's me, and I just can't right now."

"I'll figure out something. You're helping Tiana now, Tony." She squeezed his arm. "Just keep cooperating with Detective Holt."

That earned her a quick glance from Denver.

"For sure." Tony wiped his face on his T-shirt and jogged down the beach on the packed sand.

Ashlynn pulled her sweater around her as the breeze from the ocean picked up. "Wow, this is a tangled web. Tiana was playing with fire any way you look at it—a double agent."

"Maybe, but she didn't get murdered for being a mole. She discovered something more serious than dirty tricks that someone wanted to keep quiet."

Ashlynn licked her lips, tasting the salt from the air.

"I'm sorry I didn't tell you about posting that video on the blog. I had to do it, and I knew you'd object."

Denver shoved his hands in his pockets and stared at the ocean, roiling and spitting just a few feet in front of them, the spray clinging to his dark hair, making it curl at the ends.

"I have to hand it to you. You pulled a fast one, seducing me, getting me into bed so that you could sneak back and copy the video to your laptop."

Her jaw dropped. "Th-that's not... I didn't..."

"Save it for your readers. It might even make a good post for the almighty blog—how you tricked an LAPD wannabe homicide detective into leaving important evidence in your possession."

Tears stung her eyes as she reached out for him. "That's not why I slept with you. Making love with you last night was the first real joy I've felt since my brother died. The first time I've felt real and whole."

"Good for you."

As she watched him trudge through the sand back to the strand through blurred vision, one tear fell over the rim of her eye and ran down her cheek.

Looked like her brother had won again.

Chapter Seventeen

Denver's lead foot pressed against the accelerator in his zeal to get away from the beach and Ashlynn as quickly as possible—before he changed his mind about her.

Funny thing was, he'd felt the same way about last night—a connection with her, something solid and real after dozens of dates where he'd been afraid to scratch beneath any surface level.

He muttered to himself. "That's what she wanted you to feel."

He cruised down the freeway to the house of Veronica Escalante and her husband Kent Meadows. Meadows was a fat cat who had supported his younger wife's political aspirations. Escalante had recused herself from a few city council votes that had involved city planning where her husband could directly benefit. Still seemed shady to him.

He pulled up to the same drive he'd sat across from last night, but the valet attendants and lights were gone. In their place, gardeners worked the landscaping in the front of the house, the noise from their leaf blowers reverberating in the air.

When Denver got out of his vehicle, he waved and the gardener wielding the blower cut the motor. Denver called out, "Thanks."

He ascended the steps to the front door and pressed the doorbell, stepping back in case someone wanted to get a look at him from the peephole or the cameras in the corner.

A female voice came over a speaker. "Who is it, please?"

Denver unclipped the badge from his belt and held it up. "Detective Holt, LAPD, ma'am. I need to talk to Councilwoman Escalante."

"Just a minute, please."

At least she was polite as she left him out on the porch in the heat. A minute later, the door opened and a woman, her hair in a tight bun, with a tighter smile, stood before him. "Come in, Detective. Would you like something to drink? Iced tea? Coffee? Water?"

"Nothing, thanks."

She bowed her head. "This way, please."

He followed her, the heels of his shoes clicking on the tile floor behind her crepe soles. She pushed open another door off the great room, all signs of the party vanished.

She took one step into the room, a library or office, and said, "This is Detective Holt, Kent."

"Thanks, Mom." A fit-for-his-age man stood behind the desk, smoothing a hand along the side of his silver hair. He looked about the same age as *Mom*. "Detective, have a seat. I'm Kent Meadows."

Denver strode into the room and leaned across the desk to shake Meadows's hand; the older man's grip firm and practiced.

"Your wife isn't home?"

Meadows smiled, his blue eyes twinkling. "Ah, the demands of a campaign. I didn't want you to waste your time, Detective. Who knows? Veronica might show up before we're finished here."

Denver jerked his thumb over his shoulder. "Mom?"

"Rita is my mother-in-law."

"She works for you?"

Meadows waved his hands, his fingers tapering to a polished manicure. "Unofficial hostess. She lives in the appropriately named mother-in-law quarters in the back of the property—her own house—that she shares with Lulu, Veronica's sister. What can we help you with, Detective? I'm sure you're here about that unfortunate incident with that girl in the lake."

"Incident? It was a homicide, and your wife's campaign manager is on video with that girl in the lake, asking her to spy on Wexler's campaign."

"Of course, of course." Meadows folded his hands on his desk. "Tragic. I assume you've talked to Jed Gordon."

"I spoke with him. He couldn't deny the video, but said Veronica had nothing to do with the request."

The nostrils of Meadows's patrician nose flared. "Jed would say anything to protect Veronica."

Denver raised his eyebrows. "You don't believe him? Do you think your wife knew about Tiana Fuller?"

"Oh, I believe him. My wife doesn't concern herself too much with the volunteers or the nuts and bolts of the campaign. I take care of the financing and Jed takes care of the details, and Veronica does what she does best— connects with the people."

"I was hoping to talk to Veronica to find out if Jed told her anything about Tiana or what she may have discovered about the Wexler campaign."

Meadows eased back in his chair and flicked the drapes behind him, revealing a view of the meticulously tended garden in front of the house. "You're in luck, Detective Holt. My wife just pulled up to the house, but she looks busy. She's on her cell phone and she's not even out of the car yet."

"I won't take up too much of her time." Denver pushed back from the desk to get a view of Veronica Escalante stepping from a Porsche, teetering on a pair of stiletto heels, her phone to her ear, a bag slung over her shoulder.

Denver's gaze shifted from the window to a credenza behind Meadows, boasting several photos of construction sites. He pointed to one. "That's the Meadows Plaza downtown, right?"

Meadows's eyes flicked like a lizard's in his tanned face. "I hope it will be. Construction has stalled for the moment, but it should resume shortly."

"Shortly, as in when your wife gets elected mayor of LA?"

Meadows's lips stretched into a smile, but this time there was no twinkling of the eyes. "That's not how it operates, Detective."

"Are you waiting to see me?" Councilwoman Escalante's voice sounded different from her commercials and speeches. She'd lost the Spanish accent she put on for public appearances.

As Denver turned toward her, Meadows said, "This is Detective Holt, Veronica. Of course, he has some questions about that idiot Gordon and the video of him and that murdered girl. Why did he try to hide it in the first place?"

"You know Jed, my love." Veronica strode forward, her heels sinking into the thick carpet. She shook Denver's hand with a feminine hold, which she ended quickly.

She skirted him and placed a kiss on her husband's forehead. "Thank you for filling in for me, *mi amor.*"

Meadows hopped up from his chair, his wife in those heels besting him by about three inches. "You two use my office. I've had a long day. I'm going to rustle up a drink before dinner. I'll be out at the pool, *mi vida*."

The Meadows kissed again, and Denver felt in danger of choking on saccharine sweetness if he stayed in their presence much longer. Was this lovey-dovey stuff for his benefit? He didn't even vote.

Meadows touched his fingers to his forehead as he left the room. "Nice meeting you, Detective. Good to see my donations to the Police Protective League not going to waste."

Whatever that meant.

Veronica sat in a leather love seat against the wall, crossing her shapely legs. "Only my husband sits behind his desk, Detective Holt. Have a seat and let me know how I can help. I feel terrible that Tiana worked for our campaign and that Jed knew it and wasn't forthcoming when you first questioned him. I've already talked to Jed about that, but surely any dirty tricks Tiana played on the Wexler campaign didn't result in her murder. That's just crazy to think that. Nobody gets murdered over tearing down flyers."

Typical politician. He'd have to talk fast to get a word in. "Did you ever meet or talk to Tiana?"

"No, I usually don't interact with the volunteers except to give pep talks or maybe buy pizzas." She flashed a fake smile. "They're invited to certain events, like our fundraiser last night."

"Have you seen Tiana's picture? Did you recognize her from any of those occasions?"

She squinted her dark eyes. "I did see her picture—pretty girl—but I had never seen her before, and if Jed was using her for undercover work, he probably wouldn't have invited her to any of the events."

"Did Jed tell you what Tiana had discovered about Wexler?"

"I told you, Detective. I didn't know anything about Tiana until after the video, and Jed told me what I'm sure he told you—petty tricks. We don't know anything about Wexler, except that he's not for LA at this time, and we're going to turn things around, including with the LAPD. Mayor Wexler and Chief Sterling are too cozy. The LAPD needs more oversight." She winked. "Although I'm sure you don't."

Denver held out one hand. "I'm not here to discuss LAPD policies, Councilwoman. I suppose Jed had no inkling that Tiana was actually a mole."

"What?" Veronica's confidence wavered with her voice. "What are you talking about?"

"According to one of my sources, Tiana didn't support you at all. She was all for Wexler and was playing Jed to get into your campaign."

Veronica's face paled. "That little…bi…sneak. She really wanted to get down and dirty, didn't she? If you're suggesting she might've discovered anything about our campaign, I can shut down that line of thinking right now. We play by the rules."

"Of course." Denver rose, leveling a finger at the photo of the Meadows Plaza construction site. "Too bad that project is stalled. Would be nice for downtown."

Veronica flicked a strand of dark hair over her shoulder as she rose from the love seat. "I'll let you know if I learn anything else about Tiana. Does Jed know she was a mole?"

"Not yet, but I'm sure you'll tell him. I'll see myself

out." As Denver transitioned from the office to the great room, he let out a breath.

He sure hoped Escalante came across better with her constituents. She put him on edge.

The gardeners were planting a new bed of flowers under the direction of Veronica's mother as he maneuvered down the walkway. When he reached the gate, Mrs. Escalante touched the sleeve of his jacket.

He jerked his head around and she put her finger to her lips. "You're here about that murdered girl?"

"I am. Do you know something about her, Mrs. Escalante?"

She glanced over her shoulder at the house. "Just that she was here several times, *muchos tiempos.*"

Chapter Eighteen

Ashlynn glanced between her phone and the door of the high-rise office building, as she sipped an iced tea on the patio of the office complex. The tall buildings created a wind tunnel and bits of debris swirled in mini tornadoes. She pushed her hair out of her face and replied to Lulu's text.

Veronica's sister had contacted her earlier to let her know she was okay and to inquire about her well-being. Once they'd assured each other that they were unharmed, Lulu had pressed her for information about her friend.

Ashlynn had Lulu half convinced already that he was just a friend looking out for them. He hadn't even known why they were meeting.

She had asked Lulu if she'd been followed to the dog park and if she'd recognized the man who had accosted them, and now she sat tapping her toe, waiting for a reply.

Glancing up as the office door swung open, she stuffed her phone in her purse. Lulu's response would have to wait.

She jumped to her feet, her ponytail swinging behind her, and caught up with the fresh-faced young man hurrying from the office building, a stack of folders beneath one arm.

"Christian?"

He swung around, almost dropping the files. "Y-yes. Do I know you?"

"Not yet." Ashlynn gave an encouraging smile. Christian needed kid-glove handling, which was probably why Denver hadn't gotten anything out of him. Had he tried again after their meeting with Tony? He wouldn't have had time—or at least Christian wouldn't look so carefree if he'd just come from a meeting with Detective Holt.

Christian tipped his head, a shy smile curling one corner of his mouth. "I'm sorry?"

She hated to disrupt the happy vibe here, but someone had to do it. Taking a few steps in his direction, she thrust out her hand. "I'm Ashlynn Hughes from *LA Confidential*."

You would've thought she'd told him she was from the IRS with an audit request the way the color drained from his face and then all came rushing back, staining his cheeks in a crimson tide.

"I—I don't have anything to say to you. We already talked to that detective, gave him our volunteer list. That's all." He pressed his lips together, as if willing himself to be quiet.

"You talked to Detective Holt today?"

"Today?" He gulped, his Adam's apple bobbing in the slim column of his throat. "A few days ago. Is he coming back?"

"He just might." Ashlynn shifted her gaze to the side without turning her head, indicating they could expect him at any time. "But you can talk to me instead…and it's all confidential. I won't report your name. You don't have to testify to anything. Just between us."

"What do you want from me?" He hugged the folders to his chest, a poor substitute for armor. "I don't know anything about Tiana Fuller."

"I know that's not true, and Detective Holt's gonna know soon enough." She didn't have to terrify him any more by letting him know Denver already knew.

She took a step back toward the table and her iced tea. "Let's sit down a minute. I'm not going to record you or report your name. I just want to verify some information for my blog. It doesn't have to be about you, or even the Wexler campaign."

He followed her to the table, his gait stiff, and sat across from her, folding his thin frame in half. "What do you know? Or what do you think you know?"

She wrapped her ponytail around her hand and sucked in her bottom lip. "I know that Tiana did work for the CREW, that she was dedicated to re-electing Mayor Wexler—just like I am. I know that she offered to infiltrate the Escalante campaign as a spy, and then she pretended to fulfill the same role there as she actually had with the CREW. How am I doing so far?"

Christian's head dropped once. "That's what she was doing, but I didn't tell her to do it. Nobody did. That was just Tiana. She wanted to do it, thought it would be fun."

"Okay, okay." She folded her hands in front of her. "Tiana was an adult. I'm sure she made her own decisions. But what happened? What did she discover?"

"It wasn't about us." Christian crossed his hands over his chest. "I swear. She didn't find anything on Mayor Wexler. She wasn't even looking. She was digging into Escalante, not the mayor. She had no access to anything at our campaign headquarters. She never even came in."

"You think she found out something about Escalante?" She tapped her fingernails against her plastic cup.

"She must have, but she didn't tell me." He snapped his fingers. "She might've told one of the other volunteers—Tony. They were tight."

Been there, done that.

"How did she wind up in the trunk of one of your cars?"

"I can't tell you. I couldn't tell the cops, either. Honestly, nobody keeps tabs on those cars. I've known volunteers to take them out to pick up lunch and bring them back four days later, nobody the wiser. Tiana herself used the cars sometimes."

"She never gave you any hint about what she was working on? What she might've found?"

"Nothing, but she seemed…"

"What?" Ashlynn hunkered forward. "Go on."

"Secretly satisfied?" He rubbed his clean-shaved chin, which looked as if it had never experienced razor burn. "You might think she'd have been worried with all the subterfuge, but she seemed pleased about something. That's how I'd describe it. That's why I was so shocked when I found out she'd been murdered. She was happy, not scared."

"Maybe she didn't know enough to be scared, but she should've been." Ashlynn rattled the ice in her cup. "How come you didn't tell Detective Holt any of this?"

"First of all, he interviewed me with my boss. If I had said one word, I would've been fired. This is a paid gig for me. I got the feeling Detective Holt wanted to get me on my own. He's been leaving me messages, and I've been avoiding them."

"This is a woman's life here, Christian. It's not fun and political games."

"You don't think politics are life and death? Neither did Tiana, and look what happened to her." He straightened the files on the table. "Amalia doesn't want it known that one of our volunteers was murdered. It's bad enough that Tiana was found in one of our cars. Looks like the Escalante campaign didn't want to claim her, either."

"Poor Tiana. Both campaigns were eager to use her, and then disowned her when she needed them."

After she assured Christian she wouldn't use his name in her blog, he escaped to where he was headed when she'd waylaid him.

She checked her phone for Lulu's response to her most recent text, but she hadn't answered the all-important question of whether or not she'd been followed last night. She had assured Ashlynn that she had left town and was keeping a low profile, especially as Jed had accused her of stealing and then leaking the video.

She sucked down the rest of her tea and took a big breath. Before running to her blog to release this latest piece of information, she had some amends to make first.

She couldn't believe Denver thought she'd seduced him just to post that video before he could question Jed. It looked bad, but she'd wanted that man from the get-go, and it had nothing to do with *LA Confidential*—for once.

She called Denver and held her breath as his phone rang. Would he brush her off?

He picked up after the third ring. "Yeah."

"I'm going to apologize without saying sorry."

He huffed out a long breath. "You like playing games, Ashlynn. I don't."

"Yeah, like dissing me at lunch the other day after we'd been getting along great was not some kind of maneuver?"

"I think I made up for that, or I thought I did. Didn't realize I was getting handled."

"Now I'm going to make it up to you. I have some information from Christian Bushnell, and I'm coming to you first instead of splashing it all over my blog."

He caught his breath. "I have some information, too."

She smacked her palm on the table for her own benefit. "Then let's get together and return to our original purpose."

"Dinner tonight?"

Her heart fluttered in her chest. "I'd love to have dinner with you and compare notes."

"Marina, The Warehouse, seven o'clock."

He ended the call before she even had a chance to respond. There was only one response to give. Whether Denver Holt believed her not, she might be ready to put something or someone ahead of the blog.

For once, she was more excited to see Denver than to hear the information he had about the case. Would he believe her?

DENVER TOOK A sip of beer through the thick head on the top. He had to be out of his mind. He should be sharing this information with Marino, not Ashlynn, even though she had worked harder on this case than Marino had. Could he trust that she wouldn't run off to post it for her followers?

She wouldn't if he explained to her how it could compromise the case. The video of Jed and Tiana hadn't done that. He'd had no intention of tiptoeing around Jed Gordon, but this piece of knowledge demanded a certain level of secrecy.

He spied Ashlynn on the edge of the bar, surveying the dining tables. When their eyes met, he felt an electric shock.

She raised her hand and strode toward him with those long legs, her hair bright against a black top. Her black jeans and boots just made her look like one long, lean line of sexy.

She slid into the booth, across from him, and lifted the purse slung across her body over her head. She nodded at the big window overlooking slips of bobbing boats. "This is…touristy."

"It's kind of my local. I can walk here." He tapped the side of his glass. "Sorry I started without you. It's been a helluva day."

"Tell me about it. I can't believe Tony watched while two men stuffed his friend's body in the trunk of car, and then pushed that car into a lake, and didn't do one thing about it." She glanced up as the waitress approached. "Glass of chardonnay, house is fine."

"I could see where he was coming from. Even if he called the police at that point, nothing could've been done for Tiana." He sat back and folded his arms. "At least he contacted you."

She folded the corner of the napkin the waitress had tossed in front of her. "I saw Christian Bushnell today."

"Let me guess." He caught a bead of moisture from the outside of his glass with the tip of his finger. "You got more out of him than I did."

"I caught him alone, without his boss hovering. I think you would've gotten to him eventually. He's not a very good liar, and I don't think he likes lying."

"He's in the wrong business. What did he tell you?"

"Not too much. He verified Tony's story about Tiana working for the CREW. Just like Jed, Christian maintained that the spying angle was Tiana's idea."

"Hmm." He scratched his chin and gulped down some beer as the waitress delivered Ashlynn's wine.

She wrapped a finger around the stem. "Hmm, what?"

"You told me over the phone that you had some news for me. That's hardly news. We already got that from Tony."

She blinked and took a careful sip of her wine.

"There's more. He said Tiana wasn't scared or worried, that she seemed pleased about something. He also said anyone could've taken one of the vehicles. Tiana herself could've taken one of the cars."

"Okay, but he didn't know what she'd discovered over there?"

"He didn't have a clue. Sounds like she was keeping things to herself. Honestly?" She pinged her glass and the golden liquid inside shimmered. "I just wanted to see you. To apologize for how my actions appeared to you. Sure, I didn't want you nixing my post with the video, but I swear I did not use sex to get one over on you. I would've found a way to copy that video to my laptop, whether you spent the night with me or not."

"You're not apologizing for posting the video on your blog?"

Her eyebrows jumped. "Absolutely not. It drove people to the blog, and it didn't hurt your case. You know it didn't, Denver."

"It got me in some hot water with my captain, it gave Jed a heads-up. He could've bolted."

"Leaving Veronica? Never."

"There are some tips that aren't meant for public consumption. You know that, right?"

"I never revealed that Tiana was found in a CREW car, did I?"

"Ready to order?" Their waitress had finally taken the plunge after hovering every time she passed their table.

Ashlynn's gaze flicked over the menu. "I'll have the crab cakes appetizer and a side salad."

"Sea bass for me, please."

After the waitress clarified a few more details about their order and left, Denver hunched forward. "If I tell you something now, you have to promise to keep it out of

LA Confidential. This is too important, Ashlynn. More important than the blog."

"I understand." She pressed a hand to her chest. "I promise, Denver."

"It has to do with something you mentioned earlier, on the night of the fundraiser. That's why I want to run it by you."

"The argument between Veronica and Jed?"

"No, an offhand comment by the volunteers. They said Kent Meadows was a manther."

Her giggle ended in a choke when she realized he was serious. "Kent Meadows? What do his personal preferences have to do with anything?"

"I went out to the house to talk to Veronica about that video and to find out what she knew about Tiana's role in the campaign. She denied knowing of Tiana's existence."

"She's lying. She and Jed were arguing about something that night, but what does this have to do with her husband?"

"I'm getting there. Did you know Veronica's mother lives with them?"

Ashlynn nodded. "She lives in a guest cottage in the back, with Lulu."

"Mrs. Escalante was there today and, when I was leaving, she pulled me aside and told me that Tiana had been to the house."

"Well, that sort of proves Veronica was lying, doesn't it?"

"Maybe not." Denver drummed his fingers on the table. "Mrs. Escalante told me Tiana was there to see Kent."

Chapter Nineteen

Ashlynn covered her mouth with her hand. "Kent? Tiana was there to see Kent?"

"That's what Mrs. Escalante told me. She said Tiana had been to the house several times, and I just assumed she meant to see her daughter. But she corrected me, and said only Kent was home when Tiana was there."

"Unless Mrs. Escalante was lying to protect her daughter." Ashlynn toyed with her napkin. Denver was right. This information didn't belong in the blog...not yet.

"I thought about that, but then why tell me anything at all? I wasn't questioning Mrs. Escalante. I was on my way out the front gate when she grabbed me. She didn't have to say a word."

"What does it mean? I don't think Kent is even that involved with the campaign. He's strictly the money guy."

"Strictly the money guy and the guy who hits on young women. What better source of young, eager women than your wife's election campaign?" He moved his beer to the side to make room for the plates in their waitress's hands.

"Anything else? Refill on the drinks?"

They both declined the second drink, and Ashlynn shook out her napkin. "You think Kent and Tiana were hooking up?"

She wrinkled her nose as she asked the question, and

he didn't think it had to do with the savory smells coming from their food.

"Hooking up might be too strong. Maybe they were having some kind of flirtation." He dragged a fork through his garlic-mashed potatoes. "You picked up on that vibe in the video with Jed, right?"

She waved her fork at him. "Hold on. You're not blaming the victim here, are you? Whatever Tiana did or whatever methods she may have used to get information, none of that deserves a death sentence."

A muscle twitched in his jaw. "I did not say that, and I'm not implying it at all, but it might explain what she was doing with Kent Meadows. She saw his weakness and went in for the kill. We already know she was willing to take risks for the thrill of the hunt."

"She cozies up to Kent, gets invited to the house while the candidate is campaigning, and discovers...what?"

"We already established that Kent wasn't interested in the nuts and bolts of the election, but it doesn't mean Tiana couldn't discover things in that house that could benefit Wexler—maybe something so big, Kent had to keep her quiet."

Ashlynn scooted up to the edge of the booth. "And what's so big to Kent right now? We've been thinking politics all this time, but maybe Tiana found out about something else."

"Meadows Plaza. The project is currently on hold. Why?"

"I can write a post tomorrow about Meadows Plaza, see what my readers know about it."

"We don't want to tip off Meadows. So far, he believes we think he's Veronica Escalante's Mr. Moneybags, nothing more. If you and your readers go snooping around Kent Meadows and Meadows Plaza, we're giving him a heads-up." He pointed his fork at her. "You're not the only one with sources. I know a guy in Building and Planning. I'm sure he can give me the lowdown on Meadows Plaza."

Ashlynn poked at her salad, a shiver of excitement giving her goose bumps. "I think we're really on to something, Denver. Thank you for sharing that with me."

"The other night—" he dragged a napkin across his mouth "—it felt like you used me to post that video on your blog. I don't like being used, and it made me look like a fool in front of my captain."

"I know." She gripped the edge of the table. "I didn't think how it would look for you, being in the dark. At that point, it was more important for me to get that blog out."

"Why is it such a big deal for you to prove yourself with that blog? It's kind of toxic. I think you need to strike out on your own." He threw back the rest of his beer. "And that's as far as I'll go."

"I know you're right. My parents were perfectionists in everything they did when Sean and I were growing up—still are. It's just that Sean seemed to do everything right, and I was the eternal screw-up. So, I started controlling the one thing that was all mine—eating. I became anorexic and my supermodel mom didn't even realize it until I fainted. Even after family therapy, my mom didn't acknowledge her role in my eating disorder—not that I'm blaming her." She held up her hand. "That was all me, and I was no angel."

Denver reached for her hand and smoothed his thumb across the inside of her wrist. "Having an eating disorder doesn't make you a bad person."

"How about outing your own brother?"

He cocked his head. "What do you mean?"

"I found out Sean was gay. I knew he wanted to tell

my parents in his own way and time, and I should've allowed him that space, but I thought I could finally get one over on him. I figured my parents would be upset when they found out their only son was gay, so I blabbed it to them. I felt terrible when Sean found out what I'd done. And the funny thing is? My parents didn't care at all, which is how it should be, and I'm glad they reacted the way they did. The whole thing blew up in my face. I was the bad guy."

"Not cool, but how old were you?"

"A teenager—no excuse. I just wanted to be the chosen one for a change."

"How did Sean react to all of this? From what I've heard about him, he was no angel, either. I mean he called out my mom as a murderer based on some life insurance and an extramarital affair."

Ashlynn had read that whole blog series and could see where Sean was coming from, but she'd never admit that to Denver. "You're right. Sean had his issues. He knew he was the favored one. He didn't exactly lord it over me, but he reveled in it. We made our peace before he died. I'm thankful for that."

"Now this blog is hanging over your head as a way to prove yourself worthy in your parents' eyes and maybe to make up for what you did to Sean. But just like the food was controlling you, not the other way around, this blog is controlling you."

"Your father's murder doesn't control you to an extent?"

"It does, but it also dovetails with what I want to do with my life—solve homicides. I'm not sure the blog is what you want to do with your life."

"I'm not sure about that. I'm really pumped about the direction we're going with this case. It feels good." She sawed into her crab cake and held it up. "And I no longer have an eating disorder, in case you haven't noticed."

"I'm glad." He pointed to his plate. "Maybe you can help me with some of this."

"Ugh, you're not going to start watching what I eat, are you? Whenever I tell people I had anorexia, they start counting my calories for me."

"I'm sure you can handle your own food intake. It's your obsession with *LA Confidential* that worries me."

THE NEXT MORNING, Denver updated both Marino and Captain Fields, letting them know he was going to look into Kent Meadows, as he'd gotten a tip that the councilwoman's husband may have known Tiana. Marino was happy he didn't have to do anything today except talk to some of Tiana's school friends in Long Beach, and Captain Fields was glad Denver had seemingly wrested control of the investigation from the blogger.

He didn't tell the captain about dinner last night.

Both he and Ashlynn had made the decision to sleep in their own beds. His ego needed some time to recover, and Ashlynn wanted a chance to prove herself to him.

Her blog today had focused on Tiana, paying tribute to a bright and energetic young woman lost too soon. She hit all the right notes and had managed to draw even more people into the story of "The Girl in the Lake."

Maybe he was wrong and this blog was her true calling. He just hated seeing her try so hard for validation from her parents that would most likely never come.

As soon as he sank into his chair and reached for the mouse, his contact at the Building and Planning office called him. He snatched up his phone. "Ebert, what do you have for me?"

Greg Ebert whistled across the line. "That Meadows

Plaza project is in big trouble. Kent Meadows is never going to get that done. The dude owes money, he's being sued, we just rejected his most recent set of diagrams. He's going to lose a bundle."

"That's common knowledge, though, right? Or it could be if someone wanted to investigate the project."

"Sure, what are you getting at?"

"Secrets."

"I can tell you this, Holt. If that wife of his gets elected mayor, she could make a lot of his problems go away. It would have to be done on the sly, but this type of quid pro quo happens all the time."

"Okay, thanks, Ebert. I appreciate it."

Seemed like he needed to have a talk with Kent again—and this time he planned to get personal. He placed a call to Meadows and left a voice mail.

He spent the rest of the afternoon reviewing the ballistics report for the bullet that killed Tiana. He'd also gotten forensics for the car—all prints wiped clean, most evidence washed out in the lake—but the forensics team had discovered a few hairs in the trunk that didn't belong to Tiana and a few fibers.

Nobody had any idea where Tiana had been murdered, including Tony, and with the pithy evidence from the car, Denver needed something big. He needed a confession from Kent Meadows.

When his phone rang, his heart pounded when he saw Ashlynn's name. They hadn't touched base all day, and he still couldn't stop worrying about her although she'd abandoned her undercover gig at the Escalante campaign headquarters.

He picked up and said, "Is this the hot blogger who's breaking the case of the girl in lake?"

She laughed with a nervous edge. "You read the blog today, right?"

"It was good, and I appreciate your discretion. I know it wasn't easy, knowing what you do about Meadows."

"I just want you to know I'm all about solving this crime. I won't do anything to jeopardize that."

"I can see that, so I think I can tell you that Meadows is in trouble over that project."

She huffed out a breath. "That's apparent, though, isn't it? That building site has been sitting there for months with no progress."

"You're right, but my guy at Building and Planning seems to think all of Meadows's problems can magically disappear once his wife gets elected."

"If Tiana knew that, or maybe how that was going to play out, it might be motive enough for Meadows."

"Maybe. I reached out to him today. I need to do a little probing."

"I might be able to help you with that. Lulu texted me today. She's okay. She's in hiding, and she wants to meet with me."

A sharp pain lanced the back of his neck. "Is that a good idea? Have you forgotten what happened the last time you two had a meeting?"

"This is different. She's aware of the danger now, and she's in a secure location. I might be able to get her talking about Kent. I don't think there's any love lost between those two."

"Be careful. No meetings in vacant dog parks."

"I promise I'll be careful. I think I took some heat off myself with this latest blog. Nobody can feel threatened by a tribute to the victim. I think I proved the threats intimidated me into backing off. Nobody knows we're working together."

"Nobody on my end knows." Denver glanced around the room. He'd catch hell if they did. "Keep me posted, anyway, and we'll touch base later."

"You, too. Denver…"

A pulse throbbed in his throat. "Yeah?"

"Let's get justice for the girl in the lake."

He let out a breath. "You got it."

When he ended the call, he tapped the edge of the phone against his chin. He jumped when it buzzed again. Had she decided to tell him what she'd really wanted to tell him?

He glanced at the display, disappointment bursting his bubble. "Mr. Meadows, thanks for calling back."

"Call me Kent, please. What can I do for you, Detective?"

"I want to talk with you again, Kent—in person."

"I'm busy today."

"It needs to be today."

"Do you mind coming downtown? I'm going to be having a meeting at my building site here, and I can chat with you when I'm done."

A muscle ticked in Denver's jaw. *Perfect.* "I can be there. What time?"

"Let's make it seven o'clock."

"In the dark?"

"We just switched to daylight savings. It's not that dark at seven, and the construction site is lit up like a Christmas tree most of the time."

"I'll be there."

Denver didn't have any intention of meeting with Kent Meadows at a half-finished construction site downtown without telling someone first. He notified Marino and told Billy Crouch, just in case Marino didn't remember or care.

With downtown LA on the way home to the Marina, Denver decided to put in some extra time and get a bite to eat before his meeting. Could he break Meadows at the place that had the power to break Meadows?

At around ten minutes to seven, Denver drove right onto the construction site, spitting up sand and gravel with the back tires of his sedan. Other cars dotted the flat area next to a giant hole, cement pylons and steel beams crisscrossing the vast space. Definitely stalled.

He pulled into the same row as two Teslas, a Porsche Cayenne and a classic Corvette. If Kent couldn't get money out of these people, he needed a new plan.

Denver waited in his car and sucked down the rest of the soda he'd got with his burger and fries. His phone pinged, and he read a message from Ashlynn that her meeting with Lulu was on. His thumb hesitated over the keyboard on his phone. He didn't have to tell her to be careful. She already knew that. They could trust Lulu, and Lulu knew to be careful, too.

Instead of sending her a cautionary text, he gave her a thumbs-up emoji.

A few minutes later, a woman and two men emerged from the bowels of the construction site. The woman picked her way over the gravel and slid into the Corvette.

One of the guys gave Denver a hard look before claiming one of the Teslas, and the other man turned and waved at the gaping hole in the earth as he unlocked his Porsche.

Denver exited his vehicle before the others drove away, just so that they could get a good look at him in case he wound up with a bullet in the back of the head at the bottom of that pit. As he walked closer to the site, he saw a small gray building with the Meadows Construction logo plastered all over it. Now he saw what the other guy had been waving at. Kent Meadows stood framed in the doorway of the outbuilding, casual in a pair of slacks and a cashmere sweater, his arms crossed.

Lights did illuminate the construction site, and a little porch lamp cast a yellow glow over Meadows, making his silver hair glint. Denver raised his hand as he strode forward, avoiding the potholes and dips.

"Welcome to my folly." Meadows spread his arms wide.

Jerking his thumb over his shoulder, Denver asked, "Any luck with that bunch?"

"Not really." He shrugged his sweater-clad shoulders. "Office? There's light and coffee and maybe a few snacks left over from the last construction workers who were here."

"How old would those snacks be?"

"About six months old, but this stuff has enough preservatives in it to last until the project gets completed."

"When will that be?" Denver crossed the threshold of the office and knocked over a pile of folders on his way to take a seat. "Sorry about that."

"That's all right." He waved a hand. "Someone will clean this up at some point." Meadows's thin lips twisted. "Probably won't be me."

"Unless your wife gets elected mayor."

Meadows chuckled. "Is that what this is about, Detective? You found out what a bottomless pit this project is for me and how much I need saving?"

"Something like that."

"Shh." He put his finger to his lips. "Don't tell anyone, but my wife doesn't have a chance."

"Does she know that?"

He shook his head. "That campaign manager of hers keeps blowing smoke up…you know, in her face, and she believes him."

"But you weren't always so resigned, were you? You thought Veronica had a chance, and you thought this project had a chance."

"Not really." Meadows steepled his fingers. "Do you really think I killed a young woman to keep her quiet about my failing project? She wouldn't know about that, anyway. Meadows Plaza is not part of Veronica's campaign strategy, and that young woman was working for the campaign. I'd never met her. I don't involve myself with my wife's campaigns, except to foot the bills."

"You're sure you never met Tiana when she was at your house with you when your wife wasn't home?"

Meadows's face froze and the corner of his eye twitched. "Where did you hear that?"

"From a member of your household."

"Did that little snitch Lulu tell you?" He patted the side of his expensive haircut. "And after I set her up with a few of my friends, too."

"Set her up for what?"

"Exactly what she wanted, Detective. Look—" Meadows flattened his hands on the small dingy desk "—you don't have any proof that Tiana was at the house. I made sure any of our security footage showing her there was erased—and not because I murdered her but so that my wife wouldn't murder me. I had a fling with the girl. That's it. I was horrified when I learned of her death, but I wasn't involved. No motive."

"I can think of a few." Denver held up his hand and ticked off his fingers. "To keep your affair a secret. To keep her quiet about your plans for Meadows Plaza. Anger because she played you."

Meadows's head jerked up. "Played me? What do you mean?"

"Your wife didn't tell you? You haven't been following the news? Tiana Fuller was working for the Wexler campaign. She was a mole in your wife's campaign, looking for dirt. Seems that she found some."

Denver's words had sobered Meadows. His jaw tightened and his eyes narrowed. "That makes sense now. One day at the house, Tiana and I had drinks and I blacked out. I think she got into my computer that day."

"And discovered what?"

Meadows folded his hands, his knuckles white. "I'm not telling you any more, Detective Holt. You have no proof of anything and if Lulu told you about me and Tiana, she won't be able to testify to that."

Denver shot up in his chair, his fingertips buzzing. "Why is that? Did you kill her, too?"

"I didn't kill anyone, but we did send her away."

"Sent her away?" Denver's heart was pounding so hard, the buttons on his shirt were bouncing.

"After her stunt with that video, Veronica and I agreed it would be best if Lulu took a trip, so we sent her to Italy. She'd been wanting to go, anyway. She's sunning on the Italian Riviera about now, so she's not going to be telling tales about me."

Denver fumbled for his phone and jumped to his feet, sending the chair crashing behind him.

If Lulu was in Italy, who the hell was Ashlynn meeting tonight and why?

Chapter Twenty

Ashlynn crept along the path on the side of the Escalante mansion, the sparkling pool beyond the bushes to her right. She hadn't even seen the back quarters when she'd been here before. Then the path dipped to a clearing and a cozy house that merged with the canyon around it appeared like a cottage in a fairy tale. No wonder Lulu put up with her sister and the campaign. She had a sweet spot here.

Ashlynn knocked on the door, calling out, "Lulu? It's Ashlynn."

The door swung open and the other sister greeted her. "Hello, Ashlynn. Lulu had to go out, but when she told me she'd been expecting you, I thought we could meet instead. *LA Confidential* is a powerful force in the city, and I'd like to do a sit-down with you and discuss Tiana's role in the campaigns. Would you want to include a post like that? An exclusive with me?"

Ashlynn blinked. What a coup. "Of course I would, Councilwoman Escalante. Right now?"

"Sure, I'm actually free for a change." She gave a little laugh. "Call me Veronica. It's a nice night. Let's sit by the pool."

"Will Lulu be joining us later? Is she okay? Did she tell you about being followed?"

"Lulu is safe now. She'll be by later. She did mention that she'd been followed and the two of you had been accosted. I can't believe the Wexler campaign would go to those lengths." She rolled her shoulders. "Amazing what some people will do for power."

Ashlynn started to turn to take the path back to the patio of the main house, and Veronica touched her arm. "Can I have your phone, Ashlynn? I don't want this recorded, at least not now. You can take notes, if you like."

Ashlynn patted her purse. "Okay. I understand. I won't record."

"I'd feel better if you left the phone here." Veronica shook a finger at her. "I know how you journalists are, so I have to insist just for my peace of mind."

"I suppose." She slipped her phone from her purse and handed it to Veronica.

Veronica tapped the case with a long fingernail. "I'll leave this in the cottage for safekeeping. Lulu and my mother also keep a fully stocked kitchen and bar. Can I get you something to drink?"

"Nothing alcoholic. I still have to maneuver my way down Mulholland."

"Such a pain, isn't it? We pay a price for living in the hills. I'll get us a couple of sodas."

Ashlynn traipsed back to the pool area, her step light. She'd come here just to touch base with Lulu, and she'd leave with an exclusive interview with a candidate for mayor.

As she sat on one of the lounge chairs, she dug in her purse for some paper and a pen. Was Veronica afraid she'd say something that could be used against her in the campaign and that she'd splash it over the blog? Ashlynn wasn't interested in the campaign, only as it related to Tiana's death.

As she settled a piece of paper on her knee, Veronica emerged from the path carrying two glasses in her hands. "Found some soda in the fridge. Will this do?"

"Thank you." Ashlynn took the drink from her and downed a few gulps before placing the glass on the little teak table between them. "What do you know about Tiana's spying on your behalf, and did you realize that she was a mole for the CREW?"

Veronica's generous lips tightened and her nostrils flared. "Jumping right in, aren't you?"

She'd agreed not to record the interview, but if Veronica expected softballs, she'd contacted the wrong blogger. Would anyone ever try to put one over on Sean?

She tapped the paper with her pen. "I'm sorry, Veronica. I'm not interested in how you got your start in politics or why you think you'd be better than Wexler for the city. *LA Confidential* is a true crime blog, and my readers and I are investigating the murder of a young woman who was involved in your campaign and in Mayor Wexler's. I want to know what she discovered."

Veronica raised her glass to Ashlynn. "Cheers to strong women getting down to business."

Ashlynn grabbed her glass and clinked it with Veronica's. "Cheers to strong women answering tough questions."

Veronica took a tiny sip of her drink and then ran her thumb up and down the condensation on the outside. "I didn't even know Tiana Fuller was working as a volunteer for our campaign...until she started having an affair with my husband."

Ashlynn sucked in a breath and took another gulp of her drink. "You knew about that?"

"I knew about all of Kent's affairs. I had a spy of my own—my mother. She kept an eye on things."

"Y-you didn't care?" Ashlynn rubbed her eye as the lights over the pool blurred.

"Look at this house. Look at my clothes, my car, my vacations." She snorted delicately. "Not bad for a girl from the barrio. I use Kent, and he does what he wants."

"That doesn't sound like a very good recipe for a marriage."

"It works. What would you know about it? Rich girl from San Marino."

Ashlynn swallowed against her dry throat. She took another sip of her drink, cupping the ice cube on her tongue. "I didn't realize you knew anything about me."

"When we found out Lulu had given you that video, Jed and I did a little investigating of our own—mostly Jed. Anyway—" she flicked her fingers "—the arrangement worked for me and Kent, or it had worked until Tiana Fuller showed up."

Ashlynn's heart thudded in her chest as her brain struggled to make sense of Veronica's words. This was important. This meant something. "Tiana? Why was she different?"

"Feeling okay?" Veronica leaned forward and stroked Ashlynn's hand, which could barely grip the pen. "Tiana became different the day I realized she'd gotten into Kent's computer—the idiot."

"Wh-what'd she find on Kent's…?" The pen dropped from Ashlynn's fingers and rolled off the table. She watched it dumbly, without reacting.

"She probably discovered that I'd been facilitating Kent's projects in the city for years—dummy corporations, money from phony sources, votes cast to grease the wheels of Kent's moneymaking machine." She clicked her tongue. "If any of that stuff ever came out, not only would I lose the mayor's race, I'd probably be heading to federal prison. I'm not doing that."

Ashlynn should probably feel more excitement, more horror at Veronica's pronouncements, but she felt only fatigue. She opened her mouth and tried to move her thick tongue. "You...you..."

"Well, not me personally." Veronica placed a hand over her heart. "I hired a couple of professionals to take care of the matter."

"Jed? K—?" Ashlynn couldn't remember the name of Veronica's husband. Blackness hovered on the periphery of her vision. This woman had drugged her.

Veronica tossed back her thick mane of brown hair. "Neither Jed nor Kent was involved, although I think Jed suspects something. Strong women—right, Ashlynn? I don't need a man to make power moves."

"Murder." Ashlynn screamed at her muscles to move, but all she could manage was to lift one finger.

"Murder is the biggest power move of all, and I'm done with this interview. On the bright side, just think of all the hits your blog's going to get when you go missing or when some hikers discover your body in six months or a year. You'll put *LA Confidential* on the national map."

DENVER LOOMED OVER Kent's desk, and the older man reached for the top drawer. Denver lunged toward him, slamming the drawer on his fingers. Kent wailed, clutching his bloody hand to his chest, the gun in the drawer forgotten. Denver grabbed the gun and pocketed it. "Where is she? Where's your wife?"

Meadows gasped. "She wouldn't. She couldn't."

"Liar. You know what she's capable of." Denver shoved Meadows's phone into his chest. "Call her. Text her. And I'll be watching and listening, so don't tip her off."

"My wife did nothing." Meadows wiped his injured hand on the sleeve of his expensive sweater. "I'm not going to find her for you."

Denver slid his gun from his holster and leveled it at Meadows's head. "You're going to get on your phone right now, or I'm going to splatter your brains all over the plans for Meadows Plaza. You got me?"

"Y-you can't do this. I don't have a weapon. I'll sue you."

"You can't do that if you're dead." Denver smacked the phone on the table in the blood, and drops of it went airborne.

Meadows peered at him and then grabbed his phone. He entered the pass code with a misshapen finger and tapped the screen.

Denver growled. "Speaker."

The call rolled right to voice mail and a robotic voice answered.

"Text her."

Denver peered over Meadows's shoulder, the gun still aimed in Meadows's direction, as Meadows typed out a message to his wife, asking her whereabouts. The message hung there, undelivered.

Meadows coughed, cradling his hand. "She must have it turned off."

"Because she's committing a crime." Denver snatched up the phone before it could go into lock mode and scrolled through the apps until he found the one he wanted. "I knew you'd be tracking your wife's phone. Wouldn't want her surprising you with one of your sidepieces, right? Of course, she knew Tiana, figured out that she'd gotten some dirt on you—enough to sink you both."

Denver dashed the sweat from his eyes and squinted at the phone's display. He recognized the last location before she'd turned off her phone as her home in the hills above Sherman Oaks.

"Who's at the house now? Where's your mother-in-law? Do you have live-in staff?"

"I…"

Denver circled in front of Meadows, repositioning his gun to his Meadows's forehead, right between his eyes. "Not fast enough."

"We don't have live-in staff. My mother-in-law is in Mexico. We sent her there yesterday." Meadows choked. "Veronica's home alone. She'd do it there."

Denver pocketed Meadows's phone and handcuffed him to the desk so he couldn't warn his wife. He may have just ruined his chances with Homicide, but nothing mattered now but getting to Ashlynn.

As his car screamed from the construction site, he placed a call to the LAPD watch command. He ordered a unit to Escalante's address, claiming an assault in progress. At least, he prayed whatever was happening there was still in progress and not a done deal.

He turned on his blue and red revolvers and left the twinkling lights of downtown behind him as he sped down the 101, his adrenaline pumping through his system, his hands clenching the steering wheel.

Twenty minutes later as he careened off the freeway and hit Coldwater Canyon Boulevard, his phone rang and he flexed his fingers on the steering wheel. In his anxiety, he barked out, "What did you find?"

The sergeant on the other line said, "That's Councilwoman Escalante's house."

"I know that. What did you find?"

"Nothing. Nobody's home."

"Send them back."

"Detective, this isn't the Northeast Division, and we have no cause to barge into the empty house of a member of the LA city council. Don't know about you, but I value my pension."

Denver cut him off and stomped on the accelerator, his tires squealing as he took a sharp curve. If he had to save Ashlynn himself, he would.

He cut his lights and cruised to a stop in front of the Escalante mansion. Lights embedded in the flower garden lit the front of the house and guided him to the double doors. The cops had probably already rung the doorbell. They didn't get an answer, and he didn't expect one, either.

He slid his weapon from its holster. He crept around the side of the house and spotted a side gate standing open.

He sidled through the space sideways, not trusting that the hinges on the gate would stay silent. He avoided the flagstones, and his shoes squished against the dirt and grass. As he peered around the corner of the house onto the patio, his heart stuttered in his chest.

LA City Councilwoman Veronica Escalante knelt by the side of the pool, both hands in the water, pushing something beneath the surface. Had Ashlynn given up the fight? Had Escalante already killed her?

Denver charged forward, leaping over a chaise longue, his gun aloft. "Stop what you're doing! Stop!"

With her arms in the water up to her elbows, Veronica cranked her head to the side and her mouth dropped open. "I—I'm trying to save her. She fell in."

"Get away from the pool, and put your hands up where I can see them."

"I'm Councilwoman Escalante. This woman tried to

drown herself in my pool." She sat back on her heels, her arms hanging by her sides, dripping water.

Oh, God. Was Ashlynn dead already?

Denver ran to the side of the pool, knocking Veronica backward. Ashlynn was floating on her stomach, her arms splayed to the sides, her hair creating a red fan in the water. He shoved his gun in his waistband and reached to pull her toward the edge.

Grabbing handfuls of her clothing, he rolled her from the pool and onto her back. He pumped her chest and listened for her breath. "C'mon. C'mon, Ashlynn."

He applied another compression and she coughed up water, her eyelids fluttering. "That's my girl."

"Sh-she drugged me." Her eyes opened and then widened at the same time he felt Veronica snatch his gun.

He spun around, staring down the barrel of his own weapon.

Veronica's hand trembled. "I told you I tried to save her. She's one of my husband's lovers, a volunteer. When Kent broke things off with her, she came here to kill herself."

"Did you kill Tiana Fuller yourself, or did you hire someone?" Smiling slowly, he nodded at her shaky grip on the gun. "You farmed that one out, just like you hired someone to intimidate your own sister and Ashlynn at the dog park that night. You don't even know how to hold a weapon properly. It's a lot different from drugging someone and holding her head under water, isn't it?"

"I—I told you what happened."

"I know exactly what happened. You didn't care that your husband was seeing Tiana until you discovered she'd stumbled onto your little personal money train where you were funneling funds into Kent's shell companies."

Her dark eyes smoldered. "You're crazy. You came barging in here, demanding answers from me, demanding answers from Ashlynn Hughes from *LA Confidential*. When you didn't get what you wanted, you shot Ashlynn. While you were pushing her into the pool, I got your gun and shot you."

"That's a lot of setup to manage, Councilwoman, especially as it's clear you know nothing about guns and Ashlynn will have drugs in her system. How are you going to explain that?" He inched closer to her, still in a crouched position, sliding his hand up his pant leg and curling his fingers around the handle of his knife.

"Just because she's a blogger doesn't mean she wasn't having an affair with my husband. I'll stick to my original story. She came here to kill herself. I was reasoning with her until you crashed the party, desperate to solve this case, desperate to wrest it back from the blogger. It's no secret that the LAPD hates *LA Confidential*. I can pull it off." She tossed her head. "Do you know who I am?"

He lunged toward her, yanking the knife from its sheath around his leg. As she stumbled back, firing wildly into the air, he swung the blade, making contact with her side.

She screamed and dropped the gun, clutching her wound as it gushed blood.

He kicked the gun out of her reach and twisted around toward Ashlynn, her chest rising and falling, despite the paralysis of the rest of her body. He pulled her into his lap. "You're going to be okay. Everything's going to be okay."

Then he grabbed his phone and pointed it at Veronica, writhing on the patio, blood oozing between her fingers. "I know exactly who you are. You're the suspect under arrest for the murder of Tiana Fuller."

Epilogue

A few days later, Ashlynn answered her door and pulled Denver into her place. "How'd it go?"

"When Veronica saw the evidence we had against her—Kent's computer, her prints on my gun, your testimony against her, the drugs she used on you in the guest cottage—she confessed from her hospital bed. She gave up the two hitmen who killed Tiana, too. If she's going down, she's bringing everyone with her."

"I had no doubt you'd nail her either with the evidence or a confession, but I meant how'd that other thing go?" She held on to his hands, lacing her fingers through his.

"Suspended." He lifted his broad shoulders that had carried so much.

She squeezed his hands. He'd given up his career aspirations to save her. "I'm sorry, Denver. Even though you solved this case, does that mean they're not going to bring you on to Homicide?"

"I wouldn't say that." He raised her hands to his lips and kissed her fingers. "I could use a beer."

She disentangled herself and scooted past him into the kitchen. "So, there's still hope for you?"

"Let's put it this way. Billy Crouch and Jake McAllister, the two superstars of Robbery-Homicide, took me aside today, congratulated me on the case, and said, if anything, the way I questioned Meadows to get to his wife was a bright golden star next to my name, as far as they were concerned."

"Is Meadows going to sue the department?" She dipped into her fridge to grab two bottles of beer.

As he took a bottle from her, he snorted. "He can try... from federal prison. I think he's going to be busy with his high-priced attorneys for a while."

She grabbed his hand again and led him to the couch. "Poor Tiana. She craved the excitement of a political campaign and got in over her head. She never slept with Kent, you know. It was all a big tease to get into the house. Lulu told me that."

"I think Tiana watched too many TV shows. She had this unrealistic view, and didn't realize how far people would go to protect their interests."

"One thing that's been bothering me is how did she wind up in a Wexler vehicle? Did Veronica order her thugs to steal a Wexler car to frame the mayor?"

He combed his fingers through her hair. "That just fell into their laps. Tiana already had that car. She'd taken it herself and used it for her covert operations. She drove out in the car to meet who she thought was someone from the Wexler campaign. She was ambushed by the hitmen, dumped in the trunk, and pushed into the lake."

"Convenient for Veronica, but also a mistake. In the end, if Tiana hadn't been in a CREW car, she never would've been connected to either campaign. Neither campaign would've claimed her, and Tony would've been too afraid to step forward. Maybe Lulu would've come through."

"How is Lulu?" Denver rubbed a circle on her back.

"At least she tried to do the right thing, regardless of her motives."

"She's fine. She's still in Italy. She wasn't that surprised about the turn of events. She always knew her sister was ruthless, even though Lulu was supposedly the black sheep of the family."

"Is that why you two connected?" Denver tapped the neck of his bottle against hers.

"Maybe." Ashlynn scraped a nail through the foil label on her damp bottle. "What did you think of the blog?"

She hated asking, but it still mattered to her. She'd proved that by stumbling into a dangerous situation with Veronica just to get an exclusive.

"It was great. Your writing is top-notch, but is that you? Scrabbling for a story almost got you killed—several times."

Turning toward him, she traced a fingertip along his jaw. "It also brought you into my life."

He captured her finger and sucked it into his mouth. "As much as I get a thrill out of rescuing you, I want to make sure I stay in your life and you stay in mine. You're sure you don't want to go back to writing about fashion?"

"But we did it, didn't we? We did it together."

He wiggled his eyebrows. "We've done several things together. Which one do you mean?"

"Justice for the girl in the lake." She held out her fist for a bump. "Justice for Tiana."

He tapped her fist with his and then pulled her into his arms to kiss her long and hard. When he released her, he put a finger against her lower lip. "Does that mean fashion is out and true crime stays?"

"I'm ending the blog and starting a podcast." She curled a leg beneath her and cupped his face with both hands. "It's going to be all mine, something Sean never did. I'm going to put my own spin on it, my own stamp."

He encircled her wrists with his fingers. "You're going to need a contact, someone on the inside, someone not afraid to break a few rules. You're going to need me."

And then he showed her just how much she did need him.

* * * * *

COMING SOON!

We really hope you enjoyed reading this book.
If you're looking for more romance, be sure to
head to the shops when new books are
available on

Thursday 4th August

MILLS & BOON

THE HEART OF ROMANCE

A ROMANCE FOR EVERY READER

MODERN

Prepare to be swept off your feet by sophisticated, sexy and seductive heroes, in some of the world's most glamourous and romantic locations, where power and passion collide.

HISTORICAL

Escape with historical heroes from time gone by. Whether your passion is for wicked Regency Rakes, muscled Vikings or rugged Highlanders, awaken the romance of the past.

MEDICAL

Set your pulse racing with dedicated, delectable doctors in the high-pressure world of medicine, where emotions run high and passion, comfort and love are the best medicine.

True Love

Celebrate true love with tender stories of heartfelt romance, from the rush of falling in love to the joy a new baby can bring, and a focus on the emotional heart of a relationship.

Desire

Indulge in secrets and scandal, intense drama and plenty of sizzling hot action with powerful and passionate heroes who have it all: wealth, status, good looks…everything but the right woman.

HEROES

Experience all the excitement of a gripping thriller, with an intense romance at its heart. Resourceful, true-to-life women and strong, fearless men face danger and desire - a killer combination!

To see which titles are coming soon, please visit

millsandboon.co.uk/nextmonth

LET'S TALK
Romance

For exclusive extracts, competitions
and special offers, find us online:

⬛ facebook.com/millsandboon

🐦 @MillsandBoon

📷 @MillsandBoonUK

Get in touch on 01413 063232

For all the latest titles coming soon, visit
millsandboon.co.uk/nextmonth

JOIN US ON SOCIAL MEDIA!

Stay up to date with our latest releases, author news and gossip, special offers and discounts, and all the behind-the-scenes action from Mills & Boon...

 @millsandboon

 @millsandboonuk

 facebook.com/millsandboon

 @millsandboonuk

It might just be true love...

GET YOUR ROMANCE FIX!

Get the latest romance news, exclusive author interviews, story extracts and much more!

MILLS & BOON
MEDICAL
Pulse-Racing Passion

Set your pulse racing with dedicated, delectable doctors in the high-pressure world of medicine, where emotions run high and passion, comfort and love are the best medicine.

MILLS & BOON
True Love

Romance from the Heart

Celebrate true love with tender stories of heartfelt romance, from the rush of falling in love to the joy a new baby can bring, and a focus on the emotional heart of a relationship.